W9-BAD-823

R. M. Meluch's
Tour of the Merrimack:

THE MYRIAD
WOLF STAR
THE SAGITTARIUS COMMAND
STRENGTH AND HONOR
THE NINTH CIRCLE

THE NINTH CIRCLE

A Novel of the Merrimack

R. M. MELUCH

DAW BOOKS, INC.

DONALD A. WOLLHEIM, FOUNDER

375 Hudson Street, New York, NY 10014

ELIZABETH R. WOLLHEIM

SHEILA E. GILBERT

PUBLISHERS

http://www.dawbooks.com

To Jim, as always and forever.

PART ONE

Man Without a Country

1

THE BLOOD ON THE WALL was way too crimson. Didn't really look like blood. Looked more like cardinal root extract.

Cinna was alone in the barracks in the dark before dawn with the gory writing on the wall. His seven brothers were gone, their bunks in order, inspection-ready.

The savage red scrawl issued coded instructions. The references wouldn't make sense to anyone outside Cinna's eight-man squad, except for the last line, triple-underscored and all in caps: *TELL NO ONE!!*

The slashing underlines dripped a bit.

The mission took Cinna outside. The Legion base was dark. Cinna's night vision switched itself on.

All was quiet, the air warm, dry, still. A slight dust haze dimmed the stars. The rustling of Cinna's drab fatigues and the crunching of his own footfalls sounded thunderous to him.

At the specified coordinates, between the privies and the recycling building, Cinna moved a flat rock to uncover a scroll. New instructions. And a warning to obey precisely and tell no one on pain of hideous death.

Cinna's heart lifted.

Finally!

After weeks of treating him as an outsider, Cinna's brothers finally deemed him worthy of a hazing.

Cinna hurried back to the eight-man hut and washed the faux blood off the wall. That was the first instruction.

He wasn't sure how his brothers had managed to paint the wall and slip out without waking him. They must have dosed him.

What were brothers for?

Brothers were for getting you into trouble.

The second instruction bade him slip out of the Legion compound under the wall.

Do not pass the guard shack. Do not get a pass.

Cinna's nerves buzzed. Felt great.

He set off, hugging the perimeter wall, to the north end of the compound. In the blackness he found the designated escape route. He'd stepped in it.

It was a rainwater outlet. Dry as a bone now.

It hardly ever rained here. Maybe once a year. At those times the Legion compound became a forty-acre wading pool.

The egress was a shallow opening cut under the massive limestone block. Looked like a dog dug it. Cinna eeled himself under and out.

He ran all out across the flat hardpan of the surrounding badlands. He needed to get to the foothills in time.

Be quick about it, the instructions read. *Miss the appointed time and you know what happens!*

Cinna didn't know what happens. Maybe he was meant to assume the implicit deadness in the line.

His brothers would kill him? Not bloody likely. But he knew he would wish he were dead if he didn't pass this challenge. He needed to prove himself to these guys and become one of them.

Technically Cinna was already one of them. The Legion had assigned him to this squad. All but one of the squad members were variations on a single Antonian clone. And that one exception was not Cinna.

Cinna was the tyro on this squad, a year younger than the others at an age when a year was an eternity. He wasn't a boy, but he wasn't fully a man in Roman eyes. He was what Rome called an ephebe, a youth of eighteen or nineteen Terrestrial years of age. Cinna had just turned eighteen, just joined the training unit of Legion Persus. He had missed the war. So had his brothers. They were all sour about that.

He wasn't truly in the squad until his brothers said he was in. Right now they were still "they," and Cinna was still that new guy.

Cinna couldn't say he was desperate to belong. There was no desperation in it. It was a thing he must do, and he wanted it done. Now.

His brothers were waiting for him at the edge of the salt flats. Looked as severe as the rocks behind them.

Out here the land rose straight up in a natural battlement, testament of a violent creation. The Roman colonial planet Phoenix lay quieter now than when the volcanic world first thrust the Dragon's Back from the seabed and cooked off the waters.

Cinna's brothers looked like him. And maybe Cinna was vain, but he thought his brothers were magnificent.

They were bronze-skinned. Tall. Built lean and hard and all in proportion. They looked at him with the same dark, dark eyes as he looked at them. Their dark hair curled more or less.

Clones were always given individual traits for recognition and accountability. Cinna and his brothers were similar but not exactly the same. And Cinna still couldn't keep Leo and Galeo straight.

He had to wonder if the reproduction designers already knew the name of the subject clone when they doled out its distinctive genes. Did they know that Faunus was going to be a Faunus when they gave him that barrel chest, that wicked sybaritic face, and those curls? Surely they had to know he was going to be a Faunus when they gave him those curls. That head of hair was just begging for a vine wreath to crown it. Who but a Faunus could wear one of those?

Pallas was a regal, refined name. And Pallas the man was too civilized. He had a gentle look, a gentle air. His basic features were the same as the others', but he had been drawn with an airbrush. Pallas was someone's idea of ideal male beauty, and that was fine for Pallas. Cinna was glad that wasn't he. Cinna's own looks were of a sharper, rougher cut, and Cinna liked it that way.

Orissus was the hard-ass of the lot. Square, bulky, sardonic. His thick lips were made for sneering. Orissus took this insider/outsider division seriously. Orissus got clumsy with liquids around Cinna's bunk, and he tended to step on Cinna's parade-polished boots five minutes before inspection. Another reason to want this trial over with. It was getting hard not to hate Orissus.

Nicanor had a noble name, and he had nobility. Nicanor stood a gnat's breath taller than the rest. He was perfect. Not as mean as Orissus. Nicanor was cold and lofty as a hero's statue.

Leo and Galeo. Had the reprod designers gotten lazy when they cranked out those two clones? Physically, Leo and Galeo were Tweedledee and Tweedledee. But Leo was technically inclined, and Galeo was a head-basher.

And then there was Nox. He should have been taller, but there had been no choice. Nobody had designed Nox. He wasn't a clone. Nox had been born. Really born. Not gently retrieved from an incubator at term, but extruded from a live woman's very narrow you-have-got-to-be-kidding-me passage. Gotta love natural conception, but the final delivery? Cinna thanked any and all gods for giving him a penis.

Nox's mother had to be insane.

Cinna could tell at first look that Nox was a wild weed. The naturally selected had a certain chaos about them. Nox stood a full handspan shorter than his brothers, and he was fair-skinned and blond. He had been born on Earth. American, but no one held that against him. Nox was not a blood brother, but he was a brother all the same. That he was adopted meant somebody deemed him worthy to be Antonian. The venerable line of Antonius hung its gens name on him and now he was Antonius Nox, every bit as Antonian as the rest of them. Maybe even more.

You could usually tell the converts from the natives. The adoptees and the novos had to prove themselves. They had a fanatical drive to out-Roman the Romans. Probably why Nox wore a traditional knee-length tunic with no trousers and sandals instead of boots. Sand under a sandal strap either ripped up your feet or made you tough. Nox kept proving he was tough. He'd already proved he was Roman enough for this squad.

Nox was in.

Cinna, the blood brother, was still out.

Orissus spat on the hard ground at Cinna's approach. "You're late."

"I'm not," said Cinna evenly. Knew he wasn't late.

"Get moving then," said Nicanor.

Cinna didn't understand. "Move?"

Nicanor nodded his noble head sideways and backward toward the massif behind them. "Lead on," said Nicanor.

"Where?"

"Just follow the path," Pallas told him.

Cinna saw it now. A narrow footpath snaked up through rocks and weeds.

Cinna took the point position, though he didn't know where he was going. He just followed the rough path that led around and up the sloped side of the massif.

The predawn sky was getting a bruised haze to it. Cinna's night vision switched itself off.

His seven brothers hiked behind him at a distance.

As they ascended, Cinna heard them talking together behind his back. He couldn't make out what they were saying.

Cinna set a brisk pace. The squad needed to be back on base before muster.

The Legion left its new recruits little unstructured time. The idea was to run the young men ragged so they wouldn't have any energy to get into trouble. That was the plan. The squad was meant to be sleeping now.

Someone underestimated the energy levels of physically fit youths with a craving for risk.

So here was Cinna's squad, forcing themselves on another march, out of bounds, against the rules.

Rules in the Empire were rigid.

But when caught between obeying the rules or following his mates, there was no real choice.

Cinna climbed nearly half a kilometer up the path that zigged and zagged over rocks, loose stones, and scrub weeds. He mounted the summit as the sky was paling from violet to blue.

Path's end brought Cinna to the sheer eastern precipice of the rock. He recognized this place though he'd only ever seen it in pictures.

This was the crag called the Widow's Edge.

As far as anyone knew, there was no actual grieving Roman woman to go with the name of this crag. But should one want to end it, Cinna guessed the drop from here would do the job. Thoroughly.

The air moved at this height, lifting Cinna's hair from his brow. Gray-green leaves of stunted trees fluttered.

The wide vista took on color and detail, until sunlight lanced across the edge of the world and shut Cinna's eyes.

He bowed his head. Opened his eyes a slit. Looked down.

The cliff face was vertical. Striated yellow-white rock blazed with a quartz gleam in the light of dawn.

The dry hardpan lay dead flat down below. A long way down below.

Gravity on the colonial planet Phoenix was stronger than on the Roman home world, Palatine. But this drop would be lethal anywhere.

A gust of air gave Cinna an unsettling push.

He took a step back from the edge. Looked up.

Seven of the world's small moons shone in their own phases, strung across the thin dusty sky above them. The early sun threw the brothers' shadows hard and long behind them where the western horizon hugged its indigo darkness. In between lay the nightmare of the Dragon's Back, alternating jagged sharp ridges and deep pits of blackness.

The stars were fading. Only the steady white shine of a few planets and satellites persisted. The day would be clear. It always was.

Cinna knew he was up here for some rite of passage. He didn't know what his brothers intended, but he was ready. He was going to be worthy.

Nox moved to the very edge of the precipice, leaned over, and peered down. The wind moved his blond hair. His tunic flapped around his thighs. He pulled his lips back from his teeth with an inward hiss. Spoke, not to Cinna. "It looks higher than I remember."

"Well, I don't think it *grew*," said Pallas from the rear.

Leo (or was that Galeo?) glanced over the edge to see for himself and immediately shied back. "Nox is right. It's higher."

I'm supposed to be scared, Cinna guessed.

Cinna looked straight down.

It was scary.

Orissus stalked up behind Cinna and Nox at the edge and stood there for a silent moment. Without warning he seized Nox by the shoulders and shouted, "*Watch it!*"

Nox flinched. Then turned and spit in Orissus' eye.

Orissus grinned and backed off with evil chuckles. Wiped his eye.

A smile curled into Nox's snarl.

They were playing. Like wolf cubs.

No one played with Cinna like that. Yet.

There were eight men in this squad, like the old Roman *contubernium*, tent party.

In an ancient day the men of a *contubernium* shared a tent and a pack animal. These days they shared a barracks hut. Cinna's squad would form a crew of a Strig when they became fully fledged legionaries, but the term for the squad remained *contubernium*.

Latin was Nox's second language, and he was actually very good at it. He refused to wear a language module, so he missed words now and then. There was a story that when Nox first saw the word *contubernium* in print, he didn't know what it meant, so he tried to parse it. "*Con. Con.* Con obviously means *with*. Okay then. *Tuber. Tuber. Tuber.*" He'd grasped about for meaning and finally guessed, "Are we sharing a potato?"

Standing now at the Widow's Edge, Cinna asked Nox, "Is this where I get to do something with a potato?"

It was supposed to be a joke.

Nox didn't laugh. None of them did.

Cinna deflated. *I get it. I'm not one of them yet.*

They wouldn't laugh with him until he proved himself.

Well, then, let's do it. "Are we rappelling?" Cinna asked.

The other seven remained silent. An ominous kind of silence that kept Cinna from guessing hang gliding next.

Pallas stepped forward, made Cinna face him. Pallas told him, "You are going to jump."

Cinna had been afraid of that.

He took another look over the edge. "Then what?"

"You fall."

Cinna exhaled a feeble laugh.

Pallas' expression, for all the softness to his face, was impenetrable. Cinna couldn't read a thing on it.

Cinna looked to the others, faces like the one he saw in the mirror. Faunus a little broader. Nicanor handsomer. Orissus square and scarred. Leo and Galeo. Oh, hell, which was which? All of them looked solemn, remote, their expressions masked, tensed as if braced to sever a limb.

Cinna was afraid he was the limb.

Cinna asked, "Rope?"

"No," said Pallas.

"What's the trick?"

Pallas shook his head. "There isn't one."

Faunus, not a trace of mirth in his jovial face, said, "We're telling you to jump."

2

"**U**H-OH."

Uh-oh brought the Vigil of the watch over to Observer Six's station in the Sector Primus Surveillance Center.

A network of satellite eyes cloaked the Roman colonial world Phoenix. Surveillance served planetary and local weather, health, and safety departments. And it served Imperial Intelligence. Vigils kept watch for any number of things, from wildfires and accidents with wildlife to non-Roman activity.

Phoenix's resident population numbered only in the hundred millions, and those were concentrated in a few metro areas.

The satellite eyes of Sector Primus covered several Roman military bases and training centers, plus two international spaceports and their surrounding metropolises.

Sector Primus watched over the base of Legion Persus.

The Sector Vigil looked over Observer Six's shoulder at his readouts. "What do you see?"

Observer Six pointed to one satellite image. "Action on Widow's Edge." He blew the image up bigger for the Vigil to see.

The satellite eye that fed this image focused on a cadre of 'phebes—seven young men dressed in *gens* colors and one clad in burlap drab. That would be a tyro.

"Looks like a hazing," said Six.

"That's illegal," Observer Eight said from his own station.

Silence gripped the control room and extended for several heartbeats.

There wasn't a man or woman in the room who had *not* been hazed.

There were two different kinds of unlawful acts in the Empire. One kind meant Don't Get Caught. The other kind meant Don't Do It. Really. Just don't. Ever.

Hazing fit into the former kind. Hazing was done all the time, because the tacit corollary to the law of Don't Get Caught was Don't Damage Your Victim.

Senior Observer Gemma tsked at her station. She spoke laconically, "Bad boys."

Observers Two, Seven, and Eight left their stations to gather around Observer Six's station to watch the tyro walk to the edge of the cliff.

Behind the tyro were six tall, gorgeous youths who looked just like him, five of them dressed in bronze and black tunics, black cargo pants, and black boots. Bronze and black were the colors of *gens* Antonia. These boys were from the Legion base of Legion Persus.

The sixth youth was shorter than the others, blond and fair. He wore a black and bronze knee-length tunic without trousers. A gust of wind flashed his jockstrap, the modern equivalent of a loincloth. That man had to be adopted.

Satellite surveillance carried no audio, but the video was good enough for the observers to see the mouths of the 'phebes moving in a chant. *Jump! Jump! Jump!*

The Vigil knew this one. About two-thirds of the way down the cliff, a hidden net pops out of the rock face and slows you down to a stop just above the ground. Then the rope holding the net bounces you back up to where you left your last meal. And if you've hung onto your wits after the bouncing stops, you laugh and yell, "Again!"

Senior Observer Gemma covered her eyes and returned to her own station. She sat, hunched her shoulders forward, and shuddered. "Gaah. That is still a long-ass drop."

The Sector Vigil angled the satellite's cam down to find the net mechanism hidden in the cliff face. There it was. Just as it had been in his day.

Observer Six moved the satellite camera's focus back up to the tyro's pallid face and closed in tight enough to see the pinpoints of sweat form on his brow and quickly vanish, carried away by a sere wind. Widow's Edge stood over dry country.

Six asked no one, everyone, "Is he going to jump?"

The Sector Vigil said, "Of course he'll jump."

Seven: "No. He's talking. He's weaseling his way out of it."

Six: "Five denari says he doesn't jump."

Eight: "*Nego!* He will. He has to. I got your five."

Gemma raised her hand, not looking up from her own station. "I'm good for 'he jumps.'"

Seven studied the tyro's face uncertainly. His brows met. "You think? You're on."

"Plant it," Gemma said.

The other observers slapped their wagers on Six's console.

Six offered a side bet, "He's going to piss."

There were no takers for that action.

Cliff-dwelling creatures dropped from their crags, spread leathery wings wide, and soared on the thermals.

Cinna hesitated on the windy height. A silicate sting in the dry air bit his cheeks. His tunic and his trouser legs fluttered. He tried to force a calm tone into his voice, but a thin note of panic cut in. "This is pointless. I understand if I refuse, then I am not whom you want, and I deserve to die. But when I do obey, I will prove my devotion, but I'll also be dead and no use to you."

"You are assuming this is all about you," Orissus said, cold.

Nicanor said, "Ever think this might be *our* trial? *We* can't afford to be soft."

"There are things more important than you," Pallas said. "Jump."

Cinna looked straight down. *Oh, bull.* This was a loyalty challenge. There was a catch in here somewhere. He had to stop looking down. And don't stand here too long. Longer made it harder.

Fear of heights was hard-coded into a gene that most

human beings carried. Fear of heights was a survival trait—to keep you from doing something like this.

The rational mind could overrule instinct. Trust must overcome natural fear. That's what this was about.

Cinna resolved to take that step.

Fortune favors the bold.

So said the mind. The body was in full revolt. The hard-wired terror in his lizard brain subverted his conscious will. His legs were turning to gelatin.

A balk showed fear and distrust. He needed to get this over with before terror trickled down his leg.

I'm freezing up. Too much thinking. Go.

The ground below was so very far away.

Go. Just go.

"There he goes!" Observer Eight crowed as the tyro stepped off the cliff edge.

"Pay me," said Gemma, still not looking, at the same time as the Vigil's hand slapped down on the console with a victorious, "Ha!"

"Get stuffed." Seven sulked his way back toward his own station.

Six groaned.

Observer Eight snatched up the pot to divide among the winners while the jumper plummeted.

It was an eternal way down. The youth was still dropping. The camera tracked him all the way.

The Vigil shuddered, watching.

Gods, that's terrifying.

Gravity was strong on Phoenix, but the air was thick. The Vigil was not sure what that did to terminal velocity. It was still fast.

Abruptly the sour mutters of the losers and cackles of the winners cut off, and all the watchers jerked straight up like a stand of vibrating spears with a collective shout, "*Shit!*"

Nox spat a mouthful of windblown dust into a rubbery bush while his brothers leaned over the cliff edge, watching the fall. Faunus whistled a descending note.

Nox heard their sudden gasps.

Faunus' whistle sputtered short.

Nox's brothers convulsed. Clogged wordless sounds gurgled in their throats. They backed away from the edge.

When they turned around for Nox to see, their bronze-toned faces were nearly white. Their wide eyes and open mouths told Nox that the net hadn't deployed.

A delayed sound of impact traveled up from below.

"No," said Nox. It had to be a joke. They were playing him. "No."

But not one of them broke character.

Nox silently coaxed them, *Come on. Somebody crack a grin. Anybody. Faunus!*

Jovial Faunus looked ill.

Okay, they got him to bite. His brothers were razzing him. Had to be. Just had to be. Nox marched to the edge to see for himself.

Way down below lay a red spray like a lopsided flower. The compact pile in the center had to be the broken body. It was very realistic.

And there was nothing joking in the sounds of his brothers' ragged breathing behind him. Nox turned toward them.

The white line around Faunus' lips. Leo and Galeo's constricted pupils. Those were hard to fake. Tears welled in Pallas' eyes.

Nox stared at them blankly. The sick feeling rooting in his gut was unacceptable. He needed someone to make it stop. Step back a frame. Make this not real.

Nox turned round again, looked down. The horror was still down there, stark, simple, finite.

No.

Someone—Nicanor—grabbed Nox by the back of the tunic, dragged him back from the edge.

And then they were all running.

The running didn't seem to have a start. Just suddenly they were all doing it, racing down the path, back the way they came.

Nox's heart pounded in his aching chest. His pulse roared in his ears. His thoughts jammed into a ball and unraveled.

He was falling behind the others. His brothers were titans. Nox, not a natural brother, was the runt of this litter, at a shrimpy six foot tall. He was the ugly duckling.

Nox was not as powerful as a Roman-designed son. There was no stigma to adoption here. Once a family accepted your pledge, you were in. And Nox's tall, bronzed brothers considered him one of their own.

Another one of their own lay back there, broken at the foot of the cliff. Cinna.

Nox's breaths drew in harshly. He tasted dust.

Skidded to halt and turned around.

Pallas glanced back, stopped and yelled, "Nox! What the hell!"

"I need to go get him," Nox cried.

"He is *dead!*"

"I know. You go. I can't just—" He cut himself short. There was no way out of this. None. He started over, "There's going to be an inquest. They'll need to hang this on someone. I'll take the hit. You were never there! *Go!*"

Nox didn't wait for arguing. He was already running again, back to where a side path forked off. The path that would lead him to Cinna.

Nox ran. Not so much a run as a controlled fall, moving so fast he could scarcely get each foot down in front of him to take the next step as the ground came up.

By the time he got to level ground, the muscles in his legs felt solidified. He kept going, hauling his legs forward as though he were dragging and dropping tree stumps.

He closed his stinging eyes. The image came back, as if imprinted on the insides of his eyelids. A pile of bones at the bottom of the cliff.

His eyes flew back open.

He saw his future. There was nothing in it.

He hadn't just hazed Cinna, which was a crime. He hadn't just failed to save Cinna from the danger he'd put him into. He'd run away. He left him.

Even though Cinna wasn't going anywhere, Nox felt an urgent need to get to him.

The broken pile of bloody bones just shouldn't be alone.

"Deus! Deus! Deus!" Observer Six cried.

The whole of Sector Primus Surveillance Center focused on one subject only.

Gemma pushed away from her own console to come over to Six's monitor.

Wagers fell from hands as if the money were bleeding on them.

Observer Six gawked at his monitor. "They dropped him!"

"They *left* him!" the Vigil breathed.

"Can't be," said Gemma. The thought was beyond Roman comprehension. She wedged her way in with the Vigil to see the satellite image. "They're running to get him. The path winds around to the bottom. They're going back."

"*No they're not!*" Six cried, close to hysteria. "They *left* him!"

He angled the camera wider over to the cloud of dust. The seven surviving ephebes were running down the wrong path—the one that led straight away from the cliff and away from the dead man.

The Vigil commanded, "Six, keep a tracker on Snow White and the Seven Dwarves. Gemma, call a skyhook to go get Humpty Dumpty."

The Vigil paced the compartment, treading on the fallen money, rage banging inside his skull. *Cowards! Cowards! Cowards!*

Bleary-eyed, the air knifing his lungs, his throat raw and dry, Nox cast about the flat land for his brother. His muscles shook with dehydration. He couldn't find Cinna.

This was the place. The foot of Widow's Edge. But Nox couldn't see the body. There ought to be an obvious bloody mess.

He called out for Cinna.

Which was stupid because Cinna was dead. Nox had seen the blood spatter from the cliff top.

He spied a dark shadow on the sun-baked dirt, and he stumbled closer. As he drew near he saw the dark color was not a shadow.

He had found the blood. All the moisture had seeped into the thin layer of dust on the parched ground. It looked nearly black.

But where was the body?

Nox walked a helpless circle, bewildered.

His hands lifted and fell to his sides, useless.

He dropped down to sit in the middle of the bloodstain on the hard ground. He leaned over his knees, his head hanging forward. He raked his hands back through his dusty blond hair.

Shit shit shit.

A disk of bright light fell on him from above, brighter and hotter even than the sunlight, blasting away any shadow. He heard the hovercraft and a loud voice through a bullhorn: "Halt in the name of the Empire!"

Halt what? Nox stayed in his sit. He lifted his hands over his bowed head.

3

A THUNDERING RUMBLE shook Glenn Hamilton awake, rattled all the gear in the ship's lockers, and sent tremors through the deck.

Sounded like grinding rocks in an avalanche. It was a sound you never want to hear on a ship traveling faster than light in the middle of the big black empty between stars.

Glenn patted the mattress beside her. No husband. She was alone in the bed.

Another wave of crashing booms sent her scrambling under the rack to retrieve emergency life sacs for herself and her husband. There wasn't a proper spacesuit on board this crate, and any second the hull was going to rip open to the lightless, airless, flash-freeze of perfect vacuum at way below nothing Celsius.

She'd been told that it was not the cold that kills you. Freezing required the presence of other matter to conduct the heat out of your body. She didn't believe it.

But she did know for sure that eyes and lungs and stomachs and guts ruptured in zero pressure.

She didn't know how much pain you felt when dying like that. Didn't ever want to know.

Glenn scrambled for the sleep compartment's hatch.

Abruptly the noise shut off.

A sheepish laugh carried through the thin partitions of the ship. "Sorry! Sorry!"

Glenn dropped into a crouch, let her forehead rest

against the compartment's hatch. She growled, hugging the his-and-hers life sacs. She knew that voice.

Patrick. Her husband.

From another sleeping compartment someone else called a sleepy scold, "Less decibelage is required!" Sounded like Aaron Rose, the xenoaerologist.

Glenn never trusted LEN spacecraft, never imagined she would be traveling on one in the company of an international scientific exploration team. She felt much safer on board the space battleship *Merrimack* in the middle of a firefight with Romans than in this flimsy civilian box.

This ship bore the typically benign League of Earth Nations name *Spring Beauty*.

Through the vents Glenn could see lights going on outside her compartment. Feet shuffled and clomped on the ship's single deck. Apparently the scientists were assembling out there in the common area.

The other xenos would want to see what Patrick, the xenolinguist, was up to so loudly in the middle of ship's night.

Wide awake now, Glenn threw on a T-shirt and cargo pants. She pulled her sleep-tossed hair back into a tail and went out too.

The deck felt neutral in temperature under her bare feet. She smelled popcorn.

The ship's scientists collected around Glenn's husband, all of them asking variations on the same question with more or fewer expletives, "What was that?"

Patrick looked sheepishly pleased with himself. He loved an audience.

Patrick's audience was an odd collection of human beings. Intellectuals tended not to alter their natural looks. They could be defiant that way. About half the people on this research vessel looked less than attractive, lacking vital color, muscle tone, a decent haircut, a bath. Glenn wondered if some of them were marking territory with their scent.

Patrick stood out because he was good-looking, tall, with a nice build, not muscle-bound but in reasonable shape for a slender academic. His soft, dark brown hair was trimmed and usually clean.

If Patrick Hamilton were an animal, he would be a young stag, aesthetic, soft-eyed, handsome.

And he froze when scared.

His quirky manner didn't put off the she-brains on board this bus. Dr. Hamilton was among his own kind here.

"I've been listening to Zoen mammoths," Patrick said. They talk."

"Apparently," said Dr. Rose, not delighted.

Aaron Rose was a puppy-eyed man of middle years and razor intellect. His hairline was in retreat and closing in on outright desertion. Dr. Rose could be a real snot. Glenn liked him.

"Where's the popcorn?" asked Glenn.

Patrick passed her the bag.

The other xenos wore sleep-deprived dubious scowls. The ship's team leader, Dr. Poul Vrba, said what the others muttered, "*Talk?* Really?"

Senior xenozoologist Dr. Peter Szaszy challenged Patrick. "Why hasn't anyone ever heard those kinds of sounds out of my mammoths before?"

"No one ever tried buggering them before," Dr. Rose muttered. Got an elbow in the kidney from Dr. Maarstan for it. "Who's got the popcorn?"

Glenn passed the bag.

"Where did you get this recording?" Dr. Szaszy demanded, defensive.

Peter Szaszy was one of the original explorers of their destination planet, Zoe. The mammoths were Szaszy's project. Patrick was trespassing into Szaszy's field of expertise. That was a major breach of brain etiquette.

"I got it out of the database," said Patrick. "First expedition. This is your own bubble, Szasz."

"No," Peter Szaszy said. "There is no such noise on my recordings. Mammoths don't make sounds louder than a peep. That's not my audio. You jammed something in there."

"It's your bubble. And the sounds *are* on there," Patrick said, boyish. Not endearingly boyish. An irritating I've-got-a-secret kind of boyish. "I just enhanced them a little."

"A *little*," Szaszy said, vindicated.

"No, no. The volume is true to life," Patrick said. "All I did was bump up the frequency a couple octaves to transpose the sounds into the human audible range. The mammoths are communicating on wavelengths so long that their vocalizations literally go in one of your ears and out the other without registering—which is pretty much normal for you anyway."

Dr. Melisandra Minyas gasped excitedly. "Oh, I get it! Of *course*! The heads! The *heads!*"

Dr. Minyas was the junior xenozoologist on this expedition. And she was too, too perky. Had orange-blond hair. Freckles. Looked young. Maybe actually was young. Looked like she breathed country air. Her given name was Melisandra. She went by Sandy.

Patrick nodded like a proud daddy. "The heads."

Glenn made a stab at polite interest in her husband's work. "The heads?"

Patrick spread his arms out as far as he could to each side to indicate size. "The *heads*."

The mammoths' heads would of course be, well, mammoth.

"Those giant heads act as sound chambers," Patrick said. "The size of that head was my clue that there is more to mammoth communication than those few bird chirps Szasz has on record for mammoth speech."

"Speech?" Dr. Szaszy repeated, his brow tight, questioning the linguist's word choice "*Speech*. Not animal sounds? You think my mammoths are sapient?"

"Nah," said Dr. Rose with a mouthful of popcorn. "This is really a recording of Lowell's stomach, isn't it?"

"I haven't looked into the sapience of Lowell's stomach," Patrick said. "But I know the mammoths are saying a lot more than Szasz thought they were. And they're doing it over distance. Just like Earth's elephants."

Glenn asked, "Elephants are sapient?"

Patrick passed on the sapience question and said, "Elephants communicate by low-frequency sounds."

Sandy Minyas nodded knowingly and added, "Same as giraffes." She took a stance at Patrick's side with a bright smile, letting everyone know that she and Patrick were of a mind.

There really is such a thing as time travel, Glenn thought dully. *I'm back in high school.*

Glenn recognized the animal behavior playing out here.

Sandy Minyas fluttered her knowledge at Patrick. This was how brains flirt.

Doesn't even care that I'm right here with a ring on.

Patrick responded to Sandy's stroking. "Exactly." He smiled down at her. Patrick liked short women. His wife, Glenn, was short.

And the ring can go out the air lock with you, darling.

Sandy said, faux coy, "I didn't know you were a xeno-zoologist too, Patrick."

Glenn was closer to thirty than she was to twenty years old, and she was not about to play games with a junior naturalist or anyone else.

You catch him, dolly, you can keep him.

Glenn went back to their compartment. The ship was nearing its destination, and she wanted to finish sleeping.

She was an outsider on this voyage.

Patrick's colleagues didn't know it, but Glenn was a thug. Military.

Glenn Hull Hamilton served as first lieutenant on board the United States Space Battleship *Merrimack*. She thought she should've been first officer by now, but she'd been passed over. Again.

She had no hope of ever becoming the exec of a space battleship without holding an independent command first. She knew this.

She also knew that whatever ship she could get for her first command would not be the kind of spacecraft that carried a xenolinguist, so she had never requested a transfer.

The space battleship *Merrimack* had been Glenn and Patrick's home for six years. For six years Patrick served as xenolinguist on board a ship that talked with her guns. Patrick was effectively a spare part.

Glenn knew Patrick wasn't happy on the *Mack*. So it was only fair that the two spend their six-month leave where Patrick wanted to go.

Which brought them aboard the League of Earth Nations ship *Spring Beauty* bound for a planet named Zoe. Patrick was useful on the scientific expedition. He was valued.

Glenn was baggage.

Planet Zoe lay in the farthest part of the outermost arm of the galaxy in a region known as the Outback.

People showed their true colors far from home.

Glenn was afraid of her own colors. She wasn't fond of Patrick's either. Glenn was afraid this was the seven-year gnaw in the gut. Afraid she'd fallen out of love with him.

Everyone on *Merrimack* said Patrick was a lucky man to have Glenn. No one on *Merrimack* said Glenn was lucky.

She was starting to see why everyone asked, "What does she see in him?"

What does she?

She had stalled her career for this man.

She lay down on their bed.

This trip will either be the thing that breaks us apart or the journey on which I finally murder him.

* * *

Four guards hauled Nox into a wooden shed at the edge of the Legion base.

Inside the shed was hot, the air thick.

When his eyes adjusted to the relative dark, Nox saw in one corner of the shed a bloody tarp draped over a heap on a table.

A bloody boot hung out from under one side of the tarp, dangling over the edge of the table at a broken angle.

The guard nodded at the covered heap and asked Nox, "What is this?"

Nox answered, "I'm guessing that's my brother, Cinna Antonius."

"What happened to him?"

"I killed him," said Nox.

"And how did you do that?"

"I pushed him off the cliff," Nox said. He felt detached, as if he were controlling his body from a distance, above and apart.

"Anyone with you?"

"No."

"These things are usually done in packs," the guard said.

These things. They suspected this was a hazing. Nox caused his body to form the words, "This was personal. I hated him."

"You want to reconsider that statement?"

"No. It wasn't a hazing if that's what you think. It was murder." He felt an inward wince hearing himself volunteer the idea of hazing.

Too much?

He suddenly felt like he was four years old again, when he'd gone into his father's den sporting a cut on his little chin and announced, "*Daddy, I wasn't playing with your razor.*"

He fought to stay detached.

"You pushed him," the guard repeated Nox's statement back at him. No credence at all in that voice. "Why did we find you looking for the body?"

Keep digging, Nox, you'll hit bottom eventually.

"To hide it," Nox said. "I didn't want to get caught."

"You took long enough getting down from the cliff."

How do you know that?

This man wasn't a guard. He had to be an inquisitor in guard's clothing. Maybe the others were intelligence officers too.

"Yes. I am a coward," Nox said. *Stand up front and flap your arms wide enough and hope they don't look for anyone behind you.*

"We know you are a coward," the inquisitor said, dismissive. "You ran away. You came back to get the body. That won't save you."

"I know."

There would be no breaks here. Nox didn't deserve any. Imperial Inspectors had been through here recently—high-ranking men from the Roman capital world, Palatine.

The military installations on Rome's outer colonies like Phoenix had served as secret recruitment centers of Mad Caesar Romulus.

Apparently the new Caesar was shortening his leash on Romulus' Legions of the outer worlds.

Caesar Numa demanded the utmost loyalty from his armed forces.

Caesar Numa's agents were hardliners. Whatever happened to Nox would not be simple.

Legion Persus had to make an example of Nox to show Caesar how hardline it was.

The inquisitor said, "Do you imagine you'll get the sword?"

Nox's spirits actually lifted for one futile moment. There was honor in a sword. But the inquisitor wasn't offering.

Nox lost his sense of detachment. He was firmly, horribly in the here and now. He said, "I would like to. I don't expect it, no."

"You're not getting it."

"Yes, *Domni*," Nox acknowledged.

"In Romulus' day we knew what to do with the likes of you."

In Romulus' day? *That would be what, two years ago? Aye, those were the days.*

"*I* would feed you to the animals," said another guard.

Nox nodded.

"You are a faithless coward. You *ran*. *Then* you turned around and abandoned your brothers. *Now* you're here lying to us to save those cowards. How low can you get?"

I'm finding that out. It's rather amazing, really. It was like a free fall through broken glass.

The interrogators were still digging for others. The main inquisitor was trying to trip Nox into betraying his accomplices.

"I'm not covering for anyone," Nox blurted. His voice didn't sound sincere even to his own ears. He sounded guilty as all hell.

One of the inquisitors saw red.

Truly. The purple-faced man popped a blood vessel in his right eye. Nox had never faced a gaze more baleful than that angry red-smeared eye.

"There was no one else," Nox insisted. "It wasn't a hazing. It was murder. I was alone. I killed Cinna. I swear." *Oh, how obvious was that?*

The Eye spoke in a strange soft voice, a dare, "You swear?"

"I do." Nox nodded down.

They all turned away.

One guard gave the Eye a surreptitious gesture and a murmur, "Eye."

The man wiped his eye, saw the blood on his fingers. Gave a low snarling mutter, something like, "Sure. Why not?"

In the next moment a holographic image formed in the

dark shed. The floor vanished, became a windy cliff high above a sun-parched flatland. Nox was suddenly looking down on eight young men. The scene was a vulture's eye view of the Widow's Edge.

Or a satellite's view.

Video. They had a video from orbit.

Nox's despair was complete. They knew. They knew. They stood him up here and let him lie his brains out.

The holographic video played out. There was Cinna's leap. The impact. The brothers' scurrying retreat.

The image vanished.

An afterimage of brightness colored the darkness within the shed in red and green splotches.

The bloody Eye glowered at Nox. "You are not really Roman."

Oh, it goes lower still. They were going to throw that at him. Nox was willing to absorb any abuse for what he'd done, but not that. Now he was angry. "I am Roman," said Nox. His voice had gone to sandpaper.

"It makes no difference now. Confess. You are really a U.S. mole, aren't you?"

Nox hadn't thought he had any blood left in his face, but he felt it draining away now. Then it returned in a rush of heat, and he roared at the inquisitor, "NO! Rome is my mother, my father, my world! I am Roman!" He rocked with his heaving breaths. Regretted his volume.

The inquisitors ignored the outburst.
"You have a choice, Yank. You can go home. Or you can stand judgment with your squad."

Shock numbed him. It was the last thing he expected.

They were offering him his life and freedom.

The hazing wasn't the huge crime. Causing his brother's death was fairly huge. But the worst, the unforgivable, was running away and leaving Cinna behind. Brother betrayal was the lowest.

Nox had turned around to go back to his brother, but only after he'd already made the wrong decision. Rome didn't want anyone like that in her legions. Especially not under the current scrutiny from the home world. Nox had expected his punishment to be doled out in stellar magnitudes.

Yet they offered him an out.

He could go back where he came from.

Crawl back to his father.

Not ever.

They didn't want him to be Roman.

Go home.

He felt light-headed in his wrath. He looked from the Eye to the other men and back.

His voice shook with indignation. "*Domni*, I *am* home."

4

PATRICK'S SLEEPY VOICE sounded mumbly in the dark, "Where you going, babe?"

"Control room," Glenn whispered, tucked her shirt into her trousers. "Go back to sleep."

Glenn made sure she was awake for the drop to sublight on approach to the Zoen star system.

Spring Beauty was no *Merrimack*. She had minimal inertial compensators with which to sidestep Newton's first law.

At minimum, any faster-than-light craft's inertial field kept the ship's innards from bulleting out through its hull when the ship deviated from a dead-straight line.

Stouter force fields, like *Merrimack*'s, could withstand antimatter warheads.

The *Beauty*'s force field was adequate to deflect space clutter. It was not designed to stand against space weapons.

Manny, the pilot, assured Glenn there weren't going to be any warships where they were going. "We're in the bloody Outback. Traffic is thin here, even for outer space. This is good coffee. Thanks."

Glenn nodded. She slid into the copilot's seat and cradled her own cup of coffee in her hands.

The pilot said, "It's not as if space is choked with LGMs waiting to pounce on us traveling faster than light."

"Of course not," Glenn agreed.

The pouncing would be within the star system while they traveled at sublight speed.

And Glenn was not worried about little green men. "Tall, bronze, and arrogant men are more my concern."

"Romans?" Manny said, surprised. "You don't really think there are Romans out here?"

Glenn tilted her head, neither yes nor no. "*Ubiquitous* is a Roman word." She had to assume that Rome knew about the planet Zoe. Zoe was the most Earthlike world ever discovered.

Always assume Rome knows.

Glenn had a professional paranoia regarding the Empire. She still had the wartime mind-set of an officer of a space battleship recently at war with the Roman Empire. Two years was too long for a peace to last.

She watched Manny go through the approach routine. Nothing to do really but monitor the ship's programmed flight.

At the star system's edge, the *Beauty*'s engine whined, surged to full. Speeding up or slowing down, it took as much power to pass the light barrier either way you went.

The ship's engine peaked. Stars appeared in the forward viewport.

The *Beauty*'s engine quickly wound back down. Momentum carried her swiftly into the star system.

A distant yellow sun loomed ahead of them. Steadily shining bright dots that were probably planets appeared above and below it.

The ship executed a gentle quarter roll. *Beauty* had entered the system on an oblique. The lazy roll brought her on plane with the local planetary orientation—a position that made sense to humans accustomed to viewing images of laterally arrayed planetary systems.

Through the forward view screen, the planet Zoe took center stage.

Hanging in the star-specked blackness, the world appeared as a hazy blue-white marble, growing larger and larger. With the planet's yellow sun in the background, Glenn could almost imagine the *Spring Beauty* had turned around and gone home to Earth. Until she saw the moons.

As *Spring Beauty* turned, the two moons passed into view from behind the planet. The pair twisted around each other, as tight as conjoined twins. A hazy dumbbell-shaped halo surrounded both of them as they swapped atmospheres.

Glenn had been told that the tidal effect between the lunar pair and Zoe was roughly equal to the tidal draw between the Earth and Moon.

Expedition notes described Zoe as an Earthlike world orbiting in the Goldilocks zone of a singly formed G2V star.

The notes didn't do her justice. Zoe was beautiful, glowing blue and green, draped in cotton white.

"I never get tired of that view," Manny said.

They were gazing out the forward view screen, sipping coffee and listening to the quiet stirrings of waking brains behind them within the ship. Then, without prelude, a loud *crack!* jarred everyone. Splashed coffee over Glenn's fingers.

Felt like something struck the ship's hull.

Several overlapping voices sounded from aft, "What was that?"

Someone—it sounded like Dr. Rose—moved forward to the control room yelling, "Hey! Manny! Fly us *around* the asteroids."

"I didn't fly us into that," the pilot said.

"Then explain how we hit it." Aaron Rose braced himself in the hatchway.

"*It*," said Manny, "hit *us* on the beam."

"How in the help me mama!" Dr. Rose dropped in a reflexive duck as another *crack* rang through the hull with a metallic scraping.

Any spaceship's forward inertial screen deflected debris from its path. You never hear the forward strikes. This noise came from farther down the fuselage, where the *Beauty*'s energy field was thin.

Still another *crack* banged at the hull. Hard one. Sounded like there should be a dent.

Sounded like there should be a *hole*.

But cabin pressure hadn't dropped. Not noticeably. Even if there were a slow leak, Glenn would expect a warning signal from the ship's internal systems.

Glenn got up from her seat, reached around the pilot, and redistributed the ship's energy field—such as it was.

Manny stared at small hands—not his—moving the ship's controls. "What are you doing?"

"We're under attack." Glenn hip-pushed Manny out of the pilot's seat.

With more sense than ego, Manny slid into the copilot's seat without much resistance.

Most civilian pilots never needed to redeploy inertial settings. Manny would have learned how, of course, but it was dusty knowledge.

Manny seemed to recognize expertise when he saw it and deferred to it.

"Can we jump to FTL?" Manny asked.

Magical thinking, that. They both knew a jump to FTL with the ship in this condition could turn it inside out.

Letting the vacuum in, they called it on *Merrimack*.

"I think it's too late for that," said Glenn. "We're hurt."

Glenn pushed *Spring Beauty*'s speed up and maneuvered one of her exterior hull cameras outward to pick up the incoming objects.

The objects had fallen in behind the *Beauty*, chasing her now.

They were not asteroids.

The chasers were more like demon-possessed cannon balls. They looked like miniature Roman killer bots.

The old Roman killer bots were black orbs that carried antimatter loads. A killer bot would have destroyed the *Spring Beauty* on impact.

Dr. Rose, crouching in the control room's hatchway, yelped, "What are those!"

Little green men, Glenn thought. She said, "Aaron, I think you should go aft."

She would have liked to grab one of the attacking orbs for identification, but this was not the *Merrimack*. *Beauty* didn't have a hook. *Beauty* barely had a force field. Best *Beauty* could do here was survive.

Poul Vrba stomped forward to the control room, stumbled over Dr. Rose getting in, and shouted, "Get us out of the asteroid field!"

He saw Glenn in the pilot's seat. Shouted louder, "What are you doing there!"

Glenn told Vrba, "The asteroids are chasing us."

"What did you do to provoke them!?!"

Glenn ignored the question. She jinked the little ship

hard. *Beauty* did not jink well. Glenn's stomach lurched sideways.

Vrba caught his balance. "You did something! No being with the level of intelligence to achieve space travel would just attack a stranger without trying to communicate first!"

"This is their first communication," Glenn said, trying to line up an entry into atmosphere.

And realized Vrba was right. She really was provoking the orbs. They didn't want *Spring Beauty* in the atmosphere.

A second flock of orbs converged like hornets from the starboard. They glanced off the ship's inertial field as Glenn pushed the ship's nose down—down according to the ship's internal artificial gravity.

Vrba ordered the pilot, "Do something!"

"Whatever she tells me," Manny said.

Dr. Helmut Roodoverhemd, xenosociologist, climbed over Dr. Rose, staggered into the small control room, and crawled to the communications console. He spoke into the ship's com, insisting this was a League of Earth Nations vessel.

"We are peaceful. Permit us to pass." Roodoverhemd translated the message into all the languages in the universal data bank and sent it out by all known communications media.

Scientists counted on peaceful intent to get them through any hostiles.

Yes. That always works.

Glenn ignored him. Roodoverhemd wasn't in her way.

Many orbs drove into her path. They peppered the monitor display. Forced her to veer off her approach.

I am flying into a hot zone on a ship equipped with peashooters, good only for shooting peas.

The *Beauty* didn't even carry antipirate guns.

Glenn hauled the ship in ways it was never meant to move. Caught herself in a lean, then exchanged wide-eyed looks with the pilot.

"That's not supposed to happen," said Manny.

"No, it's not," said Glenn. "We're losing inertial field."

She veered the ship up and over.

"Strap in. I'm going to kill artificial gravity."

Poul Vrba roared, "What the hell are you doing! Let the pilot—"

"Pilot?" Glenn cut him off. "This boat does not have a pilot. I'm sorry, you have a bus driver."

Antigrav cut out. Vrba lifted off the deck. Roodoverhemd clutched at the com station.

Glenn's ponytail slowly lifted off her neck.

Vrba yelled at the pilot, "You can't let her—!"

"Let the woman drive," said Manny. And to Glenn, "What can I do?"

Glenn glanced aside. Manny was pale but willing. She asked, "Any combat training?"

"No."

"Get everyone into the lifeboat."

Manny nodded, unstrapped, and floated out of the control room, herding Doctors Vrba, Roodoverhemd, and Rose out with him.

After they were gone, Glenn was peripherally aware of someone else entering the cabin behind her. The man airswam into the copilot's chair, pulled himself down, and strapped himself in.

Glenn glanced aside. Double-glanced. Cried in horror, "Get out!"

"I'm with you, babe," Patrick said.

Patrick had been in several crises. Was not proud of the way he'd handled himself.

He said now, "One just cannot go around screaming every time one thinks he's going to die."

Patrick was doing an admirable job of not screaming. He was terrified here. He was *here*.

Glenn couldn't make herself demand he go to the lifeboat. She took more comfort and strength from his presence than she ever could have imagined. She wheeled the *Beauty* hard out of a swarm of attackers.

The little ship lumbered. The orbs turned clumsily after.

"Are they killer bots?" Patrick asked, his voice stretched thin.

Glenn shook her head, no. Rome had more pride than that. "Don't think so."

Rome didn't use killer bots anymore.

"They don't look right."

And had the orbs been Roman, the *Beauty* would be dead already.

Glenn circled the ship wide. More of the orbs moved in between her and the planet on her new approach vector. "They don't want us in atmo."

The *Spring Beauty* executed a sick-making roll, pulling g's.

Spacecraft never pulled g's.

The inertial compensation system went off-line. That meant no energy barrier. Without it, the ship would burn up in the atmosphere.

The energy field flickered back on. Next time it went off, it might stay off.

"This is it." Glenn stabbed into as steep a dive as she dared.

Spring Beauty slashed into the planetary atmosphere, streaming a wide contrail behind her across continents.

Glenn checked altitude. Adjusted inertials for a controlled descent. Checked her six for orbs. Noted, "They're not chasing."

"Ha!" Patrick rejoiced—

—just before the inertials glitched out.

A current of very thin air sheared off a stabilizer. The boxy ship wheeled and tumbled. Glenn's teeth clacked together. Her chin hit her chest. Her body wrenched sideways in her straps.

Inertials gasped back on. Glenn adjusted the ship's attitude so that up was up.

She nursed the ship into a lumpy, jarring descent, inertials flickering on and off. The *Beauty* was as aerodynamic as a Guernsey cow, but with a lot more mass.

Patrick must have blacked out. He lolled in his harness.

The inertials came back on. Patrick's head lifted. He gave a muddled, waking, "Huh?"

The air grew denser. Glenn tried to control the ship's wrack, shudder, and shake. Her heart seemed to be vibrating in her mouth. She bit her tongue.

As soon as the lifeboat readings showed locked, pressurized, and green across the board, Glenn threw the release.

The control balked.

Negative release.

The catches jammed. *Spring Beauty* was going down, and she was taking the lifeboat with her.

Needles of fear stabbed under Glenn's tongue.

She couldn't control the ship and fight with the release mechanism at the same time.

She banged on the lifeboat release with her palm heel. "Patrick, make this happen."

Patrick took over wrestling with the release, while Glenn fought to regain control of their descent.

White, shaking, Patrick asked, "C-can I hit it?"

Eyes locked forward Glenn said, "You can kick it. Talk dirty to it. Anything."

The ship cartwheeled. The piggybacked lifeboat tumbled with it.

Fear crowded Glenn's thoughts—the dire need to save all those people, her husband, herself. Thickness swelled in her chest. Didn't dare think about any of that.

The voices were the worst of it. She was not accustomed to hearing sounds like wounded puppies during a crisis. She shut out the screams.

Nothing existed but the job at hand.

Flame plumed out of the ship's nose and streamed fore to aft, eclipsing the view.

Instrument readings were erratic.

A hull breach somewhere topside let in the burning heat and dense air. Smoke filled the cabin. Glenn pulled the front of her shirt up over her nose and squinted her eyes. The ship juddered, heavy air bludgeoning its torn hull.

Glenn was aware of Patrick's voice from beside her. Heard him as if at a distance. "Babe? Are we going to make it?"

The most positive thing she could tell Patrick was, "The impact won't be hard enough to compromise the antimatter magnetic containment field."

That meant: *If we die, we won't take out a five-hundred-kilometer radius with us*.

Thick vegetation came into sudden sharp focus below. Ferny, feathery, leafy foliage. Glenn could imagine those were the green trees of home.

A piece of the ship's nose tore off and hit the forward view screen. Cracked it.

Open air streamed in. Heat and smoke shut the eyes. Glenn smelled the stench of scorched hair. Hers.

Muffled screaming and stomping of the trapped passengers carried forward from the still-attached lifeboat through the ship's hull.

She wished she could have saved them. She felt that failure like a physical wound.

Felt Patrick's palm press against her back. "I love you, Glenn Hull."

※ ※ ※

Pallas, Nicanor, Leo, Galeo, Faunus, and Orissus sat hunch-shouldered in a tight circle in their barracks hut. The sun angled in. The hour was coming up on roll call.

Nicanor shivered in the heat. He whispered, "What do we do about Cinna and Nox?"

"Do?" Orissus hissed. "They're kind of *done*."

"I mean what do we say when they don't show up for muster?"

Pallas nodded. A Roman was accountable for his tent mates. "We can't exactly say we don't know where they are."

When two squad members failed to show up, it would be the fault of all eight. *I don't know* was not an answer. *I don't know* was an admission of negligence.

"We can't wait for muster to do something," Nicanor said. "We need to act first."

"And do what?" said Leo.

Faunus said what no one else would, "We need to report Cinna and Nox AWOL."

With the unspeakable finally spoken, Orissus picked up from there, "We go to the commandant right now. Tell him Nox and Cinna were gone when we woke up, and we haven't seen them, and we're concerned. We ask him to ping them."

A satellite would be able to locate Nox and Cinna by the ident capsules embedded in their earlobes. The Vigil would find Cinna's body at the foot of Widow's Edge. And Nox? The brothers didn't know where they would find Nox. Nox hadn't told them where he was going.

Leo and Galeo nodded.

They all looked to Pallas.

Pallas turned his eyes heavenward, beautiful and sad as a lonely angel. Pallas said, "I can't."

"I can't get enthusiastic about it either," said Faunus. "But what choice is there?"

Nicanor said, "Nox volunteered to take the blame for us. We need to go on. We need to honor his sacrifice."

Pallas turned his back. "I can't do this."

Orissus cried in a whisper, "It's *done!*"

They were between Scylla and Charybdis. There was no decent way to go. "I can't smear two brothers with a lie," Pallas said.

"Then what do we do?" Faunus demanded. "Confess?"

Pallas shuddered.

Galeo said, "If we confess, that makes a liar out of Nox."

Nicanor blurted, "I'm going to fall on my sword."

The silence returned. It thickened, solidified. There was nothing more to say.

The best they could do was salvage their names.

It was a hard thing to accept, the dying. They had scarcely started adulthood. They hadn't lived.

Pallas turned back to his brothers. A tear trickled down the side of his nose.

No way out but this.

They bowed their heads, struggled.

Hard breathing disturbed the quiet. These were to be their last breaths.

Nicanor's midriff convulsed. He swallowed down hard.

From the far side of the door carried the approaching sound of grit crunching under boot soles.

The door opened inward. A slash of sunlight split the floor. Figures darkened the doorway. A plumed helmet defined the silhouette of an officer.

The brothers should have made their decision quicker. It was too late for sword-falling now.

5

I T WAS DECIDED FOR THEM.
The adjutant called their names.
Antonius Pallas.
Antonius Orissus.
Antonius Galeo.
Antonius Leo.
Antonius Nicanor.
Antonius Faunus.
He called six names.
And stopped.
The two omissions screamed like a telltale heart.
They knew.
The adjutant had not called Antonius Cinna. And he hadn't called Antonius Nox.
Orissus' eyes slid to his nearest brother, Faunus. The unspoken thought passed between them:
Nox rolled on us.
Orissus mouthed words without sound. *Rat. Rat. Rat.*
Then the base praefect stepped forward, his eyes raking the brothers up and down.
The praefect was a grand, austere veteran foot soldier. He wore his battle scars like medals. Breathed as if there were scars in his lungs.
He asked any of them, all of them, "Where is Antonius Cinna?"
Pallas tried to say he didn't know. The lie stuck in his throat. He said instead, "He is not here, *Domni*."

"I can see that. You don't know how he came to be at the bottom of Widow's Edge?"

The brothers stammered for a response, exchanging glances. Orissus bluffed, "You mean he jumped?"

"Were you there?" the praefect asked back.

Pallas lifted his chin, summoned up a lie. "No, *Domni*."

"Did you see it?"

"No, *Domni*."

"*Render aid?*"

Pallas swallowed hard. This one hurt because it was the truth. Pallas' voice broke, "No, *Domni*."

"*Abandon your man?*"

The words burned.

"Is that what Nox told you?" Pallas said softly, choking on resentment.

The old praefect's eyes widened into bulging orbs. He roared, wheezing. "Do you think I haven't jumped off that cliff myself! Do you think I haven't pushed 'phebes over myself!" His face purpled, veins stood out, primed to frag. "Do you think—? No. Never mind. No one cares what you think! You're a waste of oxygen." He pulled his sidearm and jabbed it at Pallas' face.

Pallas held his ground, blinking. He said nothing.

The praefect jammed his sidearm back into its holster and stalked out of the hut. The guards marched the brothers outside.

* * *

The *Spring Beauty*'s controls gave one last gasp. Her inertials kicked back in to slow her jangled plummeting. The helm had pitch and roll control but not yaw, so she came spinning down like a house out of Kansas.

She hit the treetops, flaming and shredding alien vegetation. At the very end she rallied and touched ground with a gentle *flump* and died.

Halon hissed on the lively flames inside and out. The ship settled with a sigh.

The lifeboat clamps unhooked. The escape craft slid slowly off the *Beauty*'s fuselage and stopped at an angle against a stand of trees. Its parachute deployed in a large plume that draped itself in the branches.

Glenn wiped her face. Her eyebrows crumbled off. The insides of her nostrils felt raw.

She gave the ship's console a pat. "Good girl."

Beside her, Patrick looked chalky white. He said, "I knew you could do it."

Glenn's hairless eyebrows skewed and arched, skeptical. "'I love you, Glenn Hull?'"

"I had to get that in there just in case I was wrong," Patrick said, and he shivered.

His eyes took on a glassy vacancy. Glenn unstrapped herself from her seat, then unstrapped Patrick. His body oozed to the deck.

Glenn kicked open the first aid kit, found an intradermal and gave Patrick a shot for the shock.

Within seconds he blinked back to normality. He looked up at her. "Sorry."

"You did good," Glenn said. She helped him sit up.

The lifeboat hatch opened. Its contents staggered out. Glenn closed up the first aid kit and sent Patrick aft with it to dispense to the needy.

Moaning, some screaming, and a blur of talking sounded from back there. Nothing Glenn cared to hear. She had the answer ready when the team leader stomped forward to demand, "Where the hell are we?"

Glenn read out their exact latitude and longitude.

Not the answer he'd expected. Poul Vrba had a righteous rant prepared and couldn't deliver it. He made his way back to the lifeboat and reported their location to the others.

Sounds of delight rose amid the crying.

"We're here!"

"The camp is just a klick or two away! That way!"

"How lucky is that!"

Glenn recognized Dr. Minyas' voice.

Luck. Glenn pursed her lips, shook her head. *Sure. Rhymes with luck.*

Glenn checked the engine core containment field. Found it functioning and stable. She picked up her gear from the deck and tossed it out through the gaping hole where the forward view screen used to be. She didn't want to walk back among those people to get out.

From the direction of the LEN camp, three hoverskiffs

came whipping through the Zoen underbrush. They were laden with first aid supplies and fire suppressants.

Their crews found the fires already out.

They loaded the injured onto one of the hovers. There was a broken rib, a broken wrist, a twisted ankle. A dislocated shoulder. Contusions to go around. Patrick had already treated the shock cases.

Glenn and Patrick were the only ones singed. Glenn waved off the medic. His name was Cecil. Not sure if that was his first or last name. "I'm fine," Glenn told Cecil. "Go take care of someone screaming."

The descent had been terrifying enough, but Glenn was not accustomed to the expressiveness of civilians. Glenn served among man jacks and man janes who kept glib lines ready, like *Honey I forgot to duck,* to deploy in case of emergency, so they wouldn't sound weak or cowardly. Lines like *I love you Glenn Hull.* That had been well done on Patrick's part.

Someone was shrieking like world's end. The screamer was on her feet, wasn't wearing any blood, and wasn't standing over someone else who was bleeding.

Civilian.

Civilians were allowed to scream.

The medical hover with its wounded took off the way it came, thrashing through the alien greenery.

The crews of the other two skiffs loaded heavy equipment onto their hovers. They promised to come back for the new arrivals' personal belongings.

Those who could walk set out toward the camp in a loose column, ducking and high-stepping through leafy branches, vines, thorns, fallen logs, dead leaves, and things that looked like dead leaves but hopped out of the way as your foot came down.

Glenn carried her own pack. She took up the ass-end Charlie spot in the column.

Her gear was heavier than when she'd packed it. *She* was heavier.

Bugs with cobweb wings floated on the air. Crawling bugs with lots of legs scrambled up the tree trunks. Jumping bugs she didn't see—she just felt them—collided with her ankles. Bugs that hid in the green-gold canopy whirred overhead.

The ground under boot sole was soft and fragrant as a pine needle carpet. Forest creatures chirped, piped, whistled, and trilled. The air was easy to breathe.

The expedition camp had been founded in the temperate zone on the currently summer side of the world. The temperature was comfortable. The humidity was comfortable. The barrage of smells and sounds were different but mostly pleasant.

Concepts of beauty only held up among close members of your own genome. Alien concepts of beauty and ugliness differed extremely—if the aliens conceived of beauty at all.

Even so, Zoe was beautiful.

The forest looked strange, but no stranger than life on other continents of Earth must have appeared to ancient explorers.

There was a sweet, rich tang to the forest air.

Glenn swatted something that was biting her leg. Hoped it was not the sapient species here.

Up ahead, the brush was clearing. Sunlight streamed through thinning branches and vines. Voices of happy greetings carried back from the front of the file.

Glenn arrived last in camp. She heard a bleat like a goat.

It was a goat.

The nanny goat was snubbing her hay bag and straining on her tether to tear into some local vegetation with large purple leaves. The nan's udder was swollen like a four-fingered water balloon.

Patrick eyed the goat and the purple plant. Asked, "How's the milk taste?"

"A little interesting," Dr. Rose said. This was Aaron's second gig here.

The expedition camp comprised a wide clearing bounded by six boxy spacecraft set in a half ring like Conestoga wagons, or like dormitories around a college green. There was a foundation for a seventh craft that was meant to be the *Spring Beauty*'s landing pad.

Within the loose ring of ships were huts to serve as field labs and storage units and tents, which most xenos chose for their living quarters.

And at the very center of camp lay a stone fire pit.

The LEN camp had no common language—not to deny

anyone his or her native tongue—so everyone wore language modules behind their ears.

Glenn overheard someone complaining, rather loudly, about the distance she needed to haul her gear. Patrick nudged Glenn. "You should have crashed us closer."

"Starting to wish," said Glenn.

Glenn knew from an advance briefing that Zoe had a nitrox atmosphere—heavy on the ox—with a sea level pressure of nineteen psi. The planet tilted twenty-one degrees on its axis. The planetary rotation of twenty-two Terrestrial hours would make sleep cycles tolerable.

Glenn reprogrammed her own chron to synch with Zoen local time.

Hovers transported the last of the equipment from the *Spring Beauty* to the expedition campsite. The resident scientists helped set up huts and tents for the newcomers. They patched up the wounded, calmed the hysterical, and prepared dinner.

Finally Glenn asked the Expedition Director, Dr. Izrael Benet, "Why did no one tell us the local sapience is space capable?"

Izrael Benet was not the typical xeno. He was an administrator and a fund-raiser, which required him to be attractive. Izzy Benet maintained the dashing appearance of an adventurer. He was large-boned and muscular as an outdoorsman with a thick mane of wavy hair and deep brown bedroom eyes. He was the kind of man to whom philanthropists liked to give money.

Director Benet's deep eyes looked down on Glenn blandly. His baritone voice was mellow and patronizing. "The local sapience is not space capable, Mrs. Hamilton. They are simple beings."

"Then we are not the only aliens here," Glenn said. "Someone else wants this planet."

"Someone wants this planet?" Director Benet's face took on a befuddled expression. "Where did that notion come from?"

Where didn't it? "Everyone told you about our arrival."

"So they did," said Izrael Benet. "You're taking an enormous leap to a melodramatic conclusion from a false premise. 'Someone *else* wants this planet?' Someone else? For your edification, *we* do not want to take ownership of this world."

"*They,*" Glenn said, "*do.*"

That won her an amazed condescending smile. "They?" Izrael Benet asked, disingenuous. "What *they*? Surely you don't mean the *meteors?*"

* * *

Rome kept no prisons. Incarceration was not a Roman punishment. There were, however, brigs for short-term detention.

Nox paced his confines. Three strides and he had to turn around. He sat on one of the two benches. Drummed his fingers. Got up. Paced.

Guards came. They banged on the bars and ordered him to stand away from the door. Nox took three steps back.

The cell door opened.

Pallas, Nicanor, Leo, Galeo, Orissus, and Faunus filed in. Their mouths moved as if chewing venom. A savage glint of satisfaction sparked in their dark eyes. They seemed happy to see him landed in the same cage as they.

Nox sat on a bench along one wall. The six of them crowded onto the bench opposite him.

No one spoke.

Nox was in free fall. Like jumping off the Widow's Edge. Dropping down and down, and he kept going down. He knew what his brothers thought. They thought he'd ratted on them.

And he could not defend himself. It would be whiny, groveling, and pointless. He could only salvage his one last shred of *dignitas*, in his own eyes if no one else's.

> *If you can wait and not be tired by waiting,*
> *Or being lied about, don't deal in lies,*
> *Or being hated, don't give way to hating . . .*

Hate was easier to hold than abject misery. Nox let his brothers hang on to their hatred.

The next morning the squad was marched before the Legate for judgment.

The Legate's chamber inside the Principia was hung with bronze and black colors. The imperial silver Eagle, the Legion standard, and the imago of Caesar Numa loomed over the Legate's high bench.

The guards looked shamed, as if something of the accused had rubbed off on them.

Nox stood directly before the bench.

The blood brothers made their stand at a distance from Nox, as far to the side as the guards would allow them.

The Legate spoke first to the six who stood apart from the one Other. "Death is too good for you. You are cowards. You caused your brother's death, then left him and let another brother take the blame."

Nox felt his face burn red.

"You are trash. Shame on the Empire when *semper fidelis* means more to the Yanks than to one of your own. The name Antonius will be stripped from you."

Nox could not look at his brothers. He could feel the daggers in their hearts and in their eyes.

Done shredding the brothers, the Legate turned his hawk glare to Nox. "You ran. You may have gone back, but that doesn't change the fact that you ran. Comes a moment in battle that proves the man. You proved yourself in the moment of emergency. You are no better than the rest of this sputum. On top of that, you lied to us to preserve cowards. You will suffer the same sentence. You will all be drummed out of the Legion and no longer be called Roman. From this day forward, should anyone kill you, it will not be murder. Should you fall on a sword, it gives no honor. Take them out. I can't bear to look at this offal." The Legate rose tall, quaking with rage. "Slave!" He pointed down from his high bench to where the brothers stood. "Wash that floor!"

The guards marched the brothers out of the Legate's chamber as the slave moved in to erase their footsteps.

The Legion stood at grand attention.

This morning Nox had thought to join their ranks. Now men he wanted to stand shoulder to shoulder with would not even look at him. They glared over his head, their eyes narrowed, stone hatred on their faces. Six hundred men arrayed in laser precise columns and rows.

His beloved Legion Persus assembled to spit him out.

At a command, the Legion divided. A passage opened up between its halves.

Oh, this hurts.

The exiles had to walk through that.

Just when Nox thought he couldn't get any lower, any deader, they killed him again. Was there no bottom?

He felt all the eyes.

The brothers had never been fully fledged legionaries, so there was no rank to strip from them. They'd been told to wear civilian clothes for this. Nothing black. Nothing bronze. Or it would be stripped off their bodies.

The line of the condemned was ordered to face left. That put them in a single file with Nox in the fore, facing that horrifying passage. And beyond that, straight ahead, lay the gates.

The drums started. Nox's stomach fluttered in time.

The drums abruptly stopped.

A name was called. Pallas Antonius.

Nox heard a stirring behind him. Confusion among his brothers. Pallas heard his name. Didn't know if he was supposed to do something.

No. The name had been called for the Censor to strike it from the rolls.

"No such Roman citizen," the Censor reported.

The drums rolled again. And silenced.

Another name called.

And one by one the brothers' names, their identities, their existences were erased.

At the last, a centurion ordered the file forward. That's when someone threw up. Nox heard the retch and splat behind him. He didn't look back to see who it was. Might have been any of them. Nox stalled a moment to let his brother recover. Then he began their walk down their final exit.

The drums started up again. Not a roll this time. A thudding grave march. Nox didn't have orders, but he found himself walking to the drumbeat, lurching ahead, leading the others.

The Legion ranks turned their backs on them as they approached.

Oh, and here came the breakfast he didn't eat. Nox forced it back down.

When Nox was clear of the rearmost row of legionaries, the mammoth gates of the Legion compound parted before him.

The hideous drums fell silent.

It had been a ghastly sound. The silence was suddenly worse, broken only by their own footfalls.

Nox marched his wretched file through the towering gates. Heard one of his brothers stumble and sag behind him. Heard someone else pulling him upright and piloting him out.

They made it out of the compound.

Behind them the gates shut with a resounding boom. The bar dropped.

Rome didn't use stone walls to keep enemies out in Anno Domini 2447. The stone walls were symbolic now, a reminder of Rome's ancient heritage.

The walls also kept out desert scavengers, which was what the brothers were now.

Clear of the compound, their orderly Roman file dissolved. They were no longer a contubernium. They were not Roman. They were no one. The wretched seven fanned out.

And now Nox's brothers were going to rip him apart.

It began with a fist to his kidney. Didn't see who threw it. Pain shot out his eyeballs. Couldn't breathe. Doubled over and landed cheek-first in the dust. Took a kick in the gut. Couldn't even try to breathe. Nausea had nowhere to go. Heat rose in his face. A glob of spit splatted on his eyelid.

"Wait."

They all sounded alike, but Nox knew somehow that this was Pallas talking.

And he knew Orissus by his damaged larynx. "What for?"

"Something," said Pallas. Deeply uncertain. "Something."

"What something!" someone else cried.

Pallas made halting sounds of someone grasping for a half-formed thought. His words staggered out. "The Legate. The Legate said . . ." His voice stopped.

Nox cracked an eyelid. Saw Pallas' blurry boot in his face, nudging him. Pallas leaned down. "The Legate said you lied to them to preserve cowards. What did he mean by that?"

Nox could not breathe. Even if he could have spoken, he refused to try to explain. The truth was pointless. Better his brothers not know. They wouldn't believe him anyway. They were going to kill him. Just go silently.

Pallas roared, "*What did you tell them!*"

Nox gaped like a fish on land. His diaphragm wouldn't move. Kept him from screaming in pain.

Faunus hauled him up by his armpits, dropped him on his feet a couple times. Nox's diaphragm relaxed. Nox gasped.

Faunus snarled in his ear. "What did you tell them?"

Pallas looked unnerved. "You sold us out." Those were his words. Pallas' voice said he didn't believe them anymore.

Nox said nothing. Blood oozed from his lips. From his nose. Inside his head was very hot.

Pallas screamed at him. "*You sold us out!*"

There were two Pallases. Nox's eye contact wavered.

Pallas shook him. There were three Pallases now. Breath buffeted Nox's face. "*Didn't* you?"

6

DIDN'T YOU!
Nox folded back to the ground and sprawled face up, breathing.

Pallas' faces swam before Nox's crossed eyes. A double ring of his brothers hovered above Pallas in a ferocious halo, fists ready to resume beating Nox to death.

Peripherally Nox saw Faunus working up a great gob of spit and wrapping a strap around his hammy knuckles.

Pallas demanded again. "You sold us out, didn't you?"

"We know he did, Pallas!" said Orissus, tired of this, stepping in with a cocked fist. "What's a confession going to get us?"

Pallas backed Orissus up, hand to Orissus' broad chest. *"I* need the confession," said Pallas. "The Legate said Nox lied." He turned to Nox. Shouted in his face, *"What did you tell them?"*

One eye swelled shut. There was only one Pallas now. Nox tasted blood on his split lips. Slowly he moved his head side to side; no. "Doesn't matter." He lifted a forefinger skyward. Whispered hollowly, "They have a *coiens* satellite video."

"They—!"

The menacing ring flinched wider with an involuntary look up.

The glint of satellites shone through the dusty haze. The ever-present day stars. Everyone knew the satellite Vigils were up there. You never paid them any attention.

Nox tongued a loose tooth. Rasped, "Sat eyes."

"No," said Orissus. Wouldn't believe it. "No. All the latitudes and longitudes on this planet, and they just *happened* to focus right there, right then? Why would the Vigils focus on a cliff in the wasteland?"

Nicanor said thickly, "Probably looking for guys doing what we were doing. We aren't the only squad ever to walk a tyro off Widow's Edge."

Just the only ones ever to drop one. The thought pounded in Nox's head.

Pallas' face reappeared above him. Pallas looked and sounded quietly horrified. "You didn't tell on us."

Nox gingerly gave his head the slightest shake. Croaked, "No."

His brothers backed away, stricken.

"*Skat*, Nox!" Sounded like Faunus. That was sort of an apology. It was the most remorse any of them could bear right now.

Apparently Orissus couldn't bear it at all. He moved away, snarling to himself, insisting, "No." Sounded like he badly wanted Nox to be a rat.

Nox understood that. The reality was hard to face: *We sold ourselves out.*

Nox sat up slowly, hand to his rib cage. Mumbled, "How many rings of hell are there?"

"Nine," said Nicanor miserably.

The moment they had turned to run away, it was over. Even had Nox stayed behind, it would not have helped. He had the lose-or-lose choice. Run with his brothers or split with his brothers to stay behind with dead Cinna. Nox was faithless either way. In Rome you are your unit. If one of you is bad, you're all bad. If one of you is good, you're still all bad. Nox had tried to protect them. It had been for nothing.

Useless. Useless.

Pallas reached a hand down to Nox. Nox just sat in the dust, mourning. "O Best Beloved, we did not do right by our brother. Where do traitors go in the inferno?"

"The bottom," said Nicanor. "The Ninth Circle. With Judas, Brutus, and Satan."

Nox nodded carefully. *Yep, that seems about right.*

* * *

"John!" Glenn cried when the admiral's image appeared before her.

Admiral John Farragut greeted her with a smile to light planets. "Hamster!"

His blue eyes and soaring spirit radiated energy across the resonant link.

Glenn never thought that man would ever touch ground. But John Farragut got himself stationed on Earth.

She loved him. Always had. He was the road not taken. She and he were never meant to be. Glenn was a career officer. John Farragut needed himself a girlie girl to give him home and hearth and little Farraguts.

They had each chosen their own road. Had she to do it over, Glenn would make the same choice again. But in this moment she clung to the happiness in John Farragut's eyes, the affection in his voice.

The bright blue eyes squinted in concern, and he leaned sideways to look past her. "Where *are* you? I thought y'all were going to Zoe."

It shouldn't surprise her he knew where she was going. John Farragut always kept track of his people.

"We made it. We're here. We're on Zoe. This is our ship." She moved aside to give him a better view of the devastation of *Spring Beauty*'s control room.

Glenn had slipped away from the LEN camp to contact him privately on the *Beauty's* resonator. She knew the admiral's personal res harmonic by heart.

"This planet is under invasion," Glenn told him.

His immediate question: "Are you safe?"

"Yes. We were attacked on approach. They haven't followed us down."

John Farragut put on his admiral's face. "Roman?"

Glenn hesitated. "Maybe. I don't think so."

She told him her story.

At the end, he asked, "Did you report it?"

"That's the trick, isn't it? The local authority is the LEN. This—" she flicked her hands at the wreckage around her— "is a LEN vessel. This planet is a LEN protectorate. The LEN *knows*."

"What's the LEN doing about it?"

"The LEN isn't addressing it at all. According to the LEN, I drove us into a cluster of space rocks."

Even Manny the pilot hadn't spoken in Glenn's defense. The pilot had clammed up entirely, not about to cross the people who hired him.

"I'm so mad I could cry."

"You're not a crier."

"I may start."

Sliding into self-pity was easy. She shook it off.

If you can keep your head when all about you are losing theirs and blaming it on you . . .

Glenn played back the *Beauty*'s camera records for John Farragut. She didn't need to narrate. The admiral had been in enough furballs and knew the difference between blundering into natural objects and coming under attack.

At the recording's shattering end, he said, "Nice landing."

"I'm proud of it," Glenn said. "The LEN are charging me with hijack and suing me for damages to the ship."

"Shoot 'em."

"Aye, aye," she said. Thought, *I love you.*

"Take me for a walk."

Glenn dislodged the res chamber from its console and carried it out of the ship, imager-side out, for a tour around the wreckage.

She stepped carefully through wilted, charred vegetation. The ground was seared black underfoot. But already the forest was closing back in to heal the wound.

As Glenn circled around the ship's stern, Farragut's voice under her arm sounded, "Ho. Back up. What's that?"

Glenn stepped slowly backward until Farragut said, "Stop. There. Bring me in."

Glenn moved the res chamber closer to an odd piece of wreckage wedged into the ship's fuselage. It was black, metallic, curved. It looked manufactured. It wasn't anything that belonged to the *Beauty.*

"Looks like you got a bug in your teeth," Farragut said.

"I'm setting you down," Glenn told him. She propped the res chamber against a fallen tree, then stepped into the picture and tried to wrestle the large metal shard out of the

Beauty's fuselage. She couldn't budge the fragment at all, much less pull it free.

A chuckle sounded from behind her.

"I can hear you, John!" It pissed her off that he thought she was cute. She kicked the metal. That only jammed her shin.

She stalked back to the fallen tree, picked up the res chamber and brought John Farragut close up to see the thing stuck in the *Beauty*.

Farragut spoke the obvious. "That's not a meteorite."

The metal was an oily shade of black, clearly manufactured, fashioned in a curve, bearing an artificial design shallowly etched into it, almost like a talon of a clawfoot from a piece of antique furniture.

"Local make?" Farragut asked.

"No. There's no manufacturing here. No industry on this world at all. No commerce. Honest to God, John, 'Edenesque' is the word that comes to mind. Except for these." She swatted something small and pincered on her arm. "The native sapience is primitive. I was thinking the orbs were someone's mock aliens. But who would do that?"

Farragut dismissed anyone's first thought, "Rome can do better than that."

"That's what I thought."

"The League will say it's ours."

"No doubt," said Glenn, then, just to be sure, "It's not the CIA, is it?"

Farragut's immediate expression of reassurance turned suddenly hesitant. He'd been about to dismiss the idea of U.S. involvement. Didn't.

"I'll see if I can get someone to talk to me," Farragut said. "I don't think that's one of ours. You probably have a first contact on your hands."

First contact used to sound exciting. Glenn gave a sorry smile. "Those never go well for us."

"Whose flag is on the ground?"

"No one's. Kiwi drones were the first explorers on world. They turned up a sapient native species. The planet's been flags off ever since. The only feet on the dirt are international scientists. And one scientist's wife."

"Is anyone in orbit getting this treatment?"

"There's no one in Zoe's orbit. This is the back of beyond. The LEN puts their ships on the ground. There are only six of them. The *Beauty* makes seven."

"And none of them noticed these things on their way in?"

"No. This is the first time anyone was attacked coming or going."

"What hit you could be the vanguard for something bigger," said Admiral Farragut.

"Nothing followed us down," Glenn said. "I don't know how to read that. They're hostile, they can get between stars, but they can't shoot and they can't land? All they could do was ram. I'm afraid they'll try to ram us on the ground next."

Farragut told her, "I'm sending someone."

* * *

Flight Leader Ranza Espinoza reported to the ship's hospital for a physical. Her leave had been cut short. She sat on the exam table, cooling her bare heels and twiddling her toes, waiting for permission to get dressed and return to duty.

It could not take that long for the medics to figure out she was healthy.

Ranza was built like a line backer. Big shoulders. No hips. Gap teeth. Bushy hair. Silver-gray eyes.

She crossed and uncrossed her bare toes. Listened to the ship around her. The metal partitions were thin. Sounds carried easily, and *Mack* was never actually quiet. Now she was all kinds of loud. And it wasn't just the shouting on all decks. Supply barges clunked against the wings. The ship's displacement chamber cracked away like a thunderstorm.

Dock doors clattered as transports arrived and two companies of the 89th Fleet Marine Battalion stormed aboard like they were taking a beach.

Ranza could hear the *Mack*'s new XO from the land of Oz calling out in his best American Old West voice: "Stampede!"

Real smartass, that one.

Since the war, the Marines had been deployed in the U.S. Pacific Northwest on reconstruction detail. Finally they were coming home.

The 89th Battalion's home base in Kansas was never home like the space battleship *Merrimack* was.

Merrimack was bound for the edge of the galaxy. Best speed. Unless you wanted to get reassigned, you got your ass back on her today. You miss the boat this time, you can kiss *Mack* good-bye for the rest of your tour.

The lowing of livestock in the lower hold meant this was going to be a very long trip.

Heavy boots clanged against deck grates at a run, with shouts of "Clear ladder!" just before the thump of a duffel bag dropping down the shaft and the squawk of someone who didn't clear fast enough.

And why weren't the medics clearing Ranza out of this exam room so they could poke at those guys?

Ranza curled her toes. Sniffed antiseptic smells. She banged on the partition with the side of her fist. Called, "Hey! Yous guys forget me or somethin'!"

Didn't hear nobody hurrying on the far side.

They forgot her.

Ranza called louder, "I'm havin' a heart attack in here!"

In no real big hurry a med tech sauntered in. Young. Snotty. He turned his back to her, fed something into the database. He glanced over Ranza's stats, then eyed Ranza with a gluey smile. "Had fun ashore I see."

Ranza never liked the guy. She knew the type. Only in the service to line up a position in the private sector. He looked at her with the kind of sleazy, smarmy attitude that insinuates something.

"Can I get dressed?" Ranza said.

"I guess." The tech shrugged with one shoulder. "You flunked the physical."

"Did not." Ranza sat straight up, her muscular arms akimbo, broad shoulders spread their broadest. Did he want to see how many med tech curls she could do?

"MO will be right with you." The skinny tech walked out.

Ranza threw a specimen jar after him. Pity it was empty.

She'd been spending her leave on Earth, most of the time with her three kids and her mom—who was raising Ranza's three kids. And Ranza had had some fun.

Uh-oh.

That was it, wasn't it?

The moment the ship's Medical Officer, Mohsen Shah, stepped through the hatchway, Ranza cried, "Don't tell me I got VD."

Mo gave a slow sideways nod. "V yes. D no. You are being pregnant."

"No!" She guessed it was a little late to be using that word. "You mean to tell me that son of a bitch was shooting live rounds?"

"Yes. Is there being something you are wanting to be telling me about this man?"

"Not really," said Ranza.

"Let me be speaking plainly—" Mo began.

"You can *do* that, Mo?" said Ranza.

The gentle placid Riverite doctor could meander all over the park before he completed a thought, and by the end of it Ranza often forgot what he was supposed to be saying.

Someone else answered. "I can."

Ranza turned to the other guy who had just entered the compartment. "Oh, thank God." An interpreter.

Rob Roy Buchanan. The ship's tame lawyer. Straight talker. Nice guy. Late thirties. Looked a whole bunch younger. Rob Roy was a long, tall reed with a slouch like a teenager. His rank was lieutenant, but he wasn't a line officer. He was *Merrimack*'s Legal Officer. Most of the Marines called him the First Mate because he was married to the captain.

It didn't occur to Ranza right away to wonder why there was a lawyer in her examination room.

"Look, Mister Buchanan," Ranza started, "tell Mo to just inc the little zygote and lemme get back to work. 'Kay?"

Naval regs did not permit little passengers to serve on board space battleships. And Ranza didn't want any kid of hers in harm's way either. That was why God invented incubators.

Rob Roy Buchanan hesitated. The lawyer might be able to speak plainly, but he wasn't doing it now. Something wasn't right. There was definitely something wrong here besides pregnancy. Ranza tensed up.

"Flight Leader," Rob Roy began.

Uh-oh.

He called her Flight Leader. Not Ranza.

He'd gone formal on her. *Not good. Not good. Not good.*

"If this embryo leaves your body alive by artificial means and the father is a Roman citizen, then Rome legally can — and absolutely will — take immediate custody."

"It's not Roman!" Ranza said. Afraid she shouted.

Rob Roy's voice stayed calm, even a little apologetic. "Yes, it is. And Rome has the right to claim it under peacetime interstellar law."

"Then declare war!" Ranza cried. And this man was supposed to be smart.

"I'm sorry, Flight Leader."

"This kid is mine!"

"Right now it is," Rob Roy agreed. "As long as it stays in your body, you have legal control — even to terminate it — "

"No!"

"That choice is entirely your own. But once the embryo is in the incubator, you've given Rome another citizen."

Ranza looked from the Medical Officer to the Legal Officer, helpless. Each wore the same pained sympathetic expression.

"No," she said. Went on the offensive. "What makes yous so sure I did a Roman?"

"Romans always shoot live rounds," said Rob Roy.

"He told me he was Italian."

Mo Shah said, "The male contributor to this embryo is not being in the League DNA database. That is meaning Roman."

"Could be alien," Ranza suggested. Bet they didn't think of that, did they? "Ha. So there."

Rob Roy gave a faint smile.

Mo said, "That is not being physically possible. There is being no such thing as 'alien DNA.'"

"Then where do little aliens come from?" Ranza said. Got him there.

But Mo went on, "Aliens are having their own chemistry and their own genomes. 'DNA' is being that specific genome unique to life originating on planet Earth."

"Sure. Fine," Ranza said quickly. She didn't have time for this. She had to get to her post. "I'll adopt it out."

"Transfer the embryo?" Rob Roy asked.

"Yeah. I can give it up. My mom'll prefer that anyway."

"You may," Rob Roy said. Sounded awful iffy. "But it has to be to a Roman woman."

"No, it doesn't," Ranza said.

Rob Roy never lost patience. "Legally, it does."

"I can do it in secret! I won't tell yous about it."

"Flight Leader, these conceptions are never accidental—"

"Hey! I didn't know—"

"—on their part," Rob Roy clarified. "It's always intentional on the Roman end. They will be monitoring you—"

Ranza looked around as if there were Romans in the exam compartment.

"They will know if an incubator leaves this ship," Rob Roy said.

Ever since its declaration of independence from the United States in AD 2290, the Roman Empire had been in constant need of population. Even before the catastrophic losses during the Hive years, Rome needed citizens. These days the bulk of Roman citizenry were still mass-produced. Mom and Dad often never met. Eggs and sperm met in vitro and were born from incubators. And there were also outright clones. Cloning was reserved for the brightest, the strongest, and the most beautiful. Beautiful, because Romans openly acknowledged their love of physical beauty. They claimed the bias was genetic.

Not to let their breed stagnate, Rome brought in fresh blood any way she could.

At war's end there had been two million Roman citizens stranded on Earth. A lot of those Romans were still there—collecting fresh genes for the Roman pool the old-fashioned way before they found their way home.

Ranza had been one of their targets.

Rob Roy told her, "There are only three ways to go from here."

"Uh," said Ranza, trying to think. "Can you hit me with those choices again?"

"You can abort it."

"No."

"You can give it up to Rome."

"No."

"You can carry it to term."

"You mean have the baby."

"Yes."

"An American baby?"

"Yes."

"For me to keep?"

"Yes."

"Then I'll do that." And to Mo, "So is this a boy or a girl? I ain't calling it 'it' if I'm carrying this kid the full tour."

"It is being—" Mo started, stopped. "You are being sure?"

Once you knew the sex, it was hard to turn back.

"Yeah," said Ranza. "Hit me."

"You are carrying a boy."

"Boy," she murmured. The hefty Fleet Marine lifted her brows. "My mom's gonna kill me."

"You've made your decision?" Rob Roy asked.

"Yeah. Gotta." Ranza shrugged her big shoulders and slid off the table to get dressed and collect her things. "See yous guys in nine."

Months, she meant.

7

KERRY BLUE. TRYING to get her locker to shut.

Each Marine was given a locker into which to stuff all his or her stuff. The locker was built into the Marine's berth, and it was just large enough to hold subatomic particles.

If your locker don't shut, whatever is hanging out gets spaced.

Kerry yelled through the thin partition to the men's side of the forecastle for backup. "Can I get some meat in here!"

She had lots of volunteers. Big guys trooped in to muscle her locker closed. Would have been easier if Kerry knew how to fold stuff, but she didn't. Kerry smushed. She only ever passed inspection because her mates helped her out.

The guys helping her weren't much for folding either. But they got her locker closed. Bent the door in the process. The locker door had a distinct outward bow, but it was shut.

The Yurg. Tall, hulking blond guy. Flew as Baker One. The Yurg noticed the empty sleep pod here on the girl side of the forecastle. The empty berth was Ranza Espinoza's.

"Hey." The Yurg gave a back-knuckle rap on the empty rack. Asked Kerry, "Is your Flight Leader AWOL?"

"Nah, he's here," Kerry said.

"*He*?" Last time Yurg looked Ranza Espinoza was still a she.

"Cain's in charge," Kerry said.

Dak Shepard, Alpha Two, pulled his head back. "Cain's Flight Leader? *Cain?* How'd that happen?"

"Ranza's in a civilian way," Kerry Blue said.

Cain was just walking in the hatchway. Yurg turned to Cain with a big grin and deep chuckle. "Cain! You dog!"

Cain yelped. "It wasn't me!"

"Who did that to her!" Dak cried.

"A very brave man," said the Yurg solemnly.

Cain's glance fell on the bent locker door in Kerry's rack. As Alpha's new Flight Leader Cain said, "Kerry, ballast something."

"It's shut!" Kerry cried.

"Your gear don't fit the dimensions, and I ain't bending the rules for you."

Not the little rules anyway. Just the really big ones.

"Fine," Kerry snapped. She popped the locker open. The contents exhaled and slowly tumbled out. Kerry pulled out a pair of jeans and handed them sourly to Cain.

"Oh, no! Not the jeans!" Gunner Stokes of Baker Team cried.

Kerry Blue's jeans were form fitting, threadbare across the ass. They showed off Kerry Blue very nicely.

"Can I have them?" Gunner said.

Cain scowled. "What you gonna do with them? Sleep with them?"

As if it were obvious, Gunner said, "Well, *yeah*."

Cain threw the jeans at Gunner's face.

Gunner sounded blissful from under the denim. "Thank you." He pulled the jeans off his face. "Hey, Kerry. Any time you want to borrow these you know where to find them."

"I remember where you live," Kerry told him.

"*Do* ya?" said Gunner, a lament. Been a long time since Kerry Blue been around.

❋ ❋ ❋

Space Battleship MERRIMACK SBB 63

(USA) 2434 C.E.
Class   Monitor (2 built)
Length   540 feet +
Span   400 feet

Beam	80 feet
Height	400 feet
Power	6 FMT antimatter reactors
Threshold:	26,000 c
Complement:	Crew: 425
	Fleet Marine Wing: 360
	Fleet Marine Battery: 360

Armament:

4x522mm torpedo tubes (ZSN3 tag torpedo)
6 beam cannon
24 barnacle turrets (variable load)
4 T541 Star Sparrow missiles
1 Continental Knife

Spacecraft carried:

36 Swifts
2 Space Patrol Torpedo boats (SPT)
1 Long Range Shuttle (LRS)

✳ ✳ ✳

Colonel TR Steele stood before his Marines assembled in the cargo hold. It was the only place on board where two companies of Marines could fit.

The Old Man stood six foot even. Wore his white-blond hair buzzed short. His skin was white when he wasn't crawfish red from bellowing like a drill sergeant. Looked younger than forty years, but that was because he'd needed a few rounds of repair work after the war.

The medics as well as the intelligence officers had taken a hard look at Steele after his time in Roman custody. Steele had some unscheduled body work done on Palatine. That made everyone, especially TR Steele, hugely nervous. The IOs had run him through a nanosieve before allowing him to return to duty.

Colonel TR Steele commanded a loyalty of the kind only ever seen for John Farragut. But where Farragut was dramatic, TR Steele was a brick.

Like John Farragut—like any man—Steele could get real protective around a woman.

And now Steele was standing in front of his Marines, barking orders and feeling like he had his pants around his

ankles because he knew that just about five-quarters of
these guys knew that he was practicing docking maneuvers
with Flight Sergeant Kerry Blue.

Do not look at Kerry Blue.

There was Flight Leader Cain Salvador. Alpha One. His
best man. Mixed race. Sleek and powerful as a seal. Cain
was a solid Marine.

Until this morning, Cain Salvador had been a Flight Sergeant, flying as Alpha Three. That was until Espinoza went
and got herself pregnant.

Replacing Cain as Alpha Three was a she-guy, came over
from the *Rio Grande*. Hard core. Cute face, elfin cheek-
bones, broad top shelf. The Marine was out here to fight, not
to dance. The knuckles of both hands were tattooed
DNFW—Do Not Foxtrot With. And the red X on her brow
in the third eye position announced that she was equipped
with a dragon—an appliance more vividly called a sausage
peeler. Her name was Geneva Rhine. Nothing to do but call
her Rhino.

Alpha Four. Carly Delgado. Whip thin and cuddly as razor wire. If you want your squad to take prisoners, you don't
send Carly in. Not that Carly was vicious—okay Carly was
vicious—but it took a lot more mass and muscle to take an
enemy captive than it did to make him dead. Carly couldn't
take captives. Carly could do dead. At her size it was self-
preservation.

Carly was attached at the hip to Twitch Fuentes, Alpha
Five. Quiet, calm. Steady as an anchor. Just tell Twitch what
to do; you know it'll get done. Twitch understood spoken
Americanese. He just didn't speak it. Used to. Said something stupid once and hadn't tried again since. No one remembered what it was except Twitch. Steele did not want
to know that Twitch couldn't read.

Into the Alpha Seven spot came another all-American
mongrel by the name of Asante Addai. Part Colombian,
part Mayan, part some kind of slave-descended Black, part
sub-Saharan Arab. One hundred percent U.S. Fleet Marine.
Asante had spent a year in college between tours, decided
it wasn't for him. Moved like a boxer, light on his feet. Asante kept his springy black hair shorn close to his head. He

wore a lot of scars, which he never got repaired. Medical gel would have healed those over. But, as Asante said, "I don't do the pink crap."

Steele stood through roll call of the Wing and the Battery. Then he informed them of their destination—Zoe. There had been an attack, but the initial crisis had passed. There had been no further attacks. But it was not over.

How Admiral Farragut knew that, Steele didn't ask.

We're running out to the end of the galaxy to rescue the admiral's pet hamster, and I'm not questioning orders.

Steele would do the same for Kerry Blue.

It would take *Merrimack* no less than a month to get to Zoe. The admiral could have chosen to wait for more information or more hostile activity, or he could get his big guns in motion now.

John Farragut had a sense for these things. The man could smell smoke before there was a fire.

Steele had no doubt that by time his Marines got to Zoe, hell would be loose.

∗ ∗ ∗

Director Izrael Benet stalked out of his tent.

The rest of the LEN expedition members were gathered around the fire pit at the center of camp.

Some of the xenos turned, hearing the director coming. He was stomping.

Izzy Benet shouted, "Who summoned the U.S. military!?!"

There was much looking about, eyes meeting blank eyes, quizzical murmurs.

"What?"

"What military?"

"Are they here?"

"Apparently," Benet started, making a show of struggling to keep his temper and losing. "The United States is sending a battleship here!"

"Why!" several xenos asked at once.

"*Someone*—" Benet's gaze fell upon Glenn—"told them we were under extraplanetary attack."

Dr. Suri Chin said, "Who would tell them a thing like that?" Dr. Chin had not been on board the *Spring Beauty*.

Most eyes found their way to Glenn. She was traveling under the name Glenn Hull, but, as she was married to Patrick Hamilton, the xenos could put the pieces together.

Director Benet looked to Patrick in suspicion and betrayal. "She's a thug, isn't she?"

The implicit slight in reducing his wife to a pronoun to her face did not escape the linguist. Patrick bristled. "*Glenn* is a decorated line officer and veteran of the war."

"The war," Director Benet said witheringly. "Funny how anyone who was in the war is *proud* of it." Disbelief and disgust thinned his full lips.

"Funny that," said Glenn. Rome had declared the war, and claimed the United States of America as a Roman province. "I just didn't want to learn Latin."

"Everything is an attack to your type," said Benet.

Glenn nodded. *Possibly.* "Especially an attack."

"The war is over. Your kind just doesn't get it."

No one who called you *your kind* ever meant you well.

Glenn kept her voice even. Let the facts throw the punches. "Then explain what happened to the *Spring Beauty.*"

Director Benet said, "You wrested the controls of a LEN spacecraft away from the authorized pilot and crashed it into the ground causing widespread injury and total destruction of the craft."

Glenn asked, "What do you make of the piece of manufactured metal lodged in the *Beauty*'s hull?"

"I don't pretend to have any idea what that shard is. It could be U.S. make for all I know. You're either covering up your blundering into an asteroid field, or you're staging a pretext for your country to send guns to the Outback. Your Admiral *Nelson*—I beg your pardon—*Farragut* is establishing a bridgehead to the Perseus Arm. The U.S. has no bases in Perseus space. That's it, isn't it? You're coming to take over Zoe! By God, this is monumental. It's an outrage."

"Director Benet, you are wrong," Glenn said evenly. "The *Spring Beauty* came under attack by multiple hostiles."

She glanced to Manny for support, but the pilot still wasn't volunteering his version of the story.

Benet challenged, "So where were these space invaders

when all the previous expedition ships were arriving at Zoe? Isn't it odd that your combatants mysteriously showed up only to attack *you*?"

Glenn had no answer to that.

Benet went on, "I suppose you are now going to tell me they're Roman."

"They're not Roman," Glenn said.

"Thank you. Finally, a rational statement. Now." Benet made a show of looking up at the sky. "Explain why there is no rain of aliens following up on their first strike. Funny that your attackers didn't press their advantage. Isn't that what your kind does? You must be disappointed."

Disappointment was not what she was feeling.

"There are spacecraft that can't handle an atmosphere," said Glenn.

Director Benet said, "When your battleship arrives, you will get on it and depart."

Glenn was afraid of what she would say, so she kept silent. She'd never liked the League of Earth Nations.

They wish we'd go knuckle-walk back to our caves, and we veterans, well, we just want to shoot them. That left Patrick in the middle, the worst place to be.

Patrick tried to explain, "You've got to understand, Izzy is an administrator. He's a fund-raiser. He's accustomed to overstating his case for dramatic effect. He goes hyperbolic. Don't take it personally."

"Patrick," said Glenn, her palm up. "Please stop talking."

Izrael Benet was right about one thing. When her battleship arrived, she would get on it.

❋ ❋ ❋

Space Control detained the Terra Rican racing yacht *Mercedes* in port on the planet Aotearoa in the Perseid arm of the galaxy.

Aotearoa was a New Zealand colony, but the officer who boarded the Terra Rican yacht was Roman.

The officer extracted data from *Mercedes*' control console and demanded of Jose Maria de Cordillera, "Purpose of your travel?"

Nobel Laureate Jose Maria Rafael Meridia de Cordillera was a Renaissance man. A true aristocrat, he owned an enormous tract of land on the former Spanish colonial world of Terra Rica. At one time Jose Maria had served as Terra Rica's ambassador to the United States of America.

He was a slender, gracious presence on the elegant spaceship.

"*Por favor*," Jose Maria said. "Why am I under scrutiny of Rome while I am on a New Zealand colonial world in ANZAC space? I am a neutral."

"*Don* Cordillera, if you are a neutral, then I am the tooth fairy," the officer said. "No. Back up. I actually have been the tooth fairy."

"I also," Jose Maria said.

"If you are a neutral, then I am the Little Mermaid."

Roman Imperial Intelligence suspected that Jose Maria de Cordillera had planted the nanites that had incapacitated mad emperor Romulus.

Imperial Intelligence was right.

"Are you of the Romulii?" Jose Maria asked.

The Roman officer recoiled, aghast, as if the mere suggestion of being a Romulus supporter were a lethal contagion. "No! You brought down a Roman emperor in wartime. An action, *de facto*, NOT neutral."

"I consider myself a citizen of the cosmos," said Jose Maria. "And there is no present war. May I not travel freely?"

"Purpose of your travel?" The officer demanded again.

"To establish trade relations between Terra Rica and Aotearoa."

The officer's shoulders slumped a bit in impatient annoyance. "We know your business *here*. But you are leaving *here*. Early. Abruptly. Why?"

"I answer a call from a friend."

The officer would know from the ship's communication log that the friend was Admiral John A. Farragut.

"Where are you going?"

"I am certain that *Mercedes* has already told you my destination," said Jose Maria.

A course to the planet Zoe, deep in the Outback, was loaded into the racing yacht's nav sys.

"I'm asking you, *Don* Cordillera."

"My son, sometimes redundance is not good. Sometimes it is just redundant. May we go?"

✳ ✳ ✳

A string of small moons stretched across Phoenix's night sky in their phases like broken pearls. Nox and his squad of pariahs slept out in the open in the badlands. Dry winds lifted fine dust and scattered it over their bodies.

The former Antonians had been disenfranchised retroactively. *Damnatio memoriae.* Damnation of memory. They never existed. They were not on the deme rolls. They had no *gens.* No family. They could not hold land. They had no rights, no country.

They were simply *not.*

Disconnected as the wind.

They slept outside, hungry.

All their intangible assets had been seized.

Faunus owned a small hover for getting around, but it couldn't carry all seven of them, so they hadn't traveled far from base.

They had no credit.

Nox had coin.

They had talked about going to one of the spaceports on Phoenix, one of the foreign ones, where they might buy things with coin and not get spat on.

For now they were hoarding their money and using their survival training to scavenge in the desert. Finding work without going into slavery was going to be tough.

Nox touched his blood-crusted earlobe where they'd ripped out his ID capsule. He felt its loss like a missing limb.

He wanted to go back. He wanted to be whole. He wanted to be Roman.

Never look backward or you'll fall down the stairs.

He turned his head. Leo lay next to him on the hard ground. Leo was awake too. His eyes were open, gazing up at the moons. He asked wistfully, "Hey, Nox, what's it like having a mother and a father?"

"Nothing you can't live nicely without," Nox said. "What they don't tell you is you're just a pedestal for your sire's galactic ego. I'm not going back if that's what you're thinking."

Leo stayed wistful. "Anything is better than this hole."

"No," said Nox. "This is my hole. I dug this *coiens* hole."

Galeo turned out to be awake too. He rose up on one

elbow to look across Leo to Nox. "Going back is worse than the ninth circle of hell?"

"That's another thing they don't tell you," said Nox. "Hell has a subbasement."

"You're an American, aren't you, Nox?" Nicanor said.

"No."

Yes, he was, and they knew it.

"You could go home," said Nicanor.

"Fuck you."

Why weren't any of these guys sleeping?

Pallas rolled up to sit, elbows resting on his bent knees. "Why don't you go, Nox?"

"Yeah," said Leo. "You were born in America."

Nox sat up. "Are you going to keep throwing that in my face?"

"No, that's not what we mean," said Pallas. "We mean you have somewhere to *go*. Why don't you?"

"I can't."

"They'd execute him," said Orissus. "He's a traitor."

Nox said, "I am not a traitor. Getting born in the States wasn't my choice. I *chose* to pledge to Rome."

"Well, the Americans will think you're a traitor," Orissus said. "They would execute you if you went back."

"No, actually they wouldn't," said Nox. "I'm just not going."

"Nox has a mother and a father," Leo told Orissus.

"Rome is my mother and my father," said Nox.

"Not anymore," Orissus said. "So says Rome."

"I am Roman," Nox said. "So say *I*. I am what I make me."

"And we made ourselves buzzard cud," said Faunus.

"Yes, Best Beloved," Nox said, deflating. "We did."

"What do we do now?" said Galeo. "Fall on swords?"

They didn't have swords. Rome took them.

"Too late. That won't redeem us in anyone's eyes," said Pallas. That door had already shut. "It would be another act of cowardice now. No use hurrying out that exit."

Nox felt the universe crapping on his head. It was time to stop whining, excusing, blaming. *Pick up your cards and play your coiens hand*.

"I'm with Pallas," said Nox. "Dying is not my first, second, third, fourth, or fifth choice."

"So where does going back to your parents rank?" Leo asked.

"It's not even on the list."

"But this is hell," said Leo.

"Better to reign in hell than serve in heaven," said Nox.

They stopped talking. Nox's blustering words sounded great, but they were hollow. Meant exactly nothing. The words were fine-smelling bullshit.

Yet they echoed over and over in Nox's mind, spinning in a loop.

Reign in hell.

Reign in hell.

8

AFTER NIGHTFALL THE FIFTY-SIX members of the LEN expedition sat, gathered around the fire pit at the center of camp, talking, acting as if all were clear. As if the things that nearly killed the new arrivals weren't still upstairs.

Glenn kept glancing toward the sky, flinching whenever she saw a meteor.

Sandy Minyas toasted marshmallows on a ten-foot pole.

The flames leaped bright and fierce in the oxygen-rich air.

"Hang onto your eyebrows around the campfire," someone warned the newcomers.

What eyebrows?

When Glenn stowed her gear in their tent, she'd discovered that her eyebrows had jumped ship sometime during the *Beauty*'s descent. Their absence gave her a young, astonished look.

Her red-brown hair had been singed ragged as a hornet's nest. She sheared it off. Now she looked like a young astonished Marine recruit.

Patrick talked shop with his colleagues around the fire and ate marshmallows.

Glenn walked to the edge of camp.

A wide perimeter ring of sanitized dirt isolated the camp from the surrounding native growth.

No one was afraid of alien infection. Human infection required the Zoen pathogens to have DNA. Even without a xenomicrobiologist in camp, the explorers knew there was no such thing as alien DNA.

The dirt perimeter was there to protect Zoe from invasive terrestrial species.

DNA was a robust structure. Theoretically, terrestrial species could compete with native species for basic resources. Local life was carbon-based, so there could be competition for the same proteins, sugars, nitrogenated soil, and habitat.

Terrestrial life could disturb the natural balance. So the expedition maintained a buffer zone and kept its hydroponic vegetable gardens sealed in greenhouses inside the camp.

They stopped short of raising fences. The campfire deterred most animals and birds from invading camp. The native animals were unusually wary of fire. Given the ferocity of blazes in this atmosphere, it was a good instinct to have. Predators would not approach, which was fortunate, as Zoe had some big ones.

Woven polymer shields, something like riot gear, were stacked near the camp perimeter. The shields looked like rigid spiderwebs, but they weren't sticky. Expedition members used them to confront native animals that wandered into camp and to shoo them back out.

Glenn carried a heat stick with her with which to brew a single cup of coffee. She found herself a nice granite boulder at camp's edge, sat down, and gazed up at the half starry sky.

You only found skies like this at extreme galactic north or south or here on the Rim. Half the sky was deepest, *deepest* black, pricked by a few lonely lights. The fuzzy dots in the darkness were other galaxies. The other half of the Zoen sky was heavily spangled and glowing with the full host of the Milky Way.

Another bright streak across the starfield made Glenn shrink on reflex. Felt like an idiot for doing it.

Nothing she could do now except wait for *Merrimack*. Or for the sky to fall.

A motion made her look lower.

Thought she saw something in the trees but couldn't make it out. She had removed her implanted gunsights upon taking leave from *Merrimack*. The gunsights contained night vision filters. She could have used them here. She'd forgotten how truly dark planetary nights could be.

Glenn gave an old-fashioned squint across the cleared perimeter into black foliage.

She made out the little treetop acrobat. It was a squirrel-bodied, possum-tailed, big-eared, huge-eyed thing. Seemed to have a ferret's nose for a party. It wasn't alone. There was a whole troop of them in the night trees, bouncing through the springy boughs. Looked like they were having fun. But who could tell with aliens? For all Glenn knew, swinging and bouncing could indicate aggression and fear.

She had brought a splinter gun with her on this journey. She kept it hidden, holstered across her back under her jacket. Didn't feel any need to draw it.

Abruptly the tree ferrets scattered, and Glenn heard footsteps approaching behind her.

The walker came to a stop at her shoulder, standing close enough for her to feel his body heat. She didn't turn. She knew his scent.

Patrick had come out to find her. Glenn thought he was going to ask her to come back to the fire, and she prepped a retort. But with insight Glenn didn't know he had, Patrick reached his hand down to her and said, "We don't need these people. Let's jump this ship."

She craned her head around to stare at his offered hand. She looked up into his soft brown eyes. Asked, "Don't you want to stay with your colleagues?"

"Any of 'em thank you for saving their screaming faces?"

There had been an awful lot of screaming when she'd landed the *Beauty*.

"No."

"Then fornicate 'em."

His hand waited, palm up. Glenn was touched. She set aside her coffee and put her hand in his. She rose. Their fingers interlaced. They crossed the dirt perimeter and wandered away from camp into the alien forest.

✳ ✳ ✳

Tired of wallowing in self-pity, of blaming their fate on everything and everyone, Nox, Pallas, Nicanor, Orissus, Faunus, Leo, and Galeo agreed they would take their evil luck and make a stand in their new home in hell. They put their fists in a circle. They wanted to call out some kind of team name but didn't know what they were.

They were traitors and cowards.

"We're bottom feeders," said Nicanor.

"Yeah?" said Nox. "Let's feed off the bottom. We will be pirates."

Nicanor said, "Do we not need a pirate ship in order to be pirates?" Might have been sarcastic.

"Of course we do," Nox said. "We need to get off this world. Phoenix is Roman soil, and I won't prey on Rome."

That part sounded good. It fell to Leo to ask the question so obvious it sounded dim: "How do you intend to get a ship?"

"Same way pirates always get their ships. We steal one," said Nox, then added, "Not from Rome."

Phoenix was a Roman colonial world, but it had a cosmopolitan population. Non-Roman ships came and went out of Phoenix's international ports daily.

"Oh. Sure. Of course," Orissus said. Definitely sarcastic. "*How?* We can't get near enough to a spaceship to hijack one. No one will give us passage. No one will even let us aboard. We have no nationality. I bet they don't even let us in the *coiens* spaceport."

"Think you could live on a Xerxes?" Nox asked.

Orissus snorted. "Sure. Why not?"

The Xerxes luxury transport craft was the highest of high-end nonmilitary spacecraft. The Xerxes was fast. It was beautiful—when you could see it, as the Xerxes was also stealthy and viciously armed for self-defense.

It was not Roman.

Products of Rome's largest manufacturer, PanGalactic, had issues with tracking and control.

The Xerxes was a breakthrough design from a consortium of neutral Asian colonies in Perseid space.

For a non-Roman civilian spacecraft, the Xerxes had a lot of Striker in it, but the Xerxes was bigger and better, just as agile, and supposedly faster.

Upon its debut the Xerxes instantly became the favored transport for heads of state.

The United States Spacecraft One and Two had switched over to Xerxes transports.

Caesar didn't have one, because the Asian consortium that produced the Xerxes had chosen not to sell to Rome.

A Xerxes didn't need a fighter escort. Its base model was loaded with serpent's teeth.

Faunus said, "I want one."

Nox collected a few of his things and dressed as if he had a place to go. He put on trousers and shoes. Nox never wore trousers and shoes. Nox was a tunic and sandals man.

He counted the coins from his purse. "I'm going into port."

"You're picking up a Xerc, Nox?" said Orissus. "Get me one too."

"No, dumb ass." Nox pocketed his money. "I need to get the maintenance and flight manuals first."

∗ ∗ ∗

Glenn and Patrick made their way through vines, twisting branches, ferns, and thorns. Bioluminescent moss clung to tall trunks that looked and smelled like wood of a sort. Leaves gently fluttered overhead. Glenn stepped over a rotting log. The forest litter felt soft under her boot soles.

Glenn and Patrick were not supposed to be outside the camp perimeter without exo-suits. Director Benet was going to detonate when he discovered her and Patrick on the loose. But there seemed little risk that anything Glenn and Patrick shed could wedge itself into a superior position within such a well-established ecosystem.

They stepped into the clear where a tumbling stream had cut a course through sloping ground.

The double moon rose, huge on the horizon.

Patrick started up the vale climbing the rocks alongside the watercourse.

Rocks and water were basically the same everywhere. Shale was shale. Water was water. Silica was silica. The chemistry was not exotic.

Smells from the soft organic soil were a little different—a blend like damp earth, leaf litter, lichen, acorn hulls, wet shale, leather, and thyme. Green scents of chlorophyll breathed from the forest.

Insectoids were lords of the universe. Most habitable worlds evolved something like them. Zoe had a double ration of those.

Glenn did the Australian wave as she climbed.

She and Patrick reached level ground at a highland meadow.

Got frisky in the open air.

Fell asleep under an amazing array of stars.

While it was still very dark, alien voices announced the coming sunrise—chirrups, whistles, clicks, burrs, songs, and a sound like someone running his thumbnail over a toothed comb.

At dawn Glenn and Patrick rose. They shook out their clothes. The fabric was frictionless, so their clothes did not hold dirt or odor. Their bodies did. They bathed in the cold, cold stream and dragged themselves out shivering to dry in the sun in a patch of sweet grass.

They checked their skin for crawling things, then got dressed.

They breakfasted on beef jerk, which Patrick had brought along, and drank from the clear running stream.

Glenn looked back toward the steep narrow vale they'd climbed. No one followed them. The LEN expedition hadn't sent anyone to look for them. "They don't miss us," said Glenn.

"I don't miss them," said Patrick.

Glenn wasn't sure if he really meant that or not, but it was nice of him to say.

She'd been edgy and anxious when they left, obsessing about the alien attackers she knew were lurking just beyond the atmosphere.

Fresh air, sex, and a quiet sky had calmed her nerves.

She and Patrick were on the summer side of the world. It was just past solstice. The double moon was setting; its glowing hourglass showed both sides full.

They followed the stream across the meadow.

Slouching yellow-green trees lined the water's wandering path on either bank. Tree roots hung down like bathers dangling their feet in the water.

Patrick seemed to have a destination.

Small jewel-colored creatures, like peacock eyes escaped from a tail, hopped between seed heads on the meadow.

Glenn stumbled into a nest of popping screamers. The little aliens puffed themselves out round, all their yellow quills bristling like jagged spikes with black points.

The quills were actually quite soft, the shrieks comical. Glenn couldn't help laughing at them. The screamers kept hopping, popping, and screaming until Glenn and Patrick moved on.

On gently rising ground, different sorts of trees crowded thick around the stream. Glenn caught glimpses between their rubbery trunks of the bright sunlight on another meadow beyond the watercourse.

A flash of gold glinted through the trees' gray-green foliage. "Oh, look!" Glenn exclaimed.

Patrick saw it too. He threaded through the trees and climbed down into the streambed, sloshed through the water, and climbed up the opposite bank.

Glenn followed him. They peered around either side of a massive gray-green tree trunk.

Big, dark, shambling shapes moved on the meadow, like wayward haystacks. When the shapes passed from shadow into sunlight, their dark coats shimmered watery gold.

Patrick inhaled. Held his breath a moment. Whispered, "My mammoths!"

The giant animals bore some resemblance to woolly mammoths with their hulking shapes, their trunks, their short tusks, their tree trunk legs. But these mammoths' long, fine wool was so shiny that the beasts appeared to be wearing silk pajamas. They moved peaceably in a herd.

These were the animals whose recorded calls had shaken the *Spring Beauty*.

There were no clashing grinding rock noises now. Not that Glenn could hear.

Glenn and Patrick hid at the tree line, watching the beasts.

The closest mammoth appeared to be male, biggest of the big. When breezes moved his curtain of gold locks, his undercarriage came briefly into view. Glenn knew you shouldn't assume that things were what they seemed to be among aliens, but that really looked like a bull penis.

The bull mammoth breathed deeply, slow and peaceful. He took unhurried steps and gave a slow flap of his giant ears. His trunk lifted, snuffled the air. The tiny orange eye on the near side of his head pivoted Glenn and Patrick's way. The bull mammoth seemed to note their presence, then went back to grazing.

"Are they friendly?" Glenn whispered.

Patrick shrugged. "Wouldn't know. We're not supposed to interact with the natives. Just observe."

Glenn didn't much care what the LEN supposed. "Let's observe closer."

Patrick started to call her name, but she was already on the meadow.

✳ ✳ ✳

Nox entered the taverna in a town just outside of the Legion base. Legionaries frequented the place. Nox's entrance met with mutters, stares, and glowers.

This is what we call a pall.

An ephebe named Tycho glanced, glanced twice, as Nox slid onto the barstool next to him.

Tycho had enlisted in Legion Persus at the same time as Nox. Ever so not happy to see him now.

Tycho flinched away. "Ho! *Frater*. Not good."

"*Ave*," Nox hailed him.

Tycho stared. Nox's face was battered, his eye sockets black and purple. Tycho whispered through gritted teeth, his eyes flitting nervously everywhere. "Nox. I like you well, but you are persona non grata."

"No. I am nine-day-old wet crap," Nox countered frankly. "But I'm not contagious."

"You think not?"

Tycho was slithering off his stool like a frightened virgin. Nox closed his hand around Tycho's arm and pulled him back onto his barstool. "Let the dead wolf speak."

"Nox—" Tycho tried to shrink away.

"Stiffen up. I need a favor, O Best Beloved."

Tycho hissed, panicked. "Nox, I don't even want to be caught breathing the same air as you!"

The bartender came over. Looked at Nox hard, then took down a glass, held it under the bar. Nox heard the unmistakable hiss and gurgle of the glass filling. The bartender set the glass of warm yellow liquid before Nox. "On the house."

"Yeah. Thanks," said Nox. He nudged the piss out of smelling distance and turned back to Tycho. "Can you get a copy of the complete documentation and training manual for the Xerxes?"

He was peripherally aware of someone moving across the room, getting ready to take a free swing at him.

Tycho put out a staying palm toward the menacing man. "Stay out of this."

The man gestured. "*That* belongs in the *cloaca*."

That was Nox. *Cloaca* was the latrine.

"I might acquire this piece of crap," Tycho said, as if considering taking a slave. "Don't mess it up any more than it already is."

The man backed away, disappointed.

Tycho whispered to Nox. "I always liked you, but that was before you turned yourself into worm manure. Why would I get Xerxes specs for you?"

"Why wouldn't you? You can get them."

"I can. But it's not like *you're* ever going to get near a Xerxes."

"Right," said Nox.

Tycho looked him over. Looked again. "You are going to steal one?" Tycho thought he was being ridiculous.

Nox's gaze remained steady, his blue eyes cagey within their bruises.

"You are insane."

"No, I'm not," said Nox. "I got exactly nothing to lose."

He saw Tycho's resistance waver. Spectacular disasters were hard to look away from. Tycho said, "You're going to liberate one? *How?* Whose?"

Nox said, "You do know I've still got United States citizenship?"

The United States was a LEN member. Not its favorite one, but a member all the same.

"It's going to take more than that," said Tycho.

Nox shrugged. "My crash, right?"

Tycho shook his head, but he was giving in. "The entertainment value of watching you self-immolate could be worth it."

9

GLENN STOOD IN THE SUNLIGHT, watching the mammoths for any reaction to her presence. Here and there a trunk rose in the air and sniffed. No one moved deliberately nearer. No one moved away.

No one stopped grazing.

Patrick followed her out onto the meadow at a shambling gait. He lazily swung his arm across the grass tops like a trunk.

He spoke casually aside to Glenn, his eyes locked on the bull, "If you see any ears go straight out to the sides, bag your ass back to the trees."

But the mammoths were unconcerned. One or two turned orange eyes at Glenn and Patrick for a moment, then paid them no more heed than they did the native creatures in the field.

Having never seen anything like the humans, the mammoths hadn't developed any aversion to them.

Glenn and Patrick joined in with the herd.

There were other hangers-on among the mammoth troop. Lizardlike things assumed the role of ox-peckers. Spindly-legged avians scavenged seeds in the mammoths' deep footprints.

Patrick's ambling brought him alongside one mammoth, Glenn close behind him. The mammoth's golden curtain of fiber swayed and gleamed in the sunlight. Glenn had to touch. She let the back of her hand brush the long silky strands.

"Oh!" she said quietly.

Patrick grinned, confirmed what she had just discovered. "They're feathers."

Glenn smiled, amazed, letting the silky feathers fall through her fingers. They flashed light and dark.

"The color's not pigment," Patrick said. "It's structural. The feathers are refractive. That's why they turn color in the sun. Like hummingbirds."

"Big hummer," said Glenn. The mammoth hadn't minded—or perhaps not noticed—her touch.

"There's probably a layer of down underneath her silk jammies but I'm afraid to grope her to find out."

"Her?"

"This is a gal."

The she-mammoth was tusked like the males.

Looking across the meadow, Glenn couldn't tell the boys from the girls, except for the moms with their babies.

Glenn and Patrick agreed without speaking that it was best not to go near the babies.

The babies were classically cute, chubby, round, with big round heads and big round eyes, and downy feathers. They were clumsy. They tripped over their own trunks. The smallest baby was eight feet tall.

Patrick fished out his omni from one of his many pockets. He'd known what he was doing when they set out on this safari. He was recording. He checked the chart of extremely low frequency noises.

"Someone's talking." He pointed at a line moving on the graph of his handheld.

Patrick looked around. He pointed the omni toward a particularly mammoth mammoth. "The big guy there. Long John. He's doing the talking."

"What has a mammoth to say?" Glenn asked.

Patrick shrugged. "He might be telling another herd the grazing is good over here. Or he could be giving the saber tooth report."

He pocketed the omni, moved up to walk next to their she-mammoth's head. He fell into her slow rolling gait. Imitating her, he moved his arm like a trunk and plucked a handful of seed-topped grass.

Patrick Hamilton was socially inept among most humans, except other scientists. But he had a special connection with most aliens. Maybe because he took an interest in aliens. He was an intellectual snob and a pedant. He found most human conversation tedious, and it offended people when his eyes glazed over while they were talking. He liked the puzzle of deciphering alien thought and speech. He paid attention to what aliens said and made an effort to understand them. And aliens didn't know how juvenile his conversation usually was.

"Hey, spicy hembra, is this where all the hot mammoths graze?"

The she-mammoth lifted her trunk to snuffle his head. Her large hairy nostril breathed him in. Then she curled her trunk around the grass he held in his hand. She took the grass from him and tucked it into her mouth. Chewed with broad flat teeth. Her stubby tusks moved with her chewing.

She exhaled sweet oaty breath.

"I hope this doesn't mean we're hooked," said Patrick. "I'm happily married, you see."

Glenn noted the "happily." A significant word there.

The she-mammoth gave a little chirp.

Glenn smiled at the tiny sound. "Was that her? Did she do that?"

Patrick nodded. "That's all we've got on record for mammoth vocalization. I knew they could do better than that. This." He drew his omni from his pocket and showed her the chart of bellowing low-fi noises. "This. This is their language. Maybe."

Glenn gave him a puzzled look. "Maybe?"

"The question is whether it can be called language," he qualified. "There's a wide fuzzy gray line between language and animal communication. My mammoths fall solidly in the fuzzy zone. They don't create. But they do communicate."

"Your mammoths," said Glenn. "I thought they were Dr. Szaszy's mammoths."

"Szaszy likes to think they're his mammoths."

"You're stepping in his field," said Glenn.

"Szasz deserves stepping on. The mammoths are wasted on him. He never bothered to *listen* to them. This is a language. And I *think* I've isolated a few actual words. Predator.

Water. And I think there's a difference between big water and little water. This is little water right here."

He nodded at the creek that fed the larger stream. The she-mammoth dragged her trunk in the clear running current.

"I'm pretty sure big water means the river way down below camp. They also have sky water."

"Rain?"

"That would be my guess."

Their she-mammoth companion moved away from the creek. She looped her trunk around a bunch of wheaty grass and made an unmistakable gesture of offering it to Patrick.

"For me?" Patrick said with a terrified smile. "Really?" he took the offered grass. He glanced at Glenn, unnerved. "It's probably only polite to eat it, hm?"

Glenn could tell that he wanted her to talk him out of it. Instead she said, "Are you carrying a panic button?"

"Yeah."

"Give it to me."

In case stabs of poisoning came over him, Glenn could signal for help—though she was not sure how fast the LEN would send out a rescue party.

Not the answer Patrick was looking for. "You mean you want me to do this?"

"John Farragut has been known to swallow alien substances not to give offense to aliens," Glenn said.

"I'm not John Farragut," Patrick said.

Glenn said nothing.

Patrick said, "You didn't pick up the obvious straight line. You must still love me."

"Eat your wheat," Glenn said.

"Or maybe you don't."

"Well, I can't volunteer to eat it for you. She's your girlfriend. And she's getting testy."

The hembra pushed Patrick's hand, the one holding the wheat, to his face.

"Smells good," he said, weakly hopeful.

A tasty smell usually meant something was edible on Earth. This was not Earth. Perceptions here were likely skewed.

Glenn gave his shoulder a hard pat. "Bon appetit."

"Okay then. If I keel over, we get to see how good a doctor Cecil really is."

His body visibly tensed. Patrick bit into the seed heads.

He chewed gingerly. A look of mild surprise relaxed his face. "This isn't bad."

He swallowed. Paused cautiously as if listening to his stomach.

"How do you feel?" Glenn asked.

"Good!" said Patrick, surprised. He gathered up some more seed heads for himself.

Glenn smelled his breath. The crushed seeds gave off an oaty, wheaty, sesame aroma.

The scent made her mouth water. She hoped her nose was not mistranslating the alien smell.

"This is going down easy," Patrick said.

Glenn already knew that local flora had many proteins in common with Earth and that some of the native plants were edible. But she and Patrick didn't know which ones. And ingesting alien organics was not the generally accepted way of conducting a composition analysis. You could not judge alien organics by terrestrial measures.

Well, you could, but you could also be dead.

After hours of wandering with the mammoths, anxiously monitoring Patrick's vital signs, and listening to her own stomach rumble with hunger, Glenn asked, "Anything hurt?"

"My legs," Patrick said.

Not a surprise. Patrick was no athlete. This hike was the farthest he'd walked since she'd known him.

"How do you feel?"

"Great, actually. You?"

"I'm hungry!" Glenn snarled along with her stomach.

She gave Patrick one last checkup. His heartbeat was regular. His pupils looked normal and he wasn't sweating. His energy was good. Better than hers.

As they'd been walking, he had peeled the husks off a bunch of seeds for her. He emptied a pocketful of them into her cupped hands. She wolfed into them, chewing blissfully, her head full of wheaty, oaty, sesame scent.

As soon as she swallowed, she felt a subtle rush like carbohydrates hitting her bloodstream after a long fast. She gave a happy moan.

"Know what this means?" Patrick asked.

Glenn guessed, muffled, her mouth full, "New food crop?"

"Means we don't have to go back."

* * *

The adjutant in the outer office advised Admiral John Alexander Farragut, "Sir, your father is here."

Mohammed was a whole lot less surprised when his mountain knocked on the door. *That* had been expected. *This* just could not be happening.

Not a phone call. Not a messenger.

Your father is here.

Himself.

Justice of the State Supreme Court of the Commonwealth of Kentucky, the admiral's father was the supreme master of his domain. His Honor waited for no one. You wait on His Honor.

His Honor was waiting in the outer office.

Had anyone scanned this being's retina and checked his DNA before allowing him on base?

This could not be good.

His Honor had made the first move.

Admiral Farragut shot across his office to open the door for himself. "Sir."

As soon as he saw the man, Admiral Farragut knew he was real.

Justice John Knox Farragut nodded and advanced through the open door, his back straight but with an unfamiliar humbled air. His ambivalence was familiar. So was the resentment. But his enormous pride was crushed down to a civil calm.

Admiral Farragut was an incorrigible hugger, but he resisted the impulse to embrace his father. His Honor had crossed the abyss first. The son left him his personal space.

His Honor's alpha superiority had slipped by coming here. He trudged into the admiral's office and sat heavily.

Admiral Farragut's first fear came out of his mouth, "Mama?"

His Honor waved that off. "Your mother's—" He stopped before he could say *fine*. He said instead, "Your mother is your mother."

But something was very wrong. The trouble had to be one of the admiral's twenty brothers and sisters or his fruitfully multiplying nieces and nephews. Or else something was wrong with the Old Man himself, who looked beaten down.

His Honor's hollow gaze wandered, spied the baby under the admiral's desk. He slid from his chair, hunkered down with one knee on the floor to pick her up. He gave her a sad smile, like someone grieving while holding a new life between his hands.

Bad news wasn't going anywhere.

His Honor looked into the button-nosed face, the petal lidded eyes. Managed a sad smile. "Now who is this?"

His Honor had been at Admiral Farragut's wedding—mainly because Mama had threatened him with all the devils of hell and her eternal wrath, which seldom seen was nonetheless terrifying, if he did not attend.

Father and son hadn't seen each other face-to-face since.

The admiral introduced the infant, "Your grandbaby. Patsy Augusta."

"Patsy. For your Grandmama Winfield," His Honor said approvingly. "And Augusta?" Of course he couldn't place that name.

"For a Roman."

Not approving. "Why would you give any child of mine a Roman name?"

"Sir? She's *my* child."

And here we go. The back went stiff. The familiar glower returned to the blue eyes.

And just as quickly faded. His Honor backing down.

It was terrifying.

"Who died?"

"No one. No one died," said His Honor. Didn't seem surprised by the question. With some reproach, he asked, "I can't come see my son and my grandchild?"

Yes. When entropy reverses itself and time runs backward. When little Miss Muffet invites eight-legged guests to tea. When all the laws of nature break down.

"You're always welcome, sir."

His Honor talked for a while. About family. And when he decided it was time to go, he gave his son a huge heartfelt bear hug on his way out, his eyes tight shut. He thumped his son on the back. "My boy. My boy."

Immediately he was gone, Admiral Farragut contacted Central Intelligence. "Can I get a personal data excavation — off ledger?"

"Since it's you, sir," said the agent.

Admiral Farragut said, "Can you find out if my father is dying?"

* * *

The chart on Patrick's omni spiked.

"Uh-oh."

The mammoths' lazy shuffling became restive. Ropy tails switched. Ears flapped. Trunks lifted into the air.

The bull Long John held his ears straight out to the sides.

Moving shadows swept across the highland meadow. Glenn looked up, shaded her eyes against the sun.

The silhouette of a wide wingspan circled the meadow. Then another. More of them in soaring spirals.

At first Glenn thought the lowest one was diseased, because of its naked, peeling head, but they were all like that. All of them had featherless heads, sloughing skin, and tattered rags of black feathers.

Back home, a naked head indicated a carrion eater. But there was nobody dead here on the meadow.

The circling birds had large horn beaks with hooked ends. They circled, croaking. More and more of them.

They spiraled up instead of down. The highest could see for miles up there.

Or be seen.

The mammoths picked up sticks and clods of dirt with their trunks and threw them up at the ugly birds.

"Tattler," Patrick named them. "Air jackal. Oooh, nice shot." As a dirt clod found its mark. The bird folded up in midair and tumbled tail over beak.

It recovered with an ungainly flapping before it could touch ground, where mammoths were moving in, seeming intent on trampling it.

Glenn was confused. "Jackals? Why are they gathering? No one is dead."

"Yet," said Patrick.

"Will they attack?"

"No. If tattlers don't find carrion on their own, they get someone else to kill something for them. The tattlers find a buffet and call in sabers to kill it so the tattlers can feast on leftovers."

"Mammoths?" said Glenn, incredulous. "*Anything* can spot mammoths. They picked mammoths? Why not pick something easy, like Bengal tigers?"

"Mammoth babies," Patrick said.

Chubby, chunky, clumsy, plump mammoth babies cuddled together, crying pitiably. Their mothers tossed their heads, frantic, squeaking.

Glenn looked up at the ominous birds. "What does this mean?"

A roar sounded from the tangled vegetation beyond the meadow. Another roar, very leonine, answered from the trees bounding the opposite side. Another roar of something hidden circled behind the herd. Roars kept repeating from the six o'clock, nine o'clock, and twelve o'clock positions.

The chart on Patrick's omni was scribbled nearly solid. He pocketed it and took Glenn by the hand.

"Means we're about to be attacked by sabers."

10

MAMMOTH TRUNKS LIFTED and lowered. Mammoth ears flared straight out.

The sabers were moving in a wide semicircle. Glenn couldn't spot them but knew where they were from the movements of the mammoths' eyes.

Glenn had her splinter gun out. Of course she brought her gun. She had it on her always, slung across her back under her jacket, out of sight. As Patrick was with his omni, Glenn was with her gun. She slept with her gun. Even though it was coded for her exclusive use, she never left her weapon where anyone else could get it.

She wasn't wearing gunsights. Targeting would be tricky here.

But the target sounded big.

Patrick was the expert on Zoen creatures, but Glenn was the expert in combat. Patrick listened to the saber roars and whispered, "Are they herding us?"

"I think," said Glenn. The sabers had the mammoths hemmed in on three sides. The open direction would feed them down into the stream where it tumbled down the steep rocky vale in the direction Patrick and Glenn had come.

That had been a hard slippery climb with treacherous rock walls on both sides.

"The predators are trying to spook the mammoths into the pass," said Glenn, frightened for the herd. "The mammoths won't be able to maneuver in there. Patrick, they'll kill themselves on the rocks."

"I think my mammoths are smarter than that," Patrick said. It sounded more like a wish than a belief.

But the mammoths did refuse to be herded.

The hembras were gathering up their young and hustling them into a tight group right here in the open meadow. All the adults formed a defensive circle around them, tusk-side out.

Patrick nodded up at the horn-beaked tattlers. "Tattlers have a symbiotic relationship with sabers. The saber is the only thing that will attack a mammoth."

"Sabertooth cat?" Glenn asked, gripping her gun, trying to get a look at what roared from the underbrush.

"More saber. Less cat," said Patrick just before a thick trunk encircled him and swung him up into the air and deposited him into the middle of the defensive ring with the babies.

Another mammoth shooed Glenn back there with him. The big living hose pushed her along with a stern touch, *move it, move it*.

When the trunk stopped pushing her, Glenn was trapped inside a circular wall of colossal feathery asses in the company of the keening babies. Tree trunk legs shifted and stamped. Mammoths snorted. Ears flapped. Skinny tails twitched.

The tattlers circled lower, uttering harsh squawks.

A baby mammoth looped its stubby trunk around Patrick and tucked him between its forelegs and hugged him, shivering.

Patrick pushed downy feathers out of his face. Said, "I think I just became someone's dolly."

Glenn moved around the ring, peering out through the forest of moving legs.

She spotted a motion of large shapes at the tree line.

They burst into the open.

Through moving legs and waving feathers, all Glenn could see of them at first were the sabers themselves, dirty ivory horns, straight as lances, flying at the mammoths.

Mammoth heads tossed, brandishing stout tusks.

The sabers stopped short of the thrashing tusks. They dodged, circled, feinted again.

The predators were bulky. Muscles like living building blocks moved under gray skin. Outsized heads seemed to be all mouth. They wielded two sabers. One saber jutted from under their tiny eyes, the other, stouter saber extended from their wide, armor-boned chests.

The chilling crash of tusks against sabers made Glenn drop into a crouch. Snarling and thrashing thundered from all sides. Glenn caught glimpses of retreating sabers.

The mammoths repelled the first charge.

Glenn had a horrible feeling that the sabers were only testing. They stabbed to find a weak point.

And they edged back in.

Glenn couldn't get out of the living fortress. The mammoths pressed together, side to side, swaying, crushing weights.

Glenn dropped down flat on her belly with her splinter gun aimed at ground level.

She looked down the barrel, trying to line up a shot for what might come. The mammoth legs were in constant motion. Their long feathery coats waved between Glenn and the targets.

The sabers paced with abrupt turns, in and out of view.

Glenn had no shot at all.

She jumped back to her feet. She holstered her gun behind her back, ran up to a mammoth haunch, seized two thick handfuls of feathers and scaled up its rump.

The ropy tail slapped her. She crested the mammoth's rear, and crawled up its back onto its neck. She hooked one arm over the root of one ear to keep it out of her way, and she set her sight on a saber. Fired.

The saber flinched as the splinter pierced its hide and lodged in its ribs. The saber snarled at the sting.

Glenn pulled the second stage trigger.

The splinter splintered.

The saber convulsed upward, all four feet off the ground. Its body twisted in the air and dropped to the ground. Frothing red blood ran from its mouth.

There was nervous commotion all around, mammoth and saber. The sabers held their tiny ears flat back, a very terrestrial gesture of fear. The mammoths acted confused, scared. They did not break ranks. They were already in the position they assumed when they were scared.

Glenn took aim at the biggest saber in her view and stuck a splinter into its ear. The saber pawed at its ear, shaking its head. Glenn pulled the second trigger. A piece of skull and fur burst outward in a red iron-blooded spray.

Overhead, the tattlers squawked. The sabers roared confusion, anger. The mammoths squeaked.

Glenn's mount rolled its trunk up. The trunk rose before Glenn like an enormous serpent, then the nostril prodded Glenn questioningly.

Glenn petted the giant nose away. "I'm working here."

A saber sprang up under her mount's lifted trunk. No time to aim, Glenn pulled two triggers in quick succession. The splinter caught the leaping saber in its open mouth and immediately detonated.

The saber's throat ruptured out of its neck. The saber fell thrashing on the ground coughing and gagging. It clipped one of its own pack in the ankle with its facial saber.

Glenn's mount flinched as the blood spattered its trunk. The mammoth forequarters lifted off the ground and came down to crush the wounded saber. The mammoth shook its head, tusks waving. Knocked Glenn off-balance. She slid downward, where massive sides pounded together and huge feet stamped craters in the ground.

Glenn clutched at the mammoth's ear to stay aboard. It took two hands. Her splinter gun slid away and dropped amid the stamping mammoth feet.

The ear waved. Glenn lost her grip on the ear. She grabbed at anything. Feathers. Thick handfuls of feathers. She shut her eyes, grunting, hauling herself up the moving wall hand over hand. Glenn pulled herself back over the crest of the mammoth's neck, and she clung to it, tight as skin, until the sabers dissolved back into the gray-green trees.

The two biggest mammoth males charged out of the circle to give chase. The hembras closed ranks behind them and stayed that way until the males returned. Then they all joined in stepping on the dead.

The males shook their tusks at the sky where disappointed tattlers circled, braying.

Glenn climbed down her mammoth's butt. Her hands tingled. All her nerves felt like they were sparking.

She found her gun. It was completely embedded in the ground within a mammoth footprint. She wedged the gun loose, moved apart to find a place to sit down and pick out the dirt.

A mammoth nose ruffled her short, short hair. The animal seemed to know Glenn was responsible for the exploding sabers. Making that connection had to indicate a certain level of intelligence. Glenn gave the trunk a little stroke and expected it to go away.

The mammoth kept snuffling and nudging her. Another joined in, prodded her with its trunk.

Glenn tried to shoo the trunks away without actually slapping them. Finally she cried, "Patrick, what are they doing?"

Patrick pointed up at the carrion birds. "I think they want you to shoot the tattlers."

✷ ✷ ✷

Consul Marco Camiciarossa was dubious when the young American man showed up at the Italian consulate on planet Phoenix and introduced himself as John Farragut, Junior.

"You are Admiral Farragut's *son?*" the consul asked, skeptical.

Camiciarossa had never heard that the famous Admiral John Farragut had a grown son.

"I'm his brother," said this John Farragut.

Curiouser and curiouser. Camiciarossa gave an uncomfortable laugh. This was a joke. A weak one. "Who would name two sons John?"

"You obviously don't know our father. His Honor has an ego. I'm the junior. I know it's odd, but it's God's truth."

Camiciarossa politely asked to check his visitor's DNA. He expected this obvious fraud to quickly excuse himself and withdraw.

"Not a problem." The alleged John Farragut, Junior, presented himself for testing. "Anything you want."

Astonishingly, Camiciarossa found an authenticated record that Admiral John Alexander Farragut actually had a younger brother also named John. The younger John had a different middle name than the admiral. This younger John Farragut had the same middle name as their father. The visitor's DNA and retinal image checked out to the identity John Farragut, Junior.

It was so fantastical that Camiciarossa had to make one more cross-check, in case the science had been subverted. Camiciarossa would not be gulled. In an ancient day it was common to use obscure knowledge to verify someone's identity. Consul Camiciarossa resurrected the old challenge. "Mother's maiden name?"

"Winfield."

Camiciarossa flushed, embarrassed. The young man was who he said he was. Camiciarossa tried to make amends for grilling his guest. "Signor Farragut. I do so apologize for the terrorist treatment."

The young man waved the apology away. "Understandable. Expected. You got a strange request from a total stranger. And I have to confess I can't pretend I'm on any official business. I saw one of these at an air show, and they just don't let you get within five hundred feet."

John Farragut, Junior, had asked for a tour of the Italian ambassador's Xerxes transport.

"I fell in love from afar," said the younger Farragut.

The Farraguts were a wealthy family. Camiciarossa hadn't known they were quite that wealthy.

But Camiciarossa supposed one needn't be able to purchase a Xerxes in order to lust after one. "It is a magnificent machine," Camiciarossa assured him. "I think even Rome must admit it is the premier ship of its kind."

The two strolled out to the secure area of the consulate, arm in arm, LEN fashion. The much grander Italian embassy building loomed beyond the compound wall.

Camiciarossa's eyes kept straying aside, stealing glances at the cuts on the young American's face. When a slight bump to his side made young Farragut wince, Camiciarossa took the opening to ask, "Are you injured?"

Farragut nodded. "I got thrown by a horse."

Horsemanship was an aristocratic pursuit. "You are an equestrian?"

"Not a good one." The young man touched his ribs gingerly.

Camiciarossa thought his guest had forgiven him for his rude welcome. This Farragut looked somewhat like the infamous admiral but more refined, with less brawn. He was just as blond and six foot tall. "We don't see many Americans here. What brings you to Phoenix?"

"I'm on an old-fashioned Grand Tour," said Farragut. The Grand Tour was still a custom among the well-bred gentry. "I'm seeing the cosmos. Other people. Other places. I'm thinking of becoming an ambassador when I finish school."

A very pleasant surprise. "That would be a change from your brother," said Camiciarossa and immediately checked himself. *What a ghastly thing to say*. He feared he had insulted his guest.

But this John Farragut graciously agreed, "Wouldn't it?"

The famous Admiral John Alexander Farragut was a U.S. cowboy who negotiated at gunpoint. Admiral John Alexander Farragut was not well-loved by the League of Earth Nations.

"I am *not* my brother," this John Farragut assured Camiciarossa.

That was a good thing, the consul thought.

They had come to an open area close to the ordinary transport hangars.

Energy sparked off the young man, an anxious anticipation like a boy on his first date. He searched about for his beloved.

Camiciarossa smiled. "See her?"

Puzzled. Expectant. Farragut said, "No."

Camiciarossa could not hold back his grin. "You see—or don't see!—this is beyond perfect optical invisibility." He commanded the air, "*Bernini*! Reveal yourself."

The Xerxes appeared from emptiness.

The young man's intake of breath was satisfying.

Camiciarossa enjoyed his shock and depth of emotion. The young man was profoundly impressed.

The Xerxes was an aggressive, faceted, flying wing, big as a yacht. Even revealed it was difficult to see. The harder one looked, the more diffuse its details. It took on colors of sky and ground and the maintenance hangars behind it.

"In full stealth our Xerxes refracts light and scatters the

image so it cannot be detected by any electromagnetically sensitive means. Sounders can send a ping straight at it; the Xerxes won't be there."

The young man found his voice. "That must make it tough for airspace control."

"Control is notified of its presence on a strictly need-to-know basis. And, of course, airspace control needs to know."

He took the young man for a walk around, pointed out the two antimatter engines bulging under the fuselage. They couldn't really see the topside this close up, as the ship was tall.

"Shall we board?"

His guest was having trouble putting words together, overwhelmed. He nodded, "Please."

"Signor Farragut—" the consul started, then switched, hand over heart. "May I call you John?"

The young Farragut hesitated. Camiciarossa thought he'd been too familiar. But Farragut explained, "Actually, I go by my middle name these days."

Camiciarossa had done the background check, so he didn't need to ask what it was.

"Of course." Camiciarossa nodded. "Knox."

11

GLENN AND PATRICK SPENT several days among the mammoths. At night the male mammoths paced guard duty in shifts. Mothers lay down in the tall grass, their babies between their forelegs.

Came a morning when the herd woke early. Trunks extended up in the air, sniffing. Snorting. There was something on the wind they didn't like.

Glenn reached for her splinter gun.

The herd got to its feet and shuffled away from the smell.

There was something beyond the eastern trees they didn't like. They didn't *hate* it, but they were avoiding it.

Glenn sniffed. Immediately she felt ridiculous. As noses went, she was seriously outgunned. She didn't smell anything deadish or shitty on the breeze.

"Are we going with them?" Glenn gazed after the mammoths.

Patrick gave the kind of nod that said maybe. "I want to see what spooked them."

He seemed to have an idea what it was.

Glenn and Patrick jogged across the wide meadow in the opposite direction from the mammoths. When they came to the trees, they crept softly through the underbrush to see what lay beyond.

Where the vines and bushes thinned, they hunched low and tucked into a ready-made foxhole left by an uprooted tree. Huddled against the earthen wall of their bunker,

Glenn slowly lifted her head and pushed aside a bare root to peer into the clearing.

She inhaled a little gasp. A sound of shock, but good shock. A Christmas morning gasp, or a moonlit meadow filled with fireflies gasp.

Patrick edged up to peer over the side. He breathed, "It's them!"

Glenn smiled, delighted. "They're—"

Charming was the word, but Glenn couldn't bring herself to say it. *Cute.* Another word she didn't know how to pronounce.

"Foxes!" Patrick whispered.

They were handsome animals, superficially vulpine, the size of very large dogs, wolf-bodied but with broader chests. The faces were tapered, their ears pointed and erect.

They had Samoyed smiles.

Fox language was what the LEN brought Patrick to Zoe to study.

Half of the foxes were on all fours. At least a half dozen were walking on their hind legs in a bent leg stance, and one carried something in its forepaws. Several wrestled and tumbled. One lolled in the grass. Their palms and the soles of their feet were black pads.

The foxes moved in ways that looked playful.

All the pictures Glenn had seen of foxes were taken in a winter setting. The animals in those pictures had thick lustrous pelts. The short coats of these on the summer meadow were sleek and shiny as racehorses. Only the fur of their topknots and their tails was long and bushy.

Glenn counted forty or fifty. May have missed some, and counted some others twice. They were gamboling and tumbling in the high grass.

Glenn and Patrick went unnoticed, huddled downwind under the tree roots.

Glenn noted the animals' formidable claws, the canine teeth. She whispered, "What would they do if we went out there?"

Patrick's eyebrows shrugged. He didn't know. "They share with each other. They don't pick fights. They're only ever aggressive toward prey."

"Are we prey?"

"*That*, my Hamlet, is the question."

The foxes looked sweet and cheerful. And they were so ... with each other. No one knew how they would react to humans.

"They're pack predators," Patrick whispered. "They can bring down beasts the size of a yak. There could be a reason the mammoths shuffled on elsewhere. I'm not sure what kind of IFF we'd get here."

He meant Identification Friend or Food.

Glenn watched intently for a while. Couldn't help smiling as the foxes played. She glanced aside to Patrick, who had turned around to sit with his back against the embankment, facing the other direction.

She was surprised to see him so pale. And he'd stopped talking.

The short hairs stood up on the back of her neck. Patrick's gaze was fixed immediately behind her. Glenn noticed the body heat now radiating at her back. And an animal smell. Patrick spoke straight ahead of him in a small strained voice, "Grandma, what big teeth you have."

✳ ✳ ✳

As the Italian consul Marco Camiciarossa ushered his visitor into the Xerxes' air lock, the inner hatch sealed fast against their approach. The ship spoke in a firm voice. Could have been male or female. "Unregistered person attempting entry."

Camiciarossa spoke: "*Bernini*. Register Knox as friendly."

A scanner light moved up and down the two people within the air lock. Nox held his breath.

A soft chime sounded. The inner seal relaxed. The ship pronounced: "Registered."

Nox closed his eyes.

The hatch opened for them. Camiciarossa showed Nox around the spaceship.

The overheads were higher than on military ships. This was a luxury transport for important persons. The control room was well ordered, black and steel, elegant, efficient.

The galley was sleek, clean, equipped for a master chef. The food stores were low, as the ambassador was currently in residence at the embassy.

The physical sleep chambers were small, accommodating only a very large bed and dresser. But the confines could transform themselves into illusions of anything you wanted—mountains, beaches, kingdoms under the sea.

Nox was more interested in the technical achievements than the amenities. Camiciarossa showed off the machine's engineering mastery—the helm, the sensors, the communications center, the water recyclers, the air scrubbers, the engines, which were custom built for each Xerxes, the inertial-field generators.

"What is threshold?" Nox asked.

"I can't tell you."

Nox gave him a conspiratorial smile. "It's fast, isn't it?"

Camiciarossa had to suppress his own smile. "It's very fast."

He showed Nox the arsenal of serpent's teeth. That name sounded better than "killer pencils," which better described the missiles' look. "Serpent's teeth" better defined their effect—fast, penetrating, lethal.

"They will rip through most inertial fields," said Camiciarossa. "*Bernini* is not an attack craft, but he could defend himself if he had to."

At tour's end, the consul said, "I'm sorry I can't take you up for a fly around."

"Oh, God, *please* don't apologize!" Nox said, honestly horrified. "You've been amazing."

Nox reached into his pocket. Knew this wasn't going to go in easy. He would get only one attempt.

Nox didn't carry a pocket knife, as most American men did. But he was in civilized guise, and he could carry a pen onto the ambassador's spacecraft without setting off alarms, even though a pen was the instrument of a notorious assassination in recent history.

✳ ✳ ✳

Glenn turned her head, dreadfully slowly, to look over her shoulder.

She saw the teeth first. Pointed teeth. Uppers and lowers on display in a wide vulpine smile. White. Gleaming.

The fox had very large eyes.

Glenn edged her hand toward her back, reaching for her splinter gun.

Patrick hummed.

The fox's head jerked back. Its muzzle pulled down against its snowy chest. It looked surprised. The fox barked, jumped up, and dashed around the hollow in a tight, tail-chasing puppy circle. It sat up on its haunches on the trunk of the fallen tree and cocked its head.

The teeth were still all there in a big smile. The black eyes gleamed.

Was that the look of hunger? Curiosity? Challenge? Thrill of the hunt? Alien fear?

Patrick climbed out of the root hole and performed a kind of salaam—a big full-body bow that brought his forearms to the ground and his butt up in the air. On Earth it was universal dog language for *Do you want to play*?

The fox's forepaws were armed with massive curved black claws. Before Glenn could react, one paw shot forward, batted Patrick in the chest. The fox darted away in bouncing leaps. Glenn gasped, "Patrick! Are you—?

All right? she meant to say, but Patrick was scrambling to his feet, unblooded, brushing her off, and dashing after the fox. "I'm it!"

The white tip of the fox's tail gave a wag and flick in retreat. Might have been an equivalent to sticking out its tongue.

If we are prey, this opens a new category in predators playing with their food.

Glenn crawled out of the hollow, brushed off dirt and bugs, and followed Patrick and his playmate out to the clearing, her gun at her side.

Immediately she was surrounded by curious faces and twitching noses.

She felt a nose up from behind, right in her crotch. She fought the reflex to hike a mule kick at it.

Patrick made his way to Glenn's side in the throng of foxes.

He was intact, his hair tousled, face flushed. A fox stood up on its hind legs, stuck its nose in Patrick's ear, and gave him a good sniff. Then it stuck its nose in Patrick's face, nostril to nostril, and inhaled.

It showed all its teeth.

Sometimes a baring of teeth really was just a smile.

Glenn got a nose up her armpit.

Giant claws picked at her sleeve without cutting it, just curious.

A furry muzzle found its way down the front of her shirt. Her hands closed on reflex around its head. Her fingers curled in the fur behind its ears.

The head leaned into her touch.

And I'm giving a fanged alien intelligence an ear scratch.

She didn't dare show anxiety. But didn't dare assume the aliens were harmless.

Patrick was long past daring. Patrick was already family.

Patrick tussled and rolled and boxed as Glenn hung onto her heartbeat. Patrick kept getting up unscathed.

The foxes were apparently smart enough to know that the strangers were breakable. And so far they were choosing not to break them.

A fox sniffed Glenn's face.

"Hello," said Glenn.

The fox drew back. Blinked huge eyes. It opened and shut its mouth. Another fox turned its head over sideways, as if thoroughly perplexed by the sound.

"Hello," Glenn repeated.

One fox pawed his muzzle as if he had something stuck on it. The other rolled all the way over, as if Glenn might sound different when viewed from upside down.

"Hello," Glenn said again.

The foxes hummed to each other. One touched Glenn's mouth, its big claws pulled back, its black footpads on her lips. If the fox were human, Glenn would say it was perplexed.

It really did seem perplexed.

They can't form words. The foxes didn't know how she was making these sounds.

She realized, *They look perplexed because they're perplexed.* Body language was crossing the alien barrier.

And possibly the foxes looked friendly because they actually were friendly.

When Patrick found his way back to her, Glenn pulled burrs from his hair. She said, "These creatures didn't build the spacecraft that attacked us on the way in."

"No," Patrick had to agree. He turned his face up toward the sky. "Means they're not alone."

＊ ＊ ＊

The consul's body had scarcely fallen to the deck when Nox was shouting, "*Bernini!* Emergency dust off! Execute! *Ora!*"

The Xerxes obeyed in an instant. Hatches sealed. The ship lifted off the ground in full stealth mode and shot skyward in a panic rising. The emergency command did not allow time for directions, they just told the ship to get aloft and *elsewhere* fast without hitting anything.

Nox expected to be slammed to the deck with the sudden liftoff. But the inside of the Xerc was staid and stately as an ambassador's reception room. The only thing Nox felt was the disconnect between the inner stillness of the ship and his view out the portal. It was like watching an action video.

He pounced on the ship's communications station and shut everything off. Phoenix's ground and sky controllers were not hailing him yet. The controllers didn't even know the Xerc was airborne.

Hands shaking, Nox disabled the res chamber and the auto SOS sounder. He stepped over the consul's body. Skidded in the blood.

He dashed through the ship, scouring all systems for anything that might be used as a tracking signature. He disabled the displacement collars, the landing disks, the displacement straps, and the displacement chamber itself. Turned off the emergency sounders in all the life pods and life craft. He rifled the private compartments for personal communicators and threw them in the annihilator. He pulled the ambassador's workstation out of the bulk, turned all its systems off, and removed its batteries.

He ran back to the control room to find out where in the world he was.

The Xerxes hovered like a hole in the air high over an ocean on the dayside of Phoenix.

Nox instructed the ship to no longer respond to the name *Bernini.* From now on the Xerxes was to respond only to the name *Bagheera.*

Nox purged all users other than himself from *Bagheera*'s registry. He fed the biometrics of his brothers into the ship as registered personnel.

He executed a passive scan for possible searchers. He detected no frantic activity from any base on planet. The satellite eyes would have seen nothing alarming. If they were focused on the compound between the Italian Embassy and the Italian consulate, they would have seen the Xerxes appear out of its cloaked state. They would have seen the consul board the Xerxes with a guest. They would have seen the Xerxes disappear as it returned to full stealth. There were no further visuals for them to detect. As far as they could know, the Xerxes was still in the compound, invisible.

None of the Roman Legion bases were showing alarms. None of the orbital defense stations were launching anything.

Nox knew they were going to start up—any heartbeat now. The Xerc would undoubtedly miss a scheduled call-in. Nox needed to get off world as soon as inhumanly possible.

He had already told his brothers where to be.

Now attend and listen! I'll either pick you up, or my death will be on the news.

This was going to be a flying grab.

Trouble was, Nox was ahead of schedule. Would his brothers be at the rendezvous coordinates now? Would they come at all?

Be there, be there, be there. Nox did not want to be alone on this side of the Rubicon.

The place of rendezvous came into visual range. It was a lonely stand of gnarled gray knot trees at coordinates of nowhere in particular. There was no reason for satellite eyes to monitor this place at all, much less be watching it at this particular moment in time.

Nox saw nothing at the rendezvous coordinates.

No police. No watchers.

No brothers.

Nothing but bedraggled trees, rocks, and dust.

No.

Then, at the instant of despair, *There!*

Pallas.

And behind the bleached tree skeletons was Nicanor.

Among the rocks were Faunus, Orissus, Leo, Galeo.

Nox's chest unknotted. His brothers had come. They were there, waiting.

Nox brought the Xerc straight down, abrupt as a runaway freight elevator. Set it down hard.

The brothers jerked away from the sudden noise and flying sand. They hadn't seen the ship coming. Still didn't see it.

The Xerxes unveiled in the rising dust. The hatch opened. The brothers stared, astounded, six mouths perfectly round. They looked like a tenement birdhouse.

Nox shouted, "Come on! Come on! Come on!"

Now came an alarm—sounding from inside *Bagheera*'s control room.

The Xerxes calmly spoke warnings of air and spacecraft approaching in direct lines.

Suddenly, a skyhook from the orbiting horizon guard smashed down, a fist of energy at the speed of light.

There before any of them could know it.

Either the Xerxes deflected the hook or the sky watch had targeted a thrown image. Either way, the hook missed the Xerc and captured the trees instead. Ripped them and the rock-hard ground under them out of the planet surface and hauled them up, leaving a crater behind it.

Nox bellowed, "Run!"

His brothers charged up the ramp, pelted through the air lock. Hatches sealed fast behind them. *Bagheera*'s inertial field sealed over.

"*Bagheera!* Escape!"

The Xerc rose up hard. The ascent exceeded the speed of the ship's in-atmo stealth capabilities. It left a scorch mark in the air pointing the way it fled.

Immediately clear of the ionosphere, the Xerxes assumed full stealth again. Its image disappeared from all sensors. Its heat trail scattered.

Bagheera changed course. Changed again.

Outside the space lanes, Nox jumped the Xerxes to FTL. He ordered a hard turn on a skew vector and punched the Xerc to threshold velocity.

Threshold velocity was a function of a ship's mass. Few spacecraft existed with a combination of extreme power and low mass better than a Xerxes. And no one could chase an FTL plot unless they knew exactly on which vector to look.

Roman Intelligence could locate the source of a res pulse, if Rome knew your resonant harmonic and you had your res chamber activated. Nox had deactivated or destroyed all res sources on board *Bagheera*.

Nox leaned, straight-armed, over the control console, waiting, breathing, listening.

Monitor lights blinked benignly green. Only the threshold indicator hovered near red, but Nox wanted that.

They'd got away.

Nox's brothers entered the control room with cautious, awed laughter, tentative smiles, and shining eyes.

Orissus left his mouth hanging open. Faunus smacked him up under the chin. Orissus bit his tongue.

Nicanor ran his hand over the sleek steel surfaces and the instrument panels as if making sure they were real.

Leo and Galeo prowled, unfocused, dazed, happy, horrified, amazed.

Pallas' gaze fell on Nox's shirt. He noticed the darker patch of wetness on the dark fabric and found the red-brown crust limning Nox's fingernails. There were red fingerprints and handprints on the consoles.

Everything Nox touched had blood on it.

Pallas dropped his stare to the black deck, the pool of something wet shining there. Pallas nodded down. "What'd you do with whoever that was?"

"I, um, got rid of him," said Nox unsteadily.

The mortal remains of Camiciarossa had blown out an air lock.

A moment of thick silence pressed in on Nox. The brothers were trained to be soldiers. They'd been taught how to kill.

It was still theory for the rest of them.

"I guess you had to," Nicanor said gravely, understanding.

"Not really," said Nox. "I didn't have to."

"And what was that like?" said Orissus.

Nox threw up. Spattered the deck. Got Pallas' boots.

Nox's throat stung. "Oh, screw." He braced himself, palms on his knees, head down, body bent over, waiting for anything else that wanted to come up.

"Well, then, why did you kill him?" said Orissus.

Nox spat, stood up, his nose thick. He sniffed. That was a mistake. He swallowed. His voice came out raw. "To slam the door behind me! You all think I can go 'home' somewhere! I *can't!* This is you and me! *We* are in this!"

"In a river of shit," said Leo over the pool of blood. It was a statement of solidarity.

"Face down." Galeo said as the others nodded.

"No, Best Beloved. That's only the eighth circle of hell," said Nox. "We're lower than that."

"All right. Agreed," said Faunus. "This isn't the future any of us wanted, but here we are." He ran a beefy hand along the elegantly molded trim around the hatch. "Nox, you make a superb pirate. And I think I can get used to hell."

* * *

"Where is it?"

The Italian attaché was a trim, fast-moving young man amped up on designer chemicals. He'd taken the marble stairs two at a time charging up to the governor's office. He looked around for his stray Xerxes as if it were to be found inside the governor's palace.

"Where is *Bernini?*"

Round and jovial as Good Saint Nick, Aemilius, Roman governor of planet Phoenix, answered the young man placidly, "We don't have it."

The attaché sputtered. "But you launched a skyhook at it!"

"It missed."

"How can a skyhook *miss?*"

"That's a fine stealthy ship you had," the governor assured him.

The attaché's eyes stretched. He checked himself before he could say something unfortunate.

Governor Aemilius asked, "Did you not have failsafes in place?"

"They failed," the attaché said tightly.

"That is the problem with a stealthy spacecraft. It's very hard to find when you misplace it."

"We did not—!" The attaché checked himself again. Yelling at a powerful man he needed was a bad idea. The attaché started over. "Are you going to help me?"

"I tried, sir. I did. Count me as one of your failsafes. Your ship did actually leave an exit trail. But that will point us the last direction we want to look. Which narrows the search down to the rest of outer space. You see my problem? The IFF on board your Xerxes is turned off. Its com is not receiving or sending. *Bernini* is probably traveling faster than light. Attempts at remote system overrides have failed. Your ship is obeying a new master."

"That is the *ship*," said the attaché. "What about the ambassador's system?"

"Say again?"

"Control of the Xerxes does not give you access to the ambassador's system. His data banks. His communications module. His programs. His network. His— His—"

"System," the Governor supplied.

"Yes."

"The ambassador left sensitive material in the ship?" Aemilius guessed.

"It seemed like a safe place," the attaché said dryly. "The ambassador's system is a separate entity from the ship. It has a separate security program, a separate lock, a separate ID, separate authentication protocol, its own access codes. Its own tracking code."

"Tracking code?"

"Yes. The ambassador's system is equipped with a passive tracker."

"What is that?"

"A passive tracker doesn't initiate signals. It's a catcher. You ping it, it returns a signal. Otherwise, it emits nothing. The hijacker can't tell it's even on."

Aemilius considered this. "Assuming the hijacker is somewhat clever, would he not shut the system down entirely?"

"The tracker interprets any unauthorized attempt to access the system as a ping. The tracker would return a signal. We haven't received a signal. We *know* the hijacker hasn't tried to disable it. You ping him, you have him."

"You don't suppose the Xerxes would bolt the instant we pinged your ambassador's tracker?"

"No." The attaché hesitated. He was forced to show his hole card. "It's a resonant ping."

And suddenly the attaché was facing a man who could get his feet kissed if he wanted. The governor knew it too.

Aemilius asked silkily, "Just how do you suppose to get a location on resonant pulse?"

The attaché took a breath. "I grovel before the might and mercy of Rome."

Alone among all nations in the known galaxy, Rome could locate the origin point of a resonant pulse, a pulse that existed everywhere at once in the instant of its existence.

The governor of Phoenix ordered Legion ships to stand ready to run down the target as soon as he determined its location and vector.

Aemilius left the Italian attaché upstairs in his palace, while he descended to the cellar, to sunless chambers where Imperial Intelligence agentes dwelled.

Aemilius expelled all but necessary personnel from the secure room. That left four, counting himself.

A young res tech, seated at his station, prepared to engage the resonant locator.

A tactical coordinator stood by at the com, ready to dispatch whichever Legion vessel turned out to be closest to the target.

One lone Intelligence agent remained in the room, watching, only because Aemilius couldn't get rid of all of them.

"Here." The governor held up a data slip. On it was the harmonic he had received from the Italian attaché. The man had nearly cried letting go of it. "Find this."

Aemilius gave the data slip directly to the res tech, bypassing the Intelligence agent.

The res tech loaded the harmonic into his res chamber, then stretched and flexed his arms as if preparing to work magic. "If he's out there, he's mine."

"No, he's mine," the governor gently corrected the young man. "Do this."

The res tech sent out a single res pulse.

Instantly got a resonant return in the locator. "Got him."

"That simple?" Aemilius said.

The tech caressed his locator unit. "This is the love of my life, *Domni*."

The locator unit fed the resultant galactic coordinates to the tactical coordinator's station.

Tactical confirmed. "Target located." He was about to say something else, but he did a double take at his instruments.

The res tech laughed.

Aemilius looked from the res tech to the tactical coordinator. "Something is funny?"

"Yes, *Domni.*" The res tech snickered like a boy. "His location!"

The tactical coordinator blinked at his readouts. Said, "He's *here.*"

12

"HERE?" THE ATTACHÉ ECHOED when the governor surfaced from the underground chambers with an Intelligence agent in tow. "What do you mean *here?*"

"Here," said Aemilius. "On Phoenix."

"But the Xerxes left," the attaché said. "We know he left the atmosphere."

"The fox doubled back," Aemilius said quickly. "Your Xerxes is at the bottom of the Uxine Ocean. I've sent the coordinates to the horizon guard. They will have a skyhook in place presently." A buzz sounded on his ear com. It was the horizon guard. Aemilius took the hail. "Talk to me."

"*Domni.* The target is too small."

An impatient puff passed between the governor's lips. "You won't be able to detect the target," he explained as patiently as he was not feeling. "The target is a Xerxes in full stealth mode. What you are registering as the target is only a collateral object within the target coordinates. Hook everything inside the given coordinates. As soon as you are ready, execute. Do not wait for my command."

"Deploying hook," the horizon guard said. "Hook away. And—"

Aemilius caught himself holding his breath. The attaché shifted his weight from foot to foot, almost jogging in place.

"Target acquired."

Aemilius breathed. He asked, "Is he trying to run?"

"Negative. The load is quiet."

The load had little choice but to sit quiet. Attempting thrust inside an energy hook was suicide.

"I'm beaming you a satellite view, Governor."

Aemilius activated his wall monitor to display the satellite image.

The wall vanished into a wide open sea, blustery gray-green under a half-clouded sky.

The view narrowed to where the energy hook from an orbital station was reeling its catch up from the deep. The cable of energy wasn't visible except for a static circle in the ocean waves.

When at last the energy bubble broke surface, its curved top appeared as a smooth dome of dark water, slightly shimmering. Ocean water slipped off the outer shell of the nearly frictionless energy bubble as it rose.

Suspended above the waves, tons of water churned inside the transparent energy globe.

Murky with algae, plankton, small fish, and particulates, the water appeared to swirl without the encumbrance of the Xerxes within.

Aemilius had to marvel. "Perfect stealth." He couldn't make out any sign of the captive spaceship at all. "Perfect."

The Intelligence agent snarled, "That's not stealth. That's an empty hook! There's nothing in there except a great lot of sea water and that junk at the bottom."

A cluster of objects sat at the bottom of the energy bubble. The objects were disturbingly orderly. Organized like a misplaced office.

"You're sure?" the governor said.

Was there a human being alive who hadn't snatched an annoying insect out of the air only to set it free because he didn't feel it in his hand?

"He's sure," the Italian attaché said, sounding vastly more relieved than he ought.

"We *missed?*" Aemilius said.

"No, no, no," said the attaché. "Please, please, please don't drop the junk. That's the important part. *Domni*, my nation owes you." He fluttered his hand toward the visible objects caught in the bottom of the energy globe. "*That* is the ambassador's system."

* * *

Bagheera's control room stood vacant in the moody brooding half-light of ship's night. The Xerxes bulleted through the interstellar void.

Leo had adjusted some of the ship's environmental controls. The ambassador's original settings had given the Xerxes the feeling of a planet-bound office building. Leo blew those settings away. Gave the ship a sense of motion, like a bullet train rumbling on rails, fast. Long journeys were easier to take if you felt like you were getting somewhere.

Nox paced, wide awake in the gloom.

The consul's blood was gone from the deck, from the consoles, from the air lock. Leo had activated the ship's clean-up routine and made that mess go away.

Nox told himself it was a backhanded mercy, killing the consul. This way Camiciarossa would never know what it was like to live with a screw up this big.

Nox had thought killing would be easier. He'd done it often enough in simulators. Except for garrotes. He'd flunked garrotes. He couldn't get anything around anyone's neck without telegraphing his intent.

He'd never felt any aftereffects from simulated killings during training.

He lay down in his cabin. Got up. Sat in the control room. Brooded in the dim glow of the instrument lights.

Twitched. Got up. Prowled the ship.

Ghosted into an empty compartment.

The cabin was completely empty. There used to be a full office setup in here. Leo had insisted they tear it out whole, down to the deck grates it stood on, fly it back to Phoenix and sink it in the ocean. Leo had been frantic as a caged rat about it. "That's got to go! It's got to go! It's got to go *back! Now! Now! Now!*"

He said it made the difference between them being shipjackers or being international spies, and did we ever want to sleep again. Ever?

The ambassador's office and everything in it was gone now.

Nox drifted. Ended up back in the control room.

He sat on the deck, his back resting against the bulk, elbows on his knees.

Heard someone else moving about.

Pallas leaned into the control room. Saw him. Crossed to where Nox sat and offered something down to him.

Nox looked.

It was an electronic puzzle game, wherein one manipulated moving shapes.

Nox shook his head, mumbled refusal in the direction of his ankles.

Pallas touched the game to Nox's shoulder, insisting. "It's supposed to head off symptoms of post trauma stress."

"I'm okay."

"You threw up on my boots," said Pallas and forced the device into Nox's hands. "Play the *coiens* game."

* * *

Glenn hesitantly touched the backs of her fingers to the mane of the nearest fox. She met with no shyness. No objection. And she ended up rubbing the fox behind the ears.

The fox closed its eyes in an earthly expression of contentment, then flopped down and rolled completely over on its back.

His back. The fox was male.

Glenn rubbed the fox's chest and belly, struck by the absurdity of this first contact.

The fox's tongue lolled out one side of his mouth.

Glenn decided to call him Brat.

"That is not a very dignified position, my dear," Glenn told Brat. Her words were gibberish to the alien.

Fox mouths couldn't form consonants. Apparently foxes couldn't hear the difference between most consonants either.

The foxes communicated in a whiny humming language, pitched, but mostly without whole notes.

Patrick had perfect pitch. He had already picked up some basic phrases from watching audio-video recordings on the voyage here. Fox grammar was apparently simple. The foxes were a simple species.

They were humming.

"What are they saying?" Glenn asked.

"I'm not getting all of it," Patrick said. "Mostly they're saying 'Funny.'"

"Funny, as in there's something wrong with us?" Glenn asked.

"Funny, ha ha," Patrick said. "They think we're funny."

Over the next days it became apparent that foxes found most everything funny.

They were carnivores. That was sort of obvious. Sometimes they tanned the hides of their prey to use as cloaks or sunshades or windbreaks.

"This is as advanced as their technology gets," Patrick told Glenn, inspecting a handsome pelt. The fur was golden-white, patterned with two rows of black spots. It used to belong to an antelope. The other side was cleanly finished.

"Sandy says their cranial capacity is on par with ours. Which means they should be capable of higher learning. They're just not *doing* it."

"Any idea what's keeping them primitive?" Glenn asked.

Fox whiskers tickled the back of her neck. It was Brat. Pointing out to her that she was slacking.

Glenn resumed petting the fox.

"They're not primitive," Patrick said. "They just *are*. They're not trying to advance."

Brat smiled in the grass, eyes shut, not wanting to be anywhere else.

"They have a vague concept of future. I can't get a word for 'when' out of them. I can't say 'when the sun goes down,' or 'tomorrow,' or 'when the snow comes.' But they must have some idea that it's going to get cold again if they're tanning hides."

"Maybe they just like the hides," said Glenn. "They're pretty."

"Then they're not preparing for the future at all. And the past isn't that hot a topic either. They don't write. They don't recognize pictures or drawings. And maps? Forget it. They don't have words for left or right. Directions are where they point their noses and their eyes. They don't count on their fingers or toes. They don't recognize holding up two fingers as meaning the number two."

He held up two fingers for Brat. Brat just wiggled and shifted to make Glenn move her hand a little to the right.

Patrick took out his omni and played *Twinkle, Twinkle, Little Star*.

At the sound, Brat rolled up on all fours. He pivoted his head left and right, confused, or trying to get the music out of first one ear then the other. Brat slunk in on his belly toward the omni. Sniffed it. Then puffed at it, like spitting without the spit, and trotted away.

"Aw, c'mon. Everyone likes Mozart!" Patrick called after Brat.

Patrick tried out a variety of music on the foxes, from Bach to rock to Celtic to dirty blues to Arcturan etudes.

Despite communicating with tones, it turned out that foxes didn't have a taste for any music, especially chords.

With each song, the foxes made strange gestures at the sounds, holding their heads sideways, their muzzles wrinkled. They hummed short notes and brushed their paws at their ears.

"Don't tell me," Glenn said. "They think it's funny."

"No," Patrick said. "They're calling it 'noise.'"

His playlist came to Farouq's Percussive Symphony No. 3. All ears perked up.

"Ah! We have a hit."

Foxes leaned in, ears cocked forward, interested. Bodies moved to the beat, claw tips tapping.

"They're 'cussers!" Glenn cried.

Merrimack's company and crew were great 'cussers.

Patrick turned up the volume.

The fox whom Glenn called Mama-san stood up on her hind legs to dance. Foxes hooked elbows, and the dance became a line.

The mature male dubbed Conan thumped on a hollow log with his paws and claws. Others stamped their feet, clapped sticks together, and shook shells within cages of their claws, improvising on Farouq's beat.

The female foxes shook their western ends and swished their lush tails at the males.

Glenn, who didn't have a tail, broke off a leafy branch and swished that behind her as she joined the dance. The young foxes Brat, Tanner, Banshee, and Princess rolled on the ground laughing—actual rolling on the literal ground—barking hilarity.

Winded, Glenn quit her place in the line. She tossed her tail aside and dropped to sit on the ground next to her husband. Her cheeks felt flushed. She huffed out a big breath. Said, a bit astonished, "I am having a great time."

Patrick kissed her temple. "Me too."

The 'cuss jam ended as the sun was going down.

A red-orange glow striped the horizon.

Foxes frolicked in the gloaming. Chased each other. Jumped and snapped at bioluminescent moths.

The evening was cool. The first stars came out.

Foxes were not modest but they were not as brazen as dogs either. Glenn and Patrick heard trills of fox loving in the thick brush under the trees.

They got up and walked away to find an unoccupied thicket.

* * *

Senator Catherine Mays came to Base Carolina to see Admiral John Farragut.

She found him on the baseball diamond, fielding for the team's batting practice. She tried to call him out of the diamond to talk to her.

Instead, Admiral Farragut told someone to toss the Senator a glove and made her come out in center field with him.

Senator Mays took off her suit jacket, left it folded on the bench. She pulled the fielder's glove on and walked out onto the grass. She knew to wear flat shoes when visiting her brother.

The players tipped their caps to the Senator.

Catherine took a position beside her brother John in the outfield. She squinted. Admiral Farragut passed her his ball cap. She snugged it on.

John Farragut had the energy of an overgrown boy. There was a true sparkle in his blue eyes, and he was always smiling unless you gave him a reason not to.

Team Carolina had lost its last game. Apparently that was unacceptable and the admiral was making sure it didn't happen again. Any excuse to get onto a ball field.

The crack of the bat sent a grounder sizzling off to right field, scorching all the worms.

"Cat, you're acting like you've come to a funeral." John nudged her. A big, solid man, John Farragut nudged like an ox. "They're not that bad." He was talking about the batters. "That first game against Norfolk was a fluke."

Catherine opened her mouth, but John spoke first.

"Oh, for Jesus. You didn't get a strange visit from His Honor, did you?"

"What? No. I'm looking for sublegal military operations being conducted outside of the knowledge of Congress."

"Not from *my* base, they're not," Admiral Farragut assured her.

"I don't know whose operation it is," said Catherine. "But if the room smells like decomp, it's time to tear up the floorboards."

"What do you think is under the floorboards?"

A high fly ball skied to left field. Landed neatly in the left fielder's glove. John booed the batter.

The batter shouted back from the plate, "Up your nose, sir!"

John pointed at his nose. "Put it here." Farragut hunkered down, expectant, in a mobile stance ready to sprint for a grounder his way. But he hadn't lost his place in the conversation. "You've stopped talking, Catherine."

Catherine blurted the question, "Is John John running black ops for your boys?"

"No, ma'am," said Admiral Farragut.

Crack.

The ball whistled out their way. Got stopped short by the shortstop.

John stood up straight, faced his sister, "And just what in the wide black yonder grew that notion?"

Catherine watched another grounder go foul. She spoke low behind her glove, as if she were being surveilled and someone might be reading her lips. "Someone posing as John John stole an ambassadorial Xerxes from the Italians on Phoenix."

John Farragut absorbed that shock. Said, "*That* is one ballsy pirate."

Crack. The ball soared up.

"I got it," said John, crowding Catherine.

"Back off," Catherine pushed back. She caught the ball and threw it to the shortstop.

John said, "On Phoenix. You're not talking Arizona. Is Phoenix a planet?"

"Phoenix is a Roman colonial world in the Perseid Arm. And don't tell me you didn't just dispatch *Merrimack* to Perseid space. You're out of your theater of operations, John. Are the events related?"

"No, ma'am. You know I am not dispatching a space battleship to the edge of the galaxy to run down a stolen Italian spaceship."

"So why are you sending your battleship to the edge of the galaxy?"

Your battleship. *Merrimack* would forever be John Farragut's.

"Rescuing two of *Mack*'s officers. You want this one?"

Another ball came soaring their way. Catherine backed up to catch it. She flipped it to John, who threw it home.

"Your officers are a little far from deck," said Catherine, suspicious.

"They're on leave with a LEN research expedition. They ran into some trouble. Did you ever meet Hamster?"

Catherine thought for a moment. "Little redhead? Sharp gal. Married to a gwerb."

"That's the one," said John. "Hamster and her man reported alien invaders on a planet in the Outback. I also asked Jose Maria to look in on them. He's closer."

"No half measures with you, are there, John?"

"No, ma'am—and hold on. Replay the audio. Someone posing as *who* stole a Xerxes?" The idea was so bizarre it had taken until now to register in his brain.

"Our kid brother," said Catherine. "John John."

"Someone posed as our brother to steal a ship?"

Repeating it didn't help it make sense. Just made it a farther fetch.

"Yes."

"Is he insane?"

"He got away with the ship."

"Are *you* insane?"

"The hijack hasn't been made public. It *has* been authenticated."

"How can that happen? Didn't anybody check this guy's ID before he got anywhere close to an ambassadorial ship?"

"There are indications that the consulate did run some

checks. Now there are warrants out for John John's arrest. I'm trying to back them off and bring John John home before someone can kill him, but I don't even know where he is."

Farragut's brows went way up. His first impulse was to protest. Catherine saw the protest stick in his throat.

"Your mouth is open," said Catherine. "You know something."

Admiral Farragut said, as if to himself, "I don't."

Catherine pressed. "I couldn't help but notice on the way in—as your guards checked my identity—that your base is on elevated alert status."

"Just one level above green," said the admiral. "It's not just Carolina. It's a Fleet-wide caution. Just means we don't know where Caesar is."

"You *lost* him?"

"I asked Numa to file an itinerary, but he won't do it. Last time we misplaced a Caesar, you remember where he showed up. We're just not happy unless we know what planet he's on. That's all."

"John, that is *so not* all. Fact is, either someone posing as John John stole the Xerxes or John John did it. I need to ask you. Is John John working black ops for the military?"

The admiral stared at her.

A ball came out of the sky. Landed in the grass at their feet with a thud.

Boos and raspberries hailed from the infield.

Admiral Farragut picked up the ball. He called back to the hecklers, "That was the Senator's ball." He threw it to the pitcher.

Admiral Farragut signaled himself out. Tossed his mitt to the man who came trotting out to take his place in center field.

The admiral escorted Senator Mays off the diamond.

Catherine said, "There's an international warrant out for John John's arrest. They could kill him. I need to find him first. But I need to know: is he working for the military, or did someone steal his identity?" She placed her borrowed glove on the bench. Retrieved her suit coat. "Answer the question, John."

John Farragut said slowly, "I'm thinking you should be asking His Honor."

Catherine looked puzzled. "What has Papa got to do with this?"

"He came to see me."

"Oh, Lordy." Catherine looked toward heaven.

The end of days is upon us.

And where in hell was John John?

❋ ❋ ❋

The smuggler ship *Villa Grande* was maintaining a lawful sublight velocity on an exit vector from the Phoenix star system when swamplights fell upon it out of the blackness.

Interpol ship 2186 ordered *Villa Grande* to halt.

The smugglers halted and let their vessel be boarded and inspected.

They had their black market cargo safely cached outside the star system, hidden in the infinite dark.

The Interpol officers smelled something in *Villa Grande*'s empty cargo holds, but the something wasn't here, so the police could not detain them for smelling bad.

The black marketeers were set free. They waved happy good-bye fingers after the Interpol ship.

The smuggler ship *Villa Grande* went dark again and wandered for a while so as not to give away their destination.

"We have a tail," said the lookout, a man they called Crow.

"Again?" the ship's captain said, annoyed. Spat on the deck. His name was Maurice. "They can't stop us twice."

"It's not police," said Crow.

"What is it?"

"It's a Xerxes."

"Merde muffins," said Maurice. Didn't believe it.

"It's a Xerxes, and it's flying a Jolly Roger," Crow said.

"No, it is not," said Maurice, stalking to the console to check Crow's readouts.

The other five smugglers crowded behind him. Last thing you wanted on an outlaw ship was a lookout who was missing his calls.

But the other ship truly was registering on the instruments as a Xerxes.

"What's he doing?" Gaston said.

"Looks like he wants to come alongside," said Crow.

"Let him," said Maurice.

Crow slowed the forward velocity of the *Villa Grande* to let the stranger move up on their port side.

When the instruments said the Xerxes was directly parallel, Maurice activated full portside swamplights.

"Ho!" Gaston jerked back from the viewport.

"*Hell* of a disguise," said Etienne.

The ship really did look like a Xerxes. Its Jolly Roger stood up stiff in the vacuum.

"Why is it showing a pirate flag?" said Crow.

"Because it's *stolen*," said Etienne.

"And they're *advertising?*" said Crow.

"Amateurs," Gaston said, and the others sniggered.

Philippe let his head wag, mystified. This was unbelievable luck. Unbelievable stupidity. "Why are they coming to us?"

"They must need help moving their merchandise," said Maurice. "There's always a problem with a heist that big. Where do you go with it?"

"Where would *we* go with it?" said Philippe.

"*We* didn't steal it," said Maurice. "*We* can collect the reward for returning it. Probably get something extra for snagging the lot on board too. I hope they're wanted dead. I'm not even trying to do this alive."

"And they think there's honor among thieves?" Philippe said. The others cackled like cartoon villains.

This was just plain unbelievable.

"Any warrants posted on the open channels?" Maurice asked.

"No," said Crow. "But the Xerxes is winking at us."

A light blinked on the starboard side of the Xerxes. Not flashing a code any of them knew. But the outer hatch to the air lock on the starboard side was open, as if inviting them to dock.

"What do you want to do, Cap'n?" Crow asked.

Maurice's whole face crinkled up, merrily grinning. "Dock."

"I don't like it."

"Change your diaper, Philippe."

"Let me out," said Philippe.

Etienne already had the weapons locker open. He tossed personal fields and sidearms to his mates. He motioned to throw gear to Philippe, but Philippe made no move to catch.

"No. I am serious," said Philippe. "I am leaving. Give me a moment to launch my skiff. You can keep my cut. Let me be—gah!" Philippe cried, holding his bleeding forearm. "What was that for?"

Maurice closed his butterfly knife. "That is your cut."

"Maniac!"

"You do not want in?" said Maurice. "You are out."

Maurice menacingly opened the hatch to the nearest air lock.

Philippe looked annoyed, pained. "Don't play stupid games."

Maurice seized Philippe, collar and waistband, and heaved him bodily into the air lock. Slammed the hatch and locked it.

Gaston turned uneasily to Maurice. "You are *not*—?"

Shooting Philippe out the air lock, Gaston meant to ask. Couldn't say it.

"I want him where he can't get in the way," said Maurice. "He may run away to mama *after* we have the bounty in our own vault."

"Well, that's all right then," said Gaston.

Crow maneuvered *Villa Grande* up against the Xerxes to achieve hard dock with the open lock. Crow remotely opened *Villa Grande*'s outer hatch and pressurized the joined air locks between the ships.

Maurice, Gaston, Etienne, Crow, and Raul armed themselves with everything in their arsenal that wouldn't pierce a ship's hull or engine compartment.

At Maurice's nod, Gaston opened the hatch on their side of the dock. He did not step through.

The short span across two air locks to the Xerxes' inner hatch was looking like a kill jar.

From the far side, no one was opening the Xerxes' inner hatch to welcome them aboard.

"She's all come hither, no put out," said Maurice.

"Are we going in?" Gaston asked.

"You are," said Maurice.

"I'm not going in there," said Gaston.

"Then you can have a piece of Philippe's cut," said Maurice.

Gaston snarled. He grimaced and stepped into *Villa Grande*'s air lock. He paused at the join, then stepped through the double hatchways into the Xerxes' air lock.

A soft feminine machine voice spoke an intruder warning. Commanded Gaston to exit within five seconds.

"What do I do?"

"Give her six seconds," said Maurice.

Beam fire flashed off Gaston's personal field. He fell to the deck kicking, howling.

It took Gaston a moment to realize that he wasn't damaged.

Gaston lay back, laughing himself to tears. "There it is!" he cried. The booby trap they'd been so afraid of. "It's a dud!"

Maurice chuckled. He offered a hand down to Gaston and hauled him up into a bear hug. "Good man."

Gaston growled unkind words.

The voice from the air lock repeated its warning for Maurice before it fired its impotent beams at his protective personal field.

Maurice tapped the inner hatch of the Xerxes with his forefinger, scolding. "Ah, you always say no, but you never mean it, do you." He gave the lever a tug.

He'd expected to find the inner hatch locked, but the lever turned. The seal relaxed.

Maurice pulled his gas mask down over his face. He looked back to his mates. Nodded at them to do the same.

He nudged the hatch open a grenade's width. He tossed in a gas canister and a stinger and yanked the hatch back shut. Wrenched the lever to lock it.

And waited.

No sounds of scrambling or pain carried from the opposite side. Just the hissing of the gas canister and the clatter of splinters peppering the chamber.

As the smugglers waited for the gas to degrade, they drew lots to see who took point next.

Crow got the short end.

Crow eased the Xerxes' inner hatch open a sliver.

"Hello?" Crow called into the complete darkness.

Heard nothing.

"*Hello?*" said Maurice behind him. "I give them a smoker and a stinger and you say hello?"

"Well," said Crow. A knee in his back sent him stumbling forward through the hatchway.

Maurice followed Crow aboard. He turned on his head-lamp. Saw no one else. No bodies. He called up to the ship, "Hey bitch! Some lights?"

The Xerxes did not recognize the command.

Headlamps would have to do.

Maurice was not sure what kind of chamber this was, but *that* was a definitely a Persian carpet underfoot. There were flash burns on it. Yellow threads glinted bright under their lamplight.

"Is that gold?" Crow asked, still on hands and knees.

"Get it appraised later," said Maurice. "Pay attention. Don't get flanked. And don't tell Philippe, but there is a bit of wrong here."

They moved deeper into the ship, trying to find the con-trol room. Maurice kept telling them to spread out, but they kept drawing back into a clutch.

Something sounded behind them. They looked around, headlamps moving like searchlights.

"Etienne?"

"I'm right here," said Etienne.

"Raul?"

"I'm here."

"Who is watching the hatch?"

Maurice was aware of sounds—the faintest rustling. He'd thought it was his own crew, but the sounds were on all sides.

"Shoot! Shoot! Shoot!"

"Where!"

"*Shoot!*"

They fired all directions. Needn't worry about hitting each other. Knew their personal fields would protect them from all short beams and splinters. They were bulletproof.

So were their attackers.

It took a slow blade to get through a personal field. And Maurice reached for his butterfly too late.

13

"**Y**OU WERE NOISY, NOX," Orissus said.

Nox had stabbed his man up through the diaphragm into the heart. His victim had got off a scream and some nauseating gurgles. The brothers had done quieter jobs on their victims, but just as bloody.

Immediately after slaying the smugglers, Nox, Pallas, Nicanor, and Orissus boarded the smugglers' ship *Villa Grande*. They searched all the compartments and holds for anyone left behind. There was a personal skiff stowed in internal dock, but no one in it.

They pronounced the ship clear.

Still vibrating from the slaughter, his victim's blood growing cold and sticky on his hands, Nox was not sure if Orissus was really that callous or if he was trying to show an attitude. *You were noisy.*

All the brothers had simulated hand-to-hand combat training. Real killing and actual dead bodies here unsettled most of them. They concentrated on their assigned tasks.

Leo secured the *Villa Grande*'s control room. Faunus was watching the air lock that joined the ships.

Orissus, Pallas, Nox, and Nicanor collected the smugglers' bodies from *Bagheera*'s deck to carry back to the *Villa Grande*.

"They really messed over the *Bagh*," said Orissus, passing through the antechamber. Flash burns scorched the Xerxes entryway. Shrapnel dents pocked the walls, the deck, the overhead. The smell of gas residue clung to the Persian carpet. "They didn't have to do this."

"Actually, well, they did," Nox said. "We made them dead."

"Then why did we let them board?" said Orissus. "Why didn't we just board them?"

"No surprises on our home field," said Nicanor. "We controlled the situation."

Nox added, "'Very few mongooses, however wise and old they may be, care to follow a cobra into its hole.'"

They came to the joined air locks where *Bagheera* docked to *Villa Grande*.

Faunus, guarding the hatch, asked for a password. Orissus and Nox gave him lots of words.

Orissus, Nox, Pallas, and Nicanor carried the dead smugglers through the air locks and dropped them on their own deck.

Nox saw Pallas move apart, looking fragile. Nox suggested, "Why don't you go back and order *Bagheera* to get himself cleaned off?"

Pallas' abdomen moved. He swallowed hard. "Aye," he said thickly, and returned to the Xerxes. Gave Faunus the impudent digit in passing.

Nox wiped his sticky hands on *Villa Grande*'s walls. The smuggler ship was grimy. "Stinks in here."

Then the thumping started. Muffled shouts.

Orissus, Nicanor, and Nox froze in place.

Nox felt a prickling chill. "I thought we were clear."

They listened.

Faunus called through the air lock. "Is that you?"

"No!" Nox called back. "Hold your position."

"Someone's still in here," said Nicanor. The noise carried through the *Villa Grande*'s decks and bulks. They felt it. Heard it. The definite sound of hammering fists and stomping feet—one set—of someone trying to get out of a confined space.

"Air locks!" Orissus thundered.

"We cleared them," said Nox.

"Not all of them," said Orissus charging forward toward the noise.

Leo reported over the com from *Villa Grande*'s control

room, "We have an unident in the forward starboard side air lock!"

Nox, Orissus, Nicanor, Leo, and Galeo gathered at the thumping hatch. Someone shouted on the other side.

Most ships were equipped with visual air lock monitors, so crew could see what was inside the lock before opening the hatch.

The monitor showed a screaming, thrashing man inside the starboard air lock. He had no visible weapons in there with him. He seemed dizzy, wanting air.

"The smugglers forgot to put out their trash," said Orissus.

Leo said, "The enemy of my enemy is—" he paused, leaving a blank to be filled in. "My what?"

"Not my friend," said Nicanor. "I would space him."

"No," said Nox.

"We're not going to keep him," said Nicanor. "And we're not letting him go."

"No," Nox agreed.

"What do we do with him?"

"Is this thing recording?" Nox tapped at the air lock monitor.

"Could be," said Orissus. He clicked it on. "It's recording now."

Nox opened the hatch wide enough to toss in a miniature daisycutter, slammed the hatch shut, and locked it. Turned away from the monitor and tried not to listen.

Heard a wet sound like a heavy gust of hard sleet slapping against the hatch.

"*Shit!*" said Orissus, eyes round.

"*Deus!*" said Nicanor.

Leo made a noise of disgust.

When Nox opened his eyes, there was more space between him and his brothers than normal. They were afraid of him.

Nox removed the recording slip from the monitor. Held it in his fist. His voice came out low and vibrating. "This is not a home movie. It is a warning to anyone who thinks to collect us."

His brothers drifted back in. A hand landed on his shoulder. It felt like approval. Orissus said, "Let me do the next one."

Nox nodded. "I only have one of those in me, O Best Beloved."

Nicanor briskly moved past the grisly horror. He shouted like a commanding officer, "All right, men. Are we quite sure *now* that we have secured all the hostiles!"

The brothers conducted a swift but thorough second search. Nicanor had the right idea. Stay in motion.

Pretend we're not horrified.

With the *Villa Grande* secured—for certain this time—the brothers scavenged the ship for anything useful.

"They have personal fields," said Galeo.

"Ours are better," said Leo.

The brothers were wearing PFs from *Bagheera's* stores. The Xerxes' defensive equipment was best of the moment.

The smugglers' personal fields had only held against *Bagheera's* energy barrier because Leo had dialed the power way down in order to make the smugglers feel invincible and grow careless.

"They have food!" said Orissus.

"Huzzah. Need that."

The Xerxes hadn't been stocked for an interstellar journey when Nox jacked it. They needed food stores if they were ever to get away from the Phoenix star system.

"We have booze!" Faunus sang.

"Great," said Galeo, sounding sour. "I got nothing. Cargo hold is empty. They must have ditched their load before Interpol flagged them down."

"No," Nox said. "They *parked* their cargo somewhere."

"All the same. How are we supposed to find it?"

Space was a vast place in which to hide things. You could hide mountain ranges in that haystack.

"Interpol's not allowed to search a ship like we can."

Leo took a data drill to the *Villa Grande's* computer banks. He reported in short order, "I have their drop coordinates."

Eager to get out of the smuggler ship, the brothers stacked the food and alcohol stores on lifts and hovered them back to their Xerxes. Nox told Faunus what to do with his password at the air lock.

As the brothers crossed into *Bagheera's* antechamber, they paused there, amazed.

The chamber stood pristine and gleaming, its walls smooth, the air cool and sweet, the Persian rug's vivid scarlets, golds, and ambers unsullied. Crystal fixtures sparkled.

Pallas had gotten the Xerxes to run its clean-up routine. Orissus called to the air, "*Bagheera!* Good kitty!"

"Command not understood," said the ship.

"That's all right, *Bags*," said Orissus. "You're all right."

While the others stored the food and cleaned the blood off themselves and their clothes, Pallas piloted *Bagheera* toward the site of the smugglers' dropped cargo.

They circled wide of the drop site for a watchful while in full stealth mode.

Finally Pallas arrowed the ship in, snagged the smugglers' container and jumped to FTL.

Safe at speed, they reeled the container into the Xerxes' cargo bay. They scanned for booby traps and let the container come up to temperature before venturing into the hold to rip it open.

"Drugs," said Nicanor, disgusted, opening carton after carton.

"Anything medicinal?" Pallas asked.

"No."

"Space it," said Nicanor. "We may be murderers and thieves, but I am not peddling crap to make money."

"I'm not peddling anything at all," said Nox. "Were they trafficking anything useful? Any weapons in there?"

"No weapons," said Galeo. "Only the ones they were carrying."

"Screw." This was not the haul Nox was hoping for. It was not worth the carnage. He wanted weapons. The small-arms lockers on the Xerxes were empty. What arms the Xerxes used to carry had apparently followed the ambassador and his security guards to the Italian embassy.

"Anything anyone want in here?" Galeo asked, ready to close the container.

"Throw it all out," said Nicanor.

"What about the ship?" Orissus asked.

"Throw it out," said Nicanor.

"Keep it," said Nox. "We can use it."

"For *what?*" asked Nicanor.

"Bait," said Nox.

"Just what do you think you're going to attract with that kind of lure?" said Nicanor.

"Something with better guns."

❋ ❋ ❋

Glenn got up and walked out onto the meadow before dawn.

Patrick had gone somewhere. He returned carrying what looked like two giant green acorns, big as cantaloupes.

He passed one to Glenn. "I heard the guys talking about these back at camp. They're okay to eat. They taste like strange bananas."

"I don't like bananas," said Glenn.

She felt the inside of her giant soft green acorn sloshing.

"And you're going to hate these," said Patrick. "But they're nutritious."

He took hold of the stem of his acorn and pulled the top off. It tore away easily. He lifted his soft shell in a toast. "Cheers."

Glenn opened hers.

Stringy liquid lay in the shell like something coagulating. Banana stench wrinkled her nose.

She held her breath and bolted it down. Swallowed through strings and membranes and liquid that was in turns thick and thin. When she came up for air, she tried to keep a stoic expression. Her eyes watered. She wanted to push her mouth out of her face.

Patrick passed the last piece of beef jerky to her as a chaser. They'd been conserving it for as long as they could.

A curious fox came over, sniffing. The nose worked over the acorns, then sniffed Glenn's lips. The fox hummed.

Patrick translated, "Funny."

She should know that one by now. But Glenn couldn't pick out the right note for "funny" any more than a fox could say "boo."

Glenn looked loathingly at her acorn shell. "Funny, as in this is bad meat?"

"No. Just funny."

The foxes breakfasted on insectoids, unwary birds, and small creatures that lived in the grass.

One fox, the one called Banshee, caught a scent in the

ground and launched into a sudden frenzied digging. Dirt flew like sawdust behind a spinning blade. Whatever it was got snapped up before Glenn could see it. Banshee smacked his mouth open and shut, savoring the aftertaste, and other foxes sniffed the hole for crumbs.

Patrick had figured out why the mammoths shied away from the foxes. "Foxes like to play," he told Glenn. "Mammoths don't. I bet feathers are fun."

"And mammoths don't think so," Glenn guessed.

"I bet not."

Glenn could just picture Brat and Tanner frolicking through curtains of waving mammoth plumage, dodging enormous feet and tusks.

Patrick found a hard spongy green fruit, and tried to teach the foxes the game of fetch.

Foxes only did half of a fetch. They raced each other to apprehend the flying fruit, and the winner destroyed it.

The day turned hot. The fox pack trekked through the forest to a place where the stream broadened and the water fanned out in wide sheets as it dropped over a smooth shale slope.

Foxes jumped, slid, and torpedoed down the waterfall.

Glenn sat on the bank, watching the foxes play. The female sitting next to her stood up and clawed at her own belly. Glenn thought maybe her navel itched. But the tight swirl of fur in her belly wasn't a navel. It turned out to be an opening. The she-fox widened it, reached in with a paw, and pulled out a fuzzy loaf.

A pouch. She had a marsupial pouch. The female passed the fuzzy loaf to her mate.

Glenn couldn't tell if the little loaf was a baby or a box lunch, because *he* tucked it into a pouch of his own while *she* went ottering down the shale slide.

"Patrick! Patrick!" Glenn pointed between the male and female foxes. "What did they just do?"

"Passed the baby," said Patrick. He sat down beside her. "Males have pouches?"

Patrick nodded. "He's got working nipples in there. About a week after conception, the infants—Sandy says there're two of them—they crawl out of Mama's love canal, and these two little peanuts climb up into her pouch and latch onto a nipple." He made a peanut sized space between his thumb and forefinger. "Usually only one of them survives. Mama can hand off to Papa when, well, she wants to go swimming."

"But what makes *him* lactate?"

"Sandy thinks it's the smell of the baby. You can tell a male who's carrying by who's sniffing his navel."

"I've seen that," said Glenn. Then, "Wait. They only passed one baby." Patrick had just told her they conceived in twos. "Did they lose one?"

"They always lose one," said Patrick. "Pretty early on, when the babies are knee high to a dachshund, one infant bullies the other to death in the pouch."

Oh. "How awful and sad," she said, then added, "That's probably a human take on it."

"The parents *care*," Patrick said, equivocal. "A little anyway. They dig a grave for the loser. These guys can haul dirt like a badger on sprox. It's a deep grave. The parents curl up the dead infant and place it gently, but there aren't any grave gifts, no blanket, none of that. In the recordings I've seen, they look sad. They hold their ears down, their tails down, their muzzles down. But just as soon as the grave is covered and the rocks are piled on, they get over it."

"Rocks?" said Glenn. "So the parents do mark the grave?"

"Sandy doesn't think the stones are grave markers. They're more to keep any carrion eaters out. The parents don't show resentment toward the survivor."

"Patrick? Can you call her Dr. Minyas? Unless you're talking about a beach, that name makes my teeth itch." Glenn pulled her splinter gun from behind her back and passed it to Patrick. "Hold the baby," she said and took a turn sliding down the waterfall.

✳ ✳ ✳

Nox heard a barefoot pacing through the ship's night. Not his. It was Pallas this time, haunted by the smuggler ship, which was still docked to the Xerxes, dragging along like a rotting dead limb.

Nox left his sleep compartment and gave Pallas the handheld game. Pallas tried to refuse. "I didn't throw up on your boots," Pallas said.

Nox pushed the device at him. "Either sleep or play the *coiens* game."

The Xerxes sounded a warning, waking everyone. The soft voice of *Bagheera* advised of a plot on their stern.

Their shadow was Interpol ship 2186, closing in, its red flashers going full brightness.

Nox called, "Wake up, my brothers. We go to the fight. Bay! Oh, Bay!"

14

GLENN WOKE UP when the leaves walked over her.

The leaves traveled with their shiny green sides up, their ciliate side down. Hundreds of stubby roots acted as caterpillar legs as the leaves moved in herds, foliage on a quest for a tree—or for sun or shade or water. No matter, Glenn and Patrick were sleeping on their highway.

Glenn sat up. The leaves scurried away.

Patrick foraged for breakfast. He stripped red berries off a thorny bush and offered them to Glenn. "These are okay to eat."

"Are they better than the banana soup?" Glenn asked.

"Dr. Rose makes his wine out of them," Patrick said.

The foxes were awake.

A chubby cub was making its first foray from its mother's pouch. The adults passed around the bowling ball-sized fuzzy bundle and cuddled it in turns.

The baby fox had all the same traits that made warm-blooded infant life on Earth cute—the big heads with over-sized foreheads, the pudgy bodies, the big round eyes—round once the baby got used to the light—the chubby cheeks, the little mouth.

From chicks to puppies to human babies, those same features brought out the protective instincts in terrestrial mammals and birds. That specific concept of cuteness didn't translate to most alien creatures, but the cute factor was in full force here.

"Am I allowed to touch it?" Glenn whispered to Patrick. "I'm not sure."

Glenn moved in closer, waiting to see if anyone would pass the baby to her.

And here it came. Mama-san placed the fuzzy bundle into her cradled arms.

It was a heavy little thing. It gave a big yawn with its tiny mouth.

"Puppy breath!" Glenn said, startled. "Patrick! He has puppy breath!"

She nuzzled him. The kit latched on with its tiny mouth and tried to nurse from the tip of her nose.

* * *

"Police ship secure," Leo announced over his personal com on board the ship Interpol 2186.

"*Villa Grande* secure," Galeo announced from the smuggler ship. "You can open your side of the air lock, Nox. Watch your step. Lots of blood."

Never mind the blood of the new kills of the police officers, the decomposing stench from the smugglers was enough to make Nox want to stop breathing as he passed through the dock from the Xerxes to board *Villa Grande.*

Nox forced a cocky face as he stepped over bodies. It was slick stepping. "What of the hunting, hunter bold?"

"As you see," said Galeo. He spat blood off his lips.

The Interpol officers had been more cautious than the smugglers. But they died just the same.

Nox tapped Galeo on his brawny shoulder with the bottom of his fist. "Let's see what we reaped."

The police ship yielded a wealth of equipment: small arms, riot gear, a corvus, a lot of nonlethal ordnance, some body armor that the police should have been wearing when they boarded *Villa Grande.* The harvest was all the brothers could have hoped for.

"Can we leave now?" Leo asked once all the stolen equipment was on board *Bagheera.*

They were still lurking at the periphery of the Phoenix star system. Even traveling FTL, it was a dangerous place for them to be.

"And can we cut *them* loose?" said Galeo. Them. The

Xerxes now had two grisly dead ships in tow. "Mind you, I'm going to mutiny if you say no, Nox."

"Soon." Nox checked the soles of his shoes. He had cleaned them eight times. "One more thing before we leave. We need to show off our work. We did this. We need people to know we did this. Fear. We need fear."

Upon Nox's instruction, the brothers uncoupled the ships, then propelled *Villa Grande* on a direct vector toward the planet Phoenix.

And waited for Phoenix's planetary warning system to go off.

* * *

Glenn took a seat in the meadow grass and made daisy chains from local flowers. Bright hardy blossoms of yellow and orange grew on flexible stems. She laced in some seed husks that looked like a cross between a seashell and a pistachio half shell, and she decorated the young female whom Glenn called Princess.

Princess was a pretty girl-fox, young, sleek, and shiny. She had big bright black eyes, a dainty muzzle, and sharp white teeth. Glenn wove several necklaces and a crown for her, then French braided more blossoms into the long fur of Princess' tail. Foxes couldn't braid, but they could comb braids out deftly enough when the flowers wilted.

Patrick stood over Glenn and Princess, his expression fond. "You're glowing."

"I am not," said Glenn fighting down a smile. Lost that battle.

She was glowing.

"Do you want a daughter?" Patrick asked.

"No," said Glenn. She tufted up Princess' topknot. "I just want to borrow this one."

Princess got up to show off her new look. She moved at a twinkling gait. How strange that the traits of girly flirtation translated across alien species.

At first the boy foxes acted surprised and laughed at her, as adolescent males will. But soon enough they were puffing out their manes, strutting, and flexing their muscles.

Princess twitched her tail at them, then ran and hid behind her mother and father.

* * *

Dr. Peter Szaszy's team returned from their fourteen-day field trip outside of camp. Absorbed in his data, Szaszy strode into camp without even taking off his environmental suit, his gaze locked on his omni. He almost walked into a white vicar tree.

Dr. Aaron Rose watched him advance on the unsuspecting tree and called, "Good trip, Szasz?"

"Very," Szaszy said. Looked up. Regarded the tree before him with some surprise. Then he waved his omni earnestly in the air. "Where's Ham? I need him to check out these vocalizations."

Dr. Rose coughed, confused. "Ham? You mean Patrick Hamilton?"

"Yes, of course Patrick Hamilton," Szaszy said, nearly a snap, impatient. "Where is he?"

Aaron Rose turned about face and sang out, "Izzy! Oh, Izzy!"

Director Izrael Benet emerged from his tent, annoyed by the summons. "What? Oh." He saw Dr. Szaszy. "Welcome back, Peter. Successful field trip?"

Aaron Rose told Director Benet, "Szasz wants to know where Patrick Hamilton is."

Benet's face fell slack. He stared at Peter Szaszy. Insisted, "He's with you."

Uneasily, on a rising note, almost a question, Szaszy said, "No."

"And Glenn Hull. Glenn Hamilton," Benet said. "She's not with you?"

Szasz shook his head. "No."

"They were supposed to go on trek with you, Peter."

Dr. Szaszy drew his shoulders back, head high. "Well. They didn't show up when we were ready to embark. I don't tolerate disrespect for my time."

"You left without them," Benet translated.

Szaszy answered, defiant, "I certainly did."

Sandy Minyas paled behind her freckles. Breathed into her hands, "Oh, hell, they're lost."

Director Benet demanded of whoever in shouting distance might have the answer, "Where do the Hamiltons' homers say they are!"

Other expedition members were gathering. Sandy Minyas was fastest to check her omni. "Not getting a signal. Are they even carrying? Do we know? Do we know?"

No one knew.

Benet thundered at everyone. "They've been unaccounted for for two bloody weeks! Find them! Find them!" Then he singled out Szaszy. "You. You find them. This is your task."

"What if they're dead?" Sandy Minyas breathed into her hands.

Benet heard that. "What if they're—!" He raked a big hand through his thick mane. "*Merrimack*'s coming here. If they're dead— *Somebody just shoot me if they're dead!*"

"We don't have guns, Izzy," said Dr. Rose.

Benet stalked back to his tent, speaking in tongues.

Junior ecologist Elton Langer asked Dr. Szaszy, "So what impact will it have on the environment if they decompose outside the perimeter?"

✳ ✳ ✳

Phoenix's horizon guard intercepted a runaway ship on collision course with the planet. Several news craft shadowed the chase ship and got some ghoulish images from the *Villa Grande*'s interior. It made for a sensational story.

Following up on that incident, investigative reporters uncovered the fact that *Villa Grande*'s last known contact had been Interpol ship 2186. *Villa Grande* had been boarded by the police.

Thinking they were on the trail of a police atrocity, reporters raced each other to uncover the truth about Interpol 2186, only to discover that 2186 was missing.

Now they had either a police cover-up or another victim of the same unknown horror. Interest in the story expanded.

The League of Earth Nations' bureau on Phoenix sent out a broadcast asking anyone with information on Interpol 2186 to contact them. They posted a special resonant harmonic to receive leads. There was a reward.

"What do you want to do?" Galeo asked Nox. "Tell them 'I did it. I did it?'"

"Basically," said Nox.

"I wouldn't trust the harmonic," said Nicanor. "The

League may not be able to trace a res pulse, but we know Rome can. If Rome decides to help the League with this, and we send a message on that harmonic, they will know where we are."

"They will know for that instant," Nox agreed. "But we *are* slightly mobile."

The Xerxes was fast as death.

"Anyway, Rome won't get involved. They would have to acknowledge that we exist."

Pallas was still wary. "Why is this message coming from the League and not Interpol?"

"Because of the reward," said Nox. "Interpol can't deal."

"I'd be afraid to touch the reward," said Leo.

"I'm not touching it," said Nox. "I just want to make them give it."

The LEN was no doubt receiving a barrage of hoaxes and reward-hungry false leads on their specified harmonic. The brothers needed to send a message that would immediately penetrate the fog.

Nox's message was a one-second long visual image of the Interpol officers' dog tags, along with the printed designation of a different harmonic on which to send a reply.

Soon they had a LEN representative on their given harmonic, quietly pleading, "Whoever you are, don't hurt them. Just give us our people back. In the name of mercy."

Nox returned another one-second visual. A printed message, in English: *That will not be possible. We are not merciful, and your people are dead.*

The LEN representative seemed prepared for that answer. He choked through that news and revised his plea. "We want to ransom the bodies. Those were good people."

The brothers exchanged glances, then shrugs.

Nox demanded double the offered reward. He sent a last visual message, printed: *Load the shipment into a courier missile and launch it on the vector printed below at the precise time printed below. Any improvisation, any failure, any tail, and we will send you pictures of the drawn and quartered bodies of your men so you know how they will be spending eternity when we kick them FTL, where they will never be found.*

Message sent, Leo shut down the res chamber. In case

they had been located, he jumped *Bagheera* to FTL with the 2186 in tow.

"Are we really going to do that?" Pallas asked, uneasy at the thought of drawing and quartering dead bodies.

"Shouldn't come to that," said Nox. In any case, Nox had made the threat. It would fall to him to carry it out. "They already know what we can do."

As the appointed hour approached, Leo monitored the designated vector for any sign of a courier missile. The rest of the brothers gathered round Leo's console in the control room to wait.

Faunus asked Nox if he was ready to start drawing and quartering.

"*You*, maybe," said Nox.

"Thar she blows!" Leo sang, surprised. He turned from his console to face his brothers. "They did it. They launched a courier."

"The LEN kept their side of the deal," said Galeo. Truly had not expected that.

"*As far as we know*," Orissus added significantly. "We don't really know what's in the courier."

"The mass is right for gold," said Leo.

"But it could be lead," said Orissus. "The mass is similar."

"Could be fruitcake for that matter," said Faunus.

"We'll never know what it is," said Nox. "We're not picking up the ransom. Ever. Only question now is do we park the police ship and send the LEN the coordinates to find it, or do we blow it up."

The question felt suddenly weighty. Faunus dodged it. Asked Nox, "You're not going to draw and quarter?"

"No, but you may if you want," said Nox. "O, My Brothers, what are we doing here? Do we give up our dead or not?"

"We vote," said Nicanor.

Orissus argued for no. "We'll look soft."

"We need to decide if we're to be crazed berserkers beyond the pale, or do we want to be a strong enemy who keeps our word," said Nicanor.

"We're *pirates*," said Faunus. "We don't have a word."

Nox left the control room. He came back lugging a very large wheel-made terra cotta jar. "Enough debate."

He set the jar down on the deck. The brothers formed a

ragged circle around it. Some of them guessed what Nox was about.

"It's a yes no question," Nox said. "Your decision and your reasons are your own. Just vote." He passed out lots.

The lots were the ancient kind, smooth black and white stones, which Nox had taken from the bottom of a glass flower vase in the ambassador's bedchamber.

"A yes vote means we give up the dead. A no vote, we do something else with them. Drop a white stone into the jar for yes, a black stone for no. I gave you each a bunch of stones, so no one will know your vote by what color stones you have left behind."

Nox went first. He lowered his fist into the neck of the jar. Let drop the first stone. It clinked against the ceramic base. He moved back and sat cross-legged on the deck.

Nicanor moved forward next, dropped his stone. Fell back into the circle.

Then Faunus.

Leo.

Pallas.

Galeo.

Orissus.

A strange silence followed, everyone just watching the jar that held their answer.

"That's all of us," said Leo, waiting for someone else to move.

Nicanor stepped in. He hefted up the jar and spilled out the stones.

* * *

Winged creatures rose from the trees with sharp cries.

Monkey squirrels jumped branch to branch in screeching retreat. Glenn heard their chittering calls receding deeper and deeper into the forest.

Spiderwings Glenn hadn't even known were there fluttered aloft and wheeled away in a swarm. Something startling was coming this way.

In the meadow, foxes were dancing with Patrick. The foxes didn't mind the alarms. Foxes existed at the top of the food chain, too big for most predators, too smart for the others.

Glenn and some young foxes—Princess, Banshee, and Cosmo—ventured toward the calls to check out what set off the treefolk.

The foxes' noses were going like bloodhounds but seemed to be detecting nothing at all. They were confounded by that.

At the first sight of strange whiteness in the dense greenery the foxes hunkered down among clumps of ferns.

Glenn stood up. Her shoulders bowed. The foxes observed her lack of fear, and they relaxed too. They stood up with her, sniffing, still smelling nothing.

The white strangenesses were LEN scientists, kitted in full body condoms. They looked wrong and alien in their exo-suits. They'd come equipped with rebreathers and all. No wonder the foxes were confused. Foxes lived by their noses. They could see the xenos, hear them, but otherwise the xenos might not even be here.

Two white figures advanced. They seized Glenn by her upper arms.

Princess dropped into a bent-leg starting position, seeming unsure if this were a game. The boy foxes snarled from all fours.

Glenn shook off her captors' hands, indignant. "I *beg* your pardon." She knew Dr. Maarstan and Dr. Szaszy from the *Spring Beauty*.

The xenos let go. Probably because they had upset the foxes, not because Glenn told them to.

Princess, Banshee, and Cosmo hummed, quizzical, their heads tilting the way they did when very confused.

A tall figure moved forward, forceful. Director Izrael Benet. Boomed like a truant officer to a child, "What do you think you're—" His eyes strayed up toward the meadow. He caught sight of Patrick between the trees. Izrael Benet exploded. "*What is he doing!*"

Glenn turned to see what Patrick was doing. "He's, um." No way out of this. "Teaching the foxes to fox trot."

The older female, Mama-san, stood with one forepaw on Patrick's shoulder, the other forepaw in Patrick's hand as Patrick tried to get her to execute a four-count box step.

"*That is outrageous!*"

"I know," said Glenn. "They don't really care for it. They like the polka much better, but Patrick just couldn't resist."

Director Benet bellowed to the white-suited xenos behind him, "Get her out of here." And he stalked out onto the meadow waving and roaring at Patrick: "Get away from the natives!"

Glenn watched Benet corral her husband.

Good thing he hadn't seen the bunny hop lesson.

As the xenos marched Glenn and Patrick away, Princess and Cosmo cavorted alongside for a while, getting some clue that this was not friendly. They held their tails straight up and bristling.

Banshee brought a rubbery green fruit in his mouth like a dog, offering it hopefully first to Glenn then to Patrick. Thought if he played by the rules, they wouldn't leave him.

Patrick hummed something.

The three foxes sat down and watched them go.

Glenn looked back over her shoulder to see bewildered faces and doleful eyes, Banshee with the ball still in his mouth.

* * *

Stones clattered onto the pirate ship deck.

Two black pebbles stood out. The rest were white.

"The vote is yes," said Nicanor. "Return the dead."

The result brought relieved sighs from most of them and an alarmed, "Wait!"

The brothers looked to Nox, who had shouted.

"There are too many stones here!" Nox sounded almost panicked. His palm shook as it moved across the stones to separate them. Eight. There were eight stones and seven brothers.

Nicanor said, "Who voted twice?"

Eyes met eyes around the circle.

Galeo lifted his forefinger, a confession. "I voted both ways. It's kind of an abstention."

"Damn, Galeo! You scared me," said Nox, breathing too hard.

"What?" Galeo shrugged. "I just cancelled myself out."

"*I thought Cinna was here!*"

"Are you hearing telltale hearts, Nox?" Orissus said.

Nox held his hand over his own hammering heart. "Sometimes."

Pallas said, "Before we give the LEN these coordinates, we should leave a mark on our kill."

"You want to sign our work?" said Faunus.

"Aye."

"Sign it how? Who are we?"

Pallas boarded the police ship 2186 and blotted blood in a pattern of spots on the deck.

Faunus looked over Pallas' shoulder as he daubed the spots. "What's that supposed to be?"

"Leopard spots."

"Looks more like jaguar," said Leo, who knew something about cats.

Pallas paused, his brow knotted up hard. "*What?*"

"Jaguars have the dot in the middle. Leopard spots shouldn't have a dot in the middle," Leo said.

"I dripped!" said Pallas.

"Take it out," said Leo.

"Well here, you do it, Michelangelo," said Pallas who was feeling nauseated anyway. It hadn't been easy extracting enough blood from the dead to paint with, and the stuff was not easy to work with. He started to think drawing and quartering would have been easier. Pallas pushed the bloody brush at Leo, glad to be rid of it.

Leo took over spotting the deck. The others watched. Leo daubed tight circles of five or six blots— with no dot in the middle—until the deck took on a distinctly leopardish look.

The deck had been a buff color. The blood was turning dark.

Faunus stood back. Puzzled. Vexed. He'd missed something. First Nox named the damned ship *Bagheera*, and now they'd broken out in spots. Faunus didn't want to ask the question in case the answer was obvious, but he had to know, "How did our mascot get to be a leopard?"

"It's not a mascot," said Nicanor. "It's more like an avatar."

Nox said, "The leopard guards the lowest rings of the Inferno."

They returned to their Xerxes and sent a message to the LEN: "You may approach these coordinates to collect the remains. Do not mistake this for mercy. We have none."

And they let themselves be seen. For the briefest instant they took down the Xerxes' stealth system, and flashed an image bright and deadly:

Their colors on the hull, yellow with black spots for the leopard who guarded their domain.

Their flag, the Jolly Roger.

Their standard, a bastardized travesty of a Roman standard. Not an eagle. Theirs was a blood red metal circle with the Roman numeral IX set inside it.

Their motto underneath it was written in blood, *Lasciate ogne speranza*. Abandon all hope.

So all would know who they were.

The Ninth Circle of Hell.

PART TWO

Patterns of Chaos

15

"**Y**OU JUST *NEED* TO INTERFERE, don't you?" Director Benet spoke over Glenn's head. "It's a compulsion with your kind, isn't it?"

They weren't questions, so Glenn didn't answer. She wasn't feeling well.

Benet turned on Patrick with less rancor, more disappointment. "You were not supposed to talk to the aliens."

"Then why did you bring a xenolinguist to study the language?" Glenn said. She sneezed.

Patrick murmured aside to her, "I'm supposed to spy on them."

"The term is 'observe,'" Benet said tightly.

Glenn's stomach cramped. She retched. She hadn't eaten for a while so nothing came up.

"Perfect. Just perfect," Benet said. "You brought that on yourself."

Patrick hummed something at Director Benet. A fox word. It didn't sound kindly.

Glenn shut her eyes. Dizzy. She felt Patrick's arm wrap around her back, his other arm slip behind her knees. And she was rising.

A couple weeks among the foxes, hiking, dancing, playing ball, had made Patrick stronger than he'd ever been on board *Merrimack*. Patrick carried her to the physician's hut.

The camp physician, Dr. Cecil, was surprised to have a patient. He usually only monitored his colleagues' blood pressure and bone density and treated the odd broken toe or insectoid sting and sunburn.

Patrick asked the physician, "How can this happen? How could Glenn catch a bug on an alien planet?"

"She can't," said Dr. Cecil. He tucked an intradermal blood analyzer into the crook of Glenn's elbow and made her hold it there. "Alien microbes can't infect us. If she ingested a microbe, the microbe itself is nothing. But these symptoms may be from a toxin produced by a microbe."

Cecil retrieved the analyzer from Glenn's arm. Reported, "It's not a toxin."

"I don't care what it is," said Glenn, curled up on the table. "Can you treat it? I'm inside-out here."

Cecil's face appeared tight, his mouth a straight line. His eyes flickered between her and Patrick, as if reluctant to speak in front of her. Finally he directed his answer to Patrick, "I can't treat hypochondria."

Patrick sounded pissed. "My wife is the farthest thing from a hypochondriac you will ever meet."

Dr. Cecil looked down on Glenn, "Obviously you ate something your body can't process. You shall just need to wait it out."

"This is nothing we ate," said Patrick. "She caught something."

"Caught?" said Cecil, his thin brows up, one corner of his mouth higher than the other.

"A virus," said Patrick. "You know. A germ."

Cecil moved his head side to side in a giant no. "Can't. Can't happen."

"Did!" said Patrick. "She's calling Yul."

"She is drunk."

"No, she is not," Glenn croaked.

"Histamine reaction." The suggestion sounded from the adjoining room. Cecil's colleague, Dr. Wynans appeared in the doorway.

"Smell her breath," Patrick told Wynans.

Just to humor him, Dr. Cecil leaned in for a sniff. His head jerked back. He had to admit, "It almost smells bacterial."

Dr. Wynans did not risk a whiff for himself. He told

Glenn, "It's most likely an overgrowth of your natural bodily flora."

Dr. Cecil had a clinical argument against that idea. He and Wynans withdrew from the examination room, debating the matter.

Glenn thought they were going to do research or consult with someone else.

They went to lunch.

Glenn was waiting outside the dining hut with a data bubble when Doctors Cecil and Wynans came out, their teeth slightly darkened from blueberry cobbler.

"Here." Glenn slapped the data bubble into Dr. Cecil's hand. She coughed into the crook of her arm, though she really wanted to spew in his face. "I did my own analysis."

Cecil looked puzzled at the thing in his palm. He held his hand out quite far for someone so certain that Glenn was not contagious. "How exactly did you 'run your own analysis?'"

"I hawked on a specimen slip and asked the medical diagnostic analyzer to screen for microbes. How else do you run an analysis?"

Dr. Cecil let the data bubble drop to the ground. "When you let a monkey crank the controls of a sensitive sophisticated piece of equipment, this is what you get. SISO. You put alien genetics in there, you are going to get skat."

Patrick stooped, retrieved the data bubble. He activated it and expanded the report in the air before them. "This looks awfully coherent for skat. It says she has a bacterium of unknown taxonomy," Patrick said. He looked pale.

Dr. Cecil chose not to look at the enlarged report hanging in the air. "The analyzer doesn't know what it's saying. When a computer program doesn't find a referent, it will grab the last coherent thing it had in its machine brain and give you that. Errors fall down."

His colleague, Dr. Wynans, examined the results with more interest. He had to take hold of Patrick's wrist to make him hold the bubble still so he could read the image quivering in the air. "No, Cecil. This is weird."

"It is alien," said Dr. Cecil. "Naturally it is 'weird.'"

"The report says 'unknown taxonomy,' not just 'unknown,'" said Wynans. "This implies a terrestrial organism."

"There you are," said Cecil. "She didn't pick it up here."

Glenn had dropped into a crouch. Her voice was hoarse. "I don't care where it came from! What's the treatment?"

Dr. Wynans beckoned her to the medical hut. Patrick helped her walk. His hands felt clammy.

Wynans logged the new bacterium into the data bank and told Dr. Cecil that he was taking naming rights. "Unless you insist it's yours, Cecil?"

"No. Go ahead," said Dr. Cecil. "Please. It probably has a Roman name already. After all, Rome created it."

Wynans stepped back from his console, surprised, concerned. "You don't really think so?" said Wynans. "Germ warfare is against international convention."

"When has convention ever stopped Rome?" said Cecil. "Romans love to tinker with what should be left alone. Remember, Rome created patterners."

A patterner was a monstrous creation of Frankensteinian proportion. A patterner was a human/machine interface endowed with an inhuman ability to synthesize vast amounts of data of disparate types. The ability came at a cost. Great cost to the individual patterner. A great cost to the many failures it took to create one that survived and functioned.

"Even Rome stopped making patterners," said Wynans.

"Only because patterners were loose cannons," said Cecil. "Not because the process was unethical, unconscionable, and downright macabre."

Wynans dismissed the suggestion that Glenn's sickness was a Roman invention. "More likely this microbe is actually an innocuous terrestrial bacterium that has mutated under the alien sun. The Cordillera protocol can devise a treatment in no time."

"That's good," said Patrick, just before he heaved up a bacterial colony onto Dr. Cecil's workstation.

✳✳✳

The brothers had left the Phoenix system far behind them. *Bagheera* sped toward another star system, a Chinese colonial world, to strike terror again.

For now they relaxed on a virtual beach. *Bagheera*'s antechamber had transformed itself into a deserted seashore at sunset. The ship's walls had vanished into a wide horizon. A yellow sun sank into the sea, leaving velvet blue darkness behind it. The brothers felt as much as heard the sound of open sky and open water. Gently lapping waves ridged the sand. A slight breeze carried the smell of salt air and exotic flowers. Palm trees nodded behind them.

"Where is this?" Galeo asked.

"Don't know," said Leo. "The program is called Sunset Beach."

"It's some fantasy place," said Orissus.

"It's Earth," said Nox.

Nox was from Earth. He should know.

"You've been to this beach?" Pallas asked.

"No."

"Then how can you tell it's Earth?" said Orissus.

"Moon," said Nox with a backward nod. A luminous orb was rising huge and full behind the palm trees.

Galeo twisted round to stare. "Look at that!"

"That's too big to be a real moon," said Orissus.

"No, Best Beloved. That is *the* Moon," said Nox.

Natural evolution of a star system normally resulted in planets forming with several small satellites circling them. Phoenix was typical. The planet Phoenix had a whole necklace of moons in its orbit. All the other planets in the Phoenix star system had multiple small moons around them.

Earth's moon was exceptional, even within its own solar system.

"That is Luna herself," said Nox of the giant shining disk rising behind the palm trees. "That's why in the Old Empire the Moon was a goddess, and she was singular."

Romans never forgot where they came from.

The capital of the Roman Empire was currently the planet Palatine. But Rome's real home, her birth world, was Earth. Her true name was Terra, the place where the she-wolf suckled her sons, Romulus and Remus.

The Empire failed to recapture Old Rome in the recent war.

The brothers had been cloned, cultivated, raised, recruited, and trained on the colonial world Phoenix, a long, long way from Palatine. They hadn't fought in the war.

Except for Nox, they had never seen Earth.

This was their first voyage outside the Phoenix system.

They were never going back.

"Has anyone else ever been killed at Widow's Edge?" Nox asked.

"No," said Pallas. "Couldn't happen."

"Couldn't?" said Nicanor. "It rather *did*."

"Because it should have been impossible," said Pallas. "The net *always* deploys. There's a motion sensor in the cliff face."

"I didn't know that when I jumped," said Nicanor.

"I knew there was a net," said Faunus. "I would have been a lot more scared if I'd known it was Russian roulette."

"I wouldn't have let you jump if I'd known it was Russian roulette," said Nicanor. He shuddered. "I never heard of anyone dying before."

"Why did the net fail for Cinna?" Leo wondered aloud.

Pallas guessed, "Jammed. Broke. We should have checked the equipment before we sent Cinna over."

"Don't ever say 'should have,' O Best Beloved," said Nox. "Never look backward. That river you see in the rearview? That's the Rubicon."

"Did you know there was a net, Nox?" Pallas asked. Then rephrased, "Did you know there was *supposed* to be a net when you jumped?"

Nox had to think. He shut out the sounds and images of gentle surf and beautiful moon.

He was back on that dry desert height. His brothers standing behind him, waiting. Ahead of him, that fatal-appearing drop.

"Not yes," Nox answered. *Not exactly no either.* "I was trying not to think anything. I had a feeling *something* was going to happen in between my leaving the cliff and the ground smacking my bones out."

He had been cocooned in that blessed inability of young men to conceive of a universe without themselves in it.

Nox opened his eyes to the lovely sunset. The soft sea air

from the Xerxes imager brushed his skin. The palms were casting moon shadows across the sand.

Only close his eyes and he was back on the cliff, facing that jump. He must have thought he was going to live. "But I didn't *know*."

* * *

Awareness.

His last memory had been of pain. Eyelids were stuck open, unable to blink. Harsh sun. Breath stabbing in crushed lungs. Wetness. Head felt . . . mushy.

Shooting pain of being lifted, jarring motion.

Pain ceased. Still feeling, but without pain. Grotesque sensations of dripping, crumbling. Like being a bag of sticks. Pulpy.

Woke after a moment; he didn't remember losing consciousness. Felt different.

Felt.

Different.

Opened his eyes, puzzled. The sky with its pearly moons was gone, the cliff was gone. He was indoors, the air was cool, and he could move. He had no sense at all of time having passed, yet he was not where he had been.

He sat up with an amazing feeling of well-being. Strange things moved in his body. He felt absolutely clearheaded, yet he could not remember how he got here. He did remember jumping. The fall. The landing. His hipbones had hit him in the chin.

Now there were cables protruding from his forearms, and he had no idea how they got there. Must be what he was feeling behind his neck too.

An officer was standing in the room along with several medici.

The officer told him curtly, "The medicus ruled it a suicide attempt."

So that was all real. The jump. The landing. "Not my intent, *Domni*."

"Did you think you could fly?"

"No, *Domni*."

"Then explain how you mistook air for solid ground?"

"I can't, *Domni*." Rather, he wouldn't inform on his brothers.

"Anyone with you?"

"No, *Domni*." That was a lie. The officer probably knew that. He had to say it anyway.

"Protecting anyone?"

"No, *Domni*."

"Actually, your last statement is true enough," said the officer. "The ones you would protect don't exist anymore. They are no one."

His brothers. Where were they?

His animal brain still refused to believe what his senses were telling him. His mind concocted a most desperate attempt at denial.

This is still part of the hazing. My brothers didn't drop me. This is an intricate charade to trick me into thinking they dropped me.

He clung to that thought. But even before the medici plugged in his cables, a knowing chill gripped his gut.

This is too elaborate by far.

These men were real and serious.

The cables connected. His eyes flew wide.

Horizons vanished into infinity. He knew things. Millions of links fit together, effects met with causes, randomness resolved into inevitability, chaos became order.

Against all logic, he knew what he'd become. *They don't make these anymore.*

These men, his makers, were masking fear. His mind reached through vast data stores, through endless minutiae, found the place in the documentation where one of them had made the notation: *If he's going to kill you, it will be now.*

He knew the officer had a sidearm. Its serial number was 435-X942AXZ.

The medici looked wary.

This body wasn't his.

It was.

It wasn't.

They had cultivated many of this particular Antonian clone. This was not the body that had gone over the cliff. The brain was.

They hadn't given him a new name.

He remembered his past life. His brothers. Nicanor, Pallas, Faunus, Orissus, Leo, Galeo, and Nox.

They dropped me.

I died.

16

"**T**HIS IS REALLY RATHER grotesque," said Nicanor, observing the blood spots daubed on the deck of their latest kill.

"I know."

Nox was not retching anymore. He would never enjoy killing. Didn't intend to try.

Pallas stood apart, arms tight around himself. He didn't take part in desecration. A quick kill, and he was done.

Orissus' face fissured. He nudged Pallas. "Problem, *frater?*"

Pallas lifted his chin up. "I understand what you're doing. I do. But I can't do it anymore."

"You don't need to," said Nox. "As long as the Circle is feared, no one is going to check our individual resumes. Stay the way you are."

Leo was doing worse. He couldn't sleep without a sleep program. Couldn't keep his food down without an anti-emetic program. Couldn't pick up a dagger. His hand locked up when he tried.

Leo stared at his hand, horrified. Insisted, "I can do this." But his hand fixed into a claw and wouldn't move.

"No, you can't," Nox said. He put his hands to Leo's shoulders. Giving Leo a shoulder rub was like trying to massage an elm tree. "Take care of the ship's systems. You're the only one who's good at that. Someone's gotta do supply and support."

The elm tree started to shake under Nox's hands. Leo

looked desperately to his brothers. "Really? Is that all right? Are you sure?"

Faunus gave Leo a light kick in the shin. "We got this part."

"How many killers do we have?" Orissus polled. Lifted his own hand.

Faunus signaled he was in.

Galeo lifted a finger.

Nox had started them down this road. He put up his hand. "*Ego*."

"And you're still noisy," Orissus said.

Nicanor nodded.

Pallas said, "I can kill. I can't mess them up."

Nox said, "We shouldn't need to do that much longer. The point is to establish the Leopard as the king of the jungle. We only kill what chases us, and we kill horribly. When the hunters stop chasing us and bow to the Leopard without us needing to demand it, then we can go anywhere. People will give us what we want and thank us for the privilege."

Nox hadn't thrown up after killing since the first one. The bad feeling he got after an atrocity was lessening. He was trying to become ruthless. He hadn't known he'd had that much ruth in him.

"Actually, our kills are quick and simple," said Galeo. "Even Nox's daisycutter in the air lock was quick."

"Are you afraid we're not gross enough?" Nox cried.

"Just saying." Galeo shrugged.

"It'll have to do," said Nox. "I just hope no one else figures out that messing up the dead doesn't cause pain. I can carve meat, but I can't do torture."

The horror caught up with Nox later, in the middle of the next sleep cycle. The ship was dark, and he was alone with what he'd done. He dove into a dream box that promised to weave fantasies of your deepest desires.

It started well with a dream of a woman. It turned into a nightmare of him stabbing her.

He tore off the V-helmet and leaped out bed raging. "*No no no!* That is not what I want!" He smashed the thing, stomped it, threw it, cursed it. Woke the whole ship.

Pallas calmly cleaned up after Nox's rampage and offered him another brand of dream box. The program was *Hot Trixi Allnight.* "You can't go wrong with Trixi."

* * *

It was gently drizzling in camp when Izrael Benet beckoned Glenn to a table under one of the pavilions to join him in a game of poker.

Glenn climbed onto the bench opposite Benet. Benet pushed a stack of chips across the table to her.

"What are the stakes?" Glenn asked.

"Shall we play for worlds," Benet said.

So this was one of those games wherein you sound out the character of your opponent by how he plays. "No. I don't play with worlds," said Glenn.

"That's interesting." As if to say he thought she did.

Glenn tossed in one chip for her ante. "That's my morning bagel."

Benet matched her bagel, shuffled the cards, and offered the deck for her to cut. She gave the deck a tap. "Just deal."

Benet dealt. Glenn picked up her five cards. Gave them a quick glance.

Benet studied his own hand, then asked, "How many?"

Cards he meant.

"None," said Glenn.

Benet took one card for himself, then said, "Your bet, Lieutenant. You must be holding all the big guns."

Glenn literally laid all her cards out on the table. "Director Benet. You want to know me, just ask me questions. Talk to me."

Benet folded his own hand without showing it. "Fair enough. You see, I think I already know you. You are a military officer. You have people under you who must obey you without thought. You military types abdicate your personal will and conscience to a superior. Dissent is essential to living free."

"Living is essential to living free," said Glenn. "The military makes sacrifices so that civilians can live free."

"How can you talk of living while you, your Admiral Farragut, your Empress Calli, and your battleship *Merrimack* are a galactic marauding genocidal ecological catastrophe?"

The extremity of that speech set Glenn back. Her stubbly eyebrows lifted high. "You think we should have let the Hive live?"

"No. The Hive wasn't life. It was death incarnate. It had to be eradicated. But since you mention it, Jose Maria de Cordillera and the rogue patterner Augustus were the ones who figured out how to destroy the Hive. And here you're actually claiming to have destroyed the Hive? How can you presume?"

Because we did the actual destruction, that's how. She wasn't going to argue with him about that. She returned to Benet's original accusation, "Then what genocidal eco-disaster are you talking about?"

"The Myriad."

Made her blink.

Years ago the *Merrimack* had discovered a three-world nation inside a globular cluster. The core of the colossal star system collapsed. The system was still collapsing to this day. Two of the planets were gone now. Even now the relocation of the intelligent species from the remaining planet was ongoing. The LEN was also attempting to preserve specimens of all the flora and fauna on the last world before it too fell into the singularity. It really had been a disaster.

"We tried to stop it," Glenn said.

"Only after you caused it," Benet said.

"That's what you think?"

"The Myriad was a stable system before *Merrimack*'s arrival. And then suddenly—bang—it wasn't. Do you know what it's like to organize a rescue on that scale? And to lose an entire world under your charge. A world!"

Glenn felt the hairs on the back of her neck standing on end. "I'm going to guess that you do know."

"The Myriad rescue was my project for three years," said Benet. "Trying to save all those beings. All those species. When Rea went into the singularity, I broke down. I admit it. Then, for my next project I was given paradise. Zoe. This is an extraordinary, beautiful world. I have been conservator and administrator of the LEN expedition here for five years now. And now the damned *Merrimack* is coming *here*. Forgive me if I react with hostility. No. Don't forgive me. I don't need your forgiveness."

"Here I thought you wanted to play this game to get to know me."

Benet seemed to reconsider his approach. He asked, "Tell me. Are you sorry?"

"For anything I did at the Myriad? No."

"Then I was right about you and your *Merrimack* in the first place. You come in peace and shoot to kill."

That's not true. We're a space battleship. We rarely come in peace, Glenn thought. Said, "We only shoot if something wants shooting."

"To kill," Benet specified. "You shoot to kill."

"Always," said Glenn.

* * *

The United States space battleship *Merrimack* passed through the Boomer in literally no time at all.

"Boomerang" was the Pacific consortium's term for its long-distance displacement system between Earth local space and the outer arm of the galaxy.

One moment the battleship was in Port Chalai in the Orion arm of the galaxy, the next instant she was two thousand parsecs away, in Port Campbell in the Perseus arm of the galaxy.

"Shotgun" was the U.S. term for the instantaneous connection between their two space forts. The Shotgun displaced ships in the opposite direction from the Boomerang. The Shotgun displaced ships from Earth local space toward the heart of the galaxy.

But the major difference between the Pacific Boomerang and the U.S. Shotgun in Captain Carmel's mind was that the Pacific internationals allowed Romans to use their Boomer.

The United States had originally protested the construction of the Boomerang. The Pacific nations ignored the protest.

And wish all she wanted, Calli just wasn't allowed to shoot allies.

The U.S. had a thin presence in the Perseid arm, and no military presence at all before *Merrimack*'s arrival. During the colonial frenzy of the last century the U.S. had expanded toward the galactic center. Asian nations had dominated human exploration outward into Perseid space.

More recently, just before the war, Rome had spread into the Perseid arm. Rome secretly rebuilt her legions on far-flung colonial planets during the Subjugation. Mad Caesar Romulus had been behind that project.

Romulus, the former Caesar, existed now in an induced coma, racked by crazed nightmares.

A disturbing number of people called him Romulus the Great.

Calli Carmel resented America's so-called allies granting passage to the Legions of a belligerent Empire that to this day claimed the United States as a Roman colony.

The gatekeepers of the Boomerang never checked the contents of Rome's so-called freighters, which looked a lot like Roman troop carriers. The consortium just collected the high tariff and sent the Roman ships through.

The Boomerang's displacement terminal in Port Campbell was a titanic cubical region of space scoured clear of particles of any size. Photons and cosmic rays were deflected away from it, leaving the purest black nothingness in which to displace entire spaceships across the kiloparsecs between Port Chalai and Port Campbell.

The engineers didn't wrap the ship when it displaced through the Boomer as they did when a ship displaced through the Shotgun. But the experience was the same. The traveler still saw, felt, sensed nothing at all. Departure and arrival were the same moment. The surroundings were identical at each terminus—nothingness. The ship came into existence in a lightless cubic area of vacuum exactly the same as the one it left.

Only when the port tug pushed the arriving *Merrimack* out of the pristine nothingness into the light could *Merrimack* see the port with all its stations. And all the cameras of all the stations of Port Campbell saw her.

Merrimack was the size of a large freighter, but she didn't look like one. She glided into camera view as a majestic barbarous spearhead. She had a few light-years on her, but she was still a grand, proud ship.

Captain Carmel had expected some resentment at the

arrival of her belligerent ship in the trading center. But U.S. flags were out all across Port Campbell, and there was a welcoming light show.

Port Campbell was a new outpost. Its stations had grown up fast as desert blooms, all bright, shiny, beautiful. Expensive.

The tug guided *Merrimack* on a procession between stations. *Merrimack* ran in bright mode, lit up like a minor sun. Proud. Arrogant, some said.

She passed close enough to the stations for the inhabitants on the observation decks to see her with the naked eye.

The observation decks were crowded.

Merrimack was accustomed to hate, fear, and admiration in equal parts. Calli had expected some apprehension and suspicion. But these folks were inordinately happy to see her.

"They like us," said Commander Ryan, surprised. "Why do they like us?"

"They *are* happy to see us," Calli had to admit, puzzled. Port Campbell greeted *Merrimack* like a liberator. "Something's going on here."

✳ ✳ ✳

Patrick Hamilton presented a mammoth feather to the senior of the two resident physicians in the expedition camp. "I want to run this through the DNA analyzer."

"You will not!" said Dr. Cecil and walked away from Patrick.

"Can you do it for me?" Patrick asked.

"No!"

"How about Dr. Wynans?" Patrick asked glancing around the medical hut. "Is WhyNot in here?"

"No!"

Dr. Wynans was here. Patrick could hear him in a back room.

"Did anyone determine the base structure for life on this world?" Patrick said at Cecil's back.

Cecil spun round. "Oh, no! No. No. No and no." He plucked the feather from Patrick's hand and threw it aside. "You are way out of your specialty, Hamilton, and you will not push your project in front of mine. And you won't use this analyzer! This is a medical diagnostic tool, and it analyzes DNA-based organics *only*."

"That's what I'm looking for," said Patrick. "DNA."

"The aliens don't have DNA!"

"You are shouting," said Patrick. "Why are you shouting?"

"Because you are an imbecile!"

"Imbecile is an obsolete term and inaccurate, and what has my intelligence quotient to do with the volume of your speech?"

Dr. Cecil chased Patrick out of the medical hut and threw his mammoth feather out after him.

Patrick retrieved his feather from the ground.

Melisandra Minyas overheard the exchange. She couldn't help but hear it.

She ran after Patrick and plucked the long skinny feather from his hand. Winked at him. "I'm game."

"Thanks," said Patrick and nodded toward the medical hut. "Don't get bit."

She twirled the long feather, making it flash golden in the light. She said, "You're looking for DNA? Seriously?"

"Seriously."

Dr. Minyas rolled up on her toes and rocked back down on her heels. "You know you could have picked *anything* from any animal or plant as a sample for a base code analysis."

"I know," Patrick said. "I just like the idea of bull feathers."

Dr. Minyas' freckles spread in a perky smile. "Around here? Yeah. Everything's made of bull feathers."

* * *

"You are here to kill The Ninth Circle."

Captain Carmel gave the port governor a blank blink. Afraid she looked clueless. Because she was clueless.

She stared at the holo image of Zander Kidd, Governor of Port Campbell. Calli didn't know what he was talking about.

I'm here to do what?

Merrimack had picked up some outpost chatter on her way to her main station. All the stations of Port Campbell were buzzing in fear of something called The Ninth Circle. Calli hadn't paid attention to it.

Calli answered the governor, "What is The Ninth Circle?"

"Pirates," said Governor Kidd. "Vicious. Vicious. Vicious. Came out of nowhere very recently. Now they're the terror of Perseid space."

"*Merrimack* is not here for pirates," Calli said.

"It's true then. The United States *is* staking colonies in Perseus space."

"No, sir. Not that I've heard."

"Why are you here?"

"Passing through to the Outback."

"Can I talk you into delaying your departure," the governor asked.

"I can step on a pirate if he's here," said Calli. "You point, I'll shoot."

"That's the hell of it. The Ninth Circle aren't here. And it doesn't make a damn bit of difference."

Zander Kidd had bought himself devilish good looks. He had big, white even teeth and a shock of thick dark hair with a rakish wave. His eyes were brightest blue with sunray irises. Even under a conservative business suit the man was obviously muscled like a racehorse and probably quite tall, but he was sitting behind a desk here. His bronze skin had a middle-aged texture to it, so he didn't look like a beach toy. Records said he was seventy years old.

The handsome man looked harried.

"The Ninth Circle are not here. They have never been near here, best I know, or I would have killed them myself. Some bastard in that gang of bastards knows how to play up an image. Not that they are not bad. They're ghoulish. But it's *one* pirate ship, and they've paralyzed trade across one tenth of the bloody galaxy! All my stations are hemorrhaging business.

"Cargo ships are taking wide routes off the standard lanes on approach to my port. Even though—*even though*—so far, all The Ninth Circle's victims have come to the Circle. Not one victim was ever caught in a rundown.

"The Ninth Circle have never jumped a civilian ship, but you try telling that to civilians. Everyone's holed up like sitting pheasants. Trade is *not moving*." The governor took a breath. Folded his hands, forcing himself to a dignified composure. "And the pirates are flying a bloody bleeding Xerxes."

That was unexpected. Calli said, "I'm guessing the ship wasn't lawfully purchased."

"You are correct, sir."

"Doesn't say much for the much vaunted security systems of the Xerxes," said Calli.

"No, sir. What it says is all about the pirates. The Xerxes is everything it's supposed to be, which is how the pirates manage to stay at large. It's not that the Xerxes is performing below spec. It's that the pirates are performing far beyond spec. You'd think men that clever would be doing something *else*."

"There's Interpol," said Calli. "And the League of Earth Nations has some crack pirate hunters. There is your station militia. Does enlisting a battleship not strike anyone as overkill?"

"Overkill is required," said the governor as if she'd just made his point for him. "Interpol and the militia can combat pirates. What I need is something to combat *fear*."

"Sir?" said Calli, thrown off course.

"I hate to confess this, Captain, but when I was a very small child my mother invoked a wizard to banish the monsters from under my bed. There were no monsters under there—I think there weren't—but the point is *reason wasn't working*. The wizard prevailed. Captain Carmel, I need a wizard."

"We're not dealing with children," Calli said.

"Pardon my Esperanto, Captain: the hell you say. You command soldiers. You don't know what mass civilian hysteria is."

The governor cupped his hands together. "A handful of pirates." He flung his arms wide. "Big wide galaxy. And still my people are convinced that The Ninth Circle are here. Right here." His forefinger stabbed down on his desktop. "Under the bed. And I suppose The Ninth Circle actually are as deadly as their reputation. I know they're killing me."

Calli said, "Even if I wanted to, I can't chase an undetectable ship." A Xerxes could achieve perfect stealth.

"Don't need to, sir," said the governor. "Just *be here*. Let people see *that*." He moved aside to show Calli the station's eye view of *Merrimack*, her titanic, wicked spearhead shape, bulging with massive engines, gun blisters, and torpedo tubes.

Merrimack had the power of intimidation. Not that she would scare off pirates. But she could give lawful traders a sense of invulnerability.

Civilian traffic was entrenched, afraid to move. Under *Merrimack*'s broad, deadly wing, traffic might move again.

All *Merrimack* needed to do was unfreeze the terror. Once moving again, perhaps inertia would take over, and traffic would keep moving after *Merrimack* was gone.

Calli was in a rush to get underway. But it would be bad form to bolt when she wasn't answering a well-defined emergency. So far, the alien hostiles around Zoe had not attacked the planet.

Merrimack had been riding along at cruising velocity. Captain Carmel supposed she could lay on some acceleration to make up for lost time.

She told the governor, "I can give you forty-eight hours, if you grant access for my Marines to go on liberty at the port stations. And waive their boarding fees and tariffs."

Everything in the space outpost cost arms and legs her Marines couldn't part with. Just the boarding fee at any station was beyond a Marine's budget.

"I don't want any brawls," said the governor. That was a yes. "The locals are rowdy enough."

Merrimack's quartermaster bought red, white, and blue paint from a space station and brought it on board the battleship. Colonel Steele set the Marines to painting Stars and Stripes on their Swifts. The flights were to fly rotating patrols through Port Campbell.

There would be liberty when their patrol was over.

Asante Addai couldn't wait.

The new Alpha Seven, Flight Sergeant Asante Addai, had been thrilled to death to find himself with three, count 'em, three, lindas in his squad. None of the three were knockouts but they were looking finer the longer he stayed on *Mack,* where testosterone outnumbered estrogen five to one.

But none of his three squad mates were putting out.

Not even Kerry Blue.

What to make of Kerry Blue?

Kerry Blue was easy to like. She used to be easy to like. Nowadays you look at her too long, you got guys giving you the wave-off, like you're coming in to land with your gear up.

Asante had invited Kerry Blue to a horizontal rumba, and Kerry Blue said no.

He retreated, astonished and a little wounded. He was in the maintenance hangar painting red teeth on his Swift.

Asante Addai thought he was the first man in history to get a no out of Kerry Blue.

"This is not what I expected from everything I heard about Kerry Blue." Asante confided to Cain Salvador. He sniffed his own armpits, afraid how he'd fare with the civilian lindas in Port Campbell.

"Yeah, well, Blue's got a deadly disease," Flight Leader Cain Salvador said, painting red stripes on his Alpha One.

Asante cracked an uncertain grin. "You're fugging me. There are no deadly diseases."

Cain answered with silence.

Asante cried, "It's the twenty-third century! There's no contagion the MO can't cure."

"Well, she's got one," said Cain.

"*What?* What's she got?"

"Brass poisoning," said Cain.

"Huh?"

"You touch her, and a ton of brass comes down on you."

Asante's eyes flicked upward and side to side for some precarious pile of metal about to drop. He gave Cain a blank look. Didn't understand.

On the upper-level landing of the maintenance hangar, a hatch flew open, banged off its stops. Colonel Steele marched onto the top-level catwalk and came to the rail. He bellowed down for Alpha Flight to finish up and take first patrol.

The hatch slammed behind him before anyone could come to attention.

Cain looked away, whistling an off-key ditty.

Asante looked where Cain was pointedly *not* looking—where the colonel had been. As if it were an answer to a question.

Asante lowered his voice to a whispered shriek. "*Him?*" Couldn't be. "Steele and Kerry Blue? No. He *rides* her."

Cain's face sucked in. Looked as though he'd swallowed his own lips.

Asante said quickly, "No, I mean—I didn't mean—"

Then he read Cain's face. Maybe Asante should have meant exactly that.

Asante said, "You're kidding. He can't do that. He could lose his fried eggs for that. You'll have my six, won't you, frer?"

"Sure," said Cain. "I'll dispose of your dead body with great dignity, *frer*."

Cain would never step in the way of brass. Or steele.

"And he's not gonna lose eggs or anything else," Cain warned. "Do you understand what I'm telling you? You don't fug with what keeps the dead out of you. Got it?"

"I got it," Asante said, nettled. "I'm not the village idiot." *I'm the idiot from outer space.*

Asante moved his painting gear away from his Swift and made way for the maintenance erks to prep the crate for flight. Asante got into his flight suit.

The colonel looked familiar. Asante finally placed who the Old Man looked like. Asante had been watching Roman vids of gladiatorial contests made during the war. He told Cain, "Know what? The Old Man looks a lot like the gladiator Adamas."

"Yeah," Cain said. "A little. I see the resemblance."

Marine Swifts flew in show at speeds at which they could be seen tearing through space just outside the outpost's traffic lanes. Silent in vacuum, they appeared to be roaring. They jetted white oxygen fires behind them.

The Swifts' swept-back wings gave them the look of darts. The Marines had painted their crates with star-spangled blue noses and red and white stripes down their fuselages. Navy stars were fixed on their wings. Some of the pilots added more art—paintings of arrows, teeth, claws, bald eagles, girlfriends—under their cockpits. Dak Shepard painted the name *Elegant Hag* on his crate. Geneva Rhine painted dead Romans around her gun ports.

The Swifts were flashy, fast, and fierce.

One of the local constabulary called the Marine pilots gaudy trigger-happy cowboys.

"Eyup," Lawrence sent over the com, his Swift breathing fire. "We're here to run the Dalton gang out of town."

"You know, it's not like the boys from Oz are the shyest violets in the garden either," Cain sent.

One of the local kerls flying with them sent, "No. We just don't blow things up the way you blokes do. We really need to think about invading someone so we can be taken seriously."

❋ ❋ ❋

The League of Earth Nations scientific expedition camp on Zoe lay quiet within its dirt perimeter. The night forest songs provided a gentle background noise.

A voice howled just before dawn. "Hey! Who interrupted my job?"

Groggy scientists woke unhappily. They stumbled out of their tents.

Dr. Cecil was shouting, angry.

From what any of the annoyed sleepy brains could figure, Dr. Cecil had gone into the medic's shed and found his job aborted.

"I want a head to roll! This is unprofessional! Unacceptable! Unconscionable!"

Glenn sat up in bed in her tent. She fished about for her shoes.

Patrick reached aside to stop her. "Don't go out there. Wait until he finds out what ran instead of his job. He's likely to start screaming."

"I thought he was screaming now," Glenn said.

"No. Trust me. He's not. Not yet. Sandy Minyas ran an analysis on my mammoth feather. She isolated the genetic base code for life on Zoe."

"What about it?" asked Glenn.

"The discovery. It's Copernican. It's Galilean."

"Didn't those guys do hard time?"

"Yes, well, Sandy's going to get put on the rack and roasted."

"That would be all right," Glenn said. She had guessed by now what secret the mammoth feather had unearthed.

The base genetic code for life on Zoe, the world at the edge of the galaxy, was DNA.

17

MERRIMACK'S INERTIAL SCREENS could withstand planet-killing forces. She carried an arsenal bigger than those of midsized nations. Just her presence lifted Port Campbell's economy.

Her Marines' flashy patrols convinced travelers to travel. A flood of trade passed through the outpost. Ships moved among all the stations.

The port governor, Zander Kidd, invited the captain of the *Merrimack* to dinner in his palatial residence within the main station.

At formal dinners, the captain customarily wore dress whites, with trousers and flat shoes. At Port Campbell, her host requested formal civilian attire. "We're not mad keen on uniforms out here," said Governor Kidd.

Apparently the governor's protocol officer failed to advise him that the captain in haute couture was Class One ordnance.

Calli Carmel had been thoroughly disfigured during the war. The medics had restored her all right, slapped a field face on her at the time and sent her back into action. Her artificial jaw gave her headaches. It wasn't her natural shape, and her muscles kept pretending it was the old one.

Fleet officers usually got rejuv on Uncle Sam's tab when they hit age thirty-nine, to reverse natural entropy. This officer had undergone trauma, so the Navy pretty much insisted she have the work done. So when her mileage rolled around for rejuv during peacetime, she received facial bones and eyes cultivated from her own cells. The medics also restored her scalp and hair to their natural state.

The natural Calli was idiotically beautiful. Her attitude made her looks lethal.

Before debarking, Calli stepped onto *Merrimack*'s command platform. "Mister Ryan, your boat."

Merrimack's new XO was jaunty Commander Stuart Ryan from Oz. Everyone called him Dingo. During the war, Dingo had commanded a small ship at the siege of Palatine charged with drop-kicking Rome's power stations out of planetary orbit.

Dingo Ryan stood up, eyed his captain head to heels. "Captain, you're going to kill someone."

Other personnel on deck stood up even though they'd been waved down. They didn't salute. They bowed.

"Mister Ryan, brig the lot," Calli said.

"Aye, aye, sir."

A civilian transport ferried the captain to the main station of Port Campbell. She appeared at the governor's residence on the arm of her husband, baby-faced Rob Roy Buchanan. Rob Roy had shaved for the occasion, so he looked even younger.

Rob Roy looked like the victim of an overdone rejuvenation. But he hadn't been through rejuv. Ever. Rob Roy was not a line officer. The Navy didn't rejuv his type. Anyway, if Rob Roy Buchanan ever went through rejuv, they'd be handing him lollipops.

Calli's dress shimmered cobalt, emerald, and gold. The slit in one side of the long skirt flashed a leg bracelet of laced gold from knee to ankle.

Governor Kidd beheld his guest at the door and clapped his hand over his heart as if it had stopped. "Empress Calli!"

The captain had picked up the nickname when she accompanied Romulus on a regrettable date just before he became Caesar. It was the kind of name that sticks and never comes off.

Conversation stayed on a civilized course during dinner with the governor. Only after dinner, while shooting billiards and sipping brandy in the parlor, did prickly subjects come up.

"What really brings *Merrimack* this way," Governor Kidd asked, lining up a shot.

"Our destination is a planet called Zoe," said Captain Carmel.

Kidd looked up from the table. Commented, "Oh, you really are headed out to the woop woop, aren't you?"

The planet Zoe was well away from any trade route, and it was off limits for settlement. That made the world interesting only to scientists.

Kidd took his shot, chalked his cue. "Shame about the sapient natives there. Can't build a single hotel. Can't do anything with it. And it's a pretty planet."

Kidd missed his next shot, either to be polite, or he just wanted Calli to lean over the table. Calli was certain that the governor could have run the table. He won the set, despite his attempts to let her win.

"I appreciate your making time for us, Captain Carmel. Everyone was afraid to take a ship out of its station before you got here."

"Traffic will keep moving after we go," Calli predicted.

"God, I hope so. Sooner or later they've got to realize the leopard can only be in one place at one time."

"Leopard?" said Rob Roy.

"Leopard." Governor Kidd crossed his parlor to activate a holographic image. The image displayed was a giant leopard on a star field, as viewed through a ship's porthole.

The beast was vivid, spectacular. Its bloody mouth moved in a silent roar over a kill.

"Ferocious picture," said Rob Roy.

"Isn't it?" said Kidd. "They pirated it."

The governor pointed to the belly of the beast where the Xerxes—which was projecting the leopard hologram onto the star field—was visible.

Disconcerting to see the shape of the U.S. President's ship painted in leopard spots and flying a Jolly Roger. A fiery circled IX shone on the ship's standard.

"Did the ship that took this picture survive?" Calli asked.

"No." Kidd shut off the projector. "They're a thoroughly bad lot, The Ninth Circle. Doesn't matter that half their victims are the wrong sort—no one you'd feel sorry for. Still, it's a gruesome thing picking up human remains from the vacuum. And the other half of their victims are responders. And *that* is twelve degrees past wrong. They have a large arsenal."

Calli asked, "How did they get a large arsenal?" A Xerxes only carried defensive weapons. To protect itself from pirates.

"The Ninth Circle kill anyone who tries to arrest them, then they gut the ship. So they have police-grade weapons now. There's an obscene bounty on them, so there's no end of lowlifes who want to collect. Gunrunners have tried to take them. So now the pirates have a stash of guns. The Ninth Circle do not respect the Red Cross or a white flag."

"Who *are* they?" Calli asked.

"Trace evidence says they're human and they're male," said Kidd. "They're all XY chromosomes. Six of them are similar enough to be altered clones, so someone *made* these men, but their precise DNA prints come up with no record."

"Means they're Roman," said Calli.

Rome was notorious for human cloning, and Rome did not share its DNA database with anyone. No record in the universal bank always meant the individual was Roman.

"Rome denied these men are theirs," said the governor. "Rome has no record of them either."

Calli became very still. She murmured with a chill, "They're *damnati memoriae*."

Damned in memory. These men used to be Roman. Rome hadn't just erased them. Rome pretended they never existed.

Governor Kidd said, "They *are* Roman? You mean Rome lied to me?"

"Not exactly," Rob Roy said. "And not exactly. Rome disowned them retroactively. If they're *damnati*, Rome really doesn't have a record anymore. These men aren't just dead to Rome. They were never born."

"That would make sense," said the governor. "Except there is one more pirate. His DNA print *is* in the universal system. Information on that one is blocked. The ident comes up classified."

"*Classified*?" Calli echoed. *What the hell?* "Classified by whom?"

"You. The CIA."

"Don't ever refer to me and CIA in the same breath," said Calli.

"Your side," said Governor Kidd. "The United States of America."

＊ ＊ ＊

Arguments and accusations flew around the expedition camp's fire pit like flaming arrows. Glenn expected the expedition might actually burn Dr. Minyas at the stake at any moment.

Glenn skipped dinner rather than join that group.

She found Aaron Rose in the relative quiet behind one of the LEN ships, checking his latest vintage. A white wine this time. He poured some into a shallow pan to give the camp goat a taste.

The nanny's thick tongue lapped hesitantly.

Dr. Rose looked up on hearing Glenn approach. He nodded sideways at the nanny. "She likes the red better." He poured a splash of white wine into the bottom of a glass for Glenn.

Glenn gave it a swirl. It was clear with a slight amber tint and fruity smell. She tasted it. Paused.

Dr. Rose read her face. "Too sweet?"

"Yeah," said Glenn. She passed the glass back to him.

Aaron Rose lifted his heavy eyebrows. "More?"

"Oh, yeah."

Dr. Rose topped her glass and passed it back to her.

The nanny goat nudged her pan for a refill.

All the while angry shouts carried between the ships from around the fire pit at the center of camp.

Dr. Rose swirled the wine in his glass. "Can you taste the DNA?"

He'd caught her trying to swallow. She spilled some wine down her chin. "Oh, you snot."

"Sorry."

"I don't understand the shrillness of the arguments over there," Glenn said. "The results of the life code analysis are either true or they're not true. It will all shake out. The facts aren't going to change in the next ten minutes or the next ten million years. Why is everyone screaming?"

Dr. Rose, with a few glasses of wine inside him, was taking on a rosy serenity. The angry voices might as well have been bird songs. "You really were never in academia, were you?"

✳ ✳ ✳

"Flight Leader Salvador!"

Marines' heads turned. Team Alpha had just arrived at Taz Station in Port Campbell for R and R. They were getting their bearings when Colonel Steele came striding down the concourse in dress blues, his hat tucked under his arm. He was red in the face.

Cain Salvador snapped to attention. "Aye!"

"Flight Sergeant Delgado!"

Carly snapped to. "Aye!"

"Flight Sergeant Fuentes!"

"Aye!" Twitch went rigid.

"Flight Sergeant Blue!"

"Aye!"

Dak waited with his *aye* ready, but that was the end of the roll call. The colonel was barking, moving off swiftly, "With me!"

"Sir!" Dak cried. "You didn't call me!"

"Enjoy your liberty, Marine," Steele said back.

The selected Marines fell in behind Colonel Steele at a very fast walk.

Dak blinked, left out.

Asante clapped Dak on his beefy shoulder. "Better them than us, no?"

Rhino said, "*No*. I want to go where they're going!"

Asante said, "I don't know about you, but I don't wanna spend my time out of the can on duty."

"I do," said Rhino. She trotted after the chosen Alphas. "Colonel, take me!"

"I have my team, Flight Sergeant," said Steele.

Cain, Kerry, Carly, and Twitch followed Steele out of sight. None of them crabbed. None of them looked back.

They hadn't even looked surprised.

And they didn't say anything when they returned to *Merrimack* at the end of their scheduled liberty.

They came back to the forecastle as if nothing had happened.

"Where you been?" Rhino cried.

"Special assignment," Cain said.

"Why not us?" Asante asked, starting to feel slighted. He, Rhino, and Dak had gone clubbing in Port Campbell.

"Well," Carly said. Sounded like she was stalling till a likely excuse came to her. "You're the new guys."

"I'm not!" Dak said. "What about me?"

"Dak, you can't keep your mouth shut," Cain said.

Rhino was not taking the exclusion at all well. "Why was I left out? Is someone telling lies about me behind my back? What are they saying? Why not me?"

"You got liberty," said Kerry. "Why are you skunking?"

Dak, Rhino, and Asante kept grilling Carly, Twitch, and Kerry over where they had gone. Rhino was not going to let it drop.

Cornered, badgered, Carly blurted, "I got married, okay?"

Twitch's eyes went round.

Carly said, "Now shut your mouths."

"Frer!" Asante slung his arm around Twitch's broad shoulders. "We gotta have you a party!"

"No!" Carly snapped. "I'd have told you myself if I wanted a fredding party."

"I got a marriage proposal in port," Asante said, a side thought.

"How drunk did you get her?" said Cain.

"We were both sailing," said Asante. "I let her down easy."

"Frer," said Cain, "there ain't no down easy from 'do you wanna marry me.'"

"I told her I'll never get married. Told her I can't say till death do us part. I'd immediately think one of us is gonna die."

"Yeah," said Kerry Blue. *I've had that thought myself.*

* * *

"I am mortally embarrassed for you, Melisandra," Izrael Benet said. The director and the junior xenozoologist had returned to the scene of the crime, the medical hut, where Dr. Sandy Minyas ran her incendiary analysis. "This is a mistake."

"Look at the results for yourself, Izzy," said Dr. Minyas. "Does this or does this not say DNA?"

"It does," said Izrael Benet, not looking at her report. "Because it's a mistake. You need to know that. I'll tell you what happened. Your sample was contaminated. You're holding an analysis of your own skin cells or some organism you breathed on your sample."

"I was careful," Dr. Minyas said. "There is no contamination."

"Then that bacterium is a Roman plant. Or a mutation of something one of us carried here. Or a hoax created by someone who has never respected us and has no right to be here." That last was probably a reference to Glenn Hull Hamilton. "There is no way in logical hell that your bacterium can be a specimen of independently evolved DNA."

"Never mind any bacteria." Dr. Minyas dangled a long mammoth feather in Benet's face. "*This* was the subject of my analysis."

"It's an uncorroborated analysis," said Director Benet. "You messed up the routine. It was a contaminated sample. You analyzed your own thumb. It's a mistake."

"The analyzer has a memory," Dr. Cecil, whose equipment it was, suggested another possibility. "The counter needs to be reset. The analyzer had no idea what it was looking at and reported the last recognizable thing it saw."

Dr. Benet nodded to that. He faced Sandy as if the matter were settled. "You didn't try to announce this, did you? Please say you didn't announce this to anyone."

Dr. Minyas glanced upward. "May have mentioned it."

* * *

John Farragut showed up on the Roman capital world, Palatine, in person, with baby daughter and pregnant wife in tow. The admiral was on vacation.

Palatine's planetary horizon guard allowed the civilian spacecraft to land at Nova Roma's spaceport, but the imperial palace denied John Farragut's request to see Numa Pompeii.

Consul Aban Pompeii Afrikanus received him instead.

"Caesar does not give audience to midlevel American admirals," Aban explained to Farragut.

"He's not here, is he," Farragut said rather than asked.

"Not for you."

"For anyone?"

"The emperor is about his duties," said the consul.

"That wasn't a yes or a no," said Farragut.

"Caesar is everywhere."

Virtually, Numa really was everywhere. He made regular res casts to his empire. But there had been no authenticated reports recently of Numa Pompeii in the meaty flesh.

Since John Farragut was on family holiday, Aban took him and Kathy out to the country to shoot skeet.

A great crater pocked the wide field. "Pardon the disarray," said Aban.

Farragut guessed the crater was American made.

"Looks like the ones we got back home," said Farragut.

Earth and Palatine were close to each other on an astronomical scale, with a mere two hundred light-years between their star systems. The journey between them was not a day trip by any means, but neither was it a voyage to the edge of the galaxy.

Mad Caesar Romulus' war had left both worlds scarred.

Skeet flew over the crater. Consul Aban held baby Patsy on his hip while Kathy Farragut took the first shots. She was a lean, long-limbed, athletic woman, a couple of decades younger than her husband. Her abdomen was slightly rounded.

Farragut spoke aside to Aban, "Numa doing all right?"

"The emperor is well," Aban said. "I will tell him you inquired."

Mad Romulus had reigned over the drunken rout that was the war against the United States. Caesar Numa was stuck ruling the hangover. There was nothing glamorous in cleaning up. An inevitable dissatisfaction set in when interstellar communications and commerce were not restored fast enough.

"He's in Perseus space," Farragut said.

Aban non-answered, "Were Caesar to visit the far arm of the galaxy, and I am not saying that he is, it would be his right and duty to do so."

The citizenry might be fickle, but Numa's governors and officers were loyal unto death.

"Caesar is the defender of the *entire* empire," Aban added.

"Especially those worlds that used to be Romulus' secret recruiting grounds?"

"*All* worlds," said Aban.

Farragut noted that the consul didn't specify all *Roman* worlds.

A clay pigeon broke apart.

"Nice shot, Madam Farragut," Consul Aban called, just as both his and John Farragut's resonators chimed at the same moment. Emergency messages. The emergency code overrode the callers' signal blocks.

Farragut and Aban exchanged brief stares of surprise.

"This better not be war," Farragut said, reaching for his caller.

"Amen," said Aban, reaching for his. "Your wife has the gun."

Farragut's signal was from Carolina Base. Advised him to pick up any of the galactic news feeds.

"What's this about?"

"DNA."

Farragut tuned into a harmonic. Was greeted with the caption: *God didn't rest on the seventh day*.

Kathy walked over to him, her target rifle over her arm. "What is it?"

"World's upside down," said John Farragut.

His caller showed images from the miracle planet at the edge of the galaxy where aliens shared the same genetic base code as all life on planet Earth.

Kathy pointed at the screen. "Make it big."

There was no point trying to keep it private. The news was literally everywhere. And Farragut could see that Aban was watching the same news. Different images, but the same story.

Farragut changed his caller's playback from screen image to life-sized holo.

Golden mammoths walked over the crater.

Farragut glanced back to where Aban had enlarged his own newsfeed to life-sized. "Looks like a big ol' stuffed animal!"

Aban had foxes.

They forced him to smile.

Those images had been around on nature programs since the first scientific expedition to Zoe. They were headline news now.

Now they were kin.

Farragut felt something like awe.

Okay, it was pure awe.

Until awareness slithered forward from the back of his mind of the reason why he had sent Jose Maria de Cordillera and the battleship *Merrimack* way out to that perfect world in tearing haste.

A sense that he had sent them too late.

Something wicked was already there.

✳ ✳ ✳

Every major media source across the human-explored region of the galaxy carried the report of the discovery of independently evolved DNA on a planet at the outer edge of the Outback.

"Zoe," said the com tech as the bulletin came in to *Merrimack*. "Isn't that where we're going?"

Because her XO was somewhere in port on liberty, Calli had her Chief Engineer issue the recall of all her scattered personnel.

Flight Leader Cain Salvador received the recall while on patrol.

His two flights, Alpha and Baker, were broken up into vics of three all over Port Campbell. Cain sent to all: "Red Squadron, this is Alpha Leader, pack it up. Find your best way home."

"No, wait, Cain. I got something." Sounded like Dak Shepard.

Cain answered, annoyed, "Alpha Two, what do you *got?*"

"Looks like a dinner plate," Dak sent. "Or a hub cap."

Alpha Five: "Qué?"

Alpha Six: "What's a hubcap?"

Cain: "Red Squadron, this is Alpha One. Pick up the plates before you head to ship."

Rhino: "I am not the wait staff. If they're throwing dishes they can go get them themselves. We got a recall, Cain."

Cain: "Rhino. You weren't at the siege of Fort Ike."

Rhino: "Don't rub my nose in it."

The Voice of God from on board *Merrimack*: "Red Squadron. This is Wing Leader. Pick up the plates."

Calli's XO returned to the command deck bruised, cut, sporting two black eyes and a broken-toothed smile.

Calli had promised the port governor there would be no brawling. She beheld her XO, mortified. "Commander Ryan. You did *not* get into a bar fight."

Dingo gave a cheery jagged grin. "No, sir. Friendly game of rugby."

The exec's teeth would have to wait until the ship was underway. *Mack* would be running hotter than normal. Zoe, a planet no one heard of, was suddenly the center of galactic attention. Calli wanted to get there before it became crowded.

"Are we all here? Colonel Steele?"

"Captain," said Steele. "My last patrol found something."

"Found something?" said Calli. "Your Marines were just supposed to be showing the colors."

"They found landing disks in space," said Colonel Steele. "Between the stations."

"Squid shoes!" said Dingo. He didn't want to believe it.

"How many?" Calli demanded.

"We're not sure how many are out there," Steele said. "My patrol picked up twenty-four before obeying the recall."

"Who has the ones we collected?"

"Displacement department, sir."

Calli hailed Displacement. "You have disks. Talk to me."

"Captain," the D-tech responded. "The disks are functional. Rzajhin manufacture."

Dingo murmured to Calli, "Rome uses Rzajhin disks."

"*Everyone* uses Rzajhin disks," Calli replied. The Rzajhi sold to anyone. Rzajhin disks had no memory. A displacement technician couldn't tell you the last time they were used, by whom, if ever. It was what made Rzajhin disks popular with people who had something to hide.

The D-tech recited the litany: "No marks. No serial numbers. No tags. They are functional. No one is claiming them or reporting their lost signals when we turned them off."

Dingo ran down to the Displacement department in person to retrieve a sample disk. He brought it back to the command platform. "No one leaves displacement equipment floating around between space stations. That stuff's not cheap. Well, these are." Dingo flexed his thin exhibit. "But this can't bode well."

Calli looked to Colonel Steele. "Were the disks stationary when your dogs picked them up, or did they have momentum?"

"Dead still, sir."

That was ominous. It was easier to get correspondence on a stationary disk. These disks were out there to be *used*.

"Commander Ryan, notify the admiralty. I'll advise the governor myself."

The governor didn't understand. "Who puts landing disks in space?" Kidd asked. "*Smugglers?*"

"Not inside an outpost, sir. Never," said Captain Carmel. "We have seen this twice before," Captain Carmel continued. "Both times as a groundwork for an invasion. Last time we saw this, Fort Eisenhower was attacked by the forces of Caesar Romulus."

"Port Campbell isn't a fort," Kidd protested. "We don't have a perimeter to guard. We don't have any enemies."

"You don't need enemies," said Calli. "You just need someone who wants to run a blitzkrieg through your Boomerang."

"Well, this can't be Romulus," said Kidd. "He's an incapacitated root vegetable. It took a very clever patterner to design those nanites that took him down, and it would take a better patterner to get them out. And we both know Rome is just not making patterners any more."

✳ ✳ ✳

Director Benet checked in on the medical doctor, Albert Cecil, who was madly testing Zoen biologics other than bull feathers in an effort to prove Sandy Minyas' Earth-shaking discovery wrong.

Cecil's test results came back as DNA-based every time. He kicked the analyzer. "Piece of Roman crap."

The medical analyzer was a PanGalactic product. Roman-made.

"Well. That solves that," said Benet. "This is a Roman hoax."

"The analyzer is working fine," Cecil snarled in rising frustration.

"Then Rome is here, and their genetic butchers have been playing mad scientist," Director Benet said. "Rome is perfectly capable of inventing DNA-based life. They've created strange creatures and planted them here."

"They planted a *lot* of them," Dr. Wynans sang from the back room, truly dubious.

"It's shameless. Unconscionable." Dr. Cecil sneezed. "And possibly lethal."

Dr. Minyas leaned in the doorway of the medical hut, twirling a long mammoth feather. "Izzy. Why won't you just accept the fact that these things are native life?"

"Because of the *DNA!* DNA is terrestrial. Your test subject can't be native to this world. If the mammoths are DNA-based life, then they are transplants."

"Bad news for you, Izzy." Dr. Minyas reached into her pocket, pulled out a piece of bark. "This tree fragment that Cecil already tested for DNA? It's three thousand years old. And no, I didn't use a Roman machine to get that reading. I used a Swiss-made machine to carbon-date it. *Three thousand years.* That's older than human space travel. It's older than—than—" She searched for something old enough. "Bicycles."

"Bicycles?"

"I'm saying it's old. It's older than Rome. And when I say Rome, I mean the *first* empire. Nobody brought this here."

Benet considered the tree fragment that was Dr. Minyas' test subject. "That is a fake. It cannot be separately evolved DNA."

"Why?"

"It's a self-evident truth. I can't begin to explain it to you because it is obvious and absolute. I won't stand here and explain axioms to you. Dr. Minyas, you went public with a hoax."

The arguments had been going round and round, day and night in the expedition camp. They were bracing for a media siege.

Glenn asked Patrick in private, so she wouldn't sound ignorant in front of people who already thought she was ignorant, "Why can't the DNA just be native to this planet?"

"You don't get it," said Patrick.

"Didn't I just say that?"

"The discovery is revolutionary. It's beyond Earth-shaking. It's the Holy Grail."

That answer didn't tell Glenn anything. She said blankly, "It's the blood of Christ?"

Patrick cocked his head, considering. "In a way. Yes. DNA is the base code of life on Earth. 'Alien DNA' is a faulty term for what everything else has. DNA is our genetic code. Ours. Earth's. Only ours. Each life code is unique to its world of origin. If you find an apple on an alien world—a real apple, not something apple-oid—If you find a Granny Smith on another planet, you must assume someone brought it there. You do *not* assume you found a second Garden of Eden. You dismiss it. Until you just can't possibly dismiss it anymore."

"And this is a second Garden of Eden?" asked Glenn.

"It's sure as hell starting to look like it."

Too soon to be someone coming to investigate the alleged discovery of alien DNA, a Terra Rican ship arrived in the Zoen star system. When Director Benet learned its sole pilot and passenger was the esteemed Nobel Laureate, Jose Maria de Cordillera, Izrael Benet gave the ship the landing pad meant for *Spring Beauty*.

The sleek space yacht *Mercedes* descended majestically to join the ring of boxy ships around the LEN camp.

Jose Maria de Cordillera was past sixty Terran years old now, unreconstructed, still greyhound slender, taut-muscled, and agile as a cat. His hair was shorter than last time Glenn had seen him, his black ponytail only down to his shoulder blades now, but still swept back into the same hand-wrought silver clasp. The silver blaze at his temples was wider than ever.

Izrael Benet was not pleased to see Glenn Hamilton get kisses on either cheek from the revered *Don* Cordillera. Even Jose Maria's dog wagged her entire stern to see

Glenn. The Doberman bitch was overjoyed to see Patrick Hamilton too, completely oblivious to Patrick's attempts to wish her dead.

Before Jose Maria's arrival there had been no microbiologist in camp to examine the native organisms on a molecular level.

"I am not here for the DNA," said Jose Maria. "As profound and astonishing as that discovery is."

Patrick asked Jose Maria blithely, "Are you here to make field observations of the territorial displays of *Homo sapiens academiensis?* It's a rich environment."

Benet's face became stony. Looked like he wanted to muzzle Patrick. But Patrick had the august visitor's regard, so Benet held his tongue.

"I imagine the conversations have been lively in recent days," Jose Maria said, ever the diplomat. "But no. The young admiral asked me to come. I understand there are extraplanetary aliens on world."

Director Benet said, "I'm afraid to disappoint you there, *Don* Cordillera. There are *no extraplanetary aliens on Zoe.*"

"There *are*," Glenn said wearily. Felt as if she were being flogged.

Jose Maria's hand landed warm and reassuring on her shoulder. Glenn saw two white-gold rings on his left hand, one a wedding band on the third finger, the other a more delicate band of identical design on the second joint of his forefinger. That had to be his late wife's wedding band.

Jose Maria told Glenn, "I know there are, young lieutenant. Perhaps not on the surface of Zoe herself, but at least they are around her. I met your visitors on the way in."

Director Benet looked like he'd swallowed a live ferret.

Glenn cried out, relieved and horrified at the same time. "They attacked you!"

"They tried," Jose Maria said, tranquil. His *Mercedes* was built for racing.

Benet rounded on Glenn. "They followed you here. Those things were never here before you came."

"How could they follow Glenn?" said Patrick. "They don't exist."

Benet hissed, teeth on edge. "Don't be obtuse."

"I shall try. I always saw myself as more of a reflex angle."

"Dr. Hamilton, shut up," said Benet. "*Don* Cordillera, I am sorry you had a rude welcome. But you must know those weren't real aliens. Whatever assaulted you were fakes. A hoax."

"This is possible. I cannot know without a test subject in hand," Jose Maria allowed. "But even a fake invader has to come from somewhere other than here."

18

BY NIGHTFALL IT WAS RAINING squids and muskrats in the LEN camp. At least the pouring rain was falling straight down. The tents in camp were set on raised platforms. Glenn could hear the runoff trickling underneath her tent in rivulets. Big drops tapped on the tarp.

From the surrounding forest carried chirps, cricks, and peeps like nineteen kinds of frogs. The air had cooled.

Patrick slept hard. Glenn lay awake.

She heard a sound like sniffing around the perimeter of their tent. A tent flap nudged inward. Glenn thought the wind had picked up.

Then saw a wet furry face lifting up the tarp. And another.

Foxes.

Two drenched young bachelor males slunk up and under the flaps into the tent. Glenn ducked under the sheet as both foxes launched into doggy shakes.

Brat jumped onto the bed, tracking muddy paw prints over both sheeted bodies. When Glenn peered over the top of the covers, Brat's face was there, smiling. Tanner tunneled under the sheet. Patrick gave a gagging cry, came out thrashing.

Brat and Tanner had come on a daring raid inside the human circle. They grabbed Glenn and Patrick by the scruffs of their bedclothes and tried to drag them away until Glenn and Patrick got through to them that this would go much easier if the foxes let them walk on their own.

Patrick hummed them to calmness. Brat and Tanner let them get dressed and pack some items. Patrick turned on a small light. Everywhere Glenn moved, there was a busy nose in the way. The boys had to sniff everything.

Brat saw himself in a mirror on the camp table. He knocked it over to see the back of it. Pawed at it. Hummed.

Patrick laughed and told Glenn, "He wants to know how I made the water do that."

Foxes only ever saw their reflections in water. The mirror must have seemed an odd sort of ice.

With her splinter gun holstered behind her back, rain slicker on, pockets jammed with snacks and a heat stick, Glenn was ready to escape.

They stole away into the night forest under the cover of rain. Creatures whistled and cheeped and sang. Glenn felt as if she were a teenager again, baling out her parents' window.

A snake darted out from underfoot, fled up a tree trunk in a slithering spiral.

Patrick and Tanner hummed nonstop as they climbed over rocks in the vale to the uplands.

Glenn finally asked, "What's this about?"

"Belly rubs," said Patrick. "The pack wants belly rubs."

Sometime during the climb the rain stopped.

Desiccated growths that used to look like dried dead sponges plumped out in the rain. They were now bright fungi that would not look out of place in the company of a caterpillar with a water pipe.

Glenn, Patrick, Brat, and Tanner arrived at the upland meadow in the wet hazy dawn. Silhouettes of pointed ears in the fog lifted above the mist-bound grasses. Foxes greeted their return with delighted yips.

Conan, the pack leader, stood up, planted his paws on Patrick's shoulders, and hummed happily.

Patrick ruffled Conan's mane. "Well, hey there, cuz."

Funny how *not* alien Conan looked now that they knew he came out of the same chemistry set.

Conan licked the top of Glenn's head. Her red-brown hair was growing back in. When she'd first come to the foxes, she'd been nearly bald.

The mist burned away with the sun's rising. New flowers

had just come into bloom, and Princess wanted her fur done. She had combed out the old blossoms.

Glenn walked the fields to see what was in season now that wouldn't wilt too fast. Princess knew what to look for. She went bounding through the tall grass and came back with a mouthful of hardy red flowers on nice supple stems.

Glenn got to work weaving a crown. Patrick sat beside her in the damp grass, watching mammoth signals on his omni. Princess sunned herself at their feet.

"Patrick," Glenn started, a question in her voice. "Princess knows her name. I mean she knows the name I gave her."

Princess turned her head at the sound of her name.

"Sure she does," said Patrick.

"Do *I* have a name?" Glenn asked. "In fox talk?"

"Yes. It's a quarter tone above middle C." He hummed her name for her.

Princess turned her head again, repeated the hum, smiling at Glenn.

"Does it mean anything?"

"You mean like Running Bear or Laughing Wife? Not that I know. I think it's just you."

"Now I feel stupid," Glenn said. "These animals can learn my language, and I can't pick up a note of theirs."

She had tried. Patrick had keyed in a couple of basic fox words for Glenn's reference, but it hadn't helped. She couldn't hold on to the notes long enough to hum them back. Parrots and myna birds could do better.

"They're just a different kind of smart," said Patrick. "And they have their priorities in order."

Glenn agreed. "What can be more important than belly rubs and daisy chains?" Glenn placed a lei around Princess' neck.

"Should we be afraid of infecting them?" Glenn asked. "Are they safe from our germs?"

Patrick wasn't a medical man any more than Glenn was, but he could answer that one. "We didn't bring any disease with us."

They had been thoroughly screened before boarding the LEN expedition ship *Spring Beauty*.

"But what about our natural microbes?"

Patrick paused, answerless. He said, "Don't kiss anyone."

When she'd decorated Princess, greeted everyone, and rubbed a lot of bellies, Glenn told Patrick sadly, "You know your colleagues are just going to come after us again."

Patrick shrugged, resigned. "Eventually. When they notice we're gone. They might be too busy burning Dr. Minyas at the stake."

It was not Sandy Minyas' discovery that so set off her colleagues. It was the way she did it. And the amateur hack way she announced it.

And it was jealousy. Sandy Minyas did not deserve a revelation this important. The other xenos were so busy backbiting and criticizing that they forgot to feel awe.

"There is a line that separates chaos and inevitability," said Patrick. "And here it is."

He spread his arms at the smiling foxes playing on the meadow.

"We have to love them. They've got all the cute markers DNA has to dish out."

"Including puppy breath," said Glenn.

"Well, yeah. There are pheromones in puppy breath. Works just like an interspecies Red Cross. That's why you see animals on Earth adopt each other's orphans. Even their own natural enemies. Dogs will nurse baby squirrels. Cats will nurse rats and possums. This is a fun place to be right now."

Brat came racing through the grass with a huge toothy smile. He skidded to a halt and flopped over on his back in front of Glenn. He pawed at Glenn's hands, careful of his own giant black claws.

"Why, yes, Brat," Glenn spoke to the upside-down fox. "This is why God put me on this planet." She rubbed his furry belly. Brat's tongue spilled out the side of his wide smiling mouth.

Patrick said, "You know, babe, this really does beg the question: if you and I were created in God's image, whose image is this?"

* * *

Nox and his *Damnati* had built up a ferocious reputation in the spaceways very quickly. The bounty on the Xerxes was high, so the leopard did not need to hunt its prey. *Bagheera* need only flash the image of the leopard near a planet or an outpost, then the brothers could kill and loot whoever tried to cash them in.

Space between star systems was a limitless black emptiness in which *Bagheera* could hide after a kill. The leopard need never come near a watering hole except to feed.

Except that the brothers were all aware of a lack. They had known when they started down this path.

"I want to go to a bar and talk to people I don't have to kill," said Faunus. "I want to shoot pool and throw darts. I want to drink with a bunch of assholes I don't know. I want to bet on a ball game."

"Get laid," said Galeo.

"I was getting to that," said Faunus.

Nox caught himself nodding. He wanted a real woman. *Hot Trixi Allnight* was getting tired. Just like Pallas had said, *you can't go wrong with Trixi.* And that was a problem. There were no surprises, no anticipation, no wobble in the throat when you bring up the subject. Trixi was a sure thing. There was no danger in the encounter, the uncertainty of a living mind, a real beating heart. He didn't get that prickle of fear with a virtual encounter. He wanted real flesh and a new scent. He wanted to interact with unpredictable real people, not go through the motions of pandering programs that rolled out situations some designer thought a man wanted to hear or feel. Illusions in the dream boxes were near perfect. *Near* was another word for *not.*

"Do we want to put in at a port?" Nox said.

"I do," said Faunus.

"I think I do," said Nicanor.

"Isn't this why we paint leopard spots in blood? So we *can* do this?" Leo said. "Let's *go.*"

"Find us a port, Leo," said Nicanor. "Make it a disreputable one so we don't run up against a swarm of police."

Nox put on a new image. He sliced his cheeks and colored the wounds so the scars healed into raised welts of red and blue. He dotted burns underneath the slashes and colored those yellow.

The leopard's last kill had netted them a space warehouse filled with interesting and useless junk. They hadn't yet cut it loose. Nox rummaged through its strange collection for things he could use.

He braided feathers and small bones and sharks' teeth into his blond hair, which had grown below his ears. He tattooed a leopard paw print just below the back of his neck.

On his upper arm, where fully fledged Roman legionaries were branded or tattooed with SPQR, Nox branded himself with a circled IX. The rest of the Circle followed suit.

Faunus' curls had grown wild and bushy. He donned a crown of thorns entwined with metal grapevines. He draped himself with a purple toga.

Orissus wove wool into his hair to give himself dreadlocks. He had grown a beard. It was wide and bushy, nearly black. He braided a couple of pierced gold coins into the nest of it. He gilded one of his front teeth. He struck a pose with a machete. "How do I look?"

"Too sweet for me," said Nox.

"Like hell," said Pallas.

Nicanor shaved his head and tattooed half his body in woad-blue Druidic bars.

Leo put on a studded collar and arm cuffs and a headdress made of a wolf's head and skin.

"Should be a leopard," said Galeo.

"There wasn't a leopard skin in the warehouse," said Leo.

"Are you a *veles?*" Nicanor asked.

Once upon a time the *velites* were the poorest soldiers in the ancient Roman legions. The *velites* wore wild animal skins.

"No. I was thinking something barbaric, like a Viking berserker," said Leo. He had also patterned his arms with scars.

"I thought you were an aboriginal American," said Pallas. "They wore wolves, didn't they, Nox?"

"I wasn't there," said Nox. "But I don't think there was ever an ancient culture that had wolves around who *didn't* stick one on their heads."

Pallas remained unadulterated. He looked handsome and civilized in his short tunic and trousers. Only the brand of The Ninth Circle announced that he was not civilized.

The *Xerxes* ditched its spaceborne warehouse and approached a space outpost that had grown up around a triple-star system.

Bagheera did not flash its leopard holo-image on approach.

Leo did not identify their ship when he requested dockage at the largest station in the outpost. *Bagheera* had dropped out of stealth mode. Anyone looking out a viewport would be able to see by the station lights that it was a leopard-spotted Xerxes.

The station controller advised, "You may put in at dock fifty-three." His voice hitched, not having a name to call them. He didn't demand identification. Didn't want it.

"He knows who we are," said Pallas at Leo's shoulder.

"I believe he does," Leo replied, then on the com, "No. I don't like that dock. Move that scow out of dock thirty-nine. I'll take his spot."

Control hesitated. "The owner is not on board."

"I don't care. Move him. Only him, and no other ship. No other ship departs before we do if their crew is addicted to breathing."

Station control did not actively object. He did ask, "What is your intent?"

"Drinking, whoring, shedding a lot of heavy money," said Faunus. "Or laying siege. Your choice."

The ship in dock thirty-nine pushed out from the station, cast adrift.

Leo maneuvered *Bagheera* in to take its place.

A new voice sounded over the com. Identified himself as the stationmaster, and asked, "Anything you require?"

"We're on holiday," said Leo. "If anyone tries anything, we'll go back to work."

"I want your stay to be as pleasant as possible. Please report any problems to me first. If you would?"

Leo muted the com. Spoke aside to his brothers, "Obsequious toadie, isn't he?"

"Hey, I like him," said Faunus. He reached over Leo's shoulder to activate the com. "Where's the best place to get a drink?"

"Ambrosia Club. Fifth level."

The brothers belted on their personal fields. They were all

aware that a PF only protects you against something coming at you fast, not a shiv slipped under the ribs. So they put on bronze cuirasses. Nicanor's was shaped to his torso. Galeo's was scaled. Orissus' was segmented. Pallas wore chain mail. Nox and Leo wore synthetic mesh. Faunus went bare-chested. "It's all just coming off anyway." He carried brass knuckles.

Sufficiently menacing, the pirates boarded the station. They strode onto the main concourse with an attitude that screamed: *You play by our rules, we won't hurt you. Maybe.*

They carried swords and machetes hanging from their belts. Their daggers were hidden.

As they passed, a drunken voice called blearily after blond, fair Nox and his six tall, menacing brothers, "Hey, Snow White. Where's your other dwarf?"

"We killed him," said Nox. Kept walking.

Starting at the Ambrosia Club, the brothers were treated like underworld royalty. They overpaid for everything, so the business owners in the station warmed up to them fast.

The lure of bounty was out there, but this bounty would be tough to earn—especially if this lot were who they seemed to be. And bounties were not easy to collect even if you managed to do the deed. You really couldn't trust the authorities to credit your kill and pay up. It was much easier and immediate just to take the money these cheerful monsters were throwing around.

Leo brought the ambassador's portable analyzer with him from the Xerxes. He used it to test their drinks and food. The analysis ran clean every time.

Whether from fear or fawning, no one in the station tried to poison them.

To Galeo the cloners had given musical ability the others didn't have. He got up on stage in one of the clubs and jammed with an acid Flamenco band. He left the stage with an autumn vintage señora who could teach a young man things.

"Women like pirates," Nox said, dazzled and astonished to be treated quite so well. "Who knew?"

"Who didn't?" said Faunus.

* * *

A sound like drumming on a hollow log made heads lift up all over the field.

The foxes stirred, paced, restless, ears up.

The drummer wasn't one of them.

The breeze was moving the wrong way for sniffing. The drumming came from downwind.

Noah, a big red male, frisked to his favorite hollow log and drummed something back.

More drumming sounded from the woods downwind.

A low humming buzzed through the pack. Foxes paced, stood up on their hind legs. Paced.

Glenn felt the tension. It was not quite a fear. Heads lifted and lowered. Foxes called tentative yips.

Glenn found Patrick and stood close to him, shivering. He put his arms around her. She felt his heart beating fast. He watched the trees, apprehensive, alert as a fox. Glenn asked quietly, "What's happening?"

"I think we have company."

"LEN?"

"No."

Male manes stood up. All ears pointed forward.

Glenn whispered even more quietly, "Is this bad?"

"Not sure." Patrick nodded ahead. "There."

Glenn saw them at the trees. A wide line of pointed ears like a picket fence. A row of eyes.

✳ ✳ ✳

The brothers of The Ninth Circle had money to burn. Had their money not been in the form of coins, they would have set fire to it for the hell of it. They were lords of the space station.

"Sir?" a station minion approached Faunus with a diffidence bordering on groveling.

Wallowing in a blissful half-drunken contentment, a woman on either arm, Faunus gave the man a lazy come-hither with his brass-knuckled fingers. "Approach."

The voice sounded like the stationmaster they had heard over the com. "I thought I should warn you, there is a ship of war approaching the outpost."

Faunus kept his expression neutral, not sure how to play this.

Nox pasted on a smile and sang, "Feeding time!" He jumped up, dropping the nymph off his lap. Pretended this was jolly great news.

Leo was wearing an earpiece. He opened a com link with the Xerxes. Listened. The *Bagheera* confirmed. Something heavily armed had dropped out of FTL and was approaching the outpost, on direct line with this station. The incoming plot did not announce itself or identify itself. It was not transmitting an IFF. *Bagheera*'s passive scanner had picked it up.

Nox spread the word to the others with false cheer. "All fangs on deck. Fresh meat, boys!"

Faunus dropped a caesar's ransom in coins on the informant. "Here's your kill fee."

The stationmaster bowed. "Anytime, gentlemen," he said, happy for the fortune. Ecstatic to see them leave.

The pirates bayed through the station corridors as if eager for a kill. They bounded to the lock where *Bagheera* was docked.

Dropped the charade when alone with each other aboard their Xerxes.

Leo flashed the leopard holo-image with their standard, their flag, and their motto *lasciate ogne speranza* as they departed the outpost, just to let them know, yes, we really are The Ninth Circle and you have been spared.

Nox looked over Leo's shoulder at the helm. "What's after us?"

"It's big," said Leo. "It's Roman."

"I am not going to fire on Romans," said Nicanor.

"Give them their own path," said Nox.

"They seem to want *our* path," said Leo. "And in case it makes a difference, it's *Gladiator*."

"*Merde*," said Nicanor.

"Run like a flaming rabbit," said Nox.

"Flaming," said Leo, jumping past light speed and slamming the Xerxes to threshold velocity. "And rabbiting." He changed direction.

Nicanor watched the plot reappear on the monitor on their stern. "He's following us."

"How in the hell?" Leo breathed.

"It's a Roman battlefort," said Pallas. "Imperial Intelligence can get a loc on a resonant source."

"But we're not resonating," said Leo. "Are we resonating?"

Leo changed direction. The plot changed with them.

"We must be," said Nox. "Find it!" Himself tearing open equipment panels, searching for a hidden res unit. "*Bagheera!* Did anyone other than Nox, Pallas, Nicanor, Orissus, Faunus, Leo, or Galeo board within the last six standard hours?"

"No one."

"'No one' as in somebody named No One, or no, negative, no persons boarded?"

Bagheera confirmed that the only persons to board within the most recent six standard hours were Nox, Pallas, Nicanor, Orissus, Faunus, Leo, and Galeo.

"Maybe the res source is outside," Pallas suggested. "Someone could have planted a limpet on the hull."

"*Bagheera* wouldn't let that happen," said Nox.

A dragging muddy sound churned inside the Xerxes' engines. Red warning lights flashed all across the control console.

"Leo! What's happening?"

"We have an anchor," said Leo. "We've been hooked!"

"Faster!" Orissus bellowed.

"Faster doesn't help," said Leo. "We're in a hook. No matter how fast we go, *Gladiator* comes along with us."

Both ships sped in the same direction. The Xerxes was not exactly being reeled in so much as the battlefort was reeling itself up to the Xerxes.

Gradually the distance between them closed.

"So we can't pull away," said Nicanor. "Can we push him off us?"

"You mean shoot him?" Leo said.

"Can we?" Nicanor asked. "Can we fire weapons?"

Leo turned around to give Nicanor a withering glare. "It's the *Gladiator*. A Xerxes is armed to repel pirates. This yacht was never designed to take on a Roman battlefort."

Felt a deep metal on metal clunk, hull against hull.

"He's here."

"He's inside our inertial field. How did that happen?"

More deep thunks shook the decks. "He's establishing dock."

"No. He mustn't." Nox opened a general Roman com channel and spoke, "Not your battle, *Gladiator!* Do not attempt boarding. We will defend. Abandon all hope ye who enter!"

"They're pressurizing the air lock," Leo reported.

Nox yelled into the com, reverting to Americanese, "Goddammit, this is hell! Don't try it!"

I don't want to kill Romans.

He asked Leo, "Are they forcing the hatch?"

"They don't have to," said Leo. "It's opening for them."

Despairing, Nox pleaded over the com, "Wait, ah, wait for I am Death."

Bagheera was programmed to kill unregistered boarders.

"Intruders in the air lock!" said Leo.

"*Alive?*" Nox asked.

"Very."

"No. Can't be. What's not happening here? Who turned the auto guard off? *Bagheera!* Defend!"

The ship's defenses failed.

"The inner hatch is opening," said Leo. "We are boarded."

Of a single mind, the brothers scrambled for machetes and charged to the air lock.

Legionaries were marching into their antechamber. Not just legionaries. They were Praetorians arrayed in bronze armor. They were magnificent. They were everything Nox had wanted to be. Strong, proud, noble. Roman.

Faunus flew at them in a screaming charge, his machete raised. The first guard threw him back easily with a sweep of his shield. Faunus lost his footing, fell flat on his back on the Persian carpet.

Nox wielded his machete toward a man's knees. Felt the weapon turn in his hand. Clash of metal banged at his eardrums. Shouts hammered off the walls.

We're dead. We're dead.

19

THE INTRUDERS STEPPED OUT from the trees. They were foxes. Different foxes. Glenn and Patrick knew all of their own pack individually. They had named them all.

The two packs faced each other across a wide swathe of grass. Noses were up, smelling the air. Foxes hummed, heads bobbing. The two groups edged closer to each other by starts, stops, retreats.

Then Conan stepped into the middle ground and went down in a smiling bow with a tail wag. Even Glenn knew that one.

The stately male with bold gray flanks from the other side stood straight up and dropped into a return bow. And the two were off, racing in circles, each chasing each, tag and tumble.

Tension melted into a mass frolic. Everyone sniffed everyone and batted each other with paws. They caught small animals and played tug-of-war with them until the carcass tore in half. Then the two sides traded halves.

Patrick cocked his head, listening hard. A fissure formed down the center of his brow and stayed there. He was having trouble with something.

"Different language?" Glenn guessed.

Patrick hesitated, tilted his head to one side then the other. Rephrased, "Different dialect."

Glenn couldn't hear the difference.

"I'm not getting all the words," Patrick said. "Neither is Conan."

The leader of the stranger pack, the grand male with gray sides, came over to Patrick and Glenn at a loping trot. His color was not the faded gray of age. It was an iron gray hue. Patrick dubbed him Graysides.

Graysides looked hard at Patrick and Glenn. He sniffed them. Sniffed again. Glenn got the inevitable nose in the crotch. Graysides hummed something to Conan. Before Conan could reply, Patrick hummed something back.

Conan and Graysides barked out loud with fox laughter.

Patrick translated for Glenn. "Graysides asked Conan what we were."

"What did you tell him?" She was pretty sure she knew the answer.

"'Funny.'"

* * *

Nicanor called on *Bagheera* to kill the boarders.

Bagheera wasn't helping.

Nox, with the part of his brain that wasn't flailing, wondered why he wasn't dead yet. He'd been knocked to the deck, but the kill stroke hadn't descended on him. The boarders hadn't fired on them, hadn't stabbed them. The Praetorians could have killed any of them immediately with a bronze fist.

A lordly voice of a Praetorian ordered, "Weapons on the deck! Personal fields off. Hands where we can see them."

The brothers looked to one another for direction.

Nicanor's machete dropped to the deck. Nox had already lost his machete. He let his dagger drop. It clattered down. Heard other weapons dropping.

Nox was hauled to his feet, his arms wrenched behind his back. Shackles closed round his wrists. Metal-gloved hands patted him down for hidden daggers. A kick to his heel started him walking toward the air lock. "March."

Nox advanced toward the hatch.

Here we go. Out the air lock.

But no. The hatch at the other side opened, and Nox and his guards passed through the air lock into *Gladiator.*

Nox glanced back. Felt a jolt of surprise. His brothers were not behind him. The hatch shut.

Only four of the guards had come aboard with Nox. They pushed him the way they wanted him to go.

They passed through bronze-embossed corridors. There were gilded and enameled coffers in the overhead. Aldebaran scarab crickets were heraldically placed at the tops of archways.

The *Gladiator* used to be the ship of the great triumphalis Numa Pompeii before he became emperor.

Numa Pompeii was Caesar now. Nox didn't know who commanded *Gladiator* these days.

But there were Praetorian Guards on board.

Why were there imperial guards on a ship at the galactic Rim? Someone far from the home world was acting high and overly mighty for his station.

Nox's escort passed him into the custody of other Praetorians. These were in full ceremonial regalia, with silver eagle wings embossed across their cuirasses, triple-plumed helmets, and ornate bronze greaves. They marched Nox toward an audience with someone who had a dangerously high sense of his own importance.

The Praetorian Guard and the silver eagles belonged solely to Caesar.

Who did this guy think he was?

Enormous doors flanked by marble gods parted.

The Praetorians hauled Nox bodily—still living and breathing bodily—into the throned presence of Caesar Numa Pompeii.

* * *

After a night of drumming and dancing, the two fox packs united for a hunt at dawn. No small animals, birds, and insects would do for this. They brought down a heavy, hoofed thing that looked like a cross between an antelope and a lorry. Conan clamped onto the beast's throat. Graysides' jaws closed on its spine. Other males hung onto the thing's long horns, weighing them down to the ground.

Glenn hung back, hugging her splinter gun. She desperately wanted to save her boys from those wicked horns and those lethal thrashing hooves.

Don't.

The beast fell over, kicking and bellowing.

This is what they live for. Let them do their jobs.

The bull died. Swift strokes with the razor edge of curved claws made the skinning look easy. The foxes tore off hunks of meat and sliced open the belly. A cluster of young foxes stuck their faces in the cavity.

After gorging and then licking each other clean, the young girls brought meat around to the aged members of their tribes, and to Patrick and Glenn.

Several foxes visited to make sure Glenn and Patrick got a share. Glenn tried to smile at the bloody shank proudly bestowed on her. "Thanks. Awfully."

Patrick said, "At least it's not entrails."

Glenn cooked the meat with her heat stick. She did not dare make an open flame out here. But she was not about to eat raw meat now that she knew she and Patrick were fair game for any microbes that might be in it.

Fox noses picked up the scent of cooking meat. Members of both packs moved in to find out what it was.

Whiskers tickled Glenn's cheek. It was Brat.

Glenn offered Brat a bit of the cooked part. Brat nibbled at the edge, let the piece drop. His nose wrinkled up. The others chortled.

Brat said it was funny.

When the foxes left the kill site, a circle of tattlers descended to finish the feast.

The tribes returned to the fox meadow, where Graysides told a story. Patrick recorded it on his omni.

The young ones hung on the old male's every hum as if it were a ghost story.

Glenn whispered, "Can you tell what he's saying?"

Patrick shook his head.

"I can't make it out," Patrick whispered. "Not unless smelly black thorn bushes are crossing the river."

The rest of the day was spent sleeping, lazing. Cooler breezes in the evening brought play. Then drumming and dancing.

"Uh-oh," said Patrick.

Glenn followed his gaze.

A wiry young male from the other tribe was sparking Princess. The one with the nicked ear and heavy scar across his flank. Glenn had named him Rogue.

Princess kept pacing with a haughty strut in her gait, her tail straight up like an empress' fan. She made flirty eyes. Rogue laid gifts at her dancing feet.

Mama-san and Daddy moved in to inspect the gifts.

Glenn pushed her way in there too, checking out the offerings. Patrick asked, "Is he good enough for her?" Not sure if he was kidding.

One of the gifts was a tanned hide. The furred side of the skin was spotted and striped in colors of rich auburn, tiger orange, black, and white. The other side was soft as kid leather. "This is well done," Glenn said.

Even the young male named Tanner from their own tribe gave the hide a thorough resentful inspection. Tanner could find no fault with Rogue's work.

Glenn moved back to stand with Patrick. He put his arm around her shoulders. "Is he good enough?"

"*No* one's good enough for our Princess," said Glenn. "But she wants him."

Princess was acting coy.

The bachelor males of her own tribe were agitated. Brat was biting his own tail in distress.

None of the local boys challenged Rogue.

Mama-san and Daddy appeared to approve.

When the evening drumming started, Princess and Rogue danced in a line that was just the two of them, no one else. They shared a mouse snack. They wandered into the woods in the starlight.

✳ ✳ ✳

Nox breathed an oath in Americanese. "Almighty. Almighty."

"Yes, Mister Farragut?" Caesar said, as if he had been addressed.

Nox recovered. Declared, "I am not a Farragut."

"You are not an Antonius either." Caesar's voice rumbled.

Nox was struck by the enormity that was Numa Pompeii, the enormity of his station.

Caesar Numa was a titan, brawny, fleshy. Romans like their gods huge, with huge appetites and vast grasp, living grandly.

Nox couldn't fathom what could possibly have brought

Caesar to the outer rim of the galaxy. There must be something of great importance here. And it could not be Nox, or even the stolen Xerxes.

Numa studied him in intimidating silence. Nox was not going to make another sound without leave.

Finally Caesar commanded him, "Speak."

Nox opened his mouth. Speech stopped up in his throat. He hadn't been asked a question. Caesar had bid him say something.

Nox spoke his mind, "How does puny pirate garbage rate Caesar's attention?"

"You are garbage," Caesar confirmed. "But you are not puny, and you have never *not* had Our attention."

It's my coiens birth name, Nox thought, sour. *If Caesar thinks that will give him leverage with Big John, it will not. Not ever.*

Caesar said, "You acquired a flight program for a Xerxes transport. From your friend Tycho. Did you think anyone would just hand that over to an *ignominiosissum* without higher permission?"

At this point, I'm guessing not, Nox thought.

Nox had never quite believed his luck in pulling off the theft of the Xerxes. And so he hadn't. Not without a large amount of help. Very large.

Caesar spoke, like the voice of a canyon, "You shall take your Ninth Circle to the Rim world known as Zoe, sometimes called Eden."

Strange place to send The Ninth Circle.

As if reading Nox's thought, Numa said, "It needs a serpent."

Nox didn't know that world. Zoe. There were settled worlds across one-eighth of the galaxy, so there were many places he had never heard of. He knew he would be able to locate Zoe in the Xerxes' data bank, so he didn't ask Caesar for directions. He waited for Caesar to tell him what to do when he got there.

Caesar said, "We require non-Roman Roman eyes on the ground."

Non-Roman Roman. That described him well. He wondered how Caesar knew that he was still devoted to the Empire. Nox guessed that was how Numa got to be Caesar.

Nox had to ask, "Caesar needs psycho killers?"

"We have no use for psychotics," said Numa. "They talk too much. Make no mistake, you are cowards. You *are* garbage. But you are Our garbage. You are not free. You are not citizens. We are Rome, and We own you. If We tell you to fly into a planet, that is what you shall do."

Nox thought he was about to die. Even so, something lifted inside him. Maybe it was his squashed soul. All he wanted was to serve Rome. "Am I crashing the Xerc into the planet?"

"Not this planet. Not now. But it's a future option. For now, get to Zoe, get your eyes on the ground. Gather every bit of information there is. Look for aliens."

"Caesar? It's an alien planet. They're *all* aliens."

"You will know them when you see them."

That statement implied that Numa had already seen the aliens. Caesar must already have remote surveillance on Zoe.

"Will you obey?"

"Yes, Caesar."

"Go."

Nox froze in place, a question clogged in his throat.

"What?" Caesar prompted. A deep rumble.

He's letting me go with a Xerxes. Nox had not earned anyone's trust. *All I did was say yes.* "You take me at my word I will do your bidding?"

"We would not take a syllable of yours on faith. But We don't need to trust you. We know you are telling the truth. You lie like a Farragut. Which means you are abysmal at it. You have been fortunate so far in lying only to truly gullible people."

Nox caught himself before he could raise a Roman salute. But he was not Roman. That might go over badly.

A last word rumbled from the massif, a blithe afterthought "Oh, and you might need to fly past *Merrimack* to get yourself on the ground."

Ah. There it is. It is my name. My name is not going to help. Nox assured Caesar, "*Merrimack* will shoot a pirate ship."

"Try not to get shot."

"There is a very high probability I will die trying to get my eyes on the ground."

"Yes?" Numa gave a shrug of one massive shoulder. *"Quelle dommage."*

✳ ✳ ✳

The fox tribes traded out a few of their young adult members, thus mixing up the bloodlines and sealing their friendship.

Then Graysides' pack went its separate way.

When the tribes divided, Princess went away with Rogue.

"Oh, Patrick," Glenn said with her hand over her heart, her eyes teary. "There goes our baby."

Patrick squeezed her shoulders. Sighed, "They grow up so fast."

Director Izrael Benet's res recorder saved all his incoming messages. Its capacity was advertised as: "As close to infinite as you're ever going to get."

It was full. There were inquiries from all nations and colonies in the entire known region of the galaxy.

Benet pulled the resonator out of its bracket and hauled it to the ship, where Sandy Minyas kept her workstation. Benet dropped the resonator on her desk. "Answer your messages." He turned to go.

"Izzy—"

"Get your buddy to help you," Benet cut her off.

Sandy said, "Where *is* Patrick?"

Benet took a wrong step. Caught his balance. Stopped. Thought. When was the last time he'd seen Patrick? Or Glenn?

Days ago?

At least days.

"Dead," Benet answered airily. "He's dead. I'm going to kill him."

✳ ✳ ✳

Nox returned to the Xerxes. Knew he was pale. Paler than his usual fair complexion. His red, blue, and yellow scars had to be standing out like neon.

The bronze-armored Praetorians withdrew from the Xerxes. The hatches closed behind them.

The energy hook holding *Bagheera* died. *Gladiator* separated from the Xerxes and vanished.

Nox's brothers showed tentative smiles, baffled. Leo said, "We're alive."

"We're *here*." Galeo gave *Bagheera*'s bulkhead a thump. "Why in the brane did they let us keep the Xerxes?"

"Caesar told them to," said Nox faintly.

That got him one synchronized blink from six sets of eyes.

Pallas said, "You had an audience with Caesar?"

Orissus said, "Of course he didn't."

"Oh, he did," said Nox, light-headed.

"Yo?" said Leo.

"Ho?" said Galeo.

"Caesar is in the Outback?" Nicanor said, still not believing it. "Here?"

Nox nodded. "All of him."

Nox told them about the audience. His brothers made him tell it several times.

"So that's why *Bagheera* disobeyed us," said Leo.

"He recognized a higher authority," said Nox. He couldn't fault the ship for obeying Caesar.

"How did Caesar get registered in the ship's system?" Galeo said.

"He's Caesar!" said Nox. "He wants it done, it happens."

"But how did he find us?" Faunus said. "He's Caesar. He's not God."

"*Frateri*, I didn't get to ask a lot of questions," Nox said, still rattled from the encounter. "And that topic didn't come up."

"He had to be getting a lock on a res pulse," said Leo. "There is no other way."

"We haven't been resonating," said Nox.

First thing Nox had done on hijacking the Xerxes was shut down the res chamber.

"I'm going to guess that we *have* been," Pallas said.

"A second res chamber not on the specs?" Leo guessed.

"I'll find it," said Faunus.

"Look for two," said Nox. He recalled a saying about redundancy. It was good. It was good. "And we have a handler."

"Caesar *told* you that?" Nicanor said. It was not the kind of thing one is normally advised of.

"No, he didn't tell me. But there has to be one. You know there has to be one."

Nox set *Bagheera* to searching surrounding space for something lurking in the dark that could be watching them.

"Could be one of us," said Pallas. "Actually, it *has* to be one of us."

"No," said Nox. He wouldn't stand for that idea. Not for a moment. "'You are my brothers.'" *If it's one of us, I really have nothing.* "'The strength of the pack is the wolf, and the strength of the wolf is the pack.' It's not any of you."

"Could be you," said Orissus.

Nox's blue eyes rolled. "If you think that, shoot me now."

"Is it you?" Galeo asked.

"No. And it's not you, Galeo," Nox said. "*It is not one of my brothers*!"

But it was.

* * *

Toward evening the foxes took a roundabout route back to the meadow after merrily chasing a herd of rodents cross-country all day. Patrick decided on a more direct path, which took him and Glenn across a patch of overly ripe ground fruit.

The gourds grew on long trailing vines with browning leaves. The swollen fruits looked like pumpkins and smelled like tomatoes gone wrong.

A sudden pop and a splat made Patrick give a girl shriek. He hunkered down, covering his head with his arms. "Who's shelling!"

Glenn shouted, "The vegetables are exploding!"

Another pumpkin burst.

"I always tried to tell my mother they'd do that!" Patrick said.

They had set off a chain reaction. Another gourd popped. Patrick saw Glenn get slapped with orange pulp. He shouted, "Run!"

He and Glenn came running and yelling through the patch. The foxes watched from their safe roundabout path, laughing.

When they got back to the meadow, the foxes didn't want Glenn and Patrick near them. They stank.

"*I* don't want me near me," said Patrick.

Glenn's face, coated with dried juice, was fixed in a wince. They headed through the deep-shadowed woods toward the stream to rinse off as the sun was setting.

Except for the exploding part, Patrick might have mistaken the gourds for pumpkins. Everything about this place was so very familiar—in a very strange way.

Everything except for those.

Patrick put his hand over Glenn's mouth.

He was pretty sure no one had ever done that and come away without teeth marks, and he suspected he was on the verge now. With his free hand he pointed over Glenn's shoulder through the ferny branches as he pulled her down into a crouch.

He knew when she got sight of them. He felt her tense up in instinctive loathing for something they had never seen. His own hair stood up on the back of his neck.

Instinctive meant it evolved. The loathing had been imprinted on their genes in some distant past. Though Patrick was not sure how one evolves a hatred of something no human had ever seen.

They were grotesque. They were wrong.

Patrick lowered his hand from Glenn's mouth. She had no intention of making a sound.

They stayed huddled in place, watching in creeping horror until the things moved on.

Then Glenn and Patrick turned back, still sticky and reeking of tomato pumpkin.

Glenn whispered, "Is anyone back at camp studying those?"

"Not *me*," said Patrick. "I'm a xenolinguist, and *I* don't want to talk to those! They're not local. They're not even Zoen. Those things are extraplanetary."

"How can you know that?" Glenn said. Sounded like she believed him. She just didn't know why.

"I feel it in my DNA."

20

IMMEDIATELY UPON GLENN and Patrick's return to the expedition camp, Director Izrael Benet had the two thrown into detention in a cargo container. Manny the pilot and Poul Vrba performed the actually throwing. Glenn might have put up a better fight. She just couldn't believe what was happening.

The container was built for transporting livestock so it was insulated and ventilated and equipped with a water supply and a drain. A portable crapper had been moved in, anticipating human inhabitants. There was also a mattress and some prepacked food, so no one needed to open the container to push meals in. These quarters had been ready and waiting for their return.

Patrick called out through the vents to anyone within earshot, warning them of the extraplanetary aliens in the highlands.

Glenn drew her splinter gun from under her jacket.

"We're shooting our way out?" Patrick asked.

"Don't be a crack," said Glenn. She sat on the floor and disassembled her weapon. "I'm not sure I got all the pumpkin guts out."

They had rinsed off in the stream in the dark on their trek back here but hadn't taken time for a proper bath.

"You look pissed."

"Aren't you?" Glenn asked, calm.

"Yes. I don't have a gun."

Glenn was not about to use her gun on the LEN, or even

to brandish it. She was not the bloodthirsty goon the LEN members thought she was.

"I'm not going to shoot anyone," said Glenn. "I'm pressing charges when we get out of here."

Benet had violated their most basic international right of freedom.

Patrick said, "You know that Izzy will just say he is protecting the environment."

"He can't even claim that—given that he caught us in the act of *returning* to camp. You know if we were back on Earth on a university campus, no dean or project director would ever conceive of *incarcerating* people."

Patrick considered this, said at last, "It would depend on the department."

* * *

The space battleship *Merrimack* sublighted at the edge of the Zoen star system.

"Engineering," Calli sent over the com.

"Engineering, aye."

"Transition to Zoen gravitation and Zoen sea level atmospheric pressure."

"Aye, aye, Captain."

Engineering gradually increased *Mack*'s antigrav and pushed the air pressure up to Zoe's sea level, nineteen psi.

All hands on board could acclimatize to Zoen conditions before they arrived at the planet in case Captain Carmel needed to put Marines on the ground immediately.

And she might. Something was wrong. *Merrimack* had not been able to contact Lieutenant Hamilton. The com tech had been trying to raise her since the ship dropped from faster-than-light speed at the star system's edge.

Engineering signaled the command deck. "Captain. Did you want the atmospheric gas mix switched over to local?"

"Negative," Calli sent.

"Oh, Forbin. I guess not," said Engineering, apparently seeing the percentage of oxygen in Zoe's atmosphere.

For breathing, Zoe's oxygen rich atmosphere would require no getting used to. The only adjustment would be in dealing with the threat of fire.

"Colonel Steele."

Steele stiffened to attention at the back of the command deck. "Sir."

"No beam weapons on the ground. No sparks."

"Aye, sir."

But the fight started before they could hit the ground.

As *Merrimack* swung into orbit around Zoe, she met with small spherical spacecraft that slammed themselves into the battleship's energy shell.

The attackers hit with all the fury of spitwads against *Mack*'s adamantine energy barrier. It was almost comical. But the command staff didn't laugh at something that seemed to want them dead.

Mack's field was coded to let sounds of impacts through, so the crew would know they had collided with something.

Inside *Merrimack* sounded like a tin house in a hail-storm.

The XO, Commander Ryan, questioned Tactical, "Anyone on board those spacecraft?"

"Have to be tiny if they are," said Marcander Vincent at Tactical. He gave the XO the dimensions—less than two meters in diameter. "Or one very uncomfortable person wrapped around a powerplant who doesn't need to eat, breathe, or operate equipment."

"We can't assume anything," Commander Ryan said.

"Except that they hate us," said Marcander Vincent.

Another barrage hit the ship's defensive screens.

"Are they—?" Commander Ryan squinted at the images on the Tactical monitors. One of the orbs coming in for a second strike looked decidedly *dented*. "Are they attacking without shields?"

"Yes, sir," said Tactical.

A scanner tech confirmed, "Hostiles show no energy shells. Nothing shielding them except their hulls."

"Life signs?" said Calli.

"None," said the tech. Revised, "Nothing we recognize as life."

"They appear to be under remote control," said Tactical. "But I can't pick up the control signal."

"They could be operating by an internal program," Commander Ryan suggested.

Captain Carmel spoke. "Confirm negative life readings."

"Negative life signs confirmed. Nothing living on board the alien vessels," Tactical reported, then muttered low into his console, "Would anything with a brain pick a fight with a space battleship?"

"That's enough, Mister Vincent," Calli said.

Another flock of orbs moved in and slammed against *Merrimack*, clattering.

"And *that* is enough," Calli said. "Colonel Steele!"

Steele was standing by at the rear of the control room, rigid, silent, disciplined. But the captain could almost hear him praying to be unleashed.

"Sir."

"Set the dogs on them."

The Marine Battery took to the starboard gun blisters. *Merrimack*'s port side faced the planet. There would be no shooting off the port side.

Marines of the Wing charged to the hangar decks, barking. Mustard-suited erks stepped away from the readied Swifts.

Kerry Blue suited up, snapped a displacement collar around her neck. The landing disk was already in her cockpit. She climbed up the Swift's wing, jumped into the cockpit, strapped in, connected hoses. Did a com check. "Alpha Six here."

"Copy, Alpha Six."

The elevator shaft descended around her crate. The lift started up with a jerk. She'd have thought the boffins could smooth out that part of the ride. Guessed it wasn't nobody's priority.

The elevator's top hatch slid away as Kerry's Swift rose to the flight deck atop *Merrimack*'s starboard wing.

On either side of her she saw other Swifts rising from their shafts. Above her was open black space and stars, the planet Zoe shining huge and pretty over there.

Black orbs bashed themselves against the *Merrimack*'s slightly glittering energy shield overhead. Like watching birds slam into a window. These birds didn't learn. They came back and slammed again.

Kerry activated her Swift's own shield. A Swift's energy

screen was not nearly as stout as *Mack*'s, but it would protect her from this crowd.

Kerry glanced aside. The Swifts of her Flight crouched all in a row. Kerry winked to Alpha Five. Checked in by the numbers.

Got clearance to launch.

Thrusters priming.

Three. Two. One.

Engaged.

At the same instant *Merrimack*'s shields over the flight deck disappeared and deck clamps released.

Merrimack gave her Swifts a gentle nudge. Alpha Six went catapulting off the flight deck, Kerry Blue screeching, "YeeeaAAAAH Ha Ha!"

A controller's laconic voice reported over her headset, "Alpha Flight away."

Swifts of the Baker, Charlie, and Delta flights launched from the upper and lower sides of the battleship's wings.

The Mack's wings were wings like a building has wings, not wings like an airplane's wings. It was as aerodynamic as Mount Rushmore.

Merrimack's spaceside gun blisters winked awake.

There was always a contest with the Battery for most kills. You didn't even need to dare them anymore.

Kerry heard Flight Leader Cain Salvador on the com. "Target the spaceward orbs only. No shooting in the direction of the planet."

"I got your planet, Cain," said Dak.

Cain: "Tally ho! Tally ho! Got one!"

Carly: "Got his *hermano!*"

Twitch: "Hoo rah!"

Rhino: "Come to Mama—ho! Here he comes! WASTED!"

Asante: "Got one! Got two! Let it rain, Noah!"

Planetshine made the targets visible. Really visible, not just plots on the tactical screen. The targets showed as black orbs in black space, but they had a metallic sheen to them that reflected the sunshine and planetshine.

The orbs made no defensive maneuvers. They came straight in and tried to bash you. And you just hit them.

Big Richard: "Target acquired. Target secured."

The Yurg: "They don't boom much, do they?"

It was true. Kerry noticed. You hit them and they exploded apart nicely into flying shards, but there was no blaze. No flash. No burn. No color. No proper blowuppage.

If you wanted to see the flash, you needed to look at your instrument monitor.

Colonel Steele watched his Swifts scribble paths across the Tactical monitors on the command deck of the *Merrimack*. Listened to their shouts over the com.

His Marines had spent the last two years rebuilding the Pacific Northwest. They liked destroying enemies much better. His bull mastiffs were hungry.

Around him sounded the hiss of the big ship's guns and the pounding from the gun blisters on the starboard side of the battleship.

His pilots' excited voices overlapped over the com. He kept listening for one.

Kerry Blue: "*Hey, Zeus*, what was that!"

Asante: "I don't know, but there are twelve more just like 'em coming in hot and ugly from the eights."

Cain: "Evade."

Kerry Blue's plot in the Tactical monitor was already 'vading before Cain got out the e.

Lawrence: "Got 'im!"

The Yurg: "That was *my* shot, Dickus!"

"Mine now," said Lawrence.

During the war, Rome had given the colonel a Roman name, Adamas, which was the Latin word for *steel*. Some of the Marines decided they must take Roman names for themselves. So now they had names like Nauseous, Bilious, Bobicus, and Fredicus.

Lawrence, who already had the nickname Big Richard, had become Dickus Maximus.

Asante Addai: "Got one. Got two."

Carly Delgado: "Mine."

"Dang! Look at those moons!" That sounded like Dak Shepard.

Cain: "Do not shoot the moons."

Tactical commented at his station, "Hostiles have no sense of self-preservation."

Commander Ryan said, "We like that in an enemy."

The com tech turned from his station. Spoke low, "Captain, I'm picking up low energy squawking on three radio frequencies on the planet."

Calli crossed to the com station, concerned. "From the hostiles?"

"No, sir. From the ground. There are no radio towers down there, and the signals are very low strength. No voice, no music. I thought it might be LEN wildlife tracking devices, but it's not a homing signal. It's clicking, and it has order and pattern to it. It's not coming from inside the LEN expedition campsite, and I can't get a visual on the sources. There are scattered sources in different hemispheres. Someone is sending code."

Captain Carmel snapped her fingers in the direction of the cryptotech. "Qord!"

"On it, sir," Qord Johnson acknowledged.

The com tech fed the radio transmissions to the cryptotech's station.

Kerry Blue lost count of her kills. Her crate would keep score. The Intelligence ferrets didn't believe your report anyway. The sum of all pilots' reported kills always totaled up to something like five times the actual number of enemy dead.

Merrimack's sensors located another cluster of orbs on the far side of the world. The hostiles were traveling toward *Merrimack,* but so low-powered that they seemed to be walking.

So the Swifts streaked around the planet to get them. The ship's gunners cried foul.

A new guy: "Who's ahead in the kill count?"

"Who cares," Kerry sent. "This is skeet."

"I care," the new guy sent. It was his first time firing his guns in anger. Though this action was more like firing in annoyance.

Kerry found she did better if she moved slowly and let the orbs come to her. She just needed to watch that they didn't try to fly up her tail.

Kerry sent, "Carly, get over here and watch my six."

Alpha Four maneuvered alongside Kerry Blue, facing the opposite direction. They sat still and killed all comers.

Twitch: "For why don't anyone blow up!"

Twitch was right. These colorless, flashless explosions the orbs made on detonating did not make good fireworks.

Asante: "They gotta be packing hydrogen."

Kerry: "Meaning what, Doctor Science? Anyone see a target? Ho! That one's mine, mine, mine, son of a she dog!"

Asante: "Hydrogen don't burn. It explodes."

Dak: "Where the flash?"

Asante: "It's invisible."

Commander Ryan overheard that exchange from *Merrimack*'s command deck. He turned to Captain Carmel. "That confirms there are no oxygen breathers inside the attack craft. Oxygen has a visible burn."

"Our dogs are running out of targets," Tactical reported.

Calli ordered, "Bring the birds home, Colonel Steele. The Battery can pick off the stragglers. Have them save me one. I want an intact orb."

"Aye, aye, sir."

Steele issued the recall order.

Over the com he heard Flight Leader Salvador shouting: "Cease fire! Alpha Two! Cease fire!"

Alpha Two probably didn't hear the order because he was mashing down his trigger and yelling at the top of his voice, "Grettaaaaah!"

"Alpha Two, cease fire!"

Dak annihilated his target. He ceased fire. Still hungry.

It looked like Alpha One had the last target, but Cain wasn't shooting at it. The orbs explode real easy when you shoot them, but Cain was just batting his around with the stoutest part of his Swift's energy field.

"Cain?" Dak sent, hopeful. "Are you gonna eat that?"

Cain kept batting the orb but not delivering a fatal shot. He beat it with his forward cowcatcher, circled round to interrupt its flight, then hammered it again, sending it flying another direction. Like playing catch with himself.

"Can I play?" Rhino sent.

"Back off," Cain ordered. "We need to reserve one. Captain wants a whole one."

With every hit, the orb reeled away from the impact, then gamely reversed course and came back at Cain's Swift for another try.

It took several hits to make it stop fighting.

At last the orb hurtled off and kept going.

Cain sped around to catch it and contain it. He nudged it to a near stop.

The battered orb drifted in the direction of the nudge, unresponsive.

"Wing Leader. Wing Leader. Wing Leader. This is Alpha One. Colonel Steele? Hostile neutralized. I think."

"Return to ship," Steele sent and turned to the XO. "Your target, sir."

Commander Ryan spoke over the ship's intracom: "Engineering. Ready half hook. Target the disabled alien orb."

"Ready half hook, aye. Target acquired."

Ryan: "Engineering. Engage force-field hook."

"Engineering, aye. Hook engaging."

Merrimack's distortion field extended a tendril of energy to loop around the alien spacecraft.

The half hook was a recent variation on a hook. Full containment had its perils. To put out a full hook was to enclose the target inside one's own inertial field.

A full hook on an enemy was an invitation to die. If a powerplant blew up inside your hook, you were done.

The half hook was easier for an enemy to escape from, but he wouldn't kill you when he tried it.

This enemy wasn't fighting. Best guess was it ran out of hydrogen.

Engineering: "Target captured. Alien craft in tow."

Calli nodded to her exec. "Send a Vee jock out. See what we caught."

Merrimack deployed a small unmanned surveillance spacecraft. The drone was piloted from the remote pilot center on board *Merrimack* by a V-jock nicknamed Wraith. The surveillance craft's readings were fed up to the command deck and to Ops for interpretation.

It was immediately obvious that the orbs were unarmed, unmanned, low-tech, alien-built, and not meteors.

"What jack squid thought they were meteors?" said Tactical.

The XO, who usually ignored anything Marcander Vincent said, answered, "A civilian on the ground tried to tell our Hamster that these were meteors."

"Is the ship radioactive?" Calli asked.

There was a quick conference with Ops. Tactical answered, "Negative radiation. It's a hydrogen powerplant. No hydrogen in it now."

Calli ordered, "Mister Ryan. Have Wraith strip the powerplant out of that. Keep the engine in tow. Bring the rest of the spacecraft inboard for analysis."

"Aye, aye, sir."

"Commander Ryan, organize a sweep of the debris. None of that makes planetfall."

"Aye, aye, sir."

Captain Carmel turned to the specialist at the com station. "Mister Dorset. Where is my Hamster?"

Red Dorset had been hailing Lieutenant Glenn Hamilton since *Merrimack* entered the Zoen star system. "Have not been able to make contact, Captain. I can't get Dr. Hamilton either. I do have a very angry man named Benet. He keeps telling us to go away."

✳ ✳ ✳

Thunder cracked under a cloudless evening sky. The claps erupted at ground level like shelling.

Xenos poured out of their work huts and tents. Explosions sounded all around them, but nothing fell from the sky. No dirt sprayed up from the ground.

Director Benet had not shared with his colleagues *Merrimack*'s intent to send a landing team down. He'd thought his refusal was enough to keep them away.

Now the displacement disks came blasting out of thin air in preparation for the Marines' arrival.

The thin metal disks split the air with a bang and settled to the ground.

Benet ran about, shouting at the sky, "No! No!" and to his team," Get that! Get that!" while he gathered up landing disks as quickly as he could. He carried six of them like a stack of dinner plates. "Throw them out!" He ran toward the annihilator.

Most of the expedition team—those who weren't hiding in the storm shelter—didn't want to touch the things.

Manny the pilot picked up a disk. Lights on the disk's rim turned green. Instantly a hundred-kilo Marine materialized with a *bang* on top of the disk.

Marine and disk fell hard. An oof and a snap from underneath the disk was probably a rib of the man under him. The Marine scrambled to his feet.

Other bangs sounded as Marines appeared on other landing disks.

The disks in Benet's stack showed red lights. He shoved his stack into the annihilator. He came stalking out of the recycling hut, head aggressively forward, shoulders back, lower teeth bared, indignant. The whites of his eyes flared at the Marines.

The medical doctor, Cecil, knelt on the ground, tending to Manny, who lay gaping and gasping like a landed carp.

Benet pointed down at Manny and shouted at the Marines, "What did you do to this man!"

The nearest Marine answered, contrite. "Sat on him, sir. He was under my LD."

Director Izrael Benet turned round and round, seeking the ranking officer among the invaders who materialized inside his camp.

He singled out Commander Ryan, the only formal one in the group. The one in Navy blue. The rest were in mud green and rigged like an assault team.

Commander Ryan looked rakish even in dress blues. Maybe it was his off-center mouth and inverted crescent eyes that always seemed to be smiling. He had a wide, high brow, wayward hair, no earlobes. His ears were set so close to his head it gave him a feral look.

Director Benet advanced on Ryan and demanded, "Why is there a ship of death on my roof?"

Commander Ryan said, as if it were obvious, "This world is under extraplanetary attack."

"Mrs. Hamilton's mythical attack ships?" Benet said, dripping contempt. His eyes raked the XO up and down, taking in the commander's braid on his cuffs and shoulder boards.

Izrael Benet was an imposing, forceful man. He was not accustomed to facing down so many men taller, bigger, more forceful than he. Even the women Marines looked like attack dogs. Still, Director Izrael Benet had his position of superior authority.

"You planted those spaceships here to give you a pretext to come to Zoe. There are no extraplanetaries here!"

Commander Ryan's wolf-brown eyes flicked skyward. "Not upstairs," he agreed. "Not anymore, thank you very much."

Izrael Benet didn't understand, but he wouldn't touch the bait. He played his ace. "In peacetime the League of Earth Nations has jurisdiction over any Earth presence in a LEN protectorate. Since you are here, your ship of war will accept the LEN flag."

"I'm not giving odds on that happening," said Commander Ryan. "Where is Glenn Hamilton?"

"I want green armbands on all these people," said Director Benet. "Now."

"Glenn Hamilton?" Commander Ryan repeated.

"They were contaminating the environment," said Benet.

With the kind of stillness that falls just before you need to run to the cellar, Commander Ryan asked, "Where are Dr. and Lieutenant Hamilton?"

"We had to confine them," said Director Benet.

Colonel Steele had his sidearm out in an instant. His Marines followed his lead.

Most of the civilian expedition members had never been in the presence of drawn weapons. They flinched, moaned, froze, backed away toward cover.

Commander Ryan said, "Right, then. Who's going to show me where my officers are?"

A xeno came running, shied at all the drawn splinter guns. He hissed at the expedition director, "Izzy! They escaped!"

"They—?" Benet started.

Commander Ryan asked, deadly gentle, "Escaped from what?" He guessed *they* were Glenn and Patrick Hamilton.

Steele gave a hand signal. Weapons cocked in brute unison.

Benet bellowed to everyone cringing around him, "Stand

your ground! They are not going to open fire on unarmed civilians. Who let the prisoners out?"

Benet looked around for a guilty face. It was tough to tell the difference between terror and guilt.

A serene, cultured voice sounded from behind him. "I did."

Director Benet and Commander Ryan turned toward where the racing yacht *Mercedes* sat in the half ring of boxy expedition spaceships.

A slender, dignified figure holding a wineglass advanced from the yacht's open hatch. He presented an elegant silhouette, taut and sleek as the black and tan Doberman bitch at his heels.

Jose Maria de Cordillera.

Behind him, out of the star racer *Mercedes,* stepped Patrick Hamilton and Dr. Aaron Rose, also holding dessert wineglasses. Glenn Hamilton left her glass at the dinner table.

Jose Maria strolled toward the Marines, as if this were a congenial gathering, not a powder keg in a high-ox atmosphere. He visibly took note of Steele's insignia, then nodded a greeting. "Colonel. Congratulations."

TR Steele had been a Lieutenant Colonel when last they met. He was wearing the full bird now.

Steele grunted.

Jose Maria turned to the young man in dress blues with three rows of braid on his cuffs. "Commander." Jose Maria offered his hand. "We have not met. Jose Maria de Cordillera."

"Heard about you, mate." Commander Ryan clasped Jose Maria's hand, gave it a quick strong shake. "Stuart Ryan. Call me Dingo."

Ryan turned his head sharply to Benet and said, "Not you. You call me sir." Ryan looked to Glenn and Patrick. "You right?"

Glenn nodded. "Sir."

Steele gave a silent signal. Weapons audibly uncocked.

Benet's glance moved sharply from Colonel Steele to Commander Ryan. He demanded, "Who is in charge here? You or you?"

"Not *you*, mate," said Dingo.

Benet flung an arm wide at the surrounding Marines. "Get them out of here. Get them out, get them out. No! You are not doing that!" Benet pointed at two Marines who were belting protective personal fields onto Patrick and Glenn.

"They're leaving!" said Benet. "You're all leaving." He stalked around the Marines, arms waving as if shooing geese. "Go! Go!"

Then he marched up into Steele's face, "Move!"

Steele might have been guarding Buckingham Palace for all he reacted.

Glenn spoke softly so Benet would have to stop shouting to hear her. "Dr. Benet. These men aren't hostile. This action is defensive only. Whether you accept it or not, this planet is under invasion."

"Oh, I admit we are under invasion," said Benet. "*From you!*"

"We are not the only space invaders in town," Glenn said evenly.

Benet made a show of perfect stunned outrage, his eyes round. "You dare call *us* invaders?"

Glenn threw a pointing hand out to her right. "I was talking about *those*."

At the camp perimeter, in the growing darkness, they were just visible. Eyes. Many eyes, in sets of three, craning on their stalks.

Those did not belong here.

Director Benet stared back. His mouth fell open. "Oh, bugger."

21

ON FIRST SEEING THE ALIENS at the streamside in the highlands, Glenn and Patrick had run straight back to the meadow to warn the foxes. They'd found the foxes already sniffing the air for themselves, their hackles raised, their muzzles wrinkled up at the stink, their tails bottlebrush stiff. They turned questioning eyes to Patrick.

Patrick clenched his fist before his mouth, as if closing his muzzle shut, which in fox sign-speak meant, sensibly enough, shut your muzzle and be quiet.

Patrick hummed to them. All ears pricked up and forward, intent.

Then the foxes melted away through the underbrush and disappeared into the forest, away from the stream.

Glenn had asked, "What did you say to them?"

"I said, 'Smelly black thorn bushes crossed the river. Ugly ugly. Bad bad. Go.'"

What they had seen there was here now.

Just beyond the dirt perimeter, at the periphery of the camp's minimal lights, the aliens stared.

They looked like rotten sponges perched on spindly tree roots.

They were muddy black. Each had three eyes, each eye set on a mobile eye stalk. One eye extended from the being's putative chest, another extended from its midback, and the third eye attached like a very skinny off-center neck from the top of the thing's flat, flexible slab of a spongy torso.

Positioned next to the top eyestalk was an orifice that opened and shut. One could guess it was a mouth because the aliens had no discrete heads.

Two multijointed arms attached at the top corners of the alien torsos where arms ought to connect. Thin wiry strands of hair at the corners made the creatures look as if they were fraying at the edges.

The aliens couldn't be said to have hands because they had no palms. Their arms terminated directly into fingers. Two digits extended from the end of one arm, three digits from the other arm, and all of the digits looked opposable.

Three multijointed legs were set tripodally at the bottom of the alien torsos. Glenn and Patrick hadn't gotten a look at their feet the first time, but they had seen three-toed tracks, the toes splayed at 120 degrees from one another. The tracks ran all along the streamside.

The closest person to the camp perimeter turned around to face the watchers in the forest. She was a Marine. Flight Sergeant Kerry Blue.

Kerry said, "Oh. Hello, ugly. You must be the space invaders."

Three projectiles bounced off Kerry Blue's PF with a clatter and ricochet zing. Kerry dropped to the dirt, hands to her head.

In a moment, alive and in full voice, Kerry shouted, "Who's shooting?"

With a snakestrike flick of a spindly alien arm, two more projectiles came at Cain Salvador's face and bounced off of his personal field. Cain blinked.

"Nails," he said. "They're throwing their fingernails."

The alien had thrown its nails with so much force that the Marine's personal field deflected them. The creature had flicked first its three-fingered arm at Kerry, then its two-fingered arm at Cain. Its fingers moved now like a spider, nailless.

Asante Addai moved in closer, head down, squinting between the trees. Night was falling. "Fark! They *are* ugly."

Carly Delgado picked up one of the projectiles that struck Kerry's PF. She dropped it. "And they stink like nothing on Earth."

Asante's face wrinkled against the stench as he tried to talk without breathing. "Gug. Is that them?"

The alien flipped over into a handstand, its three legs in the air. Asante jerked back. "Ho! Look at that!"

The three legs flicked. Asante flinched, blinked, as a barrage of toenails from all three legs bounced off his personal field right before his face.

"They're throwing their toenails!"

Several quick movements showed between the trees in the darkening forest, like flicking twigs. A rain of nails came flying out toward the camp.

Dak Shepard, standing farther back, where the thrown projectiles began to lose velocity, got a smattering of nails moving slowly enough to pass through his PF. Yelled, "Hey!"

Kerry Blue picked up a nail that had bounced off her energy field. She held it up for Colonel Steele to see. "Sir?" she asked, like a dog waiting for permission to bite.

A LEN xeno ran between the Marines and aliens, waving his hands. "No! No violence!"

Asante spoke, cross. "No. Hey. They started it, *frer*."

The man was the expedition's xenosociologist, Helmut Roodoverhemd. "They feel threatened by us! We are strangers on their world!"

"It's not their world," Patrick called from a safe distance. He made sure his PF was energized just the same. "Those things are every bit as Zoen as I am."

"They are strangers here. They have come to study—as have we. Don't hurt them," Roodoverhemd implored. He turned and moved slowly into the forest to say hello to the visitors.

"Watch it," Patrick warned. "They take specimens."

When Patrick and Glenn had first seen the aliens, the aliens were grabbing small animals, squeezing them dead and shoving them into bags at the streamside.

The aliens here were carrying their bags now, but these bags were empty.

"It's easy to love what is beautiful," said Roodoverhemd. "We are strangers to them. They are intelligent. They crossed the stars. They must be made to know we mean them no harm."

Roodoverhemd seemed to have—as so many xenos had—a professional self-loathing that drove them starward, far away from their own kind, to commune with things better, purer, more natural than themselves.

Dr. Roodoverhemd approached the strangers. He held his arms up in imitation of the contorted way the aliens held their multiply articulated arms.

Jose Maria cautioned from a distance, "I would not."

His dog leaned into Jose Maria's legs, standing between her master and the aliens, trying to herd him backward. She barked toward the forest.

"Would not what? Try to communicate? They're not viruses, *Don* Cordillera," Roodoverhemd called back. His gaze remained fixed on one of the aliens, trying to hold its three-eyed gaze. "If they are spacefaring, then they are civilized."

But even Director Izrael Benet, looking like a man slapped suddenly sober, said, "Take a shield, Helmut."

Benet offered the xenosociologist one of the lightweight mesh shields made of clear woven polymer that were stacked at camp's edge. Roodoverhemd refused the offered shield, offended. "What kind of message does that send?"

Sticklike arms flicked, too quick to see. Fingernails hit like bullets. Roodoverhemd jerked around in the air, twisted. Fell.

Colonel Steele bellowed, "Man down! Man down! Fire at will."

"Aye, aye, sir!"

Marines opened fire into the trees. Tags and splinters tore through the foliage. Nothing cried out in pain.

The xenosociologist, lying on the ground with three deep wounds, was not bleeding. He looked pretty damned dead, but you don't ever assume.

Against the barrage of splinters, a mass of the stilted things advanced and converged on the body. Spongy-bodied, stick-armed figures bore the dead xeno up.

Patrick cried, "They bagged Helmut!"

Surviving aliens—and there were way too many of them for the number of shots fired—spirited the body away at a lurching gallop into the forest depths.

Watching from under the camp lights, Patrick muttered, "I warned him they take specimens. Did he think they were going to ask him to pee in a cup?"

Steele thundered, "Get that man."

Cain shouted, "Sir! Either we are really bad shots, or the splinters are passing straight through the targets!"

Steele roared, "Hand to hand then! I want that man!" And he charged forward to lead the pursuit into the alien woods.

Staying behind in the LEN camp, Commander Ryan took a hail from *Merrimack*, which would be able to detect the shooting from orbit. Calli's voice sounded over his com, "Commander, what is your situation?"

"Hell, sir. We have a right regular old cluster down here."

Into the woods. Dark.

Kerry Blue's night vision switched itself on. Heard other Marines baying like bull mastiffs. The aliens didn't yell. Of the aliens she heard only the thrash of leaves and snap of twigs. There was also a squeak of something she almost stepped on.

She caught glimpses of the aliens' tottering gallop and their handsprings.

Her splinter gun was turning out to be no good against those spindly, quick, dark targets. She wasn't allowed to bring a beam weapon into the oxygen-rich air. Damn that.

Unless she struck a hard part of the alien, and there didn't seem to be too many of those, her splinter shots were passing clean through.

The aliens jumped like spiders. Big spiders. Anyone who had been in the Hive conflict reflexively reached for a sword. She reached more than once.

Saw one alien spring end over end like a bad gymnast.

The things were torqing her off. Made her feel inept. Her protective field buzzed. One of those things had nailed her PF again. She screeched. "I want my sword back!"

Twitch Fuentes and the other guys had the right idea — run in and tackle the bastards. Just grab a leg or three, swing 'em up and beat them to death against a tree. Make sure they spent their nails first though.

Cain yelled, "Grab 'em! Just grab 'em. Watch your eyes!"

Weightlifting was not Kerry's strong suit. But she could still tackle these things and twist them till something crunched.

She launched herself at one. It squished under her like a sponge, its stick legs and arms still flailing. She tried to crank its joints the way they didn't go, but they went every which way. The fummers had ball joints. Lots of them.

She bashed them with a rock.

Be careful of your eyes, Cain had said. Kerry's eyes were fine, except they were watering from the stench.

Dak got hold of two of the squigs that were part of the mob carrying the LEN guy away. He yanked them back and knotted their squiggy limbs together. "Yeah! You! Gretta! Like that? Now I'm gonna stomp on your heads!"

Dak turned them over and over. Yelped, "Where's its fragging head!"

"What? You lost it?" That sounded like Dickus Maximus.

"It don't got a head! Where's the head!"

Voices in the dark. "Head's gotta be in the body."

"You mean they have their heart in their mouth?"

"No. Their head up their ass."

"Look at this thing! I don't even wanna know what *that* is."

The aliens weren't wearing anything like clothing. They looked like stick toys assembled by an unwell mind.

They did have eyes in the back of their heads. No. That wasn't right. They had one eye behind them but not exactly in the back of the heads. They didn't have heads, not apart from the body. They were like gorgons that way—everything in one bag. Except it wasn't a bag. More like a sandwich of really coarse, soggy black bread. And they had fewer legs. A lot fewer legs and only one mouth. Kerry thought that was a mouth, up there next to its top eye.

Twitch had caught up with the crew carrying the dead xeno. He got a tree branch, hollered bloody murder, and wielded his branch like a shillelagh, beating the aliens away from Roodoverhemd's body. Twitch called for help. "*Ayúdame!*"

Kerry and everyone else ran in to help him. Forgot about trying to shoot anything. Just glom them with anything you could grab. Rock. Tree limb. Another alien.

"Colonel! We got him!"

Steele called everyone to fall back.

Twitch, Dak, Asante, and Rhino hefted up the xeno's body onto their shoulders to bear it back to camp. Roodoverhemd wasn't that huge, but gravity was strong here. Kerry walked backward behind the bearers as rear guard, brandishing a log against any chasers.

Carly carried an alien arm she'd carved off. "Anyone want this?"

Cain glanced her way. "Bring it."

The Marines returned to the LEN encampment, four of them carrying the civilian Roodoverhemd. The xeno was thoroughly dead.

Steele saw Kerry Blue with them. He died every time she went into action.

She's a Marine. You can't shelter her. Best he could do was surround her with veterans. Cain. Twitch and Carly. Dak. Geneva. Asante.

Steele walked up to Director Benet. Spoke in a quiet raspy growl. "We don't leave a man. Not even yours."

Then he glanced over his Marines. "Blue, you take a hit?"

Kerry wiped scratches on her brow. She hadn't known or cared that she was bleeding. "No, sir," she said. "Thorns."

The two camp medical doctors took custody of the dead man. A lift hovered the body to the medical hut.

Kerry moved over close to Commander Ryan. Everyone called him Dingo, so it seemed safe to ask him, "Sir? I thought these guys were all kinds of smart?" She meant the LEN scientists.

Commander Ryan hesitated. He said carefully, "They are highly educated people."

"Yeah? Well there's more common sense in a bucket of doorknobs."

Dingo swallowed down a smile. He placed silencing finger to his lips to say be quiet. A man was dead. This was not the time to say anything.

Flight Leader Cain Salvador presented himself to Colonel Steele. Cain's chest heaved with big breaths. He mumbled to himself first, a comment, "Really like this atmosphere." Then he said to the colonel, "There's not much substance to the sponge things. Splinters mostly pass right through them. Sir, I am *not* that bad a shot, but we detonated a lot of dirt. We're carrying the wrong weapons."

Steele nodded. He'd done the same.

They were all becoming aware that Flight Sergeant Asante Addai reeked. More than the rest of them. Asante had stepped into some foul-smelling mud. Afraid it wasn't mud.

A young corn-fed looking she-xeno assured him, "That is what you think it is. And those?" She pointed at moving strings in the mud on Asante's left boot. "Those are worms."

Asante went running back to the woods to find something to scrape off the crap. "Why me!"

"It's usually me!" Kerry called after him. She hiked a pant leg, checking for worms.

Commander Ryan took a call on his com from the captain. Calli told him to order the return of Colonel Steele's troops to the ship immediately.

Dingo puzzled. "Sir? We're good down here. Situation under control."

"Not up here it's not," Calli sent. She didn't sound happy. At all.

Dingo read the smug expression on Director Benet's face.

"Damn, Captain," Commander Ryan muttered into his com. "They went over your pretty head, didn't they?"

"Affirmative."

Director Benet announced that the League of Earth Nations itself had issued the order that *Merrimack* must accept the LEN flag or leave the star system. Any persons on the ground must respect the authority of the expedition director.

Izrael Benet announced, "I will not allow hostile aliens on this world."

"You're expelling us as hostile aliens?" Glenn said. "What about those hostile aliens?" She gestured toward the trees. "The ones that killed Dr. Roodoverhemd. They can't stay here!"

Director Benet spoke. "Actually, it is you, Mrs. Hamilton, who cannot stay here. We never had trouble before you arrived. We order you to leave. At once."

"I'll get my gear."

Already the loud bangs of Marines displacing back to ship echoed off the ring of LEN ships.

Night had fallen to full darkness.

Glenn packed her things. She wished she could have seen the foxes one more time. But they were gone, on their way to another, safer meadow far away from ugly ugly bad bad.

Glenn snugged a displacement strap around her assembled stuff. She took a stand on one of the displacement disks and snapped a displacement collar around her neck. She didn't know if Patrick was getting the heave-ho too. She would know soon enough. She could not endure Benet's smug face one more time. She hailed *Merrimack* to displace her aboard.

"Stand by, Lieutenant," the D-tech sent.

There was a pause. Glenn waited.

Again, "Stand by."

A longer pause.

Then, "Stand by, Lieutenant."

A very, very long pause.

22

I T WAS PAST MIDNIGHT, but most of the xenos were still awake, gathered round the fire circle, fearful, mourning the death of their colleague.

Glenn stepped in, took a seat next to her husband on a bench. Patrick's arm fell naturally around her shoulders.

Benet noticed her. His back stiffened, imperious and personally offended. "Why are you not gone?"

"I—" She faltered. This felt worse than she ever could have imagined. "Can't. I've been sacked."

"Oh, you liar."

Glenn blinked. A lot of people blinked.

"I beg your pardon," Glenn said.

Director Benet stood up. He went to his office hut and got on the com. Everyone could hear him yelling. Calling down the LEN authorities. Promising reprisals. Demanded the captain of the *Merrimack* remove Glenn Hamilton from the planet.

Captain Carmel advised Director Benet, "Glenn Hamilton has lost her commission. She is not an officer of this ship or of this Navy. This is a space battleship. No one has authority to order a Naval vessel to take civilians on board except under an SOS. A LEN vessel brought Glenn Hamilton to Zoe. She may leave the way she came."

* * *

Kerry Blue was bottled up in quarantine with the other returning ground troops in the Displacement department on

Merrimack, waiting her turn to pass through decontamination. They were going through one by one. Returning troops never had to go through this before. *Merrimack* wasn't equipped for it in numbers.

Kerry Blue sat cross-legged on the deck and played poker.

"Your forehead looks nasty, Blue," said Rhino. She tossed her ante into the pot. They were playing with potato chips.

"Does it?" Kerry tossed in her ante. "Stings."

"Looks like an infection," said the Yurg, dealing.

"Can't be," said Kerry. "MO told me I can't catch alien diseases."

"These aliens have DNA," said Asante. "Who dealt this crap?"

"DNA?" said Rhino. "Honestly?"

"What does that mean?" said Kerry.

"Means we can catch diseases," said the Yurg. "That's why we're stuck in here playing these awful cards. Asante, did you shuffle?"

Asante said, "Blue, are you in or you out?"

Kerry wasn't looking at her cards. "I have an *infection?* Does this mean I can't sleep with anyone?"

"What do you care?" said Rhino. "Who you been sleeping with?"

"Nobody," said Kerry Blue. Threw down her cards. "I'm out."

Captain Carmel had *Merrimack*'s own xenoscientists analyzing the wreckage of the alien orb that had slammed into *Merrimack*. They found the spherical hull packed solid with equipment. There was no compartment that might have housed any kind of pilot. The xenos had harbored a lingering fear that they would break the spacecraft open and find an intelligent ant colony inside. A dead intelligent ant colony.

But all was well. The orb had been operating from an internal program. Its guts were splayed across the xenos' work space.

Weng and Ski were as happy as a couple of xenogeneralists hip deep in xen.

"Gentlemen," said Calli Carmel surveying the whole of the disassembled alien craft, "What is it?"

Ski stammered. Dr. Sidowski had trouble putting words together around Captain Carmel. She was very pretty.

"Can tell you what it's not, sir," said Weng.

"And it's not . . . ?" Calli waited for the blank to fill in.

"Roman," said Weng.

"Terrestrial," said Ski.

"Local," said Weng.

"Do we have an age on these vessels?" Calli asked.

"No, sir," said Weng.

"Not yet," said Ski.

"I want to know who is driving these spaceships and from where. I need you to give me an idea when they were manufactured and how long they've been here. Then trace them back to their planet of origin."

She already knew that the orbs' control system was a program of an unknown operating system. She had sent that part to the cryptotech Qord Johnson.

Calli asked her xenogeneralists, "Are the orbs connected to the extraplanetary aliens my Marines met on planet?"

"Likely," said Ski.

"Definitely," said Weng.

When Weng and Ski said the same thing, you had to believe them.

"How so sure?" Calli asked.

"They signed their work." Weng held up a curved piece of the orb's hull. On it was etched the outline of a three-toed—or fingered—appendage.

Flight Sergeant Delgado had brought the xenos a severed alien appendage. It didn't have any nails on it because the creature had thrown its full arsenal before it got severed. But when Ski and Weng reattached the nails, the handprint matched the pattern on the orb.

The alien arm, which looked exactly like an alien leg, was multijointed. "The skeleton is not bone," said Weng.

"Which is to say it's not calcium," said Ski.

"They are not native to Zoe," said Weng.

"You're sure?" said Calli.

"These creatures aren't DNA-based," said Ski.

"And everything else from the planet *is*," said Weng.

"What's the biochemistry of this?" Calli pointed a long finger at the alien arm.

"It's a new one to us," said Ski.

"Organic," said Weng.

"Which is to say carbon-based," said Ski.

"But these are built with a whole different box of biological blocks," said Weng.

"Not entirely different," said Ski. "The amino acids are at least left-handed," said Ski. "As are ours."

"Our amino acids are left-handed," Weng clarified. "Not our actual hands."

"This has some amino acids I've never seen before," said Ski.

"We don't have a live specimen," said Weng. An implicit request that. He sounded hopeful.

"You're not going to get one," said Calli. "These things are intelligent. So the LEN would call that kidnapping."

"Which is in stark contrast to locking up Naval officers," said Weng. He'd heard about the Hamster and her man.

"Apparently," said Calli.

"Then can we get a dead one of these?" Ski asked. He picked up the appendage. "A whole one?"

Calli made a motion with her head that said maybe. "Colonel Steele's dogs were not gentle when they retrieved the scientist's body."

The aliens had not been as devout as Marines about retrieving their own fallen comrades. The alien bodies were probably still in the woods where they dropped. And since their amino acids were different from Zoen natives, it was possible the local scavengers hadn't cleaned them up already.

Captain Carmel hailed the command deck. "Mister Ryan, do we still have swords in the armory?"

✳ ✳ ✳

The next evening, a group of xenos from the LEN expedition ventured into the forest in a phalanx, carrying polymer shields, in hopes of opening a dialog with the aliens.

Instead they collected a large sample of finger and toenails in their shields' meshwork. Dr. Maarstan took a nail in the foot. The others had to carry him back to camp. They brought along a struggling "guest." It had no finger or toe-nails.

No projectiles chased the xenos on their retreat back to camp. The other creatures had abandoned their comrade to his fate, or else they had shot themselves empty.

There was no fast reload when you had to grow your own bullets.

The LEN "detained" the one creature, which was a polite word for taking it prisoner. "Not thuggish at all," said Glenn.

"You would say that," said Director Benet. "And I admit it. The action is thuggish, but we have no intention of hurting the being. It will be released immediately we have talked to it." The LEN needed to impress on the being the humans' peaceful intent and willingness to communicate.

They restrained their guest by its five appendages. They spoke soothingly, but the being would not be calmed. The humans didn't know how to safely tranq it.

The alien showed no interest in communicating. It vomited and shat on them. Now it was just writhing, its spongy sides heaving, the orifice on its shoulder moving, no sounds but gurgling and hissing coming out.

It didn't have a skin. All terrestrial life, down to the single-celled organisms, had a container, a sac, a membrane, a skin. This didn't. The oblong body was two sponges that might be lungs, in between which other ersatz organs were strung. The jointed arms and legs were stranded with sinew and chitinous ball-jointed bone.

Director Benet enlisted the expedition's resident linguist, Dr. Patrick Hamilton, to tell him what the alien was saying. "Please come communicate with it."

"No," said Patrick.

"Let me rephrase," said Benet. "Come communicate with it."

Patrick balked, loathing. "I am working on foxes and mammoths. I came here to work with fox languages. I don't have any interest in those toadstools—and by that I don't mean to call them funguses. I mean to call them the stuff that comes out of a toad."

"You are here for what the LEN needs you for, Dr. Hamilton. Tell me what this being is saying?" said Benet, as if Patrick could pull a magic translator out of his ear.

Patrick walked to the hut where the thing was held captive. Because the aliens only came out in the dark, the xenos kept the hut darkened.

The alien made no noise that might be speech, though its mouth was wide open. Its shoulder eye strained on its stalk.

Patrick gave a huff. "Okay. I think I can help you out on this one, Izzy. Nearest I can translate what this thing is saying is '*AAAAAAHHHHHHHHHHH!*'"

When the thing yanked its own arm off, there was no choice but to let it go. Upon release the alien threw rocks at the humans and scrambled in perfect terror back into the forest.

"Thank you for all the effort you put into that translation," Benet said.

"It's probably not talking at all," Patrick said.

Benet scowled. "How can you possibly imagine that spacefaring beings do not talk?"

Patrick shrugged. "Maybe because they don't have ears."

Patrick got on the com to consult with the xenogeneralists on board *Merrimack*. He had to make sure he wasn't lying when he told the director that the aliens didn't have ears. "Do they really not have ears?"

Weng answered, "Nope."

Patrick hesitated. "Nope, they don't really not have ears?"

"They have no ears," said Weng.

"That fits," said Patrick. "They have mouths but they still can't scream."

Ski said, "The clokes have no external orifice designed to pick up vibrations in the atmosphere. Doesn't mean they can't feel vibrations through solid objects same as you and I."

Weng: "But we haven't confirmed that part."

Ski: "They don't have any skin."

Weng: "Never seen anything like them."

Ski: "No external membrane. No exoskeleton."

The xenos sounded excited.

Weng: "The rigid structures in their appendages are fibrous alien proteins, similar to chitin."

Ski: "We're pretty sure they can regrow their nails."

Patrick nodded. "Yeah. They're probably reloading even as we speak."

Weng: "That would require nourishment. We don't know what clokes eat."

"Clokes?" Patrick echoed.

Weng: "That's what the Marines are calling the extra-planetaries. Cloke. It's short for cloaca."

Patrick said, "I thought cloaca was a Roman swear word."

Ski made a sound of half agreeing. "It's a Roman vulgarity. It means latrine. But it's also a scientific term. The aliens are monotremes."

Patrick rummaged his memory for that term. Came up with something that couldn't be right, "They're platypuses?"

Ski said, "So you know what a monotreme is?"

"Not exactly." Linguist though Patrick was, monotreme was not a word he ever used. "I think it was something I was supposed to know in fifth grade. A platypus and a spiny something-or-other that lays eggs are the only two of whatever a monotreme is. It means egg layer?" He took a guess. "No wait. Mono means they have only one of something. And it can't be the duckbill because the spiny thing has a long nose. It means they only lay one egg? No. I give up. I don't know. I wasn't that jazzed on biology in the fifth grade. But I'm guessing now that it's something biological you wouldn't want to go into detail about with a bunch of fifth-grade boys."

"You bet your eighth planet," said Weng.

"Monotremes have one anus?" Patrick guessed.

Ski said, "You're getting very close. Monotreme means 'one hole.' All elimination and reproductive functions use one hole."

"*All* functions?" said Patrick.

"All."

"Out *and* in?" Patrick asked.

"Yes, sir."

"That would have been marvelously gross to know in the fifth grade," said Patrick.

"It still is marvelously gross among your Fleet Marines," Ski said dryly.

The Marines were a young group. They lived hard, fought hard, laughed loud. Patrick supposed the Marines would have fun with that bit of knowledge.

Weng said, "The technical term for the multipurpose hole is cloaca. So your Marines are calling the aliens clokes."

"So are we," said Ski.

Patrick had no objection. "I guess for insults that beats asshole all to hell."

* * *

Weng and Ski finally had an approximate age of the alien orb for Captain Carmel.

"One hundred years," said Weng.

"Give or take some," said Ski.

"Durable," Calli commented.

Weng: "Very. If they weren't hostile, I'd think about buying their stuff."

Calli asked, "Why didn't they exhaust their fuel in all that time?"

Ski: "That's the beauty of using the most common element in the universe as your fuel."

"Do we know where they're coming from?" Calli asked.

Weng: "No."

Ski: "They're using a sublight powerplant. Wherever they came from has to be in walking distance."

Walkers or *crawlers* were terms for sublight vessels.

There were no hospitable worlds within a hundred light-years of Zoe. There was a reason this region of the galaxy was called the Outback.

Weng: "The orbs could have been manufactured in transit on a mobile platform."

Ski: "That opens up their outer limit to, well, anywhere."

Weng: "The LEN expedition has been here for seven years. LEN ships have been coming and going for seven years. It took seven years for orbs to intercept an intruding ship. We don't know how they knew there was something here to intercept."

"Are we looking too far?" Calli suggested. "Did the clokes come from another planet in this system? They almost have to, don't they?"

Ski went mute. He could not tell his beautiful captain how wrong she was.

Weng: "There's no other planet in the habitation zone. No manufacturing facilities on any of them. No sign that any of the other planets ever supported life. And I know you're going to ask, we did look at the moons. That there is a pretty cloud of ammonia around the moons."

"I have another question for you," said Calli. "How did the clokes get onto the planet?"

"Good question," said Ski.

Weng agreed. "Clokes can compress pretty small, but we *know* they didn't fit inside a space vessel with no oxygen, no heat, no water, and no food. These orbs don't have landing capability."

Ski hedged. "Well."

Weng: "Fine. They have the landing capability of asteroids."

Ski: "We've found no evidence of FTL capability, except for the obvious fact that they are here."

"Wormholes?" Calli offered.

"No wormholes out here," said Weng.

"We looked," said Ski.

"Collapsed wormholes?" Calli revised.

"Then we wouldn't know about them," said Weng.

"And we can never know," said Ski.

"How else could they get here?" Calli asked.

"A very slow boat," said Weng.

"Well, that's it then," said Calli. "There has to be a carrier."

Captain Carmel set Tactical to searching for something large. *Large* was a relative term. Looking for anything in space was searching for one specific microbe in an ocean.

Within the hour, Tactical sang out, "Occultation. Forty-five by twelve by nine."

The Targeting specialist checked the plot. "I have it.

It's—" he turned around to look at Captain Carmel. "It's *round*, sir."

A chill tension gripped the command deck.

Guardedly, Calli requested, "Mister Vincent, what do you have?"

Tactical reported, "Plot is large. Moving too fast to be natural and too big to be a LEN golf ball."

Calli asked the immediate question, "Is it Hive?"

The Hives were dead. No one ever wanted to face those monsters again.

"Can't tell. If it *is* a Hive sphere, it's a magnitude eight."

There was never a magnitude eight Hive sphere. There was never even a seven.

Targeting added, "Diameter of target is seven hundred kilometers."

Calli felt the nerves of every man jack and jane on deck sparking. The air felt explosive.

Captain Carmel ordered in the voice of perfect calm, "Confirm Hive." Then thought to add, "Do *not* ping."

If the target really was a Hive sphere, bouncing anything off it would wake up a billion cubic kilometers of ravenous aliens.

Targeting asked, "Can I get a parallax, sir?"

Calli responded quickly. "Helm."

"Helm. Aye."

"Take us out a few light-minutes."

"Speed, sir?"

"I don't want to walk."

Merrimack left orbit and jumped to FTL for a moment then jumped back down to space normal to give the ship's instruments another angle on the plot.

Fear instantly vanished from Tactical and Tracking.

"We were looking at the plot on end, sir," said Tactical.

Targeting added, "Target is a cylinder."

Not Hive. All hands stepped down from alarm.

"Take us back to Zoe," Calli ordered the Helm.

"Aye, aye, sir."

"Mister Vincent. Tell me about my plot," said Calli.

"It's rotating," said Marcander Vincent.

That would suggest a habitable vessel, using centripetal force for artificial gravity.

"Size?"

"Can't get an exact dimension on the length. It's a whole lot longer than it is wide."

"Is it as big as Caesar's ego?"

"Not that big, sir. It's only the size of a minor continent."

Targeting advised, "Captain, I don't think that's your carrier."

"It's big enough to be a generational ship," said Calli. "ETA?"

"Never, sir," said Targeting. "The vessel is moving *away* from the planet. If its destination was ever Zoe, it missed."

"Distance," Calli demanded.

"Five light-years."

"Did it pass through the Zoen system? How close?"

Targeting and Tactical were both shaking their heads. "Current vector is not informative," said Targeting. "Assuming no course correction, target did not enter the star system."

"Then assume a course correction," said Calli.

Marcander Vincent said, "Then—assuming constant current velocity—it could have been here five hundred years ago."

"Can't make that assumption," said Calli. "Target could have changed speed and direction since then."

The XO, Stuart Ryan, spoke up, "You're thinking that carrier dropped off Captain Bligh and the orbs?"

Targeting spoke, "If that's the case, sir, then they used to be traveling faster than they are now."

Calli had gone quiet. Dingo Ryan prompted, "What are you thinking, Captain?"

"The continental ship is moving *away* from the planet. I don't know how much of our resources I want to commit to chasing down old news," Calli said.

The XO offered, "I can organize a couple rovers to reconnoiter the continental ship."

Drone scouts were a minimal investment of resources.

Calli nodded. "Let's do that."

The drones had barely disappeared into FTL when a new ship popped into existence inside the Zoen system.

Tactical's first thought was that drones had bounced back.

But this was a new plot arriving hot and slowing abruptly on approach to Zoe.

Tac reported, "Occultation four by eighty-nine by ten."

"Friend or foe," asked Captain Carmel.

"Negative IFF, and it's a bloody Xerxes! Foe! Foe! Foe!" Marcander Vincent turned around at his station to look at her. "It's The Ninth Circle. They're here!"

23

"**S**ECURE XERXES!" Captain Carmel ordered.
"Lost him!" said Targeting.
"We only had him for three seconds when he sublighted," Tactical said. "He's gone to stealth now."

"Find him," said Calli. "Assume he will try to enter the atmosphere. You'll get three more seconds. Mister Ryan, scramble everything."

The XO got on the loud com: "Battle stations. Pilots to Swifts. Scramble. Scramble."

The summons to stations caught Kerry Blue playing basketball in the maintenance hangar. She hadn't far to run to get to her Swift. She was sticky, sweaty, and thirsty. Her flight suit clung to her skin as she dragged it on. She climbed up to the cockpit speaking every foreign word she knew.

Her erk tossed a water bottle up to her as she was strapping into the cockpit. Loved that guy.

Kerry snapped on her dog collar. Made sure her landing disk was under her ass. Got the briefing through the speaker inside her helmet.

Target was a pirate Xerxes. Target was operating at full stealth. Target would be visible for seconds while attempting entry into atmo. Objective: space the pirate. Do not fire in the direction of the planet. A skimming shot along the horizon was required. Spread out.

The elevator jerked upward. Kerry was never ready for it.

Bit her tongue. "Aw, c'mon, you'd think!" She rode her Swift up to the flight deck.

TR was going out with them. She heard him on the com: "*Merrimack*. This is Wing Leader. Confirm order, we are not trying to retrieve the Xerxes intact."

Voice of the captain herself: "Do not preserve the Xerxes. I'm only interested in dead pirates."

Kerry joined in the round of barking. That was an 89th Bat cheer for the captain.

And Kerry Blue's Swift went screaming off the flight deck with her squadron.

She watched her sensors interpreting data into visual images on her monitors. When the pirate showed up, it would be on her instruments. She could guarantee it wouldn't be a visual. The watch zone was immense.

Traveling through space, she always forgot how funormous planets were.

An advisory was coming over the com. Target will be harder to tag, harder to crack than usual. And Control reminded everyone—Wing, Battery, ship's gunners—no stray shots in the atmo.

TR's voice sounded over the com. Damn, his voice never failed to wake her up, heels to eyelashes. "Wing. This is Wing Leader. Stay low to the air. The only place target will appear is breaching outer atmo."

"Wing Leader. This is Alpha One. What are we calling the top of the atmosphere?"

The line between space and atmosphere was enormously wide and about as fuzzy as lines ever got.

Control answered that one. "Wing. This is *Merrimack*. Set your minimum altitude at four hundred klicks above sea level."

"Target sighted!"

Merrimack's targeting system automatically fed the plot to all fighters. Any fighter in the southwest quadrant of the globe pulled the trigger.

"Mine!"

"Mine!"

"Got him! Got him! No, I don't."

"Grettaaaaaaah!"

Kerry Blue hadn't even got off a tag. "Where'd he go? Did someone get him?"

"Wing. This is *Merrimack*. Target has jumped to FTL. Stay alert. He will make another attempt."

Captain Carmel turned around on the command deck. "Tactical, talk to me."

"Target is a real bastard to detect, sir," said Marcander Vincent. "He's scattering even his visual image. If he weren't trying to enter atmo, none of our instruments would be picking him up at all."

"And he's slippery," said Targeting. "Tags are sliding off. Dead shots are deflecting."

"My Marines hit him?" Calli asked, surprised.

"Yes, sir. Yes, they did. No effect."

Calli got on the ship's intracom. "Engineering."

"Engineering, aye."

"Stand by energy hook to catch the wreckage if any starts to drop into atmo."

Engineering: "Gimme wreckage, sir. I'll catch it. Aye."

"*Merrimack* to all ships, all gunners. We have trade."

The Xerxes had made another appearance over the southern pole.

"Mine!" The Yurg, shooting. Shot deflected.

"Mine!" Big Richard got a tag on the target. The tag immediately slithered off.

"Mine!" Menendez fired without getting a tone. Hit nothing.

Icarus Iverson: "Cain! IFF just came on! Says that's a civilian craft!"

Cain: "It's a Xerxes, Icky." Of course it had a civilian ident. "That's the Ninth Bloody Circle! Take the shot!"

Many voices. Sounding on top of one another.

"Where'd he go? Where'd he go?"

"*A dondé va?*"

"Did he get through to atmo?"

"Wing. This is *Merrimack*. Negative escape to atmo. Target is still out here somewhere in full stealth. Keep watch on the atmospheric horizon."

"Watch the horizon. Watch the horizon," Kerry muttered, her send-com off. It was a whole frogging planet. The Swifts might as well be a handful of gnats guarding an elephant.

* * *

Leo, seated at *Bagheera's* control console, wiped sweat from his upper lip. He jerked his fingers back through his dark hair. He had jumped the leopard back to FTL to take a breath. "We have a lot of company."

It had all happened so fast. Leo didn't like his performance back there. That truly snorted squids. But he and his brothers were still alive. That was something.

"How did this place get to be so popular?" asked Pallas, watching the monitor draw lines around the planet where the enemy plots were moving.

The fighters were traveling at sublight speeds. Still, they were a lot faster than bullets and just as easy to see. And their beam shots moved at speed of light. The fighters had converged on *Bagheera* in a heartbeat with a hail of tags and great flashes of beam fire.

The brothers couldn't count them. The ship's system was counting only thirty-seven discrete plots.

"They're good shots," said Leo, feeling as if he'd been physically pummeled. Fortunately, the Xerxes' energy field was everything it was supposed to be.

"They've done this before," said Nox, standing behind him.

"I've done all the simulations," said Leo. "There wasn't anything like this." Ran the back of his hand across his upper lip again.

"That's because the Xerxes is meant to repel pirates, not *be* the pirates," said Nox. "You're doing fine, Leo." Gave his left shoulder a quick squeeze.

Leo replayed the computer record of the encounter, slower and illuminated, to show the brothers what the human eye could not see.

One of the attackers, a small one-man attack craft, crossed the leopard's bow.

"Freeze that," said Nox.

The image froze.

Nox felt cold. "Those are Swifts."

"Significant of what?" Nicanor said testily.

"It's a U.S. Fleet Marine attack craft. That model is carried by only two ships. *Merrimack* and *Monitor*."

All eyes turned upward, as if the brothers might see the space battleship through the overhead.

Caesar *did* mention there might be a space battleship.

"*Merrimack* is here," Nox said.

"Not *Monitor*?" Leo said, puzzled. How would Nox know the ship was one and not the other?

"It's *Merrimack*," Nox said.

"Find her," said Nicanor.

It wasn't hard. One plot was much larger than the other thirty-six. That ship was running dark on the night side of the world. Leo brought the image up on the monitor.

The ship's upper and lower sails and her swept-back wings gave her the aspect of a barbaric spearhead. Her gun turrets swiveled, hunting. Her gun blisters were all open. Six huge engines gave her steroidal bulges. The Stars and Stripes were painted on her hull, alongside her name, *Merrimack*.

"Can we hit her!" said Orissus. "I'd love to take a crack at John Farragut."

Anywhere in the Roman Empire, in almost any pub, you could find a dartboard with John Farragut's face on it. At any shooting range you could get a likeness of John Farragut on your target.

"He's not on board," said Nox.

Faunus said, "*Merrimack* is John Farragut's ship."

"No," said Nox. "Not since war's end. He's got a ground assignment."

"You sure?"

"Trust me. Anyway, you're not hitting *Merrimack* with that box of pencils we're carrying. Caesar wants us on the planet."

"How do we get there?" Leo asked from the helm. "Alive."

"Wait them out?" Galeo suggested. "We're almost safe as long as we stay FTL."

Nox didn't like it. "The longer we wait, the more time they have to figure out a way to get at us. Like Caesar found a way to get at us."

"How did he do that?" asked Nicanor. "Do we know?"

"We don't," said Nox. "All I can guess is he got some kind of tracking code from the Italian government or from the manufacturer."

None of them liked the idea of waiting.

"We have our choice of executioners," said Leo. "There's a whole bunch of little skat. Then there's the space battleship."

"All we need to do is get into the atmosphere before they get a lock on us. Even the Americans won't blow up an antimatter-powered vessel inside the atmosphere," said Nox.

"That's all," said Leo fatalistically. "Piece of cake."

Nox told him, "Keep us in as tight to the atmosphere as you can without losing stealth before we try entry. At least it will take out most of their possible shots. They can't shoot downward."

"Just what makes you think they can't shoot down?"

"Because they're not shooting down," said Nox. "Play back the tactical log again. You'll see. They don't want to shoot at the planet."

Pallas saw what Nox meant. "They're guarding the planet. They don't dare miss."

"Neither do I." Leo slammed the Xerxes back through the light barrier to sublight speed. The transition made the ship instrument-visible for a moment.

That moment brought not just a shower of tags and shots, but converging hostiles.

The Swifts were coming off their positions hugging the planet.

The Xerxes regained its stealth after its transition to sublight, and Leo changed course. Changed course again. He drove the undetectable ship on a jagged path around the world, while the Swifts swarmed toward each of its last sightings.

* * *

"Wing. This is Wing Leader. Do not let yourselves get drawn off the horizon! You will be flanked!"

* * *

Bagheera ran in, unseen, under the Swifts, straight at the planet.

"Too steep! Too steep! Leo, we're too—"
Shit!

* * *

Tactical: "Target sighted! He's entering atmo!"

Targeting: "There he goes. There he goes."

Tracking: "Here he comes! Here he comes!"

"He *bounced!*" Tactical cried, coming out of his seat. "He bounced off the air! Get him! Get him! Get him!"

Merrimack's tracking system automatically sent the Xerxes' loc to the targeting systems of all fighter craft.

The Swifts opened fire.

"Got him got him got him—"

"Tag! You're—"

"Gone."

"*What?*"

* * *

Bagheera escaped with a panic leap to FTL.

Leo bent over his console, breathing hard. Finally spoke. "Screwed that, didn't I?"

"We're still here, *frater*," said Nox. Spilled milk was never on the menu. "Get us ready to sublight again. We know they'll see us. And we know there'll be another barrage of shooting. We can survive that."

"Shoot back," said Orissus.

"To what end?" said Nicanor. "Realistically."

"It could back 'em up," said Orissus.

"No. It will just scatter *our* attention from what we're trying to get done, and it will annoy *them*," said Nicanor.

Nox added, "These hombres and hembras do not back up."

Galeo said, "Sure we don't want to back off and try again later?"

"No. This is it," said Leo. "Get this done. Nox, where do you want me to drive?"

"Snug in close to the battleship," said Nox. "Get right under her."

"We'll be vaporized," said Faunus. "That's the *Merrimack*."

"I know it's the *Merrimack*," said Nox. "She can't see us.

Get us between her and the planet. Tuck up close enough to smell her."

Leo, getting fanciful in the face of death, said, "You can't smell in vacuum."

Leo piloted *Bagheera* into the shadow of the planet where *Merrimack* lurked. The space battleship had her running lights off. The view through the Xerxes' viewports was black.

Only *Bagheera*'s instrument display told the brothers when they passed silent, unseen, underneath *Merrimack*.

"I can smell her," said Nox.
Merrimack will not shoot me.
I think Merrimack will not shoot me.
I hope it's quick if Merrimack shoots me.

* * *

The Swifts fanned out tight to the horizon, watching for the next appearance of the leopard.

"Target sighted," Marcander Vincent reported at the Tactical station. "We're sitting on him!"

Targeting: "He's right here. And we don't have a shot."

Commander Ryan sent: "Wing! This is *Merrimack*. You have the plot. Take him! We are already shielded against enemy fire. Take off your IFF and shoot us if you need to."

Red Dorset, at the ship's com, reared back at his station. "*Hell*-o!"

"Mister Dorset?" said Calli, her patience brittle. "Something more informative."

The com tech gave the captain his astonished report.

Everyone on the command platform except for Targeting stared at Red Dorset.

Heard a lot of words you didn't ever hear out of Captain Carmel.

Beam fire from racing Swifts lanced and deflected underneath the battleship, drawing a star spray pattern across the tactical monitors. Voices shouted over one another on the com.

"Mine!"

"Hit! I got a hit! Didn't do snot."

"Gretta, Gretta, Gretta!"

"I got a tag! Oh, *stick*, damn you!"

"Target is entering atmo."

"He's going stealth."

"He's gone."

"He's not gone!" Kerry Blue cried. "He's leaving a wake. I'm going in!"

The Xerxes had assumed full stealth, but its stealth didn't mask the atmospheric turbulence behind it.

TR Steele: "Alpha Six, you are below minimum altitude."

"But I'm not shooting!" Kerry cried. "I'm getting *under* him."

If she could just maneuver herself under that invisible plot she could knock him back up where the others could finish him off.

TR Steele: "Alpha Flight! This is Wing Leader. Get down there and back up Alpha Six. Wing, stand ready to shoot what she throws at us."

Then it was Dingo's voice on the com. "Wing. This is *Merrimack*. Cease fire. Abort operation. Return to ship."

Kerry Blue's screech carried over the com: "No!"

It was not a refusal. It was disbelief.

"Obey orders, Flight Sergeant." That was the captain's voice that time.

"Aye, aye, sir," said Kerry. She had a whole lot more to say with the com switched off.

It was nothing Captain Carmel hadn't just said for herself.

Captain Carmel ordered, "Continue tracking the Xerxes."

"Lost it, sir," said Tactical.

"You can't have," said Commander Ryan.

"I did, sir," said Marcander Vincent. "And it was easy."

* * *

"We're in!" Leo said, astonished to be in the atmosphere. Relieved to have that damned fighter out from under his keel.

"Can they see us?" Nox demanded, urgent.

"I don't know. I'm driving." Leo was changing direction at quick intervals. "Somebody else look." He flapped a hand toward the systems monitors.

Nicanor checked all the readouts. "Stealth engaged."

"Why are you still worried?" Orissus asked Nox. "You said they wouldn't shoot us in the atmosphere."

"They won't," said Nox. "But they can still hook us and reel us back out to space."

"And then shoot us," said Orissus.

"Yes. Then they would shoot us," said Nox.

Leo changed course again, slowing down so not to leave an unnatural wake in the air. "Can they see us?"

"We'll know in a moment," said Nicanor.

"We should know already," said Nox.

No shots followed them down. No hooks enclosed them. No chase ships appeared on the monitors.

"I think—" Leo paused for luck. "We might—" He looked out the viewports. Looked at his instruments. "Be in the clear."

"We made it?" said Galeo. "Really."

It took a few more course changes before they were sure.

"When that Swift came up under us, I thought we were done," said Faunus.

"We should have shot it," said Orissus.

"Where are we?" said Pallas. "Where are we going?"

Leo called up the coordinates of the LEN encampment. "We want to be here." He tapped the readout. "Now I need to find out where we *are*."

They were in the wrong hemisphere. That was good, because there was snow on the ground here. They'd all had arctic training. Hated it.

Leo piloted them to the summerside of the world and put the ship down six kilometers from the LEN camp.

The LEN camp was where Caesar wanted his non-Roman Roman eyes.

Leo shut down propulsion and artificial gravity. He kept the inertial shield on full. Kept the internal atmospherics on. Kept full stealth engaged. "We're here."

Nox clapped Leo on the back, just below his neck. "We owe thee—I think—our lives."

"Aw—hell, Nox," said Leo, shaky. He leaned back in his chair and let his arms dangle. He exhaled as if draining his lungs. He said, as he suddenly realized, "That was fun."

Galeo punched him in the biceps. Orissus snorted.

Leo got up. "I am going to drink heavily and sleep for a week." He left the control room.

Faunus hooked an elbow over the back of his chair and tilted his saturnine face at Nox. Faunus squinted to see around the red, blue, and yellow scars. Recognition sank in. "I know who you look like."

Nox's head bowed. The teeth and bones and feathers braided into his blond hair hung forward. Nox spoke wearily toward his own feet, "I know exactly who I look like."

※ ※ ※

Merrimack's tracking systems lost their target's last trail in the atmosphere.

Tactical scanned the ground for any sign of the Xerxes. Marcander Vincent muttered, "Nothing, nothing, nothing."

"I'm getting a real appreciation for a Xerxes' stealth capability," said Tracking.

Colonel Steele stalked up to the command deck, still in his flight gear except for the helmet. He appeared in the hatchway, red in the face. Red to his whole head. Angry.

He needed to know why his dogs had been called off the pirates. He was too disciplined to demand an explanation from his commanders. He could only stand here on the command platform fuming and hope he got one. He deserved one.

Captain Carmel noticed him. She didn't ask what he wanted. She said, "There was a reason, Colonel."

Maybe not a good one. But there was a reason.

"Hell-o!"

"Mister Dorset? Something more informative?"

"One of the pirates. He's a Farragut."

"He's a what?"

"He's a glory hallelujah Farragut."

"Can't be a relation to our John Farragut."

"This one's birth name is John Knox Farragut, Junior."

"Imposter. Did the State Department verify that?"

"I didn't get this from the State Department. I got it from a Roman bulletin. Nox Antonius, birth name John Knox Farragut Junior, stripped of Roman citizenship and gens name Antonius along with six others. They're damnati."

Calli had instantly known that the report was real. Farraguts didn't do anything small. John Farragut, Junior had come out of his brother's shadow with a big bang. Junior had *joined the other foxtrotting side!*

Calli was furious that she hadn't heard about it from the State Department or from U.S. Central Intelligence or from Naval Intelligence. She'd had to learn about it through a Roman news source in the middle of battle. An announcement revoking the citizenship of Nox Antonius.

And she'd called off her attack dogs.

The U.S. Space Battleship *Merrimack* would not shoot a John Farragut. This John Farragut was a pirate and should be shot.

But someone else would have to do it.

24

ADMIRAL FARRAGUT'S VOICE sounded confused over the com. "Where's your vid, Cal?"

"I don't want you to see me," said Captain Carmel. "It ain't pretty."

"Cal, I've seen you with your skin off."

Captain Carmel turned her video on.

John Farragut recoiled. "It's too terrible. Turn it off."

Cal gave him a twisted smile.

Captain Carmel was wearing an armband of LEN green. A green flag stood next to Old Glory on *Merrimack*'s command deck. Cal said contritely, "You never let this happen when she was your boat."

"What in creation did I send you into?" said Admiral Farragut.

"It was a righteous call," said Calli. "There are extraplanetaries here. The extraplanetaries are not friendly."

"Then why are you showing a green flag? You can declare martial law if the world is under alien attack."

"That's the snag. The LEN are not denying the extraplanetary presence anymore. But they are denying their hostility."

"The aliens attacked the *Spring Beauty*," Farragut said. "That's a LEN ship. How is that not hostile?"

Calli said, "According to the LEN report of the incident, Hamster crashed the *Spring Beauty*."

"She didn't."

Calli nodded to that. "You can't imagine the depth of denial here."

"What about the hostiles in orbit? What does the LEN say about those?"

"The LEN is right. There aren't any hostiles in orbit," said Calli. "Now."

Admiral Farragut knew what that meant. "How many did you destroy?"

"Buck and half," said Calli. "The only hostiles now are on the ground. And they *are* hostile, but the LEN won't admit it. The clokes even killed a LEN xeno. Doesn't matter."

"Clokes?"

"Don't make me explain that term, John. It's what we're calling the extraplanetaries."

"The LEN took a fatality?"

"The LEN ruled that a misunderstanding. The clokes were 'just protecting themselves.' And we have more hostiles than the clokes. It's why I'm contacting you."

"More hostiles?"

Calli didn't want to speak. She moved into the cryptotech's compartment off the command deck and picked up the call in there, hatch shut. She pushed the words out. "John, do you know where your brother John is?"

The captain emerged from the cryptotech's shack, demanding, "Mister Vincent, where is my pirate ship?"

"Um," said Tactical. "Everywhere."

The Xerxes emitted infinite fractured echoes with no apparent nexus.

Suddenly Marcander Vincent cried out in surprise. "I got him! I got him!"

"The pirate ship?" Calli moved to the Tactical station to see.

"I don't got him." Tactical quickly backpedaled. "It's not a Xerxes. I got something else."

"Exactly what do you have, Mister Vincent?" said Calli, patience thinning. Wondered why she had promised John Farragut she would keep this man on board.

"It's—I think it could be a cloke ship," said Marcander Vincent.

"Say again."

"A cloke ship *wreck* actually." Marcander Vincent

brought up a visual of the target. It had the look of a fuselage, mostly buried, with vegetation grown over it.

"Antimatter containment?" Calli asked.

"No. No radiation either. It's inert," said Marcander Vincent. "Actually, it could even be a Nissen hut for all that."

It couldn't be local make because there were no manufacturing facilities on Zoe.

Commander Ryan agreed, "Cloke ship. Has to be. Would have been launched from our giant unidentified cylinder on a near pass by the star system."

The immense rotating continental ship might be a cloke ship. It might be the carrier that launched the orbs. It might be the carrier that launched this unidentified craft. It might be none of those. It was five light-years away and retreating. Calli said, "Do we have a data feed back from our drones on that carrier yet?"

"Negative," said Commander Ryan. "The drones are barely underway."

"Where is this?" Calli tapped at the image of the shipwreck on the planet.

Computer-enhanced images did suggest a spaceship rather than a metal hut. The images also suggested a harsh landing. "Is it near the LEN camp?"

"No, sir," said Tactical. "This is on another continent."

"Then it didn't bring the clokes," said Dingo. "Not the lot I met anyway."

"Are there any more of these?" Calli asked.

Now that he knew what to look for, Tactical located eleven of the alien craft scattered across the globe. None of them were putting out energy. All of them were more than half buried, and they were completely derelict.

The distribution of the ships was confined between latitudes thirty-seven degrees North and South, except for one ship crashed in the arctic. That one had gone thoroughly wrong and was strewn across kilometers. The aliens' target zone appeared to be the tropics.

"These ships might have been the vanguard," Commander Ryan suggested. "The scouts made it. The mothership didn't,"

Tactical said, "Or maybe the mothership didn't like the scouting report and kept going."

Calli asked, "Are these ships the sources of the low-level radio signals we've been detecting?"

"Negative," said the com tech.

Tactical said, "The shipwrecks are inert."

"Yes, you did tell me that," Calli said, pacing.

Dingo Ryan asked, "Could the radio transmission have to do with our pirates?

"How could they? The pirates just got here," said Calli. Then, "Mister Dorset. Raise the LEN camp."

"Aye, aye, sir," said Red Dorset at the com.

When Director Benet responded at last to *Merrimack*'s hail, Captain Carmel advised him of the presence of pirates on the world. She suggested the director put up a defensive dome over his LEN expedition encampment.

Director Benet refused. "This is a scientific expedition site. I know you're creating a pretext to come back down here. But honestly. *Pirates?*"

"The pirates are real," said Calli.

"And they're not here. Do not unleash your thugs anywhere near here!"

Benet broke the connection.

Man's as mean as a low-level bureaucrat, Calli thought. Said aloud, "I want to get a look at one of those shipwrecks. This one." She pointed at the site of the wreck two hundred and fifty klicks from the LEN expedition camp. "I want to set troops down here without being detected."

"Detected by the LEN or by the pirates?" Commander Ryan asked.

"Either," said Calli. "Both."

"We don't know where the pirates are," said Commander Ryan.

"And I don't want them to know where *we* are. I have to assume they'll be alert for displacement rifts."

Traumatic insertion of matter into an atmosphere was as stealthy as a thunderstorm.

"And Swifts and SPTs and drones don't have stealth capability," she added.

"The pirates don't have a large staff," said Commander Ryan. "We might be able to slip a small craft down. We don't know how vigilant they are."

"Assume they're bloody brilliant," said Calli.

"Then they will know the moment any ship enters atmo," said Commander Ryan.

Colonel Steele had been listening from the rear of the command deck. He answered before he could be asked, "I don't see any way to get Marines down to the target site quietly."

"Neither do I," said Calli. "So we won't be quiet. Colonel Steele, you're going to fall."

The Swifts were going down in a meteor shower.

The boffins measured the optimum point of atmospheric entry and ran the operation through computer simulation five hundred times with varying air currents. The boffins guaranteed touchdown within fifteen klicks of the target, but no closer than two.

They factored in the precise measurements of the Swifts, including their limpet nets.

Because particles physically cannot adhere to a frictionless inertial field, the Swifts' inertial fields were encased in filament nets embedded with fine grains of particulates, which would burn off during descent.

The particulates were chosen to be clean-burning. Nothing incendiary was to survive to touch Zoen ground. The objective was to cloak the falling Swifts in shells of fire without setting a fire on the ground.

"This will make for an interesting view from the cockpit," said the operation engineer at the preflight briefing.

Interesting.

Kerry Blue and the pilots of Red Squadron listened. Interested.

"Your Swifts overheat in atmosphere. Most of you know that firsthand. We're starting you out with your internal temperature low—you and your Swift. It's going to hot up fast," said the briefing officer.

The boffins were calling this landing Operation Fried Ice Cream.

"You will be in free fall the entire descent. Keep your hands off the controls. Your inertials will engage a hard stop at ground level. We have programmed the engagements into your Swifts. Do not switch to a manual operation. No unscheduled mining operations, *Flight Sergeant Blue*."

The boffin raised his voice to make sure Kerry was paying attention.

"Yeah, yeah," Kerry Blue muttered, arms crossed. "Sir."

Bury one Swift one time and they think you're a gopher for life.

Calli waited on the command deck for the drop.

She assumed the LEN and maybe the pirates would see this.

She was hiding her Marines in spectacularly plain sight.

The LEN *might* be able to tell that the meteor shower was not normally falling debris, but only if they had instruments in place specifically looking for such things.

"What about the pirates?" she asked, wanting reassurance.

"The pirates are not going to be able to parse the difference between falling rocks and intact Swifts with sand on their noses," said Dingo Ryan.

"Unless they have a patterner," said Calli.

"They don't," said Dingo.

"Neither do we," said Calli. She remembered Augustus with a shudder. The name was almost an obscenity.

Augustus had been a Roman patterner. He'd been enormously useful, and the most intentionally offensive being ever to tread these decks. The patterner was dead. *Gloria in excelsis Deo.*

The Swift pilots got a marshmallow's eye view of the campfire.

Over the res com Calli could hear Marines going down in flames. The pilots sang-chanted the latest of a long line of songs titled "Fire." Thumping out a jungle beat on their consoles, punctuated with grunts. "Fiiiiii-*yuh*! *UGH!*"

Across the command deck Calli could catch covert toe-tapping and head-bobbing in time.

✳ ✳ ✳

The pirates of The Ninth Circle spent the night locked inside *Bagheera*, parked on the Zoen ground. The Xerxes scattered its passive signals, making the ship effectively invisible. The brothers waited to see if anything descended on them.

The Xerxes' defensive systems watched *Merrimack* and watched for any displacement rifts planetwide. The sensors detected some meteors. There were no ships coming or going from the LEN camp.

In the morning the brothers ventured outside.

The oxygen-rich air was easy to breathe. The gravity felt normal to them.

They belted on personal fields. No PF could protect them against a beam of the strength *Merrimack* could send down. *Merrimack* could drill a hole in the world. So the brothers' survival strategy was not to become a target in the first place. These PFs were equipped with scatter tech. They could elude *Merrimack*'s sensors, giving her nothing to shoot.

The visual scatter tech of a PF was not as perfect as the ship's visual scatter. With the naked eye Nox could still see where his brothers were, though he couldn't tell *what* they were, unless he already knew. They appeared as blurs in the air, like waves of heat over a fire.

The brothers sat down for breakfast outside, near a purple sticky vine that waved in the air, trolling for winged insectoids.

The air smelled summer sweet. Alien sounds like birdcalls were cheery. Crawling insectoids were irritating. The purple vine was doing all right with the flyers.

The brothers, except for Nox, had grown up on an alien planet, so they were accustomed to drinking water from running streams without a second thought for infectious microbes. Nox drank too, but he thought first.

By afternoon Nox heard one of his brothers clearing his throat a lot. The throat-clearing turned into bouts of coughing.

"Who is hacking up a lung?" Nox asked the spectral shapes around him.

The cougher threw up.

"That's Faunus," came Orissus' voice.

By afternoon, Faunus had a chorus behind him.

Pallas, Nicanor, Leo, Galeo, Orissus, and Faunus were sneezing, then retching. All the brothers were sick.

Except Nox.

They sat under a broad-boughed tree. They turned down

their personal fields' visual scatter so they could see each other.

They looked abysmal.

"Nox! You're okay!" said Orissus, surprised. Resentful. "We all have it! You don't!"

Nox said, "It only makes sense that if one of you caught it, you'd all get it. You're all the same guy."

Despite their individual designer traits, Pallas, Nicanor, Leo, Galeo, Orissus, and Faunus were clones of the same man.

"Do you think this is American germ warfare?" Leo said, his eyes watering. "You know. Maybe the Yanks came up with some disease to target Roman clones?"

Orissus hawked, spat. Growled, "Could be. You know the Yanks wouldn't design anything that would target a Yank."

Nox leaned forward and threw up.

"Though I could be wrong," Orissus said.

"It was a hypothesis," Leo said.

"Then we've caught an alien virus," said Faunus. "That's not supposed to happen."

Pallas swallowed painfully. Said, "It did."

Galeo bent over his knees, talked into the ground. "So what do we do?"

Nox spat, stood up. "We do what we were sent to do."

25

KERRY BLUE SLID BACK her canopy. It got snagged halfway back on the limpet net.

The net dispersed heat, so it was cool to touch. Kerry unlinked it to make a hole for her to get out of her Swift.

She climbed out of her cockpit, laughing. Looked around to see where everyone else was.

Great big lake over there. No bubbles that she could see. Nobody landed in that.

A voice in her headset sounded like Big Richard. "Can we do that again?"

The colonel was barking at them to call in by the numbers.

They'd come down in daylight into an area that couldn't decide if it was field or forest. The rolling land was covered with high grasses of green, red, brown, and yellow, with clots of gray tree-ish things throughout.

Dak had come down in a stand of trees. He assured everyone loudly that the trees were thorny.

The air was warm. Kerry got out of her flight suit, then snapped her displacement collar back on. She tucked her landing disk into her field pack to bring with.

Not sure why they were lugging displacement equipment. They had orders to call for rapture only in the direst emergency.

Kerry pulled out the old-style camouflage netting from the Swift's storage compartment and draped her Swift. She mustered with the others at the colonel's coordinates.

The Marines were pretty well scattered, so mustering took a while.

They looked out for clokes, but there was nothing like a rotten stick-figured sponge in sight.

Tall grasses nodded in the yellow sunlight.

Asante Addai pulled up the coordinates for the cloke shipwreck on his omni to get oriented. With his eyes focused on the handheld, he pointed. "We need to go that way. South."

"Into the lake," said Kerry Blue.

"What?" Asante looked up from his handheld.

"There's a BFL in the way," said Carly.

Big lake. Very big. Actually it was more like an inland sea.

"Yes. Yes, there sure is," said Asante seeing that now. "Good news is the shipwreck is on dry land. Three klicks as the crow flies."

"That's just wucking fonderful," said Cain. "How far is that in dry miles?"

"More like eight klicks around the lakeshore."

Colonel Steele got off the com with the *Merrimack*. He ordered his squad, "Bring your gear. Move out. We're hiking around. This way."

Steele took first point. Kerry Blue took ass-end Charlie. She was usually found in the farthest position from the colonel when they were on the ground. Wasn't fooling anyone. But her comrades appreciated the charade.

The lake had shrunk from some past age, leaving a high, heavily forested and thorn-vined ridge around it.

Below the ridgeline lay a wide, flat shore of pebbled sand. The going was much easier down there, so that's where they hiked, with the Old Man yelling at them once every klick not to bunch up.

Faces appeared up on the ridge, peeking between the gray trees. The faces had pointed muzzles and bright black eyes.

"What are those?" Kerry pointed up. "Are those foxes?"

"They look like foxes," said Asante.

The pre-drop briefing said that the foxes were not aggressive toward humans. That was good because there seemed to be a whole tribe of them up there.

After a while, a trio of foxes came scampering down the incline. They were youthfully sleek. One was jet black. The other two reddish gray. They had huge claws.

The Marines were carrying swords, but no one felt an impulse to reach for his.

Steele had been issued a language nodule, but it didn't seem to be working. The foxes came up to him humming the damnedest mash up of off-key notes, but the nodule was not translating a word.

The three creatures ran rings around the Marines like dogs playing, then they ran toward the steep slope and looked back, as if expecting the Marines to follow.

The Yurg tried throwing a stick, but the foxes didn't seem to understand the concept of fetch.

"Stop playing with the animals," Steele bellowed. "Keep up the pace."

They continued their march toward the crash site.

The foxes acted increasingly frantic. And they were definitely trying to lead the Marines away from the shoreline.

Walking was easier on the lakeshore than up on the wooded ridge. Asante checked his omni for any activity that might have set off the foxes. He didn't see anything threatening.

The foxes abandoned them. The trio threaded up the incline and disappeared with their troop into the trees.

Dak Shepard hiked in the shadow of the steep ridge rather than in the sunlight at the water's edge. He set his pack down to adjust his boot. He'd picked up a thorn from somewhere.

A sudden *splat!* made him jump, lose his balance.

A tree, way up on the ridge, had dropped a soft-skinned bright orange pumpkin in front of him.

It splattered with an overripe stench.

Off to his right, an arc of water lifted. A silvery dart came at him—a dart more the size of a bus—opening up vast jaws as it came.

Dak dove out of the path of the oncoming mouth.

The lake serpent snapped up the pumpkin and writhed backward to the water.

Asante checked his omni. "That has to be a scylla."

Dak cried, "I don't give a—"

"Look out!" A silver blue-white flash just below the surface made the rest of the squad move away from the water's edge.

Another scylla, or the same scylla, came arrowing up onto the beach. Rows of razor teeth showed inside the mouth that seemed to be a third of its endless body. It snatched something in its massive jaws and pushed the length of its eternal self back toward the water with its wide front fins.

Dak chased it, yelling, "It's got my pack! Get it! Get it! Get it!"

The squad filled the lake monster's head with exploding splinters. The beast died in the shallows.

It took all of the Marines to drag the thing up the beach, except for Asante who set his omni to watching out for other scyllas in the water.

Apparently it was every fish for himself. No one came to help this scylla. No one came to eat him either.

Dak's pack was not inside the huge jaws.

"Oh, crap, he swallowed."

Cain cut the scylla open with his sword, starting at its throat. He kept sawing down. And down. He had to hit stomach sometime.

"Are you sure this is the one that got your pack?" said Cain, sweat running down his face. "You better be sure."

The Yurg took over sawing. He came to a big bladder that might be a stomach. It was undulating.

"Ho! Look at that!"

The Yurg sliced the bladder open. The inside of the bladder was entirely ringed with row after row of teeth. Even with its brain demolished, the scylla's stomach was still chewing on pungent orange pulp. And on Dak's field pack.

The Marines used shovels to fish Dak's pack clear of the teeth. They left the stomach, still chewing, at the water's edge.

Steele led the squad away from the lakeshore and up the steep embankment to take their hike through the trees on the high ground.

And they picked up their entourage of foxes again. This time it was the whole fox troop—maybe thirty of them—

and they wanted to play. They frisked alongside the Marines, sniffing, bowing, running circles.

Asante looked up scyllas on the omni. He read aloud, "'Freshwater aquatic carnivore.' Hey. Get this. 'Scyllas have been known to pull themselves thirty meters up the beach to get a stink pumpkin fallen to the ground in season.'"

"Really?" said Dak, sour. His pack reeked.

"You know? I don't think that thing was going for your pack," said Asante. "I think it was after the pumpkins. Your pack was collateral damage."

"I don't care!" said Dak. "How close are we to the spaceship?"

"According to this, we just passed it." Asante lifted his hand, signaled the column to halt.

Dak stopped. "How far past?"

"You and I are past it. The rest of us aren't." Asante turned around. "I should be looking at it."

"We walked over it?"

Asante backtracked ten paces. "We're here. Yurg, you're standing on it."

Yurg looked down. "Not." He stomped on solid ground.

Asante beckoned the rest of the column to come forward.

The trees were thinner here and smaller.

The foxes didn't like this place, but they were not so emphatic as they'd been on the lakeshore around the scyllas. Here they held their tails over their noses. They didn't like the smell.

"I don't smell anything," said Dak.

"I do," said Carly. "It smells . . . clokey."

It was the same dank smell that clung to her hand after she carried the severed cloke arm back to camp when they'd retrieved Roodoverhemd's body.

The squad had been issued shovels and archaeologist's trowels. Kerry looked at the trowel. Looked at the hard dirt. Looked at the trowel. "They are kidding."

Big Richard jabbed his shovel at the dirt. Its blade cut a quarter inch in. He stopped. Backed away. "Exactly *how* far under is this thing?"

The foxes caught on to what they were about, moved in, and took over.

"Ho! *Frommage!*" Dak yelled. "Look 'em go!"

Hard-packed clay, pebbles, rocks, and roots went flying from under the foxes' digging claws.

They soon hit curved metal and kept digging down around it.

The Marines stood back and watched. Steele couldn't even order them in to assist. They would just be a drag on the operation.

A clumsy, fuzzy-coated baby fox waddled through the weeds and pawed at Dak's boots. Dak picked the pup up. It had some weight to it, but a lot less than his field pack, and it was a hell of a lot cuter. Dak liked cute things. The pup was pudgy, its downy fur reddish-gray with black socks. "Hey ya, little guy."

The fox puppy licked Dak's chin.

"Flight Sergeant. What are you doing?" That was Colonel Steele.

Dak nodded his head down sideways to where the foxes were unearthing what was starting to look like a spaceship. "Supervising, sir."

The fox pup curled into a comfortable ball in Dak's arms and shut its big eyes.

"They're doing a good job, sir," said Dak.

The excavation crew had uncovered the whole alien spacecraft. Now they were cleaning their claws and combing their fur.

The alien ship's design was a basic flying cigar. The bulk of it was an antiquated hydrogen powerplant. The rest of the vessel was a cylinder no bigger than a Swift.

"Skat. That's not very big," said the Yurg.

The dimensions were not human-sized. Neither were the clokes, so that made sense.

"Those things came in *this?*" Dak said, dubious. "This barge must have been stuffed like Kerry Blue's locker."

Mama fox came to collect her cub from Dak. She took the sleeping furball and popped it into her belly pouch. The opening contracted so fast, Dak wasn't sure what he just saw.

"Did you see that?" Dak cried.

"Ignore the foxes!" Steele bellowed.

Icky Iverson found a round hatch in the spaceship's fuselage. He pulled on it. And immediately dropped it back in place, surprised.

"It's not locked!"

"Something must have come out," said Rhino. She pulled the hatch back open.

"They came out a very long time ago," said Asante, counting the strata in the dirt walls of the excavation pit.

"Look for a radio," said Cain. "We're supposed to check for radios."

"Look how?" said Rhino. "I can't get in there. Hell, I couldn't get Carly in there."

The hatchway was small. You couldn't get a fox in there, and the foxes were not volunteering to try.

"Who's got the crowbar?" said Rhino.

Steele dropped the red crowbar down into the excavation pit. Rhino caught it. She started breaking the ship's hull open.

The curved panels came apart without too much effort. The black metal alloy looked similar to the hulls of the orbs that attacked *Merrimack*.

"I got a cloke-print!" Rhino held up a piece of decking that bore a distinct three-toed star track on it.

"Captain's gonna like that," said Cain. "Are they seeing this upstairs?"

Steele signaled *Merrimack* on the harmonic exclusive to this operation. "*Merrimack*. Are you reading this?"

"We see it, Colonel." That was Captain Carmel.

"It's a cloke ship, sir."

Foxes had a cat's compulsive need to sit on whatever you were working on, and a young white she-fox set her chin on Steele's wrist com as he was talking to the ship. Steele tried to shoo the animal away.

"What is that?" the captain said. "Is that what they're calling a fox?"

"Yes, sir. This is our excavation unit."

Even Carmel had to say, "They're kind of cute."

"They're annoying, sir. But they brought the right tools for the job."

The inner passages of the ship were small. Even a cloke could not have stood up in there.

With the crowbar, Rhino cracked open the ship's control center. She uncovered no radio. No communications equipment of any kind. But there was evidence that some pieces might have been removed a long time ago. The Marines found brackets that held nothing.

The Marines pulled the wreck apart and ran scanners over the pieces. The readings went up to the *Mack* by res pulse for analysis. The ground troops couldn't send up the pieces themselves, in case the pirates were watching for displacements.

Wherever in the world the pirates were.

* * *

LEN scientists posted no sentries.

Nox, on point, crossed the dirt perimeter into the LEN expedition camp in daylight. He gestured toward one large hut at the outer edge of camp, which bore a red cross blazoned across its roof. A red cross was an international do-not-shoot symbol. That was a good place for the brothers to be. The red cross also indicated there would be medical help inside.

The brothers nodded in silence and proceeded to that hut.

The door hung open. Leo went in first. When he signaled the all clear, the rest of the brothers hurried up the ramp and in.

Leo kept watch at the door while the others rummaged through the medical supplies and looked over the machines. They had no idea what half of them did. They didn't know how to operate the other half.

Leo hissed. Someone was coming.

Leo and Faunus flattened themselves against the wall on either side of the entrance. The others pulled back out of sight.

Someone came stumping up the ramp at an uneven gait. A male voice called, "Cecil! Cecil!" He put both hands to the doorjambs and leaned his head in the entryway. "Cecil?"

"Not Cecil." Faunus seized the man by his throat and

pulled him inside the hut. Faunus growled into the man's face, "You heal us or die."

When Faunus loosened his grip on the man's throat, the man squeaked, "I'm a xenoaerologist, not a doctor."

The man was wearing safari shorts. There was a giant angry red swelling on his left calf, a large black stinger still in it.

"*Skat*." Faunus hadn't caught the doctor. He'd caught a patient.

Faunus hauled the man into a back room and parked him hard in a chair. "Have a seat. If you require immediate attention, I can amputate that for you." Faunus' machete swung on its hanger.

The xenoaerologist shook his head, finger before his lips, promising silence, and assumed an attitude of very patient waiting.

A shadow fell in the entryway. Another man stood framed in sunlight, blinking, his eyes not adjusted to the inner dim. But he was immediately aware of the presence of strangers in his hut. His voice suggested it was *his* hut. He demanded, "Who are you?"

"Boy Scouts of America," said Nox. He closed a fist on the man's lab coat, yanked the coat up under the man's chin, and pulled him inside. Leo shut the door behind him.

Half strangled, the white-coated man began noticing bandanas, earrings, bones, scars, feathers, dreadlocks, brass knuckles, and machetes.

Nox told him, "You are going to heal us, or you will be up to your eyeballs in eyeballs."

The man lifted his open hands, spoke through clenched teeth. "No violence."

"That's not your call to make," said Orissus.

The man's eyes moved, inspecting the faces around him. Nox could tell the man, who was apparently a medical doctor, saw the illness in them.

Nox released the physician with a rough push toward a workstation.

The physician recovered his balance and caught sight of the xenoaerologist sitting in the back room with his bee-stung leg puffed up. Alarm crossed the physician's face.

The man in the back said meekly, "Hi, Cecil."

"Aaron! What did they do to you!" the physician—Cecil—bellowed.

"Tiger bee sting," the xenoaerologist, Aaron, said quietly. "I can wait. They were here first."

Dr. Cecil smoothed down his white coat. He turned on a piece of equipment and beckoned one of his patients to come toward him.

The pirates stood huddled in a glowering pack, not moving except to cough or swallow down bile.

The physician prompted, impatient, "*Some*one?"

Nox stepped forward.

"Look out for nanites," Leo warned. "He could put nanites in us."

Horrific things had been done with nanomachines.

Nox told Leo, "These are not that kind of people."

"Thank you," said the physician stiffly. He had taken grave offense at the suggestion that he would use medicine as a weapon. The Hippocratic oath was older even than Rome. *First do no harm.*

Dr. Cecil made Nox spit on a slide, then checked the sputum under magnification so the pirates could see the microbes for themselves.

"I've seen quite a few cases of this recently," said Cecil. "I can treat this."

Leo watched him prepare the remedy, watching for evidence of nanites.

"They say the madness of Caesar Romulus came from nanites," Leo said. "The work of the rogue patterner Augustus."

"How can a patterner go rogue?" said Orissus. He had never believed that rumor. He cleared his throat loudly. "Patterners are programmed."

"The patterner didn't go rogue, and he didn't break programming," said Nox. "The devil is in the definitions. Augustus was loyal to Rome. But what is Rome? And what is *that?*" Nox moved forward, pointing at the concoction Dr. Cecil prepared.

Leo pointed, "Watch him. Watch him. He's got two things in there."

Dr. Cecil was loading an intradermal with two different antisera.

"It's a two-stage treatment," Cecil said, proud, irritated. "One to kill the infection. One to neutralize the toxins given off by the dying bacteria."

"Prepare eight treatments," said Nox.

There were only seven pirates. As commanded, Dr. Cecil loaded eight intradermals.

Nox picked up one intradermal at random. He handed it to Cecil, "Do him first." He pointed at Aaron, sitting in the back room.

Dr. Cecil administered the shot to Aaron and walked brusquely back out to the front room. He crossed his arms, waiting for his next command.

Nox called into the back room. "How do you feel?"

"Honestly?" said Aaron. "My leg hurts. But I'm not complaining. Truly."

Nox picked up one of the other intradermals. He pushed it into his own arm, the same way Dr. Cecil had administered it to Aaron.

"This stings, Doc," said Nox. Tingling. Something was definitely happening.

Dr. Cecil pronounced, "You are healed. Next."

None of the brothers hurried to step forward. They watched Nox.

Pallas asked, "How do you feel, Nox?"

Nox considered this. How did he feel? "Not bad." He inhaled, exhaled. Felt something falling away inside him. Tightness loosened from his chest. His abdomen was quiet. His head was clearing. He coughed up a satisfying loughie and spat on the floor. He breathed more freely. "I feel pretty damn good, actually."

"Great," Faunus said thickly. He gave a juicy cough. His stomach whined. He pushed Nox aside. "I'm next. Orissus, if I die, kill him." Faunus jerked his head toward Dr. Cecil.

"You know I will, *frater*," said Orissus.

Dr. Cecil provided a receptacle for any further spitting.

It felt so good to be rid of the infection, the pirates actually used the spitoon.

Leo was the last one treated.

Orissus checked Leo up and down, frowning gravely, concerned. He lifted Leo's eyelids with his thumbs, inspecting Leo's eyes. Orissus growled deep dismay. "Worst case of nanites I've ever seen."

The physician took off his diagnostic probe, placed it in the sterilizer. He set an automaton to clean the deck. "I have done my duty. Go now."

Faunus stared at him with an amazed smile. Puffed a derisive laugh. "Go?" He didn't even bother telling Cecil no.

Nox pointed to Aaron waiting in the back room with his ballooning leg. He told Dr. Cecil, "Fix him." It was probably good to have healthy hostages, so he could threaten to mess them up later.

Cecil said, offended, "I don't need to be told to heal the sick."

"And I don't need an anesthetic to cut out your tongue," said Nox. "Do what you're told, when you're told."

Cecil extracted the stinger from Aaron's leg and administered antivenom.

Nox ushered Cecil and the limping Aaron out the door with a rusty machete.

Faunus swaggered out to the fire pit at the center of camp, where many of the LEN expedition members were sitting on benches, talking. It was apparently their favorite gathering spot.

Several heads turned as the pirates came into their midst. Faunus boomed brightly, "What's for dinner?"

More xenos looked up in alarm at the newcomers dressed like brigands.

Someone's muttered aside to a colleague carried louder than he'd intended, "Where'd they come from?"

"Mars," said Faunus.

"Mars needs women," said Orissus, flashing a gold-toothed grin from within his black beard.

Tentative expressions started to look adequately frightened.

Nox, Leo, Galeo, Nicanor, and Pallas fanned out to the ships, huts, and tents to round up all the xenos who were not already assembled in the center of camp.

Inside the parked LEN ship *Amber Dragonfly,* Dr. Sandy Minyas crouched over the resonator. Her fingers were clumsy keying in the emergency harmonic. She fumbled. Had to enter the harmonic again. Her breath came in shallow gasps. "This is LEN expedition base Zebra Oscar Echo. We ha—have—" Her whispering voice hitched. She was horribly aware of someone behind her, a large presence, smelling wrong.

The hilt of a machete smashed down on the res chamber. Sandy Minyas reared flat back into a pirate. A shriek flew out of her throat.

Then she was rising by her shirt collar.

"Move along," said the pirate. He steered her around to face the hatchway and gave her a push. She stumbled out to the sunlight and let herself be herded with the others gathered around the fire pit. No one, not even Benet, said anything to her.

"Family conference," Faunus sang to the assembling xenos. "There's been a little regime change. I'll wait till we're all here."

"Oh, look at that," Leo pointed suddenly. "I want that!"

Set in the half-ring of uninspired square-built spacecraft, looking entirely out of place among the prosaic boxes, crouched a silvery late-model racing yacht.

Smaller than the other ships, smaller than the Xerxes, the Star Racer was fast, high end, gorgeous. It was too good for these people.

The pirates hadn't searched that ship yet.

"Let's take it," said Nox. He marched up the ramp and tried the hatch. It was locked. Nox rapped on the hatch of the racing yacht with the hilt of his machete.

A dog barked inside. It sounded large.

Nox shouted through the hull, "Don't try to take off. We'll shoot you out of the sky and kill all your friends behind you."

Leo added, "We'll carve your name into their carcasses."

The dog barking silenced.

The hatch opened.

Nox blinked at the figure in the hatchway—a trim, elegant, older man with a dignified youthful posture. He wore his long silvering black hair swept back in a tail.

Jose Maria de Cordillera gave a gentle smile and said happily to the pirate standing at his hatchway, "John."

The other pirates gaped at Nox, their eyes big as full moons.

Jose Maria stepped out through the hatch, arms wide, and greeted the stunned pirate with an embrace and a kiss on either scarred cheek. "John Farragut."

26

CAPTAIN CARMEL SUMMONED her cryptotech. "Mister Johnson, what can you tell me about the radio transmissions on the planet?"

Merrimack had detected low-level radio messages on first arriving at Zoe. The staccato patterns were not any signal that would ever occur in nature. Some intelligence on the planet was clicking.

"It's not a code," said Qord Johnson. "It's a language."

"What's the signal strength?" Calli asked.

"Weak," the com tech answered that one. "Less than fifty watts. Frequency five hundred ten kilohertz."

"That's near the old Morse range, isn't it?" said Calli.

"It is," said Qord Johnson. "But this is not a code, Captain."

"Is the LEN scientific expedition conducting wildlife radio tagging?" said Calli. "Could this be wildlife telemetry?" In that case she could be chasing literal wild geese.

"No, sir. It's not ours," said the com tech. Then specified, "Not human."

"It's an alien language," said the cryptotech. "I'm the wrong man for this job."

Code breakers did not untangle languages.

Calli paid an in-person visit to the xeno lab where the xenogeneralists Weng and Sidowski had their full cloke specimen spread out on a table.

Calli immediately zeroed in on the wiry filaments that looked like strands of coarse hair protruding from the cloke's shoulders. "What are those?"

"Antennae," said Dr. Weng.

"*Radio* antennae?" said Calli.

"Not necessarily," said Dr. Sidowski.

"*Could* they be?" said Calli.

"Do you want them to be?" said Weng.

"Someone on the planet is talking on the radio," said Calli.

"These are the radios?" said Ski, staring at his alien.

"Are they?" Calli said back.

"This is dead, sir," said Dr. Weng of his specimen. "Perhaps if I had more to work with . . . ?"

"Is there such a thing as a biological radio?" said Calli.

"Don't see why not," said Ski.

"Because there should be more signals if the clokes are all walking radios," Weng snapped at Ski. "That's why not."

"There are only a few dozen signal sources worldwide," said Calli. "The signal strength is too low for those sources to be talking to each other."

"Maybe they're *listening*," said Ski. "Maybe only the group captain's talking."

Calli's eyebrows went high. She absorbed that thought.

"Captain?" Weng prompted.

Calli said, "If only the command-and-control cloke talks, do the foot soldiers not talk to each other?"

"Maybe like ants talk." Ski touched his fingertips together like conversing ants. "Couldn't begin to tell you what they're saying."

Weng said, "Where's the ship's xenolinguist when we finally need one?"

"Yeah," said Ski. "Ham. Where's Ham?"

Patrick Hamilton.

"Dr. Hamilton is on the planet," said Calli.

"Need him, sir," said Weng.

Calli signaled her exec on the ship's intracom. "Commander Ryan, I need to consult with Dr. Hamilton."

The XO responded, "Sir, the LEN put up a shield dome ten minutes ago. We can't see anything in camp. The expedition is not answering hails. And—"

Calli heard a quick exchange of voices before Commander Ryan returned to the com. "They just activated displacement jammers."

Weng heard that. He looked to Calli. "I know the LEN don't like us, sir, but what the Fortran?"

"Oh, foxtrot," Calli said, eyes to the overhead.

We just found our pirates.

* * *

Nox was aware of heads whiplashing round his way. He returned Jose Maria's embrace mechanically, because he couldn't bring himself to stab the man. "My name is Nox."

"Nox," Jose Maria acknowledged. He stepped back from the embrace and somehow managed to turn Nox around so they were both facing the staring camp gathering. "Nox, this is Glenn Hamilton, and her husband, Dr. Patrick Hamilton. That is Dr. Melisandra Minyas. There is Dr. Poul—"

"You are trying to humanize them," Nox said.

"Of course I am," said Jose Maria, warm and calm. "And that is Dr. Aaron Rose, who makes excellent wine."

It was harder to kill people with names.

"It won't work," Nox said.

But Jose Maria had already got inside Nox's guard. Jose Maria had been a houseguest of his father back when Nox was still John Farragut, Junior. Jose Maria had never called him John John. Or worse, John John John. Jose Maria had recognized him through his scars and tats and bones. It meant Jose Maria had looked at him, really looked at him, and remembered him.

Nox felt his brothers' stares. Felt a physical nudge behind his knee. A snuffling nose.

Jose Maria reached down to the nose's owner. "This is my dog, Inga. I don't think I had her when I visited."

Oh, hell. He's introduced his dog. He's throwing the whole arsenal at me.

The bitch's warm brown eyes, doggie smile, and wagging stub tail dared Nox to kill her.

Nox tried to salvage his authority, his ruthlessness. Had to make an example of someone. He put his hand on his machete hilt and spoke loudly past Jose Maria, "I seem to have everyone's attention. Who is in charge here?"

Before anyone else could speak, Jose Maria said, "I am."

He wasn't. But apparently Jose Maria guessed that Nox had intended to cut off the expedition leader's head.

Nox couldn't kill Jose Maria.

We have broken bread.

"Son of a bitch," Nox muttered.

Nox needed to keep up his role of vicious killer.

I am evil.

The thought of killing Jose Maria was making him physically ill. He couldn't do it.

Nox was agonizingly aware of his brothers stealing looks at him and pretending they weren't as shocked as anyone else to hear him called John Farragut.

Nox gave up the idea of killing someone for now. He pushed ahead with the rest of the Circle's plan. "Your presence is required around the campfire, *Don* Cordillera." Nox motioned Jose Maria out of his elegant ship.

Jose Maria complied. The dog trotted at his heels, stub tail wagging.

Orissus was keeping watch over the flock around the fire pit. Orissus told them that anyone caught with a com would lose his hands. Out came the coms onto the ground. Then Faunus searched everyone. He didn't find any hidden coms. Orissus, with his black bushy beard, his wild hair, his gold tooth, and his machete, looked just too eager to cut off the hand of a holdout.

The brothers searched all the ships and all the tents and huts for anything that could be used against them. Nicanor acquired a list of all expedition personnel and called roll to make sure no one was AWOL.

"Anabelle," Nicanor called. "Which of you is Anabelle?"

Met with silence.

Nicanor roared, "Where is Anabelle!"

The scientists were cowed speechless.

A small voice offered, "The goat."

Orissus' eyes bulged menacingly.

The voice got smaller. "Really. Anabelle is the goat."

Nicanor looked to his brothers, "Is there a goat?"

Pallas said, "I saw a goat."

Pallas left the fireside and walked out between huts and parked ships. He returned within moments suppressing a grin. He waved a feed bowl embossed with flowery letters: Anabelle. "Explains why Anabelle doesn't have a last name."

Satisfied now that everyone was seated around the fire pit under Orissus' guard, Nicanor, Pallas, Faunus, Leo, Galeo, and Nox did a second more thorough search of the camp. Then they closed up the ships and sealed the hatches with nothing more formidable than tape.

The tape might as well have been radioactive iron bars.

The expedition members did not need to be told not to disturb the tape.

Nox noticed a glassy shimmer in the air overhead. Leo had got a defensive energy dome up. There would be no bolts from the blue now. No skyhooks either. If *Merrimack* found them, she would need to put soldiers on the ground to root them out.

We have hostages.

The civilians were as docile as livestock, hoping they were dairy cows, not beef cattle.

"That was a productive meeting, folks," said Faunus. "You can go back to your beakers."

One scientist seemed about to tell him that his "beakers" were inside one of the sealed ships. He thought better of it.

* * *

Data and pictures had begun streaming in from the drones that *Merrimack* sent to scout the titanic alien ship five light-years out from Zoe.

It was a vast rotating cylinder, using old style centripetal force for gravity. Newer parts had been constructed and kluged on over a series of generations.

The huge ship had a manufacturing plant in tow, big and dirty. As there was no need for pollution containment in interstellar space, the plant churned out smoke and radiation behind it.

"It's a nuke," Commander Ryan told Captain Carmel.

"The cloke ships weren't nukes," said Calli. "Even their orbs were hydrogen powered. Are we sure this vessel is a cloke ship?"

"Affirmative. Their three-toed prints are all over it. They had a little accident in there. It's hot."

"What do you mean hot?"

"Radioactive," said Commander Ryan. "It ought to be glowing in the dark."

Little accident apparently meant *catastrophe*.

"Does any part support life?"

"The drones are still scouting, but it doesn't look hopeful," said Dingo. "If anyone is hoping. I'm sorry, I don't like the squiggy little things. Our drones can't board. The ship is sealed up tight, and a sounding indicates its passageways are too small for a drone to move inside."

"Where is the cloke home world?"

"We don't know."

"Why don't we know?" said Calli.

"There's nothing back in line the way this barge came. Not in this galaxy. They must have changed course at some point, or at several points."

"It's leaving an obvious trail," said Calli. "Dispatch a drone to back-trace the carrier's emission trail."

"Aye, aye, Captain," said Dingo Ryan.

He sounded reluctant. It must have seemed a diversion of resources when they had a crisis down on the planet.

"I want to clear my six," Calli answered his unspoken objection. "That generational ship has been in transit for centuries, but you know their home world technology has not been standing still waiting for this crew to report back. They planted squatters on a planet that already has a resident intelligence. They wrecked a LEN ship and they attacked us. They could have FTL technology by now for all I know. If I want to line up an end run against the clokes, I need to know where their end is."

Dingo nodded down. "You'll have it, sir."

✳ ✳ ✳

Dinner at the LEN expedition camp was always taken around the fire pit. This evening, seven of the xenos had pirates eating off their plates and drinking from their mugs.

No one talked.

Nox avoided making eye contact with his brothers.

He caught the woman whom Jose Maria had introduced as Glenn Hamilton stealing glances at him. Not that everyone wasn't stealing glances at him. Nox was sure he didn't know her. She was petite. Kind of pretty. Several years older than he. She held herself tall, but she was actually nearly a foot shorter than he was. She was the only one besides the pilot who wasn't called "Doctor." Her red-brown hair was cut very short and not styled. It was kind of a hack job. Her eyebrows were funny, as if she'd shaved them off and they had grown back wild. It was strange because she was dressed neatly and had pretty hands. And a wedding ring.

After dinner, bags, clothes, and belonging came flying out of one large tent. Nicanor leaned out the entrance, and looked round for his brothers. "Is this one okay?"

Nicanor had chosen the best tent for the pirates' quarters.

Five xenos scurried to retrieve the jetsam as it came flying out of their former lodging.

Orissus moved in to help Nicanor clear out what the Circle didn't want from the tent. It became a game of who could get more distance.

The dislodged residents quietly looked for someone to take them in.

One of the displaced xenos hovered at the tent flap, wary of flying objects. He leaned into view and called in politely, "Pardon me. Will the beds be—?" He trailed off, finishing with a heave-ho motion with his hands. *Coming out?*

"No," Nicanor said. He counted up the beds in the tent. There were five. "We need two more."

Pallas and Galeo set out to liberate two more beds from elsewhere. They took a liking to the split-log bed frame in one of the other tents.

Poul Vrba watched them haul the bed away. It wasn't Vrba's bed, but he made a show of quiet indignation. "You are pirates?"

Galeo blinked at Vrba a couple of times. There were silver pieces of eight worked into Galeo's corn-rowed hair. His neat goatee was dyed a brilliant red. The number 666 was tattooed on his forehead in red, a black cross between his eyes. Galeo asked Vrba back, "You are a moron?"

Poul Vrba said evenly, "You know I have the legal right to kill you without legal process."

No sooner said than Vrba's throat opened up, smiling bright red, blood spraying, an artery spouting a pumping stream. His body thrashed, slumped, dropped to reveal Nox behind him, patched wetly red down the front of him.

Nox's eyes flared at the others, who were staring at him as if he'd grown an extra head.

"Don't look at me like that!" Nox shouted. "It's natural selection! What kind of dung sniffer tells a pirate 'I have the right to kill you' like inviting us to tea! This outfit isn't called the ninth ladies sewing circle!"

❋ ❋ ❋

The Marines on the ground received orders to proceed toward the LEN camp, best speed, and under no circumstance to be detected.

Avoiding detection would not be difficult to do for the first leg of the journey. The ground rose between them and their destination.

The Marines were on the march when *Merrimack* received a hail from Flight Sergeant Asante Addai. Commander Ryan took the hail.

"I can't get a hold of Ham at the LEN site," Flight Sergeant Asante Addai said. "Is he upstairs?"

Patrick Hamilton was likely a prisoner within the LEN camp. Or dead. But the XO was not sharing half-cooked information just yet.

"Dr. Hamilton is not available at present," said Commander Ryan.

"Well, sir, tell him his fox translator don't work worth a skat."

"What is the language module not doing for you, Flight Sergeant?"

"Anything! It doesn't recognize anything these foxes hum at us."

"You're over two hundred klicks away from the LEN settlement," said Ryan.

"Yes, sir," said the Marine.

"Your foxes are probably speaking a different dialect than the foxes Ham talked to."

"Oh," said the Marine. "Well, have him come over here and talk to these ones."

"Priority?" said Commander Ryan.

"They're building cages," said Asante. "The foxes are. I got a bad feeling about those cages."

"Figure it out, Marine. Dr. Hamilton is otherwise engaged."

27

NOX STALKED into the woods. He found a stream and lay in it, pissed, quaking, letting the cold current wash the blood away.

His brothers were waiting for him when he came stalking back across the dirt perimeter under the edge of the energy dome into the LEN camp as night was falling. They had sent everyone else to their tents.

Nox made straight for the fire pit, took a spot on the bench closest to the fire, and leaned in, shivering.

Pallas was the first to dare talk to him. "John Farragut?"

Nox spat toward the fire. "My name is Nox."

Faunus sat on the ground, cross-legged. "Tell us a story."

Nox let his shoulders drop for a moment, then straightened up. He inhaled for strength. "Once upon a time, O Best Beloved, when the famous Admiral John Alexander Farragut was not yet famous and not yet an admiral and only eighteen years old, he pissed off his father. And his father, the Honorable Justice John Knox Farragut, decided that his eldest son was an unacceptable heir to His almighty name. So John Alexander was cast out of Farragut heaven—or he left, I'm not sure which way it went. Because I didn't exist at the time, O Best Beloved. And Justice John Knox Farragut, Senior, who art in Frankfort, created a new being in his own image and bestowed upon this later-born son his full name, John Knox Farragut. Junior. And this boy child grew up thinking he was ever so special. He was the Chosen One. He had His Honor's name.

"Well, O Best Beloved, I can be slow to learn, but I did catch on finally that big John Alexander is, was, and ever shall be the center of the Farragut universe. My name, my special name, was given to me as a slap at big John Alexander. John Alexander is the Chosen One. I am the bluff and discard."

"And what does that make us?" Orissus asked, standing over him, his muscles bulging in his crossed arms. "Are we your tools to get back at your father?"

"That would only make sense if His Honor knew what I had done," said Nox. "He doesn't know. I haven't told him. I just left without a look back. You are my brothers."

During the war, Roman warships had flown right over the house. Nox remembered His Honor ran out there roaring. Nox had looked up and thought they were the most glorious things he had ever seen. And he'd gone to Rome. Decided to be Roman.

"You don't need to do anything to be American other than be born on a piece of U.S.-flagged dirt.

"The province of America was founded by Romans. Columbus. Jefferson. It's become a bastardized travesty of Rome. You don't need to serve your country to be an American. Full citizenship isn't earned. It's just dropped on you by birthright. You can dance on a burning flag, and no one can take your U.S. citizenship away.

"Rome always treated me as me. When I swore allegiance to Rome, there was no braying news flash from Palatine back to the States to say, 'Ha ha, we got a Farragut to change sides.' Rome took me as I was. And when Rome threw me out, it was for something I did."

"But you said the inquisitors asked you if you were a mole for the United States," said Nicanor. "*Somebody* didn't accept you as you are."

"He was wrong," said Nox. "I am and will always be Roman."

* * *

The foxes were sunny and curious. They had been a huge help to the Marines digging up the cloke shipwreck. Now they were just in the way.

The Marines had orders to get closer to the LEN encampment. The foxes had decided to come with them.

The Marines were passing through a shallow pass between low hills when the foxes began gathering thick woody vines and weaving them into large lumpy balls, like double cages.

The balls had an inner compartment and a woven outer shell equipped with a vine-hinged door. The foxes rolled their finished creations along with the file.

"They're cages," said Dak. "Look at that. Fourteen of us. Fourteen cages."

"They're steamers," said Rhino. "They're going to try to slow cook us. I bet there are hot springs around here."

The tight set of twin moons that circled Zoe every thirty-five local days were on the wane, following the sun over the western horizon.

As the dusk gathered, the foxes told the Marines to get in the cages. At least that's what the Marines thought all that humming and gesturing meant. The foxes even held the doors for them to get in.

"I knew it! I knew it!" Dak yelled toward the darkening sky. "I knew it!"

Kerry Blue told the foxes to bite her asteroid.

The slivers of the double moon, nearly new, looked like a pair of grinning Cheshire cats as they touched the horizon.

The foxes stopped trying to coax the Marines into their cages.

But here came the weird part. The foxes rolled out more cages from a forest glade. They climbed into the cage balls and lashed the hatches shut.

Kerry looked at her squad mates. "Do you see that?"

Flight Leader Cain Salvador ordered the squad, "Get in the cages."

"No, I don't think so," said Dak. "We need shelter? I'm checking out the caves."

Dak marched up in the direction of the caves in the rocky hillside.

The foxes rolled their cages like giant hamster balls alongside Dak. They rolled into Dak's path, humming. Agitated.

They were afraid of something.

The pack leader unlashed the door of his own cage,

climbed out and jumped around Dak. The leader's gestures—if you could read alien gestures like human gestures—seemed to say: No, no, no. Caves bad.

The alpha male scampered into and out of a cage as if to show Dak how to do it.

Dak told the fox, "Look! I get what you're telling me to do, Fur Face. I'm just not doing it. Look at me! I'm Black!"

Colonel Steele, who had been marching rear guard, hiked up to the scene of the noise. He demanded, "What is the issue, Marine?"

Flight Leader Cain Salvador told him, "The foxes don't want us near the caves. They want us to get in those cages."

Steele's night vision turned on in the gathering darkness. He looked from Cain to Dak to the caves to the empty woven cages to the antic foxes inside their own cage balls. "What's in the caves?"

"I don't know, but I bet it comes out at night during the new moon," said Cain.

Steele's eyes moved over his Marines, the twitching foxes, the caves, the sky.

The sliver moons were slipping below the horizon.

Here at the edge of the galaxy, at this hour, the world turned this face toward the starless side of heaven. When those moons disappeared, the sky was going to be pitch black.

Steele ordered, "Get in the cages."

Kerry Blue woke to something. Immediately forgot what it was. She knew what was happening while she was still asleep. Now she was awake and couldn't remember what it was. She thought her cage shook.

She remained still, listened. Heard insects buzzing, crickety chirps, notes like birdcalls.

Big fronds rustled, waving in the warm breeze, but she couldn't see them. She heard Dak and Cain snoring. Smelled green scents and earthy musk. Saw nothing. May as well have her eyes closed. It was foxtrotting dark out here.

Kerry Blue shut her eyes. Dozed off again.

She smelled something rank. Felt something big. Now *that* really was a shake this time. She woke up rolling. Over and over, bouncing.

Things that came out to feed under the moonless sky on the blackest night of the year were here. She hadn't seen anything in the daylight like those she sensed clawing at her cage. Heated gusts breathed on her. These things must have been in the caves.

She switched her night vision on. It didn't help much. There wasn't any ambient light to enhance. She got an infrared image of a jagged gaping mouth. Claws raked at the outer bars of heavy vine. She felt the swiping paw roll her cage.

She grasped at one of the inner vines to hold on as she rolled hip over shoulder.

Someone else yelled. Dak. He sounded upside down. "What's happening?"

"Something is trying to eat my feet!" Kerry shouted.

Hot breaths seethed between teeth. Kerry unholstered her splinter gun. Rolled.

She heard Rhino, fluent in blasphemy.

Someone else yelled, "I dropped my fragging gun!"

Kerry got off a shot. Her target gave an angry snort so she knew she'd jabbed a splinter up the thing's broad nose. She pulled the second stage trigger. Fragged it.

Felt a wet spray with an ungodly squeal. She hadn't killed it. Not near.

Oh, crap. It's angry. And I've got gunk on me.

The thing batted her into a furious roll. She held on till she crashed into someone else's cage.

Someone else was yelling, "Get this thing off me!" Sounded like Taher.

Kerry Blue tried to get a bead on the mouth that latched onto her cage. The mouth and her foot were in same direction.

She braced for a sting in case she nailed herself. She fired.

Didn't feel anything in her foot. But a sharp cry came from the mouth.

She detonated the splinter.

The thing threw her, cage and all, screaming. She heard the wrenching screeches diminish behind her. Her springy vine-framed ball rolled and bounced down a hill, picking up speed, with Kerry inside it.

The ball rolled off an edge. Dropped. Bounced. Splashed. The rolling slogged to a wet stop.

And now she was sinking.

Kerry dropped her gun. In the blackness she felt quickly around with her hands at the hard vines for the lashing that held her cage shut. She was clawing at the knots. The twined ropes were wet. They seized together tighter. She drew her knife.

And her cage was sinking. It was already up to her waist.

And took a roll for the worse.

Kerry screamed, "*I'm in the water!*"

With water up to her chest, she floated, the top of her head pressed against the hard vines. She took her blade to a vine. Barely scored a couple of grooves in it. Water was rising at her chin. She took in a giant breath.

Water rose up over her nostrils, filled her ears, shut her eyes. She felt around for the ropes that held her cage shut.

Thomas will save me. He always does.

The cage rolled slowly upside down. *Don't get water up your nose. You cough and you're done.* She'd lost touch with the ropes on that roll. Leaves and dirt swam in her face. Algae brushed against her in slimy veils. She snorted them off her nostrils. Hard bubbles tapped her face.

Her head was singing. Lungs burned.

Needing to breathe.

Did anyone even know where she was?

I want to breathe. I want to breathe real bad.

Hold it. Hold it. Hold it.

She'd lost her place during the last roll. Lost her knife. Couldn't find the twine to claw at it. Grabbed the bars and tried to shake them. *Stupid. Stupid Stupid.* The vines were hard enough to keep out giant creatures. She wasn't going to shake her way out. Her motions were heavy and slow under water.

Thomas will be here.

Lungs felt to be splitting.

It didn't look like Thomas was coming.

Why the hell did she have to say till death do us part?

* * *

Jose Maria de Cordillera was the only person in camp not afraid of the pirates. He knew they were deadly. Jose Maria was at peace with the concept of death.

He sat at the fireside, in the depth of the darkest night, his dog's head on his knee.

Nox sat down on another bench. Said, "Thank you for respecting my name."

"A man is not who he was," said Jose Maria. "He is who he chooses to be. I am familiar with men who have more than one existence."

Nox struggled not to feel shame at what he'd become. "I had damn few choices."

Jose Maria picked up a stone. "Not mine to throw." He let the stone fall from his hand.

Nox said, "I can let you inside your ship to get something to sleep on."

Jose Maria motioned the idea away. "I have a hammock out here."

No one was confined to his tent, but all the xenos were hunkered down anyway. Except for Jose Maria. And the one woman. She had taken a matter-of-fact walk across the grounds to the head, then stopped in the galley, then walked back to her tent with a glass of water.

Nox had caught her looking at him during dinner. Not the way the others looked at him. Nox could tell that she recognized him, or someone like him.

He knew he had never met her. But her name was familiar. Glenn Hamilton. Glenn Hamilton.

Mrs. Hamilton.

✳ ✳ ✳

A snag. A jerk. Kerry sank to the bottom of her cage. Her cage was rolling.

And rising. Head up. Huge breath. Rolled back under. Rolled up. Another gasp. A voice. "We got her! You still with us, Blue?" Dragging up on land. Rolled her upside down.

"Oh, *frag a hag!*" she rasped.

"She's okay!"

Someone got a red light on. She could see, sort of.

Thomas Ryder Steele. And Cain Salvador. They were out of their cages, hauling her cage away from a pond. Twitch and Carly were there too. Kerry dimly saw the others, their backs to her, arranged in a defensive half ring, splinter guns at the ready, watching for monsters.

Steele growling, "God *dammit*, Blue! Stay out of the water!"

Kerry felt warm. The growling was sweet. He'd been scared out of his head for her.

Asante Addai took the hail from the ship. Of course *Mack* had monitors all over them. *Merrimack* had detected splinter fire.

The XO's voice: "Do you have pirates down there?"

"Negative," Asante responded. *Pirates?* "We have wild animals."

"You really oughtn't be shooting the native wildlife."

Oh, yeah. This from a guy called Dingo.

Kerry heard that. Yelled, "It was trying to eat my feet!"

"That's the being's nature," said the voice safe, way high and dry on the space battleship. "You need to allow for alien nature."

"Yeah, sir?" said Kerry Blue. "It didn't allow for my nature!"

TR Steele stalked away from camp in the night blackness while the others slept in their cages in a stand of trees that kept them from rolling anywhere.

Carly was the sentry this watch. She let him pass.

She let someone else pass too, dammit. He'd crossed the perimeter to be alone.

Snapping twigs and that voice sounded behind him. "You mad at me, Thomas?"

He snarled at her in a whisper without turning around, "You were underwater, and I couldn't breathe!"

He brought his fist to his chest. Felt all locked up in there. "*I* fucking told you to get in the fucking cage. I put you in there! *I* did! Dammit, Blue, I can't protect you!"

"Hoo bloody ra," said Kerry Blue.

Very philosophical she-man, his Kerry Blue.

He seized her and kissed her hard. Her lips were cold and rubbery under his. He tried to press warmth back into them. Her clammy fingers held the back of his head.

I can't lose her.

He couldn't protect her either. She was a Marine.

Hoo bloody ra.

* * *

After two days that lasted forever, Glenn stole away from the LEN encampment. Her mouth felt as if it were full of nettles as she crossed the dirt perimeter behind the storage huts.

The defensive dome that the pirates had energized over the LEN camp did not extend down to ground level, so she was able to walk out. The pirates were not guarding against walkaways. They had confiscated all the displacement equipment and had jammers going, so attempting displacement would be fatal.

The pirates weren't worried about escapees, because there was always the hanging threat, if one person torqed them off, the pirates could execute nine or ten of his friends.

Everyone was taking great care not to upset The Ninth Circle—even Director Benet.

Glenn moved at a casual walk. She picked wildflowers for the first hundred yards into the forest, as if that were what she'd come out here to do.

She was taking an enormous risk. It seemed safer than doing nothing.

Beef cows did nothing.

She moved slowly not to set off any of the woodland sentinels. Those blue things had calls like crows.

She stopped, crouched down, waited, and listened, in case she was followed.

She continued by starts and stops. Even when she made it two klicks out, she was still afraid to breathe.

She found the *Spring Beauty*.

The forest had recovered quickly. If she hadn't known, Glenn couldn't tell that there had been a fire here. The tree trunks, scarred from the falling wreckage, had healed over. Vines had grown over the fuselage, and something was nesting in the life craft.

She climbed carefully over weeds and bits of wreckage to get to the ship, and crept inside.

There was a chance that the pirates hadn't secured *Spring Beauty*'s res chamber. She wasn't sure if the pirates even knew the *Beauty* was out here.

A scatter of animal droppings pelleted the control room deck. Something was cocooned in the copilot's seat. Blunt shards from the shattered viewscreen lay strewn across the deck. Panels from the overhead had dropped. Glenn moved them aside to uncover the res chamber. She cringed with every loud metallic creak. Her hands shook with her pulse.

The res chamber was gone.

Dammit. They took it.

They knew this ship was here. She had to get out of here. Now.

Then remembered. Of course the res chamber was gone. She felt incredibly dim. Incredibly relieved. She herself had pulled that res chamber out of the console to take Admiral Farragut on a visual tour around the shipwreck.

She found the res chamber where she'd left it, stowed in a corner aft of the control room. A stretch of the overhead had buckled in since then. She had to climb under that to get at the res chamber. The chamber was wedged in between panels, but it looked intact. She reached in. Touched the control.

Held her breath.

The unit powered on.

Glenn fed in the harmonic. She hoped the Navy hadn't changed codes since she'd gone on leave. She whispered, "*Merrimack. Merrimack. Merrimack.* This is Glenn Hamilton."

Waited. Nothing.

She didn't know the current code words. "Gordon? Red?" she called the com techs by name. "It's Glenn Hamilton." She made sure her face was on camera.

She imagined the crew on the command deck were trying to determine her authenticity.

Finally a voice answered without video. "Lieutenant?"

The voice of Calli Carmel.

"Captain!" Glenn whispered a shout. "Pirates have taken over the LEN expedition camp. I'm in the *Spring Beauty*, a few klicks outside camp."

"Is this a hostage situation?"

"We're not locked up, but yes, I'd say we were hostages. Except I don't know what they want. They killed one man. John did."

"John John?"

It shouldn't have shocked her that Calli already knew

John Farragut, Junior, was here. "Yes, sir. He's—" Glenn didn't know how to describe what happened to him.

"Is John John a CIA operative?" asked Calli.

Glenn's voice stopped up entirely. Not a question she ever expected. She recovered. "I don't *think* so. He's mad as a cut snake. The pirates know that you are up there."

"Yes. We met," said Calli.

Glenn guessed there had been some shooting involved.

Calli said, "Lieutenant, do you know who you've got there?"

"I—" thought she did. "Guess I don't."

"These pirates call themselves The Ninth Circle. So far as we know, everyone who has ever seen them is dead. They're not shooters, so don't rely on a personal field for protection. They use blades or garrotes. John Junior goes for the heart. The others are cutthroats."

"John can take out a throat too," said Glenn. "I saw that for myself. He calls himself Nox."

"What are their numbers?"

"Seven."

"You mean John plus seven," said Calli.

"No. Seven total."

"A Roman *contubernium* is eight," said Calli. "These men used to be a tent party. Where's the eighth?"

"They haven't mentioned anyone else."

"There has to be one."

"Maybe he's dead?" said Glenn.

"That could be, but, to be safe, assume there is an outlier. Probably left guarding the Xerxes."

"Say again, sir. Guarding the *what?*"

"Your pirates hijacked a Xerxes class transport on a planet named Phoenix. They're smart, they're vicious, they're trained, and they have nothing to lose. Find where they parked their ship. It will be under extreme stealth. I have a map of your expedition camp here. Where do the pirates stay?" *Merrimack*'s video turned on and presented the camp layout toward the resonator.

Glenn was able to point out the pirates' tent. "They all spend the night there. But sooner or later you're going to find one in Dr. Nooan's tent instead." There was some heavy flirtation and Stockholm Syndrome happening between Dr. Ilsa Nooan and the big sybaritic one named Faunus.

Far removed from civilization, mating behaviors change, and well-educated civilized women go for the biggest savage in the pack.

"Nooan's tent is the singleton on the east side, closest to the fire pit."

"Do the pirates post sentries?"

"No. They count on intimidation to keep us in line. They're probably counting on our presence to keep you from blowing the site away. They have a dome up."

"We've seen that."

"We're accessible on ground level. The pirates are tall, and they don't duck to get outside."

"How often do they leave the dome?"

"Random times. Never all together."

"Do they bring anything back from their ship?"

"No. They're never gone very long. They wear personal fields. They do what they want. They graze like sacred cows."

"How did they arrive? Did they displace in?"

"They came on foot. I didn't hear displacement."

Displacement was loud.

"Outstanding," said Calli.

That narrowed the search radius. It meant the pirated Xerxes was within hiking distance of the LEN camp.

"You realize I didn't actually revoke your commission, Lieutenant," Calli said.

"Yes, sir. I guessed that." Glenn had fervently hoped that. But at the time she'd really thought she had been pushed down a mineshaft.

Calli had only done it to give her an excuse to leave Glenn in place over LEN objections.

"Get close to John John," Calli ordered. "Find where they left the Xerxes and how many men are in it. There has to be an eighth man. Failing that, keep the pirates in place. Call in when you can."

"Aye, aye, sir."

Calli's audio and video ceased.

Glenn turned off the resonator.

So Captain Carmel was sending in the Marines. Glenn knew that from what the captain had asked. And from what she hadn't said. With Glenn a hostage, it was best to tell her as little as possible.

Glenn crawled back out from under the collapsed overhead. She dragged a charred seat cushion in front of the gap to mask the resonator from view should anyone look down there. She left no footprints as she moved forward to the exit.

Stopped in the hatchway.

Bones and feathers braided into blond hair. Red, blue, and yellow scars on his face. Nox stood on the ramp. A rusted machete in his hand.

28

"**H**AMSTER."

Glenn felt as if her mouth were full of pins. Her face drained of blood. She eyed the machete. Its cutting edge was nicked and scored from heavy use. Every blink brought back images of Poul Vrba, dying.

Nox said, "You're the Hamster."

Captain John Farragut had given Glenn Hamilton the nickname. Glenn wanted to lie. Knew she couldn't pull it off.

"Small universe," Glenn spoke without voice.

"The universe is infinitely vast, but the paths of human travel in it are as narrow as ant trails," said Nox, sounding bizarrely cultured.

Glenn came down a degree from blind panic. Nox hadn't overheard her reporting him to *Merrimack*.

Hamster. He knew she was the Hamster.

The "Hamster" name hadn't gone away even after Admiral Farragut left *Merrimack*. The name was thoroughly stuck to her. She had a petite build and delicate features that made her seem smaller, a command presence to chase lions down the stairs. Even *Mack*'s new XO—who had assumed the position Glenn considered rightfully hers—called her "Iron Hamster."

Nox took a step toward her. Glenn was afraid she flinched. She regarded him warily. Wished she didn't need to look *up* to face him when he arrived at the top of the ramp.

"Don't be afraid of me," said Nox.

"Why not?" said Glenn.

He had a machete.

"That back there?" Nox said, gestured with the rusty blade toward camp. "That man? I was only as brutal as that man was stupid. You're not stupid."

Nox brushed past her in the hatchway to board the shipwreck. He strode to the control room console and moved away clutter to uncover the empty place where the res chamber should have been.

Glenn said, "My presence here won't give you any influence with the *Merrimack*."

"Okay, maybe you're a little bit stupid," said Nox. He prowled through the debris, threw sheets of metal aside.

Then he moved aft. He tossed the burned seat cushion out of his way, which revealed the res chamber. No chance he wouldn't see it. He crouched down and pulled it out from its hiding place. He heaved it up and set it on a console. Powered it on.

After a moment he said darkly, "You deleted the harmonic."

Maybe he *had* overheard her. There was nothing for it. Glenn had to tell the truth. "Yes."

Unless she left the harmonic loaded in the chamber, the harmonic was irretrievable. Irretrievable from the machine. But not from her.

"Doesn't matter," Nox said.

Up flew the rusted blade. The machete came slicing down with a crash that made Glenn shrink back.

Nox cleaved the res chamber nearly in half.

He seesawed his blade free from the sheared metal. He told Glenn, "I can get the harmonic out of you if I need it."

* * *

It was raining where Colonel Steele's patrol was. Steele received a resonant call from Commander Ryan advising him that the pirates known as The Ninth Circle had taken the LEN camp.

"One fatality that we know of. The position of the pirates' Xerxes is unknown but it has to be within walking distance of the LEN camp. A Xerxes has true stealth capability, which makes your mission objective a bit on the tricky side. Find the Xerxes. Do not be sighted. Lives depend on that."

"Sir?" Steele began. "What do you mean by 'walking distance?'"

"It means the pirates walked," said Dingo. "At one time they were Roman legionaries, so use whatever *you* consider a walking distance. That's a big area, but you've got to get a lot closer than you are now. Give us your best, Marine."

"Aye, aye, sir."

❋ ❋ ❋

Rain tapped on the energy dome and came down in odd trickles, as if the raindrops hit a plastic bubble. But the expedition members couldn't see the surface of the bubble except as defined by the flattened undersides of the raindrops.

A heat pocket collected at the top of the energy dome. A cool damp breeze came in at ground level.

Because it was unshielded around the edges, the camp would have been vulnerable to a ground siege, if not for the hostages.

Any one of the expedition members could walk out across the dirt perimeter, if he had anywhere to go.

There wasn't anywhere to go. The pirates had set up jammers to prevent displacement. And Orissus let them know, "If one of you escapes, you had better all escape."

"Woe betide anyone you leave behind," said Nox, his gaze fixed on Glenn Hamilton.

Nox reported back to Caesar. Advised him that his non-Roman Roman eyes were on the ground and inside the LEN camp. Nox told him of the presence of *Merrimack* in the Zoen star system, though Caesar already knew that before he sent The Ninth Circle here.

"Is the DNA a hoax?" Caesar asked.

"If it is a hoax, people down here think it's *our* hoax," said Nox, then corrected himself, "Rome's hoax, I mean." Nox kept forgetting that Rome did not consider him Roman. "But there's a lot of evidence to say it's real."

"Send all data contained in all the scientists' information

banks to Us. Send all the raw data from the scientific equipment. Send everything on the extraplanetary beings they are calling 'clokes.' Is that truly short for cloaca?"

"Yes, *Domni*. The U.S. Marines came up with that name for them."

"Are there Marines on world?"

"There were. The LEN ordered them off. I don't see any. *Bagheera* hasn't detected any displacements or landings since we got here. There are two officers on leave from *Merrimack* down here in camp as part of the scientific expedition. One is a civilian in uniform. A xenolinguist. The other is a line officer. She's just here because she's married to the xenolinguist. So I'm told."

"Rank?"

"Lieutenant."

"Glenn Hamilton."

Nox's voice hitched. "Yes, Caesar."

Was there anything Numa Pompeii didn't know?

"Send Us complete personnel files on the xenos. Include their medical records. Send every record they have, all correspondence, notes, diaries, games, family pictures, porn. Collect everything. Omit nothing. We will sift out the useful from the chaff. After any transmission to us, erase this harmonic behind you. Kill anyone who suspects that we are in contact."

Knowledge was power. Caesar wanted all of it.

Nox got his brothers to work immediately. Galeo questioned, "Caesar specifically asked for personal records?"

Nox nodded. "He was adamant about that."

"Why is Caesar doing background checks on the xenos?" asked Faunus.

Nox shrugged. "Looking for a DNA hoax? I don't know."

"No. Not in their personal records," said Nicanor. "He's looking for something other than that."

"He must be looking for someone who is not what he seems to be," said Orissus. "Hopefully not another Farragut."

"Leave it," said Pallas.

"Does Numa know who you are?" Faunus asked.

"You're dumber than a dead xeno if you think he doesn't, O Best Beloved," Nox told Faunus.

"This is almost like a mole search," said Leo.

Rome was known for creating and inserting moles inside other societies. Rome was not known for having moles inside itself.

Pallas inhaled a small gasp. Realized, "He's looking for Romulii."

The others froze for an instant, then turned to stare at Pallas.

The Romulii were subversive supporters of former Caesar Romulus. Romulus was now comatose and completely crackers. His diehard followers were rabid. And clever.

"Do you really think so?" said Nox.

"You have a better idea?" said Pallas.

"No," said Nox. "But I don't like that one."

"I liked Romulus," said Leo. Sounded wistful.

"You did?" said Nox. "He was a patricide."

"No," said Galeo. "He wasn't. That was Claudia."

"Or Empress Calli," said Leo.

"I enlisted under Romulus," said Nicanor.

"We all did," said Pallas.

"I enlisted under Numa," said Nox. "But I fell in love with Rome under Romulus." He remembered the fighters passing over the house, rattling all the windows.

"The man did things," Faunus said, nodding. "Would've done more except for the traitor Augustus. It was a hell of a ride."

The brothers couldn't help but look at some of the data they collected. Leo questioned the references to "orbs" around the planet. What orbs are they talking about? Did they mean the U.S. Marine Swifts? Swifts were definitely not orb-shaped, but they were the only things up there in orbit other than *Merrimack*.

Pallas asked the xenos around the fire pit, but most of the xenos were too afraid to talk at all.

Jose Maria answered for them. "The orbs were cloke spacecraft. You would not have seen them when you came in. They attacked *Spring Beauty* and *Mercedes*. Then they attacked *Merrimack*."

"They attacked the *Mack?*" said Nox.

That explained why there were no more orbs.

"Why didn't the orbs attack the ships that came before *Spring Beauty* and *Mercedes*," Nicanor demanded.

"We do not know," said Jose Maria.

"The orbs were asleep," Nox said, an epiphany. "They were the Little People. Just a lot slower to wake up."

Glenn hesitated, afraid for her life. But she had orders: *Get close to John John.* The next thing she said would either get Nox's attention or get her dead quickly. "The buck lived."

Nox's blue eyes got very wide, amazed. He spoke the next line in *The Jungle Book*: "Because he came first, running for his life, leaping ere the Little People were aware."

In this case, the first several LEN ships to approach the planet survived—getting down to the planet before the Little People—the clokes—were aware. Once aware that ships were coming to *their* planet, the Little People had swarmed around the next intruders to come and tried to kill them.

"Just so," said Glenn.

At nightfall Nox took Glenn Hamilton for a walk out from under the dome.

This close to the galactic Rim, space was true black at this hour. Later, the Milky Way would rise, but for now, the sky was black.

And those widely spaced, fuzzy points of light up there weren't stars. They were galaxies unimaginably distant in the incomprehensible abyss.

"What are the constellations called here?" Nox asked.

"No one has named them," said Glenn.

"Really?" He looked up. No stars yet. They wouldn't rise for hours yet. "Someone should."

"You think in symbols, don't you?" Glenn said. Not a question.

Nox seemed startled. Glenn didn't want to startle him. She thought he knew that about himself.

"I guess I do." He hadn't known.

"Not everyone does," said Glenn. "Think in symbols."

It seemed to explain something to him.

"Ever kill anyone, Lieutenant Glenn Hamilton?" Nox asked. "I mean hand to hand."

Her turn to be startled. "Only monsters," she said.

"And what am I?"

"I don't think you're a monster."

"What am I then?"

Any answer could be fatal. She said, "A runaway Star Sparrow without a target."

He thought about that. She didn't want him to think too long. She said, "We should come out here later when the stars are out."

He nodded as if that were a fine idea. He walked her back to her tent.

She turned at the entrance. She didn't know if Patrick was inside or not. She did not want Nox in there. She said to Nox, "Thank you for the walk."

He stood over her, like a first date on the doorstep. His eyes shifted, his gaze moving across her face. "The Second Coming ever hit on you?" Nox asked.

Glenn hesitated. Nox meant his older brother. Admiral Farragut. Glenn couldn't muster up a convincing lie. Said, "Yes."

"What'd you do?"

She gave a brief chagrined smile. "Same thing I'm doing right now."

She was twisting her wedding ring.

Nox touched her cheek. "Good night, Mrs. Hamilton."

✳ ✳ ✳

The Marines advanced toward the expedition camp. This leg of the trek was all uphill.

The foxes kept up. Sometimes they ran ahead, which was good. It motivated the squad to keep up the pace. But this was a long march, and sooner or later the foxes had to turn around and go home. But then again, what else had a fox to do?

The gray-brown she-fox whom Rhino dubbed Fur For Brains pawed at Rhino's navel as if her belly button could open up.

Rhino yelled to no one in particular, "What the fecund is this furball doing?"

Kerry Blue cackled. Carly Delgado and Twitch Fuentes snorted. Asante said, "She's trying to look in your pouch to see if you're carrying a baby."

Rhino gave the fox's face an annoyed shove away from her. "Sister, you have the wrong address."

✳ ✳ ✳

"*Merrimack*," said Leo, like a man suddenly making a mental connection.

"What of her?" said Nox.

It was after dinner. Most of the xenos had abandoned their usual seats around the fire pit. That left only the brothers, Jose Maria, Aaron Rose, and Glenn and Patrick.

"Is *Merrimack* still upstairs? Is Adamas aboard?" Leo had the bright-eyed look of a fan. Adamas had been mad emperor Romulus' gladiator. Adamas had been known to serve on *Merrimack*. His real name was TR Steele.

Nox lifted both hands. "How would I know?"

Glenn clammed shut.

Patrick blurted the answer without thinking, "Usually."

Glenn shot him a glare. Patrick was nominally an officer, but he was as discreet as a civilian. You never offer information to an enemy. Not even seemingly harmless stuff.

Galeo spoke up, another fan. "I would like to see Adamas."

"You don't," Glenn said quietly. *Adamas will take your head off.* "You really don't."

TR Steele was a confirmed Roman hater.

Nox told his brothers, "I've heard Steele hates all things Roman."

"We're not Roman," Orissus reminded him. "We're pirates."

"That's probably worse," said Nox. "Everyone hates pirates."

✳ ✳ ✳

The leader of any pack got all the finest hembras. A snow-white she-fox in the furry band of camp followers took to twitching her tail at TR Steele. The white vixen ran past him, brushing herself against him, then stopped and looked back, tilted her foxy head to say, *Ain'tcha gonna chase me?*

"I can translate that," said Kerry Blue sourly and yelled to her compadres, "Hey! Can someone tell Fluffy here the Old Man's not interested?"

A twitch too far, and Kerry Blue was on her. Kerry dropped her field pack and lunged. Big claws and sharp teeth be damned.

Gyrene green and snowy white rolled over and over on the ground.

"Girl fight!" Dak cried.

Before Steele could bark his Marine back into line, Kerry Blue had already wrestled the she-fox over onto her back and roared into her huge rounded eyes, "Hey, perv! I AM THE ALPHA BITCH!"

Then Kerry was on her feet, collecting her field pack.

The white vixen shook herself off and gamboled away to flirt with a knot of young fox males.

"Good thing foxes are not aggressive," Asante told Kerry. "Fluff could've torn your guts out."

"*Muy estupido*," Carly said. "*Chica linda*, you gotta know the furball wasn't never no competition."

* * *

Patrick Hamilton had figured out that Leo was the technically inclined one among the pirate band, but he had no idea what inclined Leo to amass all the data in the expedition's computer banks, even to Patrick's language files.

Scarred welts that extended from Leo's shoulders to his wrists made him look like a cutter. But then again, Patrick supposed there was no "looking like" about it.

The jovial one, Faunus, fashioned a panpipe out of cloke bones he'd collected from the forest. Faunus made Patrick help him tune it. It terrified Patrick to tell the pirate when his pitch was slightly off. But Faunus, despite his brass knuckles, was one of the better-natured ones of the Circle. Faunus didn't seem likely to break a tool that served him.

The proud one, Nicanor, was humorless. Never laughed. Which was okay, because Nicanor didn't get angry either.

That Orissus was nasty for the fun of it.

Galeo, with his red goatee and red 666 on his forehead and his penchant for barbaric body paint, looked worse than he was. He had a mean bark, but if you obeyed the bark, he never bit.

Pallas was the one you wanted in your pocket. Pallas

looked handsome and normal except for the circled IX brand on his arm. Pallas was almost kind, and he was close to Nox. You wanted Pallas between you and Nox.

And Nox. Nox was flash-tempered and unpredictable and too interested in Patrick's wife.

Something about my wife attracts Farraguts.

After Faunus got his panpipe tuned, he made himself a crown out of local vines and broke into Aaron Rose's wine cellar. Faunus came out waggling four bottles. "They're holding out on us, *frateri!*"

The brothers gathered where Faunus led, to a long table under a tarp where Glenn, Patrick, Jose Maria, and Aaron Rose were sitting.

Faunus thumped down the bottles and leaned in to Aaron's face. "Aren't you?"

Aaron Rose, the amateur vintner, warned nervously, "Uh, that batch is an experiment. I really can't promise that's even drinkable."

It looked as though Dr. Rose feared the pirates would kill him if the wine was bad. It was a reasonable fear.

"Where's the corkscrew?" Faunus boomed.

Nox reached for one of the bottles. "I'll open it. Let's see what happened to Schroedinger's cat."

Patrick was unclear on the details of Schroedinger's famous experiment except for the part everyone knew. Dr. Rose said it, looking ill, "That experiment sometimes ends with a dead cat."

"Yes, it does," said Nox, ominous.

"I believe the experiment was theoretical," Jose Maria offered.

"I prefer the practical," said Faunus, grinning.

"Physics are fun," said Nox. He set the wine bottle on the table edge. He checked it for level. Then he took all the rings off his right hand.

Nox gave the rings to Glenn to hold. Then he lined up a knifehand strike on the bottle neck below the cork.

His torso moved in a slow twist through a couple practice passes. The brothers' chuckles rumbled.

They started up a low chant: "Nox! Nox! Nox!"

Ready, Nox put up his hand for silence.

His body coiled back, his right hand cocked behind his

head. Then he unleashed his massed power. His leading arm flew round first as a counterweight, his right hip thrust the momentum through the turn of his body, like a major leaguer swinging mightily for the fences. The bottle's neck sheared clean before the edge of his right hand. The bottle mouth, with the cork still in it, bulleted out of the pavilion. Nox's lips pulled back in a white snarling grin.

His hand was unscathed.

The brothers thumped the tables, hailing his success.

Nox put out his hand to Glenn for his rings. She spilled them into his palm.

Nox held up the opened bottle toward Dr. Rose, softly menacing. "Here, kitty."

Apparently the life or death of the vintner hung on the quality of the contents.

Olive-skinned Aaron Rose turned ghastly pale. Couldn't move.

Jose Maria stepped forward in Aaron's stead. "Are you a physicist, Nox?"

Nox said, "I know enough to be dangerous."

Jose Maria leaned his nose over the cutting edge of the bottleneck. He sniffed. "The cat lives."

It wasn't until Nox threw back his head, poured wine into his own mouth, and confirmed the verdict that Aaron Rose passed out with relief.

The brothers collected more bottles of the wine and took their party elsewhere.

Left behind under the tarp, Patrick, Glenn, and Jose Maria revived Dr. Rose. They had only water to offer him, which was probably a good thing.

Dr. Rose asked, "Would they have killed me if the wine was bad?"

"Don't ever want to know," said Patrick.

Trying to push past his terror, Aaron Rose told Jose Maria conversationally, "I never understood Shroedinger's cat."

"The problem is the cat," said Jose Maria.

Glenn blinked up at him. "You're serious?"

"The cat is too big."

"You're not serious."

"I am. At issue is decoherence. A cat is a complex system, subject to interference from its surroundings and even from itself. It is not an isolated quantum object, and the premise that a cat can exist in two states at once, both living and dead, is wrong."

"You don't know cats," said Glenn.

"Apparently not," Jose Maria admitted.

Inga lifted her head from her paws, looking around for cats. Glenn hadn't noticed her under the table.

"I suppose that is why it is not Schroedinger's dog," Jose Maria said. "One always knows where one stands with dogs. Ah, there's the sun."

The sun had come out from behind the clouds.

"What makes Schroedinger's illustration unworkable is that the state of the cat inside the box is either alive or dead before Schroedinger lifts the lid and observes it. Even though he is leaving the fate of the animal to a subatomic event, the only uncertainty here is in Schroedinger's mind, not in the state of the cat. This is not the case with quantum objects, which exist in two states at once. Is a photon a particle or is it a wave? The answer is yes. It is a particle. It is a wave. It is both until one observes it; and then the observation itself forces the decision. What the quantum object is depends quite literally on how you look at it.

"The observation of one aspect renders the other aspect unknown and unknowable. There is no equivalent of quantum behavior in the macroscopic world."

Oh, yes there is. Glenn turned her head in the direction Nox had gone. She could hear a panpipe playing. *There is*.

The clokes came out that evening. Clokes only ever came out at night or when the day was overcast. They didn't like sunlight.

The pirates had demanded to be notified next time the clokes showed up at the edge of camp. The xenos sent Jose Maria to be the messenger.

When the brothers followed Jose Maria out to see, the xenos returned to their tents. They left a red light aimed out toward the forest. The clokes didn't seem to notice the red light.

The pirates moved silently.

"You need not be quiet," Jose Maria said at a conversational volume. "Only do not move quickly."

"They can't hear us?" Leo asked, oddly compelled to whisper.

"No ears," said Patrick Hamilton.

Faunus squinted between the trees. Scowled. "I've seen prettier cases of gangrene."

"What do the clokes want here?" Nox asked.

"They want us dead," said Glenn.

And it was too easy feel the same way about them.

※ ※ ※

Drone surveillance craft had been streaming sensor data from the distant cloke generational ship back to *Merrimack* continuously. Computer programs sifted through the mass of data to flag readings of interest.

Commander Ryan brought Captain Carmel the status report.

"Life on board?" Captain Carmel asked.

"No, sir. Not yet. And it's not looking likely. The drones detected a lot of dead cloke bodies. The major find is the presence of res chambers."

"That is major," Calli agreed.

One never expects a sublight culture to have resonant communications.

"Are we sure that's what we found?" said Calli.

"Yes, sir," said Ryan. "The res chambers aren't sending and they're not receiving. But they're functional."

"What's the harmonic?"

"Undetermined. We can see the designation of the harmonic loaded into the cloke res chamber, but we can't translate those alien symbols into anything we can dial into from one of our own res chambers. The boffins did get the drones to send a ping from one cloke chamber on one of our own harmonics. The other cloke chambers picked it up. So we know the units really are res chambers, and we know they work. The boffins have a drone monitoring the chambers for any incoming messages, but so far, except for our ping, they're silent. Looks like everyone's dead and nobody from the hometown is trying to reach them."

※ ※ ※

On the long trek toward the LEN expedition camp, the Marines advanced to a dying bog. It was a sunken area of gray-white pillars of dead tree trunks spiraling up from black ground. It might have been a once-upon-a-time lake. It was just damp and dead now. Dried algae mats and layers of fallen reeds made the walking soft, like on a bed of pine needles but not as good smelling.

Their entourage of foxes sniffed the brackish air. They hummed and tried to lead the Marines off in another direction. The foxes didn't want to go there. They wouldn't follow.

"Should we pay attention to our scouts?" Cain asked Colonel Steele.

Steele marched back to where the foxes were. The animals had sat down, watching their friends go. They looked confused. The white fox, Fluffy, stood on her hind legs, her head down, her muzzle on her chest, her paws folded over her pouch.

"What do you think got into the fur heads?" said the Yurg. "Do you think there's something bad here?"

"*They* think so," said Cain. "And they know the place better than we do."

"It can't be scyllas," said Steele.

The foxes didn't look near as frantic as they had when the scyllas or the cave monsters were around. But they were scared.

"I don't like that they're scared," said Steele.

"I don't see anything," said Asante. "There's nowhere for any monsters to hide really."

The area was flat decaying ground with tall gray spikes in it.

"The foxes just don't like the smell," said the Yurg.

"Neither do I," said Cain.

"We need to get closer to the LEN camp," said Steele. "A lot closer." He didn't want to detour around the stinking ground without a good reason. He signaled *Merrimack* to get their view of the terrain.

Merrimack could detect nothing menacing in the area. Steele ordered the squad forward.

"It smells clokey," said Carly Delgado, shouldering her field pack.

"You think there's something bad here?" said Dak, sniffing.

"*Where?*" asked Rhino.

And Dak dropped. Straight down.

He'd stepped in a hole, and his leg was in it now, up to his groin.

"Man down!" Carly cried. "Dak's in a hole!"

Asante ran forward. "Dak! How deep is it?"

"How should I know! Longer than my leg!" Dak yelped. "Just glad I didn't land on my boys!"

Twitch and Rhino moved in, took hold of Dak's beefy arms, and hauled him out of there.

Asante shone a light down the hole.

The squad gathered round.

Cain Salvador said, "What's it look like?"

"It's a hole, Cain," said Asante.

Steele barked, "Spread out."

And the ground gave way under all of them.

Suddenly Marines were scrabbling, scurrying up the sliding dirt, falling in. Earthen walls collapsed as men clawed at them.

Steele planted a boot in the ground, and it kept going down and got stuck. An air pocket broke underneath him. He dropped. Black clods filled in from above. He couldn't move his legs. Soil dropped on his head, spilled in his face. He shook his head. Spat. Couldn't lift his com to call for rapture. He didn't have his displacement collar on, but some of his squad might. He could get some of them out of here.

He couldn't. He couldn't open his mouth. Couldn't open his eyes. Losing the light.

Knew someone had got clear of the sinking ground. Voices called to those going under.

He heard his name in Kerry Blue's voice.

Thought as the light died, *Don't never say, Till death do us part.*

Kerry Blue found the solid rim. Watched the alien earth consume her squad. She lay down flat as if on the edge of a breaking ice floe. She clawed at the dirt with her hands. Her hands never looked so small. Even the pitiful amount of soil she did move immediately slid back down from where she dragged it.

Hurry, hurry, hurry. It didn't take much earth to crush a man. She leaned farther over the edge. Hauled armfuls of soil up toward her. Reached down for more. Balance shifted forward onto her hands. The ground gave way under her hands. Air pocket! She fell in, hands and head first, hips following over the rim.

The ground packed in around her.

29

SOMETHING TORE KERRY'S pant legs. Hands that were not quite hands closed hard on her hips and pulled. Made her grunt. Scarcely moved her. Her field pack anchored her in the ground.

Something slicing like box cutters at the straps. Another tug at her hips. Her teeth scooped up dirt. Filled her mouth. Stuffed her nostrils. She was moving up and backward, chest squeezed.

She broke to open air. Exhaled hard, expelling earthen plugs. She coughed, snorted. Inhaled. Coughed again. Spat. Tears washed her eyes. She blinked and blinked.

Through a blur of tears she saw dirt flying in arcing sprays. Rooster tails of it rose up from the sinkhole. Furry tails, held straight up like flags, marked the source of each fountain. The foxes were digging like sons of vixens.

Kerry moved around the rim of solid ground to see where the white fox, Fluffy, was working like a machine. Kerry wanted to get down in there with her but knew she would just be in the way.

She watched, helpless. Seconds passed in lifetimes, like an approach to light speed. *Please please please.*

White paws unearthed a broad white hand. Springy blond hair lifted off the skin that looked bluish pale.

Kerry jumped down into the pit, stumbled toward him.

The white fox was scooping dirt away from his chest. Kerry Blue uncovered his face. It was pasty, his brow pinched, eyes shut hard, lips a hard line.

Eyelids flickered without opening. His mouth opened, his chest rose inhaling. He snorted dirt from nostrils.

Cursed.

Tears splashed down on his cheek.

TR Steele cracked an eyelid. Saw Kerry and the fox.

He croaked at Kerry, "Everyone else out of here?"

Kerry immediately moved over to help uncover someone else, who turned out to be Dak.

Kerry knew Fluffy would get Thomas out of here. Tears streamed from her eyes, not just from the grit.

When all the Marines were standing, sitting, or lying on solid ground around the sinkhole, and the foxes stopped digging, Colonel Steele drew himself up to attention. Tried to. Fluffy stood up, planted her paws on his chest and licked his face. "Yeah, okay," he growled, gave her a quick scratch behind the ears, and pushed her off of him. "Good dog. *Marines!* By the numbers!"

"Alpha One, here!" Cain yelled, then, nudging Dak, "You're up, you boon!"

"Oh. Yeah. Alpha Two, here!"

Rhino: "Alpha Three, here! My pack's not."

Carly: "Alpha Four, here."

Twitch: "Alpha Five, here."

Kerry Blue: "Alpha Six, here." And because Asante was still gagging and spitting, Kerry said, "Alpha Seven's here too."

The Yurg: "Baker Team all here, sir!" Added, "Some of our stuff is not."

"Like my shovel," said Big Richard.

"How the hell do you bury a shovel?"

TR Steele contained his internal tremors and mentally beat himself up. He'd almost lost his squad. His men could have been crushed. Easily.

He relied too much on personal fields to keep his Marines safe. PF's deflected beams and projectiles only. There was a lot more out here that could kill you than beams and projectiles. The pirates of The Ninth Circle showed everyone that.

And then there was Kerry Blue. TR Steele was trying not to think about Kerry Blue. He felt stark terror when he thought about Kerry Blue. He never used to feel fear.

So here he was pretending he hadn't felt as if he'd had a rib torn out back there when he'd heard her screaming for him. He was not looking at Kerry Blue. Knew where she was. He always needed to know where she was. He really should beach her.

Yet he felt he couldn't breathe if she weren't here.

He looked down into the sinkhole. The bottom had dropped at least two meters. The skeletal trees were still in place, the tops of their roots exposed. The walls of the crater were pocked with holes the diameter of basketballs.

"Tunnels!" said Cain.

"This place is shot with cloke tunnels!" said Icky Iverson.

"Explains why we never see them," said the Yurg.

"They're underground!"

"There's no conduit. Those are just naked tunnels," said Taher.

"Sure those aren't wormholes?" said Kerry Blue. "I mean for really big worms?"

Rhino said, "Why do we think these are cloke tunnels?"

"Are you breathing the same skat I am?" said Asante with his shirt collar pulled up over his mouth and nose.

"Delgado said it when we first got here," said Cain. "It smells clokey."

"If it's clokes, they've come a long way from their spaceship," said Colonel Steele. "They had to cover the same distance we did. Addai! How many clicks out are we?"

Asante checked. "About a buck and a quarter, sir."

Steele wondered how many clokes there really were. Their spaceship wasn't that big, yet there were a lot of openings in the dirt walls.

The Marines stood around the rim of the sinkhole, wondering if it was safe to climb down into the crater to search for their gear.

Steele hailed *Merrimack* to get a sounding of the solidity of the crater floor and the location of all tunnels that could undermine their path.

Merrimack sent the map. Tracking also sent Asante the precise coordinates of the Marines' buried equipment.

Retrieving their stuff was easy. All a Marine had to do was start digging at a spot, and a fox jumped down to take over. They retrieved field packs, landing disks, swords, can-teens. A shovel.

Fluffy ate a package of C-Rats.

The foxes leaped back out of the crater. They cleaned their fur and their claws, then started back the way they'd come at a dogtrot.

Finding themselves not being followed, the foxes circled back round to the Marines. The looks on their alien faces clearly said, *Can we GO now?*

Steele ordered his squad, "Wear your LDs on your backs. D-collars around your necks. D-gear will be turned on at all times."

He had *Merrimack* chart a path for them over solid ground to get them closer to the LEN encampment. The ship's sensor techs plotted the cloke tunnels and sent the locations to Asante's omni.

There were an ungodly lot of them.

"Any clokes in those tunnels?" Asante asked.

"At current settings our sensors can't tell the difference between a cloke and dirt," the tech said.

"Can I suggest you adjust your settings?"

Technicians didn't take suggestions well.

Colonel Steele bellowed for his squad to move out.

The foxes came along.

* * *

The expedition members continued to take their meals all together around the fire pit. The pirates insisted. No one ever knew who was getting a pirate to share his plate.

Patrick Hamilton could never be trusted not to say something inappropriate. He just had to comment on The Ninth Circle's fondness for leopard spots and leopard paw prints.

"The leopard choice doesn't make sense," Patrick said.

Glenn cringed.

Nicanor shot Patrick an odd look. Told Patrick coldly, "The leopard guards the lowest circles of hell."

"Yes," said Patrick. "The *other way around*. The leopard's not there to protect the lower circles from outsiders. The leopard is supposed to keep the damned *in!*"

Glenn's eyes shut themselves, pained. She breathed, "Nox, please don't kill my husband."

"The leopard, Dr. Hamilton," said Nox, chillingly reasonable, "joined the other side."

* * *

When the subject of DNA came up again around the fire pit, Nox asked anyone, "Why is this just coming out now? Your expedition has been rotating scientists in and out of here for seven years. Why did no one notice?"

Peter Szaszy answered hotly, "Because SOMEONE never brought a microbiologist on board." That directed at Izrael Benet. Benet had little enough to say these days.

Sandy Minyas, who never let an I-told-you-so get by her, said, "Our resident physicians were asleep at the switch. They saw the signs and did everything to sit on it."

"Alien genetics is not in the scope of our project, and you know it," said the senior physician, Dr. Cecil. "We weren't sent here to chase unicorns."

Wynans gestured toward Glenn and Patrick. "Before those two went wandering unprotected off reservation, no one caught an infectious microbe. No one had any reason to analyze the base life chemistry."

"And then you got rear-ended by a unicorn," said Nox.

"That's a good summation, sir," said Wynans.

Dr. Sandy Minyas told Nox, "They've known for a long time that Zoe has proteins in common with Earth. And proteins don't just replicate themselves."

"You're out of your area of specialization, Dr. Minyas," Cecil warned. "There is more than one way to build a protein. Protein doesn't indicate DNA. Other worlds have other ways of manufacturing sugars, phosphates, and bases. There are as many different ways to build life as there are inhabited worlds. No two of them alike. There was no reason to look for DNA just because we found compatible proteins here. And may I say the question of how we missed it strikes me as trivial, petty, and pointless. That question misses the colossal picture. The real issue is how did this happen."

"It was *my* question," said Nox, cleaning his nails with a stiletto.

Cecil blanched.

"So how did this happen?" said Nox.

"Easily," said Dr. Minyas. "We are all—all of us, everywhere in the known universe—built from the same basic blocks—the elements. All elements abide by the same rules of construction. Two hydrogen atoms bond with an oxygen atom to make water. Given same pressure and temperature, that combination will behave the same every single time. There is a logic to the universe. An element is, well, elemental."

"DNA is a *little* more complex than a water molecule, thank you very much, Dr. Minyas," said Dr. Cecil, teeth on edge.

"But the DNA macromolecule is still made up of just five common elements from the skinny end of the periodic table. Hydrogen, oxygen, carbon, nitrogen, and phosphorus."

"That's it?" said Glenn. "What about iron?"

"Iron is in your blood," said Sandy Minyas. "Not in your genetic makeup."

"I don't understand."

"DNA is the blueprint for terrestrial life. You're reading iron off the construction materials list for the finished product."

Szaszy said, "Sandy, your view is far too simplistic. You're leaving out the infinite variables, the aeons needed for a solar system to coalesce. You gloss over everything that might happen to the planet as it condenses and cools. There's no predicting what kind of atmosphere will form or whether it will even stay there. You need some kind of cyanobacteria to organize itself and make the nitrogen atoms let go of each other long enough to bind with carbon, hydrogen, and oxygen to make the formation of organic life possible. Your blithe 'easily' ignores the infinite variables and complex orchestration of processes that resulted in that chemical self-organization that is terrestrial life."

Sandy Minyas said, "The variables are not quite infinite and apparently not random. And it *is* simple. Even our twenty amino acids are made of only hydrogen, oxygen, carbon, nitrogen, and some have sulfur. These are not exotic ingredients, guys. As for fitting them together, all elements have limited ways of forming bonds. Reactions of amino acids with other amino acids is preferential. It's a complex game board, but there *are* rules."

"And you're obviously all about rules, Sandy," Dr. Cecil muttered.

"Could someone burp Dr. Cecil?" said Sandy. "We have an Earthlike planet here. It is not unimaginable that similar forces would come together to create this pattern twice."

Cecil said, "Except that you're completely ignoring the fact that DNA and RNA are chemically difficult to produce. *And* there is a chicken-and-egg conundrum at work here. DNA manufactures RNA, but DNA consists of two strands of RNA. Nucleic acid is needed to make a protein and proteins are needed to make nucleic acid. It's an informational tail chase. How can a substance spontaneously organize itself into living existence when a living system is required to form those base substances?"

"Suffice to say that it *did*," said Sandy Minyas. "Twice. And why not? DNA *works*. The basic units are simple molecules. Maybe DNA's particular combination of molecules isn't the only template to build life, but it's a really good one."

Senior xenozoologist Peter Szaszy lamented, "Everything I knew about the origins of life has gone out the window."

"Out the window? Szasz, what you knew was never in the building."

"Thank you for that, Dr. Minyas."

Cecil said, "The rise of DNA was so improbable as to be miraculous. *Therefore* the first time was a miracle. A second time is fraud."

"Give it up, Cecil," said Wynans, who had tested a hell of a lot of Zoen organisms. "This is no fraud. That genie's already out and granting wishes."

Sandy Minyas said, "It is precisely because it happened once that a second time is possible. And because it is possible, it is inevitable."

"Back up," said Wynans. "How do you figure that? Where are you getting the inevitability from?"

"Because it *did* happen, that means it *can* happen, and when something can happen in nature, it *will*. The same forces that culminated in the first formation of DNA are still at work in the universe."

Glenn tossed out a word she'd heard once, "Is this Panspermia?"

Pained faces around the fire pit told her it was an ignorant question.

"Panspermia was a bit of a joke really," said Dr. Minyas. "The chicken-and-egg conundrum was so confounding that the early theorists resorted to importing their eggs from outer space."

"I don't get it," said Glenn.

"According to the theory of Panspermia, the same comets or meteors that salted Earth with amino acids necessary for life also scattered those same molecules onto other planets in the Solar System. Which still left hanging out there the question of how those amino acids formed in the first place."

"How did they?"

"We don't know. We can make DNA in the laboratory—"

"*You can?* Can you, Sandy?"

"Oh, back into a unicorn, Cecil. We can make DNA in the laboratory, but we can't re-create the *evolution* of DNA in the lab."

Wynans added, "We're probably overlooking a strategic variable. The presence of chaos means the smallest critical variation can change the whole picture."

"So we have the same genetic code as the Zoens," said Dr. Rose, whose specialty was alien atmospheres. "Does that mean we can mate with them?"

"Can you mate with a dog?" Dr. Minyas asked back.

"That's been suggested to me," said Dr. Rose. "More than once."

"Yes, I think I made the suggestion," said Dr. Minyas. "I think I suggested baboon though."

"I dated some of those in college," Glenn offered.

"I am not touching the recreational *mating* question," said Peter Szaszy. "But *insemination* requires more than a DNA genome in common. Procreation is species specific. The genetic design of a species is complex beyond measure. Not even Sandy Minyas can say duplication of a species is inevitable."

"She won't," said Sandy Minyas.

"Forms of life will vary as much as they can," said Wynans. "There is a level of complexity above which the probability of duplication is beyond the threshold of chaos."

Glenn said, "What's the threshold of chaos?"

"The threshold of chaos divides the inevitable and the impossible," said Wynans. "Things that will happen and things that happen once."

Peter Szaszy said, "You can't find an Earth species duplicated here. And you won't. You can find something analogous to a bird, but there are no birds per se, let alone a species of bird. Life on Zoe is all similar to life on Earth but not the same. The way dinosaurs were similar to mammals and birds. Dinosaurs seem alien, but they were actually DNA-based creatures. They were chordates. Dinosaurs had lungs and hearts and heads and spines and four appendages, a head and brain, eyes, noses, and ears. Skin. All standard construction of the chordate model out of a deoxyribonucleic template."

Patrick asked, "So who got DNA first? Earth or Zoe?"

"We did," said Cecil. "Earth."

"Then this is the Second Creation," Patrick said.

"Who cares which is first?" Cecil said.

"Scientifically, it doesn't mean spit," Patrick said. "Theologically, it could disturb some folks—who came first, Man or foxes. The Biblical Creator has a track record of being disappointed with His heirs and starting over."

Nox turned to Jose Maria de Cordillera, whom he knew to be a devout Old Catholic. "What does this do to your Creation story?"

Jose Maria answered serenely, "Creation just gets more and more miraculous."

"What's happening here doesn't bother you? A separate Creation?"

"One cannot argue with Creation," said Jose Maria. "One can only marvel."

In the morning, the pirate Faunus swaggered out to the fire pit where the xenos sat at breakfast. Faunus waggled a long strip of tape from one stout finger.

"Who is going to die for this? Don't gawp at me. You look like fish. Tell me who it's going to be."

Sandy Minyas squinted at the strand hanging from Faunus' finger. "What is that?"

"Tape," several people murmured.

Szaszy whispered to Sandy, "Someone broke into one of the spaceships."

Faunus boomed, "Who did this?"

Nox quickly rounded on Jose Maria de Cordillera, who appeared about to confess, "NOT you!"

Faunus scanned all the other horrified faces. "Pick someone else."

"No," said Director Izrael Benet.

"Yes," Faunus said back. "Give me someone or you all die. Come on, people, I need someone to die for this." He gave the tape another shake. It coiled and stuck to itself.

"Her!" Tom Cryscoch cried out, shrill. "She did it!"

His outthrust finger pointed at Glenn.

Glenn inhaled a gasp. Didn't exhale.

Faunus moved in on Glenn. He bent down to push his face right into hers. "Is this your work?" Wild hairs of his beard grazed her chin. He smelled of last night's liquor. "Did you do this? Verily?"

Glenn choked, "Yes."

"Well, then." Faunus took a step back.

"No!" Dr. Cecil cried.

The machete swung.

With an edge honed nano-fine and a mighty arm behind it, Faunus severed the neck clean through with one stroke. The head rolled.

And came to a rest at Glenn's feet. Glenn shut her eyes and shuddered.

She opened her eyes. Looked down.

Tom Cryscoch's head rested against the toes of her boots. His body was doing a fish twitch, pulsing brightest red from its stalk.

Faunus picked up the head by its hair. Talked into its slack face. "Oh, come on. You were just not paying attention." He tossed the head to Nox, who tossed it to Orissus. Cryscoch's head made the bouncing rounds of The Ninth Circle until Nicanor threw it into the fire pit. Nicanor told the xenos in a lordly voice, "We control your lives. We control your deaths. Do not make us remind you again."

Glenn felt fizzy, her nerves dancing. Wondered what she'd ever done to Tom Cryscoch. She didn't even *know* him. And maybe that was why he'd picked her to give up for slaughter. He didn't know her.

Even as she was thinking it, Nox seized Glenn by the arm, snarled at her softly, "And you. You really need to figure out who is worth defending to the death." He threw her arm back at her. His bloody handprint on her sleeve slithered off the slick fabric.

Nox moved back to Faunus. "Problem, O Best Beloved."

"What problem?" Faunus grunted.

"I don't think that's our culprit." Nox nodded at the head in the fire.

"I'm sure it's not," Faunus said. "I don't give a rat's ass as long as someone is dead and it's not Ilsa. Or the smart guy. Or the winemaker. Or your girlfriend. Or the goat. Or the dog."

The pirates seized food from the xenos' plates and moved away to breakfast by themselves. Orissus spoke back over his shoulder to the xenos, "Clean that up."

The expedition members converged to care for the dead man. They retrieved the head from the fire and cleaned the body as best they could and held a hasty, somber little funeral.

Glenn felt a buzzing inside. Thought she might vomit. She murmured to Dr. Cecil, "Thank you for speaking up for me."

"Wasn't for you," Cecil said. "I just don't participate in human sacrifice."

Patrick, who seemed to be trying hard not to scream at her, asked Glenn, "What in name of sanity made you admit to a fucking lie?" His lips were rimmed in white.

"I'm a soldier among civilians. It's my duty to stand between them and enemies." She swallowed down bile. Confessed, "Just between you and me, I'm glad I'm not dead. I didn't want to die for Tom Cryscoch."

Glenn got up in the middle of the night. Got dressed.

Patrick's voice sounded from the bed. "Babe? Where are you going?"

"Just act like you think I'm having an affair."

Patrick sat up. Whispered, "Can you get a signal up to *Merrimack*?"

"I won't even try. If I go near a com, I'm afraid Nox will kill someone."

"Nox wouldn't kill you," said Patrick.

"I wasn't talking about me."

Glenn and Nox lay side by side on a blanket outside the energy dome to stargaze. They had to stay up very late to do it.

Glenn hugged herself, waiting for the starrise.

"You're upset," said Nox.

"Yes."

She was lying face up, staring at the black.

Nox was resting on his side, facing her.

"Don't waste yourself on the dead guy. That was natural selection."

"I just don't know what whoever really did it is thinking."

"I wouldn't worry about him," said Nox.

Glenn turned her head toward him. "You know who it is?"

"I'm pretty sure it was Faunus."

She stared at Nox in the dark. Couldn't really see him.

She felt his shrug. He said, "Y'all were getting too comfortable."

They fell silent. She dozed.

Nox nudged her awake. "Glenn. Stars."

She opened her eyes. "Oh, my God."

In the hours before dawn, half of the cloudless sky was brilliant with stars, the other half a black bottomless pit.

They talked about John Farragut. The other John Farragut. Nox brought it up. She wouldn't.

"Your John Farragut never did anything bad to me," said Nox. He was on his back. Eyes fixed heavenward. "I only saw him a few times. He never called me John John. Senior avoided the house when big John visited. And I avoided him too. I was snotty to him. He was funny, made everyone laugh. He was larger than life. I hated him for my father's sake. Then I hated him because I was his replacement.

"Then I hated him because I wasn't his replacement. I was just a shot across big John's bow." Nox suddenly rolled over sideways, propped up on his elbow, facing her. "You're thinking something. Tell me. And don't lie. I'll know."

Glenn confessed exactly what she'd been thinking. "It just sounds so very *Farragut*."

"What does?"

"Why light a candle when you can set off a nuke?"

"You can't be saying we're alike."

"No and yes."

This nut fell from the same tree. John Alexander was born in sunlight. The shadows were much deeper where John Junior fell.

She could see the familial resemblance under the scars, the tattoos, the feathers and bones. But underneath even that, Nox reminded her more of Augustus—a really big gun pointing in an uncertain direction.

"You're not safe here," said Glenn, a tremor in her voice.

Nox said, "You must know nothing scares me anymore."

Glenn exhaled an unsteady breath. *Oh, you are too easy*.

She had learned in judo, if you want an opponent to step away from you, you pull him. If you want him to step toward you, push him away.

She pushed.

Glenn was not good at deception. But the hell of it was, she could deceive with perfect honesty. "I'm afraid for you."

A puff of air passed between his lips, dismissive. "Don't be."

Nox was not leaving her now.

And Glenn was dead certain Captain Carmel had Marines on the ground. She just didn't know how long it would take them to get here.

Senior xenozoologist Peter Szaszy said at dinner, "We are a greater threat to this world than the clokes."

Sandy Minyas looked at him sideways. "Where did you get that idea?"

"The clokes are respectful of the ecosystem."

"If you don't count murder," said Aaron Rose.

"Murder?" said Peter Szaszy.

"Yes, murder. Remember Helmut? Our late colleague?"

"That was a mistake. The aliens misunderstood Roodover-hemd's intentions."

"We saw the clokes carry off a baby mammoth and raid a monkey squirrel's nest," said Glenn.

Dr. Szaszy rolled his eyes as if Glenn had said something incredibly tired and naïve. "Scientists collect specimens. The visitors haven't upset the balance. They don't pollute."

"They even bury their shit," said Dr. Maarstan.

"They bury . . . ?" Patrick started in alarm.

Glenn asked cautiously, "You mean they dig latrines?" The Latin word for latrine was *cloaca*.

"Not exactly bury," Maarstan revised. "They insert their cloaca into the mud and excrete. But I suppose you imagine they're humping the ground."

"You *boon!*" Glenn cried.

Maarstan opened his hands, looked blank. "What?"

Patrick breathed, "Holy Mother of Mercy."

Sandy Minyas said, "Monotremes are egg layers."

"They're breeding," said Patrick.

"Where are they doing this?" Glenn demanded.

"Go down to the river," said Sandy Minyas. "The banks are pocked with insertion holes."

"No one is going down to the river," said Orissus.

Dr. Szaszy told Glenn, "It's not as if the visitors are polluting the river. The ground is soft on the riverbanks."

"Joy joy for them," said Glenn.

"They're breeding like roaches," said Patrick.

"There aren't that many," said Maarstan. "We would have seen them on one of the surveys."

"They're hiding," said Glenn.

"Of course they are," said Dr. Szaszy as if humoring a mad woman.

And apparently the clokes were still taking specimens.

When the clokes came out very late into the night, several xenos gathered at the camp perimeter to watch from behind a wall of polymer shields. The xenos shone spotlights on them through red gels. The red light didn't seem to bother either the native wildlife or the clokes.

A spindly procession of clokes lurched through the forest like oversized mangled ants carrying a bigger load. Perhaps they were headed down to the river where their eggs were laid.

Glenn spied the thick vulpine tail swinging from the shoulders of a clot of bearers. They had taken a fox this time.

They passed into a patch of the red lights, giving a glimpse of the head lolling back loose and lifeless. And recognizable.

The dead fox was Princess.

30

A WALL OF RED descended over Glenn's eyes. A wall of noise filled her head.

"No!" Blood roared in her ears with her own raw scream. She felt something deeply rooted yanked out of her. Glenn grabbed up the wicker shield before her, seized a machete from the nearest pirate's hangar—Nox's—and charged out screaming. *"That's my baby girl!"*

Glenn flew at the clokes, crazy angry. She slashed down every cloke within reach in a mindless rage, then chased the others. They went springing into the forest depths. Glenn charged after them, reeling back at times from the force of thrown nails that stuck into her shield. She caught her footing and forged ahead, screaming.

The pirates did not exist. Danger did not exist. Hurt, rage, and sorrow were all that existed.

The pirates stared after Glenn startled, amazed.

Patrick dashed after her. He tensed, expecting a shot in the kidneys from angry pirates. *OgodOgodOgodOgod.* The muscles in his back tightened. They felt solid and shrinking.

Not sure why he wasn't gunned down.

The path before him was black. He followed the grief-charged screaming.

He tripped over messes of carved clokes.

Then blundered into a warm lump and fell across it. It was furry. He'd found Princess.

He picked her up. She weighed maybe a hundred pounds. Her fur was soft, her body warm, limp.

A funny mist descended over his eyes looking at her. No pirates were chasing him. He was lost.

He turned his face up toward the treetops. Through the lacy fronds he saw the glow of starlight. Where the highlands rose the sky was perfectly black. He trudged, heavy footed with his heavy load and heavy heart, upward.

Glenn's raging screams had turned to gasping ragged bleating.

Princess weighed mightily in Patrick's arms. He tried to call, "Glenn." A weird broken sound came out of him. He hiked through underbrush. Tears glinted on fur in the starlight.

"Glenn!" he croaked.

Thrashing of brush and snapping twigs sounded nearer.

Glenn found him. She moved like a lost waif.

She had already dropped her polymer shield somewhere. She dragged the machete at her side.

Patrick set Princess down. He took Glenn into his arms. She cried on his chest. There were scratches and nicks in her skin. Her frictionless clothes held no blood. There were burrs in her short hair. She stank.

Patrick kissed her forehead.

Patrick took up his burden again. He needed to take Princess home. Glenn walked ahead of him, hacking out a path with the machete back to the vale where the forest parted and the stream tumbled down from the highlands.

They had to stop every hundred yards and rest. It was a long trek up to the highland meadow. They could not know where the tribe had gone, but they trusted somehow that they would find the foxes.

In the light of dawn, Patrick could see that Glenn had been grazed by cloke nails. The caked blood had to be hers. Clokes didn't bleed.

Glenn washed off her own blood and the cloke gore in the stream.

At the high meadow, the foxes found them.

The two tribes had come back together. They milled, agitated. A cry went up from both tribes on seeing Princess.

Patrick set Princess down, his arms sore, his back and knees aching.

Rogue came forward. He nosed at Princess' lifeless body. He keened, utterly bewildered.

Hamster, who thought she was all cried out, sobbed.

Princess' Daddy sniffed her. He smelled something hateful on her. Snorted. His hackles lifted up.

Mama-san rubbed Princess' fur with aromatic herbs to get the cloke stink off.

And already dirt was flying as foxes augured out a grave.

Glenn watched the arcs of dirt. She breathed, "Oh, no. So soon."

Rogue nosed his mate. He gave a strange little cry that seemed to beg of her, *Wake up*. There was a question in it, an upturned note. *Please?*

The hole was quickly deep enough to hide her from predators.

Rogue stood up on his hind legs and walked away into the forest.

The others curled Princess' body into a shape to fit into the deep round hole. Her legs wouldn't stay curled. The foxes gently folded them back up and tucked them into her belly.

The body relaxed again as if exhaling, uncurling. The motion was eerily lifelike. Princess was eerily, starkly, absolutely dead.

Foxes patiently moved back in to refold her so they could lower her into the hole.

Hamster stepped in. "Wait."

She was sure they didn't understand her word, but there was no hurry here. The foxes sat back on their haunches, their muzzles bowed to their chests. Waiting.

Glenn combed through Princess' belly fur to find the puckered navel that was the opening to her pouch. The opening was tight, becoming stiff. Glenn pushed her fingers in, and worked her hand inside. The pouch entrance closed around her wrist in a tight ring. She gave a careful grope.

Princess' skin still held a tepid vestige of living warmth. Glenn's hand found and closed around a warm little body. It was fuzzy. No bigger than a hamster. It squirmed in her palm.

She pulled the tiny baby off its teat. The mouth closed on her fingertip, sucked. Glenn pulled her hand out through the tight opening, trying not to squeeze what was in her palm.

She brought it out into the light. The bluish eyes were covered with a thin membrane. Its toothless mouth opened wide. It made a tiny noise, an unhappy yowl that was barely a squeak. It exhaled baby smell. Squirmed, helpless.

The foxes moved back in, recurled Princess, and settled her into her grave.

Glenn ran into the forest after Rogue.

It was easy to follow Rogue's aimless crashing. His forepaws flailed. He was not walking. He was falling forward by lurches, stumbling into trees and thorns.

When Glenn closed the gap between them, Rogue finally noticed her behind him. He turned. Looked like he'd been flogged.

Glenn didn't know how to speak to him. She hummed an upturned *hm?* She could have been saying mumble socks for all she knew.

Rogue came to her on all fours, his head lowered, ears back, tail firmly between his legs, submissive. He sniffed her feet. He stood up and sniffed her wet face. His whiskers tickled.

He sniffed the baby in her hands.

Glenn had seen couples pass infants before. She gestured toward Rogue's pouch.

Rogue took the baby in his paw and slipped it inside his pouch. He took a moment rearranging things in there. He withdrew his paw. The pouch opening contracted shut so it looked like a navel. Rogue combed his fur over it with his claws.

Glenn turned to go. Rogue followed her docilely back to the tribes.

The burial was done by then, the earth stamped down, the rocks piled over top. Princess was safe from predators. And that was the end of concern for the dead.

Glenn washed in the cold stream. Her tears ran hot. When she came back out to the meadow, the foxes were already dancing.

They lived in the moment. Foxes shook off sorrow and got on with living. Rogue danced.

The line beckoned for Glenn to hop in.

Patrick shouldered her, "You should go."

"I-I can't," said Glenn. Knew she should. But she couldn't. "Go for me."

Patrick got into the line.

Glenn could not dance. She wasn't a fox. The loss lodged in her human heart. She sat, hugging her knees, rocking, grieving and angry.

Toward sundown it occurred to Glenn just how reckless she'd been. She and Patrick had escaped from the pirates. But without landing disk or displacement collar or com, they could go nowhere.

"We need to go back to camp," Glenn told Patrick.

He agreed. "They could hurt the others."

Worse, they could hunt us down and hurt the foxes.

"Scientists collect specimens for study?" Glenn said, returning to the LEN expedition camp at daybreak. "I got you a specimen." She slapped the dead cloke down like bagpipes retrieved from a peat bog, its arms and legs jutting in every direction. Its body wheezed.

"Study that!" she said.

The pirates stared at her, astonished.

"What!" Glenn yelled at all the staring faces. She stabbed Nox's machete into the ground.

Director Benet hissed at her, "You stupid bitch! You could have got us all executed!"

Nox took a step forward. He retrieved his machete from the ground. He walked up to Glenn, the blade held vertical. "I knew you'd come back."

Glenn said quietly, almost surprised, "I didn't even know I left."

She had been out of her head. She knew what that phrase meant now.

Lost it. Just lost it.

She felt a sudden revelation. Her anger, back when she'd been passed over for the XO spot on *Merrimack*, had been entirely out of line. Someone made the right call there.

I shouldn't be XO. I should be shit-canned.

She turned away from Nox and the machete.

She hadn't known she had that unbridled savagery in her. It was gone now. It left a deep hollow behind it. She could only hurt, hurt, hurt for her baby girl. Only close her eyes and she could see those big shining black eyes and bright innocent smile. She couldn't look at wildflowers without crying, because she wanted to braid them into Princess' fur.

She knew people lost themselves in a strange land. Her latent maternal instinct surfaced here. She never knew she had one at all. She had imprinted on a pretty young fox who became her daughter.

And lost her.

Even the pirates gave her a wide berth.

Nox murmured, "The female of the species is more deadly than the male."

Loss had transformed her into that most dangerous of creatures, a bereft mother. Hell had no fury like it. A woman scorned didn't even come close.

Dr. Patrick Hamilton had made a life of talking to aliens. All he wanted to say to the clokes was drop dead.

His wife was in their tent, hugging a pillow, trying to sleep. His wife, who never cried, sobbed her heart out for the loss of their pretty baby princess.

Patrick got up from his worktable.

The LEN camp stood on a narrow plateau of level ground set into a rise between the river in the low land and the highland meadows where mammoths roamed and foxes played.

The stream that ran outside the LEN expedition camp cut a rocky passage from the highlands down to the wide river below, where clokes buried their eggs in the muddy banks.

Patrick loaded himself like a pack mule with audio equipment. He emerged from his work hut draped with leafy camouflage netting. He looked ridiculously like a furtive bush. He glanced around for pirates and crept out between parked spaceships. His light footfalls sounded like cymbal crashes to his own ears.

He crossed the dirt perimeter and walked out from under the energy dome.

He hiked through thick tangles of late summer brush to the rocky stream. He started once more up the rocky ascent.

By now he was starting to recognize stones and trees.

And he stumbled upon a pirate.

It was Nox, crouched quiet as a forest creature at the streamside. He was shaving with a dagger. His hair was wet.

Scared fearless, Patrick kept hiking. His survival instinct completely failed him. He was on a mission.

Nox's head turned slowly as Patrick, the walking bush, climbed past him. The expression on Nox's scarred face looked like odd disbelief.

Patrick nodded up at the route through the steep narrows ahead of him. His voice came out a growl. "Nox, if your pirate ship is hidden in this pass, you might think about moving it."

Like a mouse telling the baddest kitty in the litter to move its furry ass.

Patrick expected he was about to leave this world as Poul Vrba had, smiling from his throat. Yet he couldn't make himself care.

My wife is crying.

I've never done anything for her.

Our daughter is dead.

He continued upward.

Nox's bemused expression hadn't changed as Patrick passed him.

Patrick climbed one step. Another step. Balanced on a rock. Shifted his load of audio equipment.

Audio equipment. Oh, hell. I'm carrying audio equipment.

Sometimes the smartest people could be the dumbest.

Patrick could not contact *Merrimack* with the equipment he carried. But could he expect the pirate to know that?

I just murdered the whole camp. Another step. *Starting with me.*

Nox's voice sounded at Patrick's back. "You're letting the jungle in."

The words startled Patrick. The unexpected insight of the pirate. The man was insane, not stupid. Nox knew exactly what Patrick intended.

Patrick tried not to react. Faced forward. *Don't acknowl-*

edge. Just keep climbing. His back tensed. He waited for a machete to cleave him open like a side of beef. He did not want to know what that felt like. Should have thought about that a minute ago.

Nox's voice sounded behind him again, not closing in, still crouched at the water's edge. "Jungle favor go with thee."

31

A RUMBLING DISTURBED the expedition
camp. All the xenos felt it in the ground.

"Quake!" someone whispered.

From the surrounding forest animals yelped, barked.
More took up the calls. Sounds of alarm lifted. Flocks of
winged creatures rose from the trees. They passed over the
camp in mixed flocks, headed away from the highlands,
down toward the river.

"I do not think so," said Jose Maria. His dog stood with
her ears up.

The nanny goat bleated and yanked on her leash as if
to choke herself.

The rumbling sound didn't have the timber of grinding
bedrock. It was the pounding of hooves, paws, and many
many feet. Insects swarmed in rising clouds.

"Stampede!" someone shouted.

Snakes, monkey squirrels, furred and feathered creatures
scampered through camp. But the loudest roaring came
from the direction of the stream. The vale was where all the
highland animals were descending, fast.

"This is possibly a fire," said Jose Maria.

A rush of panicked animals funneled down the vale, all
charging down toward the river below.

"They're trying to get down to the river!" Dr. Minyas
cried.

"Oh, my God! Fire! Fire!" Not sure who was screaming
that.

Nicanor, Pallas, Orissus, Faunus, Leo, and Galeo collected together around Nox because Nox was as serene as a hurricane's eye.

"Is *Merrimack* trying to flush us out with a ruse?" Pallas asked. "Or should we be running."

Nox said quietly, "There's no fire."

Sabers and antelopes, fleeing side by side, seemed to think there was a fire. Night-flying monkey squirrels flew in broad daylight, their giant eyes slit-lidded against the brightness.

Benet shouted, "Where's the fire? Who started a fire?"

"We haven't found it yet, Izzy," said Dr. Rose, checking his shaking instruments. "Stop yelling. Wow, look at that."

Overlapping echelons of majestic birds passed over.

Dr. Rose noted the direction of the wind. It was coming out of the highlands, from where the animals fled.

"If there's a fire up there, it will spread this way."

The expedition members begged the pirates to allow them to take shelter inside their ships.

Nox told them, "You break any hatch seal, I'll burn you myself."

Many of the xenos noted that the pirates weren't running for their lives. They wore no displacement collars that could blink them to a place of safety. The pirates weren't afraid.

Jose Maria de Cordillera and his dog had climbed on top of his Star Racer *Mercedes*. That would not protect them from fire, but it got them out of the way of the torrent of beasts that were now galloping and bounding through camp.

The pirates collected a few bottles of Dr. Rose's wine, climbed up to the flat topside of one of the spaceships in the half ring, and settled down to watch the parade of strange creatures.

"Damn, there goes our tent," said Nicanor blandly.

Most of the xenos climbed atop other ships and watched. Someone brought the goat up. They scanned the horizons for fire.

No plumes of smoke appeared. The only smells were of animals.

Mammoths came lumbering down from the heights,

their long golden feathers waving, their short tusks lifting and lowering. They raised their trunks, squeaking.

Herds of glass deer ran through the camp, their transparent flesh revealing their organs and bones, their hearts beating very fast.

Boxcar mice snaked along the ground in long segmented chains like toy trains, nose to tail.

Armored land squid pelted along backward, and furry little bellows voles propelled themselves in high arcs, jumping breath to breath.

From their high shelter atop the ships the xenos could see over the treetops, down to the wide river, where animals of all kinds muddied the water.

The beasts stomped on the riverbanks.

Glenn climbed up the ship where the pirates were gathered. Her eyes were red and hollow and wet. There was a meek set to her shoulders that were always so proud. "Nox? Do you know where my husband is?"

"He's doing just fine," Nox said, and moved over to make a place for her. "Have a seat."

Glenn sat down between Nox and another pirate, the nice one, Pallas.

"You need to see this." Nox tilted his head toward the lowland.

Down in the wide river crowded with creatures, predators and prey milled together, none particularly hungry. Giant flightless snakemouths—birds with powerful legs like ostriches, their beaks able to unhinge to swallow prey whole—didn't snatch anything from the assembled buffet. They jostled with the sabers, slipping in the sediment. They trampled the riverbanks with their hooves.

Mammoths' wide feet sank into the mud under the weight of their gargantuan bodies. Water swirled brown around their tree trunk legs.

Anything buried in the riverbanks was obliterated and washed away.

By nightfall still no flickering glow of fire appeared up on the heights. No waft of smoke carried down on the wind.

Strange animals wandered through camp, disoriented.

By dawn it was clear that there had been no fire.

The animals started returning to the highlands at a more leisurely pace than they had left. Many of them strayed into camp.

Xenos with polymer shields guided them around the compound.

The creatures couldn't smell the gas fire at the center of camp, but they bolted as soon as they saw it.

Patrick stole back into camp. Not many people had noticed that he'd been gone. He stowed his sound equipment inside his tent, which was still standing, though there were many strange animal tracks around and through it.

The tent flap moved. He gave a guilty start.

It was Glenn, looking curious.

She seemed to guess that Patrick had said something to the mammoths.

Patrick had broadcast a message, very loud. Up in the high country he'd blasted on wavelengths between eighteen and twenty-three meters, too long for the human ear to detect.

Glenn whispered, "What did you *say?*"

"Fire."

There hadn't been a fire. Not now. Not in ages.

So how had he known what to say?

Glenn said, "You know the mammoth word for fire?"

No one had been monitoring mammoth lo-fi speech long enough to have ever heard mammoths utter that particular word.

Patrick shook his head no. "I said it in elephant."

It wasn't so much a word. It was a literal note of panic that provoked an instinctive reaction, a fear written on one's genes.

Patrick sounded the alarm. The mammoths led the charge. Other animals took up the call in the audible ranges, which sent everyone rushing down to the river.

To trample the clokes' seeding area.

Glenn threw her arms around Patrick. She clung to him tightly.

Patrick put his arm around her. He felt tall. *I am the man.*

"Now I can dance," said Glenn.

In the evening Glenn danced the hora around the fire pit. It was a white gas flame in the pit. Still, the light caught the red in her hair and made the civilized young woman look purely savage. Hers was a defiant, angry dance.

Glenn said, "I need to teach the foxes this one."

Nox met Patrick's gaze across the fire pit.

Patrick had not told Nox anything of what he'd done in the highlands. But Nox knew. He'd let the jungle in.

Nox closed a fist that said *well done*.

Director Benet was calling the stampede an ecological disaster—because of the crushing of the cloke egg deposits on the riverbanks.

Patrick's back stiffened straight up. "What hole did you excrete that idea out of, Izzy? The clokes are an invasive species."

"The clokes are endangered," said Izrael Benet. "We must protect any other clutches."

"Endangered?" Glenn said. "We have no evidence of that. The planet could be lousy with them."

"It's not. We would have seen them on the global surveys."

"Why do you think they deserve protection?"

"*Why?*" Benet said back, as if she'd asked why he should keep breathing. "They're infants."

Glenn fought to keep the shrillness out of her voice. "Infants? You call those infants?"

"Nymphs," said Benet. "Eggs."

"And you would let them *hatch?*"

"We must protect them. We must let them live and breed. Or else what *are* we?" Director Benet declared and stalked away from the fireside.

The answer to that question came from behind her, murmured into Glenn's ear for only her to hear. "Pirates."

Nox was there.

Glenn turned, lifted her brows at Nox, questioning.

Nox said softly, "Your man had the right idea. It's just that a bigger mammoth is required."

Patrick's stampede had taken out just one clutch. There were more. There had to be a lot more.

"Got one?" Glenn asked. She thought her question was ironic.

Nox may have nodded.

* * *

There was a saying on *Merrimack*: *If anything's gonna happen, it'll happen on the Hamster Watch.*

Lieutenant Glenn ("Hamster") Hamilton was not here, but the middle of ship's night on board *Merrimack* would always be the Hamster Watch.

There had been a wildlife stampede two days ago. The LEN encampment had caught the edge of it. *Merrimack*'s Intelligence Department sifted through the recordings of the event for signs that any human beings might have slipped out of camp under cover of the chaos. They turned up nothing. They also analyzed the patterns of animal movement, searching for any evidence of creatures avoiding an invisible Xerxes-sized object. That also turned up nothing.

Now Chief Engineer Kit Kittering had the deck. She was expecting a quiet watch.

Commander Stuart ("Dingo") Ryan, the XO, was in the maintenance hangar, which doubled as a rec area. He had a V-mask on. From outside Dingo seemed to be shadow boxing. From his own point of view, Dingo was in the ring with Ali, who floated like a butterfly and stung like a jackhammer.

Dingo was collecting his virtual teeth off the deck when his V-helmet abruptly went blank and an oh-so-polite voice advised him that this program had terminated due to the ship's elevated alert status.

He tore off his V-mask, cursing but happy to have all his teeth, and ran through the ship's tight corridors and up the ladder one level to the command deck.

Kit advised him as he barreled past the Marine guard flanking the hatch, "Plot coming in, sir. Big one."

"Define 'big.'"

"Not big like the clokes' mobile continent but bigger than us. Sir, it's the *Gladiator.*"

Oh, bullyrings.

The image of the gargantuan Roman battlefort appeared on the monitors.

Romans. Who invited Romans?

"Who's in command?" Dingo demanded.

The com tech answered, "Same guy as last time we met."

"Wake up the captain."

"She's awake," said Calli, striding in. She waved down

the Marine guard's announcement of her entrance and any-one's attempt to stand at attention.

"Sir," said the XO. "We have Romans. Hisself is here."

"Caesar," said Calli.

"Yes, sir."

"Load a torpedo."

"Shot across the bow, sir?"

"No. Hit him."

Commander Ryan spoke. "Targeting. Firing solution on *Gladiator*."

"Targeting, aye. Firing solution acquired, aye."

"Fire Control. Stand by forward beams."

"This is Fire Control. Forward beams powered up and standing by."

"Fire torpedo. Fire beams."

* * *

Asante Addai ran up to the front of the column to bring the squad's resonator to Colonel Steele. The link was more se-cure than a normal tight beam. "Sir. We have Romans on the roof. Actually, we have Caesar."

Steele immediately bellowed to his squad, "Personal Fields active! Everyone!"

Steele took up the resonator to confer with Commander Ryan on *Merrimack*.

The Marines at the rear of the file came forward. Some of the foxes shouldered into the huddle with them. Rhino whispered to Carly. "*Qué pasa*? Are we at war?"

"No," said Carly. "But that don't mean they won't shoot. Caesar's upstairs."

"Caesar Numa?" said Rhino. Her eyes lit up. "You don't mean he's here? I mean, *him*. Really here?"

"Yeah," Asante nodded. "That's what the Dingo told me." He pushed fox whiskers away from his face.

"No big surprise," said Kerry Blue. "We always end up at the same party."

"The captain and the emperor always get into a pissing contest," said Carly. "And the cap'n can piss pretty far for someone who don't got a pistol."

Kerry added, "I think he kinda likes her. She kinda hates him."

Rhino's grin made her elfin face look wolfish. "I knew I boarded the right boat."

Asante turned to see that Steele was still talking to *Merrimack*. Couldn't tell what the presence of Romans was going to do to their orders. Right now the Marines had orders to search for a pirated Xerxes within "walking distance" of the LEN expedition camp.

Rhino questioned the order. "Why don't we just storm the camp?"

"We need to secure the Xerxes first," said Cain. "Otherwise the pirates can call the Xerc to come rescue them."

"Yeah. Like Superman's horse," said Dak.

"Where are we?" said Kerry Blue.

Asante checked his omni. "We're still over a hundred klicks out."

"I don't think that counts as walking distance," said Kerry. Her trousers were shredded into long flapping strips that left her strong lean legs on display.

Dak said, "Can you walk in front of me, Kerry Blue?"

"Shut up, Dak."

"Wait, wait, wait," said Rhino. "A Xerxes has full stealth."

"Yeah?" said Cain. His tone said, *so what?*

"We have orders to search for something *invisible*," said Rhino.

"Yeah?"

"How are we supposed to do that?"

"If you walk into it, say ow. Throw rocks and see if they bounce," said Cain. "Nobody cares how we do it. We have orders to find it."

Steele got off the resonator. He shouted at the file to spread out.

They crossed over the ridge crest. The trek was mostly descending from here, except for that last leg up from the river. The land was more open, the trees more scattered. In the distance lay a wide river.

The Yurg called forward from the Charlie spot. "Colonel? The Vols aren't coming with us."

Steele turned around. "*What?*"

"Our volunteer unit," said Cain, pointing rearward. "The foxes."

Steele looked back and up.

The foxes were gathered at the ridge, a whole row of them, watching the Marines descend.

They didn't look frightened this time. They just weren't coming. The ridge top was some kind of boundary for them.

TR Steele marched back up and reviewed the band of alien volunteers.

"Yeah. Um." *I'm trying to address a bunch of fluffy animals.*

Exactly how did one thank impossibly cute creatures for saving one's life without getting terminally gooey?

This is ridiculous. I'm not doing it.

Steele frowned seriously. He spoke, gruff. "You did good work. And um. Thank you."

The bright-eyed foxes smiled at him. Ears up, listening.

"That will be all." TR Steele turned, rigid, and marched down the incline where his human squad waited.

He didn't look back. The damned silly things better not be following.

✳ ✳ ✳

"Why are We taking friendly fire, Captain Carmel?"

"I'm sorry, Numa, I mistook you for a pirate," Captain Carmel said innocently over the com. "Are you here to extract your pirates?"

Caesar said, just as innocent, "We see no pirates in orbit. Of what pirates do you speak?"

"On the ground," said Calli.

"If you have pirates on the ground, then kill them yourself. We have less than no interest in common outlaws."

"What brings you here?" Calli demanded.

"Rome has colonies in Perseus space," said Numa. "*You* do not."

"This is the Outback," said Calli. "Zoe is not one of your colonies. Zoe is a LEN protectorate."

"We are here because this planet is under alien invasion."

"It is *now*," said Calli, glaring pointedly at the image of the large invader before her.

"Not us," said Caesar. "We are no invader. We are here to defend a kindred world against alien invasion."

"That's just your pretext to be here."

"What is yours?"

"The United States is a member nation of the LEN." Calli was wearing the green. "I'm protecting."

"The world needs more protection than that," Numa said.

Calli clicked the com off.

This planet is under alien invasion, he'd said.

She thought out loud, "How the hell does Numa know about the clokes? He just got here."

There had been a broadcast about the discovery of Zoe's DNA, so there was no surprise that Caesar knew Zoe was a "kindred world." But no one ever announced the presence of the extraplanetary aliens, the clokes.

Dingo spoke the only possible answer, "Caesar's got someone inside the expedition camp. Either someone on the expedition or else those really *are* his pirates."

✳ ✳ ✳

After the midday meal, Nox took Glenn on a walk outside the camp. The day was clear and brilliant, the sky so blue and deep Glenn felt if she gazed into it long enough, she might fall up. A high-soaring lizard-bird stooped into peregrine dive and disappeared below the treetops.

Glenn felt a brush at her cheek. Nox. His fingertips touched a ragged edge of her hair. "What's with the hair?"

"A little incident involving crashing and fire," said Glenn.

"Then you came here on that ship in the woods?" asked Nox. He had seen the *Spring Beauty.*

"I landed that ship in the woods," said Glenn.

Nox had a bright American smile. He almost laughed. "That's brilliant."

Glenn tilted her head noncommittally.

Nox said, "Nobody in camp cuts hair?"

She had orders to get close to Nox. She didn't like how close she was getting to Nox.

Anything she said could get her killed. Blunt honesty had gotten Poul Vrba killed. Then again, no one had asked Vrba a question. Glenn said, "Prettying myself up in captivity strikes me as philosophically wrong."

Several of the women on the expedition had taken to wearing makeup and jewelry since the pirates' arrival.

Glenn didn't sense anger from Nox at her answer.

Felt more like approval.

Nox himself was clean. He'd gotten the blood out of his linen-colored tunic. His black cargo pants showed no dull spots. His hair was freshly washed, and the teeth and bones braided into it were polished shiny ivory white. He had added in fresh blue feathers and gold-flecked porcelain beads.

"Bagheera is an easy place to live," Nox told her.

"Bagheera?"

"We named our ship *Bagheera.* We do grisly work, but we don't live that way. Our home is really beautiful. It looks like anything we want. It could look like this."

"Why are you telling me this?" said Glenn. "Are you going to show me your ship? Would you trust my motives if I said I wanted to see it?"

Nox stepped in front of her, facing her. "I wouldn't trust you if you hadn't said that."

She couldn't hold his gaze. She spoke at his chest. "We both know what I am."

Both his hands rose to her cheeks. His fingers laced back through her shabby hair. He shook his head. "Only one of us does," said Nox. "We be one blood, thou and I."

32

NUMA INVITED CALLI to his battlefort *Gladiator* for a drink.

"That is not a terrific idea," said Captain Carmel.

Numa chided, "You went on a *date* with Romulus."

"And how *is* Rom?" Calli asked too politely.

"The same," said Numa.

That would be incapacitated, twitching, comatose.

"You must come," Caesar commanded. "Bring Dr. Cordillera. We were told he was here."

"Jose Maria is a hostage downstairs with your pirates," said Calli.

"Do not attribute the pirates to Us," said Numa. "It is irritating and insulting to Us."

Calli said, "I don't know if Jose Maria is even alive. I have no knowledge of what's happening under that dome. You'll need to ask your inside man."

"More accusations," said Numa.

"Any of them true?"

"Of course not."

Refusing hospitality was not done in space. Even during a hot war, which this was not, it was not done. Sharing food and drink was the most ancient and basic human intercourse. It was a duty beyond sacred out here. Civilized spacefarers were bound to maintain their humanity in the most hostile of environments. Space was stark, ruthless. Everyone was vulnerable.

Dinner or drink invitations were a social mandate. You

could shoot each other after dinner, but, unless the guy killed your mother, you must attend dinner. To do otherwise put you on a level with a pirate.

So when the head of the Roman Empire invited Captain Carmel for a drink, she must go.

Calli boarded *Gladiator* in dress whites with trousers and flat shoes. Her hair was pulled severely back, held by a heavy golden cicada. Rob Roy Buchanan came with her. They both wore armbands of LEN green.

Heads of most states adopted a dignified, reserved, subdued garb. The emperor of Rome went the other way. Numa Pompeii made all his entrances like a circus rhino: big, flashy, loud.

In an empire that adored beauty, Numa was as lovely as a tyrannosaurus.

But you don't need beauty when you are *Rex*.

Because more than beauty, Rome loved the biggest, strongest, brightest, cleverest, loudest.

The reprod scientists broke the mold after they made Numa. Probably right after they beheld their creation and said *Oh, Gods, what have we done?*

Caesar advanced into his dining chamber as if claiming the field. He was built like a stack of boulders, well padded with brawn, even to his craggy face. The fabric of his tunic moved like liquid steel. The bronze toga over that also looked molten. His oakleaf crown was bronze.

Numa recognized Rob Roy. "Ah. The first mate." Numa's voice boomed even in conversational tones.

Rob Roy brought a bottle of single malt for their host. Numa passed the gift to an attendant. There was already a red wine breathing in a decanter of Roman glass on the olivewood table.

The attendant withdrew. It was just the three of them in the chamber. They didn't sit or recline, which was more the Roman way. For now they stood.

Caesar poured the wine.

"To Zoe." Numa lifted his glass.

"To life," said Calli.

The ornate bronze pillars ringing the dinner chamber might be real. The gentle sea of Mediterranean blue beyond them was illusion. The slight breezes were balmy.

Numa said, "Callista. You reverted to your natural looks."

"Since when are my looks subject for imperial comment?" said Calli.

"A face has been known to launch a thousand ships," said Numa. "Ships in that volume get imperial attention."

Calli said, "The sack of Troy was never really about Helen."

"And Rome's presence here has damned little to do with you," said Numa.

"And Rome lets its emperor go dashing out to the edge of the known galaxy?" Calli asked.

"Rome expects it."

"Numa. Why are you here?"

"We are reviewing Our secret empire," said Numa.

That was a joke. But not really.

Admitting that he had less than absolute power over his vast empire was admitting a weakness.

Odd that Numa would speak of it. But he must know Calli was already aware of the possibility.

"I don't think Romulus made it this far into the Outback," said Calli. "This is ANZAC space."

"Never trust where Romulus' tentacles might have reached," said Numa.

Calli agreed. "Romans are like heartworms that way."

Numa said, "Romulus is here."

Calli's mouth opened and some words or others ought to be coming out of it, but she didn't know which. Numa could always enrage her, but she hadn't thought he could still shock her. "What?"

"Not Romulus, the physical creature. His tentacles. His Romulii. There is a secret society within Rome. You know that one."

She had heard of it.

Under the reign of Numa Pompeii, the followers of mad Caesar Romulus had gone underground. There were still an appalling number of Roman citizens loyal to the incapacitated mad emperor. Romulus had been the most cunning, manipulative, grandiose, conscience-free, beloved, hated Caesar of the new Empire. His adherents, the Romulii, denied, ignored, dismissed accusations that Romulus was a patricide. Romulus was the one Caesar who nearly returned Rome to her true glory.

Instead, he'd brought Rome to the brink of disaster. Even sane people forgot about that part.

Like a drunk recovered from a massive banging hangover, a part of Rome looked back fondly on the reign of the mad emperor Romulus and wanted to try that again—the swaggering belligerence, the unapologetic excesses, the intoxicating power. The war.

A secret society moved now within Rome—the supporters of mad Romulus. The Romulii.

The secret kept itself. Most times when the existence of the Romulii was mentioned in public, the immediate reaction was, "You have got to be kidding."

So Rome herself had existed very well as a secret society within many nations of Earth during the Long Silence.

The shoe was in the other closet now.

Calli gave a stalking-cat smile. "Oh, and how does *that* feel?"

"A surprising lack of civility for someone of your rank and training, Captain Carmel."

"It's a lack of hypocrisy, Numa. You and I have a long history of shooting at each other."

"Which is why We trust you."

"Can't say the same."

"Romulus concerns Us," said Numa. "There is nothing like being dead to improve one's image."

"Did Rom die?" Calli felt something. Not sure what. Definitely not sad.

"Romulus is not actually dead," said Numa. "Effectively dead, but with a very dangerous possibility of resurrection should someone devise a way to extricate the nanites from his brain. If he dies in fact, there will be accusations of assassination."

"Will they be true?"

"I have tried."

The blunt statement startled Calli. She believed him. She couldn't believe Caesar said it to her. But he hadn't used a royal plural when he confessed.

"Not while Romulus was Caesar, I did not. But Romulus the raving vegetable ..." He let the rest of the sentence hang. Sighed. "That is one heavily protected vegetable."

"You tried to have Romulus assassinated," said Calli. "Why would you tell me that?"

"Why would We not? Repeat it if you like. No one will believe you."

"Numa, there are *two* of us here." Calli's eyes flicked aside toward her Legal Officer.

"Married," said Numa. "You two have vowed to stand together come what may. You are less than useless vouching for each other. I want Romulus dead. That should not be a shock."

"The shock is that you can't get it done," said Calli. "He's in your custody."

"The not getting blood on my hands is the difficult piece of it. But it must be done. I cannot have the vegetable's name spoken in the same breath as this world's. This place holds a significance unlike any other."

"You think the DNA is real?" said Calli. "As a natural, independent evolution, I mean."

"It is real. Beyond a doubt, reasonable or otherwise."

So says the man who just got here.

Numa went on, "The discovery is profound. Earthshaking, you would say. Some tremors were felt through Palatine too, be assured. This world is too important to leave in the hands of its natives."

"You mean it's too important to entrust it to the beings God gave it to?" Calli said.

"The motto of Rome is *not* In God We Trust," said Numa.

"No," Calli agreed. "It's not. It's *Senatus Populusque Romanus.*" SPQR. The Senate and the People of Rome. "Just where do you fit into that, Numa? Are you the Senate or are you the People?"

"Verily? That's our motto?" Numa said with all the innocence he didn't have. "I thought our motto was *I came. I saw. I conquered.*"

The moment Calli returned to the *Merrimack*, she ran up to the command deck with a controlled panic she hadn't shown to Numa.

She blew through the hatch barking, "Get me Colonel Steele."

The com tech got the ground unit on the res link.

"Abort the search for the Xerxes," Calli ordered. "Redirect operation. Get to the LEN camp. Get our people out. Caesar may be making a move. The pirates could panic, and there's no one in camp that Numa can't spare. Get in there first."

Calli looked at the chron. It was five hours before sundown on that part of the world.

"Get there before next sunup. I'm sending all the information I have on the site and on the pirates."

Steele didn't object to the impossible assignment. Her XO did.

"A forced march over three marathons in strong gravity?" Commander Ryan said after she cut the connection. "They can't make it before sunrise."

Calli knew that. Said, "I don't think whatever's about to happen will wait any longer."

"What is going to happen?"

"Numa Pompeii," said Calli. "Numa Pompeii is going to happen. Never mind that Zoe has sapient life—which never stops Rome anyway—but this planet is already a LEN protectorate. Which should stop Rome. And it won't. Numa has come to Eden. Imperial presence, his big personal presence, means Rome isn't on a humanitarian mission. Caesar Numa Pompeii is going to stab the planet with his eagles."

"I'm sure you're right, Captain," said Dingo. "But this is an emergency?"

Calli said, "First scenario: The pirates are just pirates. Numa breaks atmo. The pirates start carving up hostages.

"Second scenario: The pirates are agents of Numa. Numa breaks atmo. The pirates kill all the hostages, clearing the entire League of Earth Nations presence from the planet for Numa. All roads from Rome lead to dead hostages."

Tactical reported, "Scenario Three, off the starboard stern." Marcander Vincent enlarged the image on the tactical monitor.

A LEN ship had entered the star system.

Calli knew this one, the LEN ship *Windward Isles*. Despite its idyllic name, *Windward Isles* was a pirate hunter.

I don't think he can help me. Still, she was happy to see him. She hailed *Windward* over the LEN channel and bade the captain come aboard.

She met him at the dock with open arms. "Ram Singh!"

Captain Carmel gave and received a kiss on either cheek.

"Calli Carmel." Ram's grin was very white in his dark face. Even his mellow voice smiled. "You look good in green."

"Don't," Calli warned. "Just don't."

Ram knew how she hated to wear LEN colors and to have any flag near Old Glory.

Ram's *Windward Isles* had come here responding to an interrupted message from the LEN scientific expedition team. A breathy female voice: *This is LEN expedition base Zebra Oscar Echo. We ha—have—*

"We believe The Ninth Circle might be on Zoe," said Ram.

"The Ninth Circle *is* on Zoe," said Calli. "They have control of the LEN expedition camp. And as you *might* have noticed, Rome is here."

"Rome is here," Ram said. The battlefort *Gladiator* shone like a star.

"Numa is going to make a move," Calli told Ram. "And I'm afraid Numa's idea of a surgical strike might be amputation."

"What hour is it at the target site?" Ram asked.

"Daylight. For another few hours."

"How many civilians. How many hostiles. What weapons and armor do they have?"

Commander Ryan snapped to Tactical, "Mister Vincent. A layout of the camp for Captain Singh."

Quietly urgent, Calli said, "Ram, I have people down there. Two officers in the camp. They sleep in this tent." She showed him the location on the aerial view. "And Jose Maria Cordillera is down there too."

"Is the Star Racer his?" Ram asked of the sleek ship amid the boxy LEN circle. Then answered himself. "Of course it is. Does *Don* Cordillera sleep in there?"

"The last and only intel I have said the expedition people weren't confined at all, but they weren't allowed inside the ships," Calli said. "I have a squad of Marines moving in from the northwest. Here. But they're still over sixty miles out."

Ram's *Windward Isles* had already spotted the Marine unit on the ground.

By now there were also multiple ships of unverified identity in the Zoen star system. They came at the news of alien DNA. *Merrimack* prohibited any of them from approaching within an astronomical unit of the planet as long as the camp was hostage.

Ram asked, "Is there any chance someone upstairs with us is keeping the pirates informed of where your Marines are?"

"Dammit, Ram, there is every chance. And we can't set anyone else down without alerting the pirates."

Ram proposed to put a team down in the Xerxes' blind spot.

"That would be lovely if there was such a thing," Calli said. "A Xerxes has a blind spot?"

Ram hesitated. Answered, "May have." That was a yes.

"Design flaw?" said Calli.

"Failsafe," said Ram.

"And how did you get it?"

That would be secret information of a kind Italy wouldn't part with easily, if at all. Ram wasn't parting with it either.

"My country is on very good terms with Italy," said Ram. "We are also a member of the Pacific Consortium."

The Xerxes was properly an Italian-flagged ship. The Pacific Consortium manufactured the Xerxes.

Ram shrugged. "And everyone knows I live to make pirates dead."

* * *

It was very late, closer to dawn than to dusk. Patrick couldn't sleep. Glenn should have turned in by now. Patrick trusted his wife. He didn't trust the pirate she was keeping time with.

My wife is out with a pirate. A pirate once named Farragut.

Patrick sat at his desk in their tent with a study light on. He reviewed his notes on fox dialects to keep his mind occupied.

The light disappeared.

Something—a hood?—dropped over his head.

Can't see.

A hand clapped over his hooded mouth. He inhaled through his nose. Fabric of the hood smelled sweet. All conscious thought fell into darkness.

Came to. There was a hand over Patrick's mouth. He could breathe through his nose. The hood wasn't there anymore. He opened his eyes. He wasn't in the tent. He wasn't even in the camp. It was still dark. He saw stars through the trees. Stars meant it was close to morning.

He focused on the insignia of the man holding his mouth shut. He lost colors in the dark but knew this insignia was green. The LEN officer put a finger before his own lips to tell Patrick to be quiet. Patrick recognized the broad dark face of Ram Singh.

Ram withdrew his muffling hand from Patrick's mouth.

Patrick whispered angrily, "Why are you kidnapping me?"

"It's a rescue," Ram whispered.

"Thanks awfully," Patrick said wryly.

"Where are the pirates?" Ram whispered.

"They have the nice big tent with anemometer on top."

"They're not there," said Ram.

"They were there at sundown."

Ram helped Patrick stand up.

Ram's LEN pirate hunters buckled a PF onto Patrick. It wasn't going to help much. Patrick whispered to Ram, "The pirates don't shoot. They slice."

Ram whispered, "So do I."

The black silhouettes of Ram's people fanned out shadow silent through the camp, though they were already getting the idea that the pirates were gone.

Patrick looked around him. "Glenn! Where's Glenn!" he whispered, "Glenn!"

Blood appeared black in the dark. A leopard-spotted pattern was discernible on the wall of a hut.

Patrick darted a zigzag path like a panicked rabbit, trying to see everywhere at once. Could hardly see anything. Whispered, "Glenn!" The pirate hunters tried to hold him, but he wouldn't be held. He blundered into more leopard spots. These were on the ground. They stuck to his shoe soles. He danced as if he could levitate off the spots. "Glenn!"

Then, in the gap between ships, he sighted the body lying on the ground, like a low mound, outside the energy dome.

He knew the shape of her. The angle of her shoulder, the curve of her hip.

"No. Oh, no." He crept quickly nearer, his breath all but frozen in his chest. Closer, the shape became more distinct.

No. Please no. He prayed to divine powers he didn't believe in.

He put out a trembling hand.

The body stirred. Glenn rolled onto her back. Her eyes opened, focused on Patrick's face above her, then shifted focus over Patrick's shoulder where Ram Singh leaned in. She seemed to realize what was happening here. "Ram." Her voice came out gravelly from sleep. "You got them?"

Ram Singh shook his head. "Where are they? The pirates?"

Glenn's head turned to her side, to the flat spot on the blanket next to her. "I don't know. Nox was right here. That was—" She checked her chron. "Two hours ago."

Patrick saw the pattern in the blanket where someone had been lying next to Glenn.

"He beached me?" said Glenn. She sounded strangely offended. "I thought I had him." She rolled up. Stood up. Took a dizzy step. Put a hand out to Patrick for balance. "I think I've been dosed. He must have seen through me."

"Did you tip him off?" Patrick heard himself say.

Glenn scowled surprise. "And who was supposed to tip *me* off? Oh. My. Head." She crouched down before she could fall over.

One of Ram's men pointed over at the spotted ground. "Whose blood is that?"

"I hope it's the dog," said Patrick. "Where's the dog?"

The expedition members came out of their tents as the pirate hunters took names and searched the grounds. Ram's men broke the tape seals over the ships and searched inside. They were fairly certain the pirates were gone. That didn't stop the search.

"The pirates must have run away when *Windward Isles* showed up," said Patrick.

"But who told them *Windward Isles* was here?" Ram said.

"Their Xerxes has to be keeping watch of who is in orbit," said Glenn.

"If that were the case," said Ram, "then why did they not run when *Gladiator* arrived?"

Patrick pulled back in surprise. "*Gladiator* is here?"

"*Gladiator* arrived hours ahead of *Windward*," said Ram.

Glenn reached up her hand for Patrick to help her stand up again. She told Ram, "Those pirates ran under *Merrimack's* guns to get down here in the first place. They're not afraid of anyone."

That left the questions: Why did the pirates brave the guns of *Merrimack* to come to Zoe in the first place? And why did they run away now?

A shout sounded from the camp perimeter with the alarmed cocking of a lot of guns: "Who goes there!"

It turned out to be a squad of U.S. Fleet Marines approaching the camp from the northwest.

They were old friends.

Ram's men hailed Colonel TR Steele, "Adamas!"

Steele glowered.

Ram stepped forward smiling broadly. "Adamas, I know you are Superman, but how did you get here!"

The Marines had covered a lot of ground in inhuman time.

"We caught a ride on some—" Steele stopped, fishing for the right term.

"Dinosaurs," Dak supplied.

"Big animals," said Steele.

The camp physician, Dr. Cecil, set off on a tangential rant about the Marines not wearing protection.

"Calm down, Cecil," said Patrick. "They're equipped with personal fields."

"They—?" Cecil looked confused, then aghast. "I don't give a damn about your Marines! What is protecting the *native ecosystem* from your infested Marines?"

"Hey! I am not infested," said Kerry Blue.

Cecil threw up his hands. "But who am I talking to? You

dared provoke the pirates while they held us hostage. Get out of here!"

"Geez, Cecil, you sound just like Izzy Benet," Patrick said. "We don't need two Izzies. Nobody needs two Izzies."

"Where *is* Izzy?" said Cecil. "Did the pirates take him?"

Patrick looked up to the hut roofs, which were festooned with he didn't even want to imagine what. The first glimmer of predawn was showing the color. He spoke unsteadily, "Oh, I think he might be around here."

* * *

"Numa, where are your pirates?"

Numa's expression on the video com was impenetrable rock. He told Captain Carmel, "Caesar does not deal with pirates."

"You have no idea, have you?" Calli said. "I am talking about the *Roman* recruits whom *Rome* disenfranchised before they hijacked the Xerxes."

"We are somewhat familiar with the hijack report. It was not a Roman ID that the hijacker flashed at the Italian consulate," Numa said smoothly.

It had been a United States ID.

"Perhaps if you had advised us, Captain Carmel, you would not now be in the position of misplacing *your* pirates. We can attempt to capture them, if you will share information with us."

"No. Actually, I'll find them myself," said Calli. She cut the connection.

The pirates were back in the vacuum. There would be no finding them.

"Captain," said Dingo Ryan. "We're assuming the Xerxes has left the planet. But no one saw them go."

"No one would," said Calli.

"The pirates left the expedition camp on foot within the last two hours," said Commander Ryan. "For all we know the Xerxes is still on the ground. The pirates may still be down here."

Calli turned to Tactical. "Mister Vincent. Pirates!"

"Sir," said Marcander Vincent. "The Xerc was designed to protect heads of state. If that ship don't want to be found, we're not going to find it."

"Yes, we will. We have a place to start, and the pirates left camp on foot. They can't be far."

"But their personal fields have scatter tech. They are sensor-invisible. You can't even see them with the human eye."

"We have the beds they slept in downstairs, and *I have dogs*."

The ships' dogs—Nose the bloodhound, Rommel the shepherd, and Godzilla the rat terrier—arrived at the LEN camp with displacement thundercracks along with fresh Marines from Green Squad and Silver Horses for the Marines to ride after the dogs.

The handler let the dogs sniff the pirates' beds and Nox's place on the blanket, then turned them loose.

The dogs picked up a scent immediately and ran with it. Jose Maria's Doberman, Inga, took off from her master's side at a joyful run to catch up with her old shipmates.

Patrick pointed after Inga. He warned, angry, "That dog is a killer! She murdered an ambassador!"

Ram Singh knew. He had been there.

"Then it is a good thing they are hunting pirates and not ambassadors," said Ram.

The ambassador had been seaweed, and possibly already dead at the time, but Inga was not supposed to chew on it. She'd lost her commission for that.

Dogs could run twice as fast as a man. The Marines of Green Squad rode their Silver Horses after the baying Nose.

Calli had an ear to the beam when Flight Leader Bjorn Kim of Green Squad called in. She heard Colonel Steele bark over the com, "Report!"

The whining and barking dogs were audible in the background.

Flight Leader Kim said, "We found where the Xerxes was, sir."

Was. The word sat inside Calli in a lump. *Was* meant it wasn't there anymore.

"They're gone?" Steele demanded.

"Yes, sir," said Kim.

Calli got on the com, "Flight Leader. This is *Merrimack*. Are you sure?"

"Sir!" said Kim. "Yes, sir. We're sure it was here, and

we're sure it's gone now. There's flattened grass, residue, some well-aged vomit, the imprint of trademark landing gear, and . . ."

Calli waited for it. She heard the Flight Leader's reluctant cough.

Kim plowed ahead, "And a bottle of rum."

33

THE BLANKET ON WHICH GLENN had lain when Patrick found her was still there—still with the rumpled imprints of two reclining bodies. Patrick asked his wife, his voice forced casual, "What were you doing out here? You and Nox."

"We were making up constellations."

Patrick's voice hitched. "You were . . .?"

"Picking out star patterns and giving them names," said Glenn.

"Oh." Of all things he imagined, he hadn't expected that answer. He could only blurt, "Why?"

"No one on this planet has made up constellations. The foxes aren't going to do it. We thought they needed naming."

Those words fell like a rusty machete. "We did?"

Glenn closed her eyes, gave a weary sigh. "I had orders to hold him here."

"How hard did you try?" Patrick asked. Heard himself sounding like a jealous oaf. *So I'm a jealous oaf. I'm allowed.*

"Not hard enough," said Glenn. "Or too hard. In hindsight, I think he saw right through me from the beginning."

"If he saw through you, why didn't he hurt you?" Patrick couldn't bring himself to say the word *kill* next to the word *you.*

Glenn was at a loss. "I don't really know. Maybe he knew I had orders and respected that. Maybe he didn't see my loyalty to my country as a personal betrayal? I can't answer for him because I don't know how his mind works. I'm not in his head. I am so glad I'm not in his head."

A murderer who wears bones, quotes Kipling, and names the stars.

The expedition members collected Director Benet's remains together, then cleaned off the rooftops. They washed the leopard spots off the hut walls and shoveled the marks off the ground.

Dr. Cecil, now acting expedition director, ordered Captain Carmel to recall her Marines and take her battleship out of the star system.

Calli tried to tell him that the world was under alien invasion, so she had jurisdiction here. She knew Numa Pompeii would challenge her, but that was a separate battle.

Cecil told her over the com, "How many times must you people be told? We are not under attack. The visitors came here with no weapons except their own nails!" He would not call them clokes. He knew what the word meant.

"They came with no weapons other than lethal projectiles," Calli sent back. "Is that what you just told me?"

"They are a Class Nine Intelligence," Cecil sent. "They travel between stars. They aren't savages."

"They may not have been savages when their ancestors left home, but they are clearly savage now. And hostile."

Cecil shut off his com.

Dr. Rose's voice carried across the camp. "Where's the goat?" He came walking between ships, holding Anabelle's tether. "Anabelle? Anabelle?"

"She escaped?" someone asked. Maybe Sandy Minyas.

"Not by herself. Not unless she has opposable thumbs." Aaron Rose opened and shut the clasp.

The expedition members collected around the goat's stake. They found tripodal tracks and a hole.

The Marines and Ram Singh's men stayed back, fanned out.

Colonel Steele roared at Dr. Cecil, "Get this damned dome off my roof!" and he shouted into his com, *"Merrimack, Merrimack, Merrimack.* This is Colonel Steele. We need a sounding at this location."

The camp geologist said, affronted, "I assure you this camp was sited on a solid foundation."

"Seven years ago," said Glenn.

Steele bellowed at all the xenos clustering around the hole. "*Spread out!*"

Jose Maria standing at a distance from the group called to his dog, "Inga, come!"

As the stake and the ground around it caved in.

Men, women, and the dog sank into a black nest of flailing multijointed arms and legs.

On solid ground, Steele barked at the nearest Marine, Asante Addai. "Him." Steele jabbed a forefinger at Dr. Cecil. "Dome."

"Sir!" Asante seized Dr. Cecil and hauled him in a running march to deactivate the dome over the camp that shielded them from aid from *Merrimack*.

The sinkhole was taking on shape. It looked to be six feet deep—eight feet in places—like a dirt swimming pool filled with gyrating people and alien stick figures. And it was screaming.

The Marines advanced toward the hole two by two—one man forward, one following behind—in case the edge gave way. The forward Marines seized the reaching arms of any people who made it to the sinkhole's wall and pulled them out. Clokes clung onto them.

"Swords!" Steele bellowed.

The Marines slashed down the clokes that came near the edge.

Not like gorgons. These things had the sense to retreat—pulling themselves and their victims away from the swords. And oh, no, they are not retreating into that tunnel!

Steele sent Marines to cut off that escape hole.

Kerry Blue jumped down into the mess of it.

Dimly aware no cloke fingernails were bouncing off her personal field. Were they saving their ammo?

Hacking at black things. Tough to get a clean slice, the clokes were intermingled with flailing people. People in agony just won't hold still.

Slash down two clokes. Hold up while Twitch grabs a human and drags him clear.

Kerry cut down a cloke through its spongy middle.

Kicked its pieces behind her. Advanced one step. Boot snagged on a stick. Cloke arm. She was about to kick it away. It was too thick. Bloody. Had flesh on it. Five fingers.

Kerry Blue screeched, "CARLY!"

There was the rest of Carly over there.

Twitch was suddenly there. Seized Carly. Carly was all floppy. Twitch holding Carly's bleeding stump closed in one big hand, ran back for the dirt wall. Passed Carly up to the Yurg. Climbed up after her.

"Twitch!" Kerry cried from the sinkhole.

He turned. She threw Carly's arm up to him.

About face. Sword ready.

All those Slash/Don't Slash drills come right back. Like falling off a bike.

On the left. Don't slash. Shove that civilian behind her toward the wall. Slash that and that and that. Jump out of the way of that hook thing zipping out of cloke's shoulder hole on a black string. Slash the string. Movement left and right. Friend left. Foe right. Hack the right one down.

Black mass rocketing past her left. Don't slash. That's *Don* Cordillera's dog.

Big dead guy in front of her. Might not stay dead if she could get him out in time. Need more muscle here. "Rhino!"

"Got him!" Rhino came in low on the left. "Cover me, Blue."

Rhino grabbed the dead guy, ankle and a wrist. Dragged him out of the melee. Kerry thrust up at a cloke jumping at Rhino's head.

A slight constriction tugged at her thigh. Kerry hardly felt it till her leg stopped working.

Saw a spurt of bright red blood. Someone had popped an artery. Someone was really screwed. Looked around for who.

Self jumping clear out of her body. Those slo-mo sensations that can't be real. A wire tightened around her thigh. Cut to the bone.

No blood in her head. The world closing into a tunnel. Ground smacking her in the cheek. A gray haze of boots and alien toes.

Someone shouting in the closing darkness, "Go displacement! Go displacement!"

Roger that.

Over and out.

Knew before she opened her eyes that she was back on the *Mack*. Her body didn't feel as heavy as it did on world. And she could smell that pink medical goo they used to glue people back together. She was in the ship's hospital.

She flexed her legs. Both of them. Hoo ra.

She sat up, and *ho mo*, there were a lot of people in here. Mo Shah's river was *full*.

She relaxed a little when realized the wounded weren't all grunts. The two guys in the Lazarus tubes were civilians. She'd have to ask them what God looked like. She only ever got as far as the white light.

The Roman battle barge up here really coulda stepped up and taken those guys to their hospital. Lazarus tubes were all right, but no one could raise the dead like Rome.

Kerry turned around. No Thomas. That was either really good or really really bad. "Where's the Old Man?"

"On duty, *chica linda*."

That was Carly. Count her arms. Two. Check.

"Anyone know where the clokes got the piano wire?" Taher called from his cot. Pink medical gel around his neck.

"Wasn't piano wire," said one of the civilians. "It was superfine filament. They must have stolen it from our camp. What I want to know is how they used it without cutting their own fingers off."

That silenced the room.

Kerry Blue got up and asked Mo Shah to clear her for duty.

Merrimack's Medical Officer told Lieutenant Glenn Hamilton upon her return to ship, "You are being a garden of unclassified flora and fauna."

Mohsen Shah had put Glenn through a nano scrub before allowing her to leave the ship's displacement chamber.

Clean now, in uniform, Glenn felt herself psychically decompressing. She'd gone island happy down there. She had killed alien intelligences.

But her party had been attacked and incurred a fatality, so her use of deadly force against aliens was not going to be a blot on her record.

Still, she knew her force had been excessive.

Captain Carmel called off the search for the *Xerxes* and brought the rest of her Marines back on board. Once the *Xerxes* left the ground, further search was useless. The pirates could have gone anywhere. Literally anywhere. And Captain Carmel was not the police to continue the chase.

Glenn murmured on the command deck, "You can find anyone if you know where he wants to go."

"Do you know where the pirates are going?" the captain asked.

"No one told me," Glenn said. But she was afraid she did know. "I think the pirates may be going to strike the clokes' home world."

Commander Ryan turned fully around to stare at her. "Why would they do that?"

"My reasoning is very thin," Glenn said. She couldn't begin to explain the concept of a bigger mammoth. "It's more a feeling than a reasoning. And I could be completely wrong."

A bigger mammoth was needed to stomp out the cloke eggs. All the clokes. All the eggs.

Calli said, "Mister Ryan. Do we know where the cloke home world is?"

"We may," said the XO, provisionally. "Our drones aren't there yet, but the generational ship's trail looks to be leading to a K-type star forty light-years rimward. Long-range readings indicate the probability of hospitable planets is very low. But we don't know what is hospitable to a cloke."

"Forty light-years," Calli echoed.

"That's twelve hours out," said Commander Ryan, anticipating her next question. "A *Xerxes* has a higher distortion threshold than our *Mack*. If this is a race, we can't win."

"You're assuming the *Xerxes* is running at threshold," said Calli.

Threshold velocity was a big strain on a ship's system. Threshold required constant acceleration to maintain.

"Don't ever stop running until the race is over," said Calli. "The pirates don't know they're being chased."

Apparently *Merrimack* was about to chase.

"And we don't know if they're running that way," said

Commander Ryan. He turned to Glenn. "Lieutenant, are you sure?"

"No, sir," said Glenn. *I said I wasn't.* "Not at all."

Commander Ryan challenged her, "Why would pirates hit a planet?"

"It might be convenient for Caesar if they did," Calli answered for Glenn. "Rome always takes the war home."

"There's a war?" said Commander Ryan, missing something.

"Numa is going to plant eagles on Zoe," said Calli. "He's making sure no more rival claimants can come in the back door."

"In that case, he could be drawing us off Zoe," said Ryan. "Don't we need to be *here*?"

"Colonel Steele!" Calli barked.

"Captain."

"Take the Spit boats and half your Wing. Get outside and hold the fort till we get back. Mister Ryan, organize best course to the cloke home world. As soon as Steele's unit is outboard, punch us to threshold."

"Aye, aye, sir."

Merrimack launched Space Patrol Torpedo boats One and Two. Red and Blue Squadrons scrambled, launching off of the space battleship's wings.

The two Spit boats received the Swifts at all their docks until both blocky ships looked like they were being eaten alive by space predators.

Captain Carmel then ordered, "Mister Ryan. Get us out of here."

"Aye, aye, sir," said Ryan.

Calli heard the reluctance in his acknowledgment. Said, "I can't let Numa kill the planet."

"I don't think a Xerxes carries planet killers," said Commander Ryan.

"The pirates will find a way," said Calli. "One strategically placed antimatter blast will close your shop for a millennium."

"You really don't think it's beneath Caesar to destroy a world?"

"Numa? No," said Calli. "Not if he can pin it on pirates."

"Sir, I just can't see where you're getting the pirate-Caesar connection."

"Mister Ryan. The pirates have no reason whatsoever for being on Zoe. They have every reason *not* to be on Zoe. Yet here they were. On Zoe. And here is Caesar."

Glenn hung back near the hatch of the command deck, hoping the captain was right. She didn't want to believe the Xerxes was heading to the cloke world so Nox could slay dragons for her.

But that was exactly what she believed.

We be one blood thou and I, he'd said. The finish of that quote was: *My kill shall be thy kill if ever thou art hungry.*

It was silly to think everything was about her.

But Izzy Benet called me a stupid bitch in front of Nox, and he's strewn across rooftops.

Calli paced the ship's corridors late into ship's night. *Merrimack* was moving faster than imagination, but the distances were vast. She felt as if she were rowing the battleship across an ocean. Her heart raced as if that could make the ship go faster.

Merrimack couldn't move any faster than she was now.

Eight hours into the twelve, Captain Carmel let the Dingo drag her onto the racquetball court. Calli smashed the little green ball with particular ferocity.

"Unusually savage tonight, aren't we, Captain?" said Dingo Ryan, serving.

Calli slammed the little green ball off the front wall. "I keep envisioning those bloody pirates setting off an antimatter blast in atmosphere right before my eyes." Slam. "We're going to get there a heartbeat too late." Slam. "I can see it." Slam.

"It won't play out that way, Cap'n." Dingo lunged to make a volley. "I promise you."

Slam. "You promise?"

"Absolutely." Missed the volley. The little ball made shallow thuds across the floor. Commander Ryan mopped his sleeve across his dripping brow. "If we're late, I promise it will be by more than one heartbeat."

* * *

Bagheera sublighted before a ruddy sun. Leo piloted the Xerxes toward the dull planet orbiting at one astronomical unit out from the star.

Announced, "We are here, *frateri*."

The Ninth Circle gathered in the control room for the approach to the cloke home world, still deciding how best to kill it.

An ambassadorial transport ship was not rigged for mass destruction. *Bagheera* had enough armament to defend itself and to engage in some piracy. It wasn't a ship of war.

During the voyage here, none of the brothers had figured out how to arm one of the Serpent's Tooth missiles with an antimatter warhead without killing themselves.

They agreed they needed to locate a volatile target on the planet surface and break containment of one or twelve of those.

"Nukes would be good," said Leo. "Nukes would be great. I hope they have nukes."

"I've got missiles loaded into the rack," said Orissus. "Find me some nukes. I'll break them open."

Nox took a seat at the console next to Leo, looking over the sensors. "You're going to have to get us a lot closer if I'm supposed to pick out a nuclear facility on the ground," Nox told him.

"Aye, aye, Captain Farragut," said Leo.

"Shut up."

Nox was not going to feel bad about this. He felt no empathy, no kinship with the clokes.

And he had promised Glenn a bigger mammoth.

✳ ✳ ✳

On approach to the clokes' home system, *Merrimack* pushed out the Swifts of Green and White Squadrons ahead of her.

Overheard their chatter.

"I can't see it."

They were on the lookout for the Xerxes.

"We can never see it, you boon."

"It's got to be ahead of us."

"We could have passed it and not know it."

"We could get there first."

"We'll know when we get there."

"What's the threshold of a Xerc?"

"That's not public knowledge."

"Faster than us."

"We think."

The Swifts stabbed into the solar system and homed in on the only planet in the temperate zone. They made a hard jump down from FTL.

Came the immediate report from Delta One: "Xerxes sighted!" Couldn't believe it. "I got a reading! All ships open fire!"

Delta Two: "I have him!"

Delta Three: "I'm firing!"

Delta Four: "Firing."

Echo Two: "Where!"

Echo Three: "I can't get a tone!"

Echo Four: "Gone!"

Delta One: "Skat, he was just there! *Merrimack*! Target went FTL."

Dingo Ryan leaned over the intership com. "Squadron, this is *Merrimack*. Target could still be in the area. Watch your Tac monitors. He will come in again for another run. Do not let him at the planet."

The planet was coming into visual range on the daylight side of the world as *Merrimack* followed her Swifts in.

"Oh, no."

Captain Carmel, monitoring the pilots' com channel, heard the sinking notes in the voice. Sounded like Delta One.

"Oh, no."

That was the sound of *too late*.

Merrimack's monitors showed what the Swifts saw.

No misty blue glow shone around the world, no white reflections bounced off the clouds.

The world was dark.

Delta Five: "Is it supposed to look like this? Is this cloke home sweet home?"

Closer, they saw an endless dust storm of hurricane winds.

Echo Two: "Look what they did!"

"It's dead!" Delta Five cried.

"*Merrimack. Merrimack. Merrimack*. We lost," Delta One sent.

Captain Carmel picked up the caller. "Squadron Leader, what is your status?"

"Too late, sir," Delta One responded. "The pirates did their work. Looks like we have a dead planet."

Calli turned to her exec. "Is *anyone* alive down there?"

Tactical scanned all the continents. The com tech listened on the full range of cloke radio frequencies. But no one on world was clicking.

Commander Ryan pronounced, grim, "That's nuclear winter."

Scanners filtered out the turbid atmosphere to show visual images of the surface. It was apparent that there used to be industry on most of the planet. It was half buried now under sludge lakes. Had been that way for a long time.

"The pirates didn't do this," said Commander Ryan. "Someone beat them to it."

That was why the planet had gone unnoticed by the early drone explorer vessels. It was uninhabitable. Drones didn't stop at dead inhospitable worlds.

"It's *dead!*" Delta Five cried over the com. "They trashed it! The clokes trashed their own planet!"

Echo One sent, "Actually I don't think we can tell whether the clokes did this to themselves or it's a natural disaster."

Delta Five: "What's the difference! It's dead!"

Captain Carmel lifted her eyebrows, said nothing.

What *was* the difference?

Dingo Ryan said off com, "Makes a difference how sorry we feel for those that remain on Zoe."

It appeared now that the vast dead cloke generational ship trudging through space had not been an explorer vessel or even a pilgrim ship.

It was an Ark.

And now it was as dead as its home world.

The only ground left to the clokes was Zoe.

* * *

"I'll turn us around back to Zoe," said Leo.

"Why?" said Nox.

"*Why?*" Nicanor asked back.

"Why," Nox. "Why go back to Zoe?"

They had all assumed they would return. They forgot there was a choice.

Pallas considered. "What are you suggesting? We go on our merry pirate way?"

"*Gladiator* is back at Zoe," Nicanor said, like a reason to go back to Zoe.

"*Gladiator* is back at Zoe," said Nox, like a reason not to.

"We don't have any orders," said Faunus, following Nox's lead. "We could keep running. We wouldn't technically be defying Caesar."

"You want to run?" said Nicanor.

"We're not Roman," said Orissus. "Numa never said we were Roman. He said we were pirate garbage. Right, Nox? Why would we go back to him?"

"That was my question," said Nox. "We need not walk into Shere Khan's mouth."

"So we have heard from Mowgli," said Nicanor. "Who else?"

Leo was considering the logistics. "If we don't resonate, Caesar can't find us."

The Xerc's prox alarm sounded.

Leo convulsed at his station. "How in hell—!"

"Caesar found us," Nox guessed.

"Oh, of all things buggered!" Faunus roared. "How does he *do* that?" Starting to think Numa had supernatural powers.

"That's how." Leo pointed to the monitor that interpreted the sensor readings into a visual image.

It wasn't *Gladiator*.

The ship closing on the Xerxes was a Roman Striker. It was black and bronze. Antonian colors.

"A Striker is a patterner's ship," said Leo.

"There are no patterners," said Nicanor. "We stopped making those." *We.* He meant Rome. Nicanor still thought of himself as Roman.

"Apparently Rome made one more," said Nox.

An Antonian one.

"Hook!" Leo cried.

"We don't have a hook," said Nox.

"I mean *him!*" Leo cried. "*The Striker has a hook on us!*"

It was a partial hook. A full hook would have cooked both ships.

The tiny Striker had latched onto the larger Xerxes and was reeling itself in.

"Kick him off!"

"I don't know how!"

"Maybe the ship knows how," said Nox. Yelled at the overhead, "*Bagheera!* Defend!"

Heard and felt a physical clunk of ships touching. The system monitor on Leo's console lit up the indicator for the lower starboard dock.

"He's here. He's making hard dock."

Sounds carried through the deck of the Striker's hatches opening. The patterner was trying to board.

Bagheera's hatches would hold against the intruder.

All the brothers saw the green light on Leo's monitor.

"Outer hatch opened!" Leo bolted straight up from his seat at the control console.

The seven of them barreled down to the lower level. *Bagheera* must fry the intruder in the air lock. He must.

But already the brothers heard a voice from the far side of the hatch—the voice sounded like one of them—demanding the Xerxes to recognize him in the name of the Empire. The patterner did not give his name.

Without introduction, the voice of the traitor leopard *Bagheera* intoned: "Welcome."

The brothers fanned out, crouching in the compartment adjoining the dock, daggers drawn and ready.

Measured footsteps passed through the air lock.

Leo stole a quick peek through the hatch, then drew back horrified, his bronze face gone ashy. "No. Oh, no."

"What!"

"Screw everything!" Leo cried in a whisper.

The footfalls advanced toward the inner hatch. Leo shrank in terror, yelling, "Shut it! Shut it! Shut it!"

"What the hell *is* it!" Orissus snarled.

Nicanor leaned in to see through the hatchway. His face slackened. "It's Schroedinger's bleeding bloody cat!"

The patterner stepped through the hatchway onto the inner deck.

It was Cinna.

PART THREE

Full Circle

34

CINNA. IN THE FLESH.

He was younger now. Looked seventeen and beautiful. His eyes had black irises and a bottomless stare. Dark loose curls wreathed his young face.

The brothers had all been good-looking until they'd scarred themselves and made themselves terrible, but even among good-looking clones, this man was an Adonis—except for the inhuman cables protruding from his forearms and behind his neck.

He might have been any clone of theirs, as they were all clones of a single Antonian man. Still, there was no doubt. Not even for an instant. Each and all knew, immediately knew, against every impossibility, that this was Cinna.

Even though this was not possible.

"It takes decades to make a patterner," Leo blurted.

"That may have been true decades ago," said the handsome Cinna-thing. He had a smooth deep voice.

"Technology marches on," Galeo murmured faintly.

None of the brothers could understand where Cinna's new body came from. They really didn't want to know.

All the king's horses and all the king's men hadn't had Caesar Numa's resources.

Cinna asked his brothers, all of them, any of them, "Did you really run?"

They had dropped him and left him for dead at the bottom of Widow's Edge. Last thing any of them ever thought was that Cinna would come back to haunt them.

Did you really run?

They all hesitated in choking silence.

Nox answered, "We could have medaled."

Pallas told Cinna, "We are working for Caesar." As if that would save them.

Cinna appeared to consider this. Said finally, "Then only one of you will die."

The brothers exchanged glances in hollow shock and disbelief.

Pallas, who did believe, asked as calmly as he could, "Why does anyone need to die?"

"All for one," said Cinna. "One for all."

Nox stepped forward. He looked Cinna dead in the opaque eyes. "Then I will be the one."

"No!" said Leo and Galeo at once, as Faunus cried, "Nox! No!"

"You can't," said Pallas.

Nicanor shouted, angry, "No! Not you! Not any of us!"

"You murderous cur!" Orissus bellowed at Cinna.

As Cinna looked from one shouting man to another, Nox shoved his dagger up Cinna's diaphragm into his heart.

The patterner folded to the deck.

There should have been more blood.

Nox withdrew his dagger, wiped off his blade and his hand on his own tunic, furious. "Oh, for cryin' tears. Did anyone *not* see that coming?"

The brothers shook their heads. The pattern had been plain a long way off.

"They don't make patterners like they used to," Leo said.

The patterners of yore had been nearly unstoppable. Unless they wanted to be stopped.

"Numa's not going to like us killing his patterner," said Galeo.

"Then Numa should have told us!" Pallas shouted. "You okay, Nox?"

Nox looked like he might pass out. His face was waxy, as if he himself were bleeding. His arm felt sticky up to his elbow. "Doesn't feel any better than it did the first time round. *Dammit, Cinna!*" he cried at the body.

I killed my brother. I killed him twice!

* * *

Merrimack caught up with her Swifts around the dead cloke home world. She brought the squadron inboard.

The orange sun was catalog number PB (for Perseus Benthus) 41X1900X12. The planet didn't have a name. But everyone on *Merrimack* called it cloke world.

Cloke world shrieked. Stones and sands scoured exposed bedrock. Muddy skies roiled in constant violence of thunder and lightning and lashing winds.

Merrimack's instruments scanned the world for technology and population centers.

The industry was built above ground, caked with soot and cold except for the nuclear plants. One of those gaped, cracked open from an apparent earthquake.

Under the surface the world was riddled with warrens of bunkers and tunnels.

Men couldn't fit inside the tunnels. These tunnels were larger than the naked dirt passages on Zoe and lined with conduit. They were big enough to send drones through.

The drones found no bodies. The clokes' hollow bones decayed quickly, but the drones could still find traces of the larger bones, enough of them to say there had been clokes down here. A while ago.

Scanners found a wreck of some kind of vessel on the surface. Huge one. The thing's crash left a long wide path of destruction behind it stretching a quarter of the way across the continent. It had been a giant ship or maybe an orbital construction platform that came down. An enormous hot crater of lethal radiation marked the place where it finally buried itself to a stop.

A search on another continent turned up less industry and cruder tunnels. There were mounds of cloke nails and hollow bones on the surface, the bodies decomposed, as if masses of the beings had poured out of the ground to die.

"It's starting to look like the clokes on Zoe are the only ones left," said Dingo. "I guess we can't drive the little squigs out after all."

"Yes, we can," said Calli.

"But they have nowhere to go."

"They can come home."

"Home is a little bit dead," Dingo pointed out.

"Not my problem," said Calli. "They killed their own world. Or maybe they just let it die. Dead is still dead. They figured out how to get to the stars. They could have cleaned up their home, but they decided to cut and run instead. Here's the bed they made. Stick 'em back in it."

Dingo didn't argue too hard. "I'm not in love with them, Captain."

Standing at the rear of the command platform with the Marines, Glenn Hamilton thought, *All the people like us are We, and everyone else is They*. It was something Nox would have said.

* * *

Nox washed his hands of Cinna's blood. He changed into a fresh tunic. He threw the bloody one into the annihilator.

When he came back out, he found that *Bagheera* had cleaned the deck, and the brothers had moved Cinna's body into one of the other air locks.

It looked like they intended to send their brother into the Deep. Nox guessed there was really no other choice.

Galeo despaired. "I am the proverbial dead horse. Why does Fate keep beating me?"

Nox told him, "Get up. I need you." *And oh, fug, I sound like Him. That other guy named John Farragut.*

The words always worked. Galeo rallied. He grasped Nox's hand hard. "I'm here for you, *frater*."

"Do we say something over the body?" Pallas asked.

They looked to one another.

"Does anyone believe in anything?" Orissus asked.

"Us," said Nox.

Nicanor nodded. "He was one of us."

They said their good-byes in the air lock, their regrets, and withdrew into the Xerxes one by one.

The last one left, Nox knelt down and kissed the patterner's forehead and murmured. "We did wrong by you, O Best Beloved. Shit, Cinna. Why did you let me kill you again?"

Nox's throat closed up. Cinna's hand was gripping it.

Cinna's eyes opened. "You're right," Cinna spoke to

Nox's bulging eyes. "There wasn't anybody who didn't see that coming."

Cinna rose, holding Nox's throat closed, talking conversationally, "Doesn't being in The Ninth Circle of Hell require you to be dead?"

❊ ❊ ❊

Lieutenant Hamilton hadn't been given back her command duties. Still, it happened in the middle of ship's night—the Hamster Watch—that *Merrimack*'s drones discovered a res chamber on the clokes' home planet.

Chief Engineer Kittering advised the captain and the XO as they converged on the command deck, "The cloke resonator is not sending. It *is* receiving something."

Resonance had no age. It existed in the right now. That the res chamber was receiving something now meant the message was being sent right now.

"Who is bloody sending?" Commander Ryan demanded.

Captain Carmel asked, "Is the message coming from the clokes on Zoe?"

"That is the problem, sirs," said Kit. "It's not any cloke talk we have on record from Zoe."

"A different language?" Ryan asked.

"It's not cloke talk at all. Clokes click. This is just intermittent noise."

But the res tech spoke Calli's worst fear: "The message is arriving in packets."

Relativistic distortion affected resonant messages when the sender and receiver were not both traveling FTL.

Resonant messages only smashed together in packets when the receiver was in normal space-time and the sender was traveling faster than light.

The res tech said, "The cloke resonator on the planet is picking up an FTL source. It doesn't have a compensator to separate the instants."

Commander Ryan immediately ordered the helm, "Take us to FTL."

"Destination, sir?"

"Don't care. Around the block. Just get us FTL."

All became clear when *Merrimack* made the jump.

The resonant signals expanded.

"Confirmed," said the res tech. "The sender is moving faster than light."

He transposed the frequency of the message into the range of human hearing, then put it on audible.

It was clicking.

Somewhere, right now, there were clokes traveling faster than light, sending messages home.

Calli spoke low, "More than one. More than one. More than one. *De Eendracht. Mayflower. Niña, Pinta, and Santa Maria.*"

"Sir?"

"More than one. We are dealing with an entire planet. On any naturally evolved world, there is more than one nation. Their levels of technology are not always in synch. There is *more than one cloke ship out here*! More than one nation. More than one era. This planet *did* develop FTL capability while their generational ship was slogging away in sublight transit. There is another cloke ship. Where is it?"

"We have its resonant signal," said Dingo significantly.

Calli knew where he was going with that. She headed him off. "I will not ask Numa Pompeii to give us the source on a res pulse."

Her husband, the ship's Legal Officer was on deck. He murmured very low, "Pride, Cal. Pride goeth."

"I am not asking Numa for anything," Calli said.

Tactical spoke up. "Don't need to, sir."

Sentinels at the edge of the Zoen star system had picked up a new plot. A ship had just dropped out of FTL outside the farthest orbit. Its profile fit no known nation.

"IFF?" Calli demanded.

The com tech said, "It's clicking."

Tactical said, "Plot is on approach vector to Zoe. ETA fifty-six hours."

"Type of craft?"

"Vast," said Tactical. "It's another Ark."

35

CAPTAIN CARMEL SET the *Merrimack* on course back toward Zoe at moderate haste. At this pace, the battleship would beat the Ark to the planet with days to spare.

A signal came in from the League of Earth Nations headquarters with orders for the *Merrimack*.

"Take the message," Calli ordered Red Dorset at the com station.

"They won't talk to me, sir. They want you."

"Then let's have it."

A voice like an assistant God issued from the com: "Captain Carmel, you will not go near the alien spacecraft. And your weapons will not fire."

My weapons fire very well.

"I have no intention of going 'near' the Ark," Calli said. "*Merrimack* is on course to Zoe. If the Ark comes to Zoe while I am there, know that I will prevent the invaders from off-loading on Zoe. You do not command my weapons against an alien invader."

"Why do you assume an invasion? Why can the ship's passengers not be there to explore and to talk?"

"They brought a moving van."

❋ ❋ ❋

Admiral John Farragut picked up a resonant hail on the personal harmonic Glenn Hamilton used to hail him.

It wasn't Glenn Hamilton.

Admiral Farragut didn't show shock at the face on the screen. Surprise, yes. The major emotion coming through the resonator was concern.

He saw a face like his own, a couple of decades younger, colored and scarred, with beads and feathers woven into the same blond hair as his.

Admiral Farragut greeted the pirate with a nod. "Nox."

That left Nox momentarily mute. John had addressed him as he would have demanded. Nox had expected his older brother to insist on calling him up by his birth name. But big John conceded that fight straight up.

John Alexander had the touch. Not too many cow pies that man ever stepped in. And when he did, it was a big splashy stomp with a purpose. He was the favorite son. The first. The best.

Nox wanted to hate this man. And couldn't.

"John." Nox nodded in return.

John Farragut didn't say anything off course. He went straight to the heart of things. "Is there anything I can do?"

Nox shook his head. It was too late for miracles.

John tried again, "Why are you calling?"

Nox said, "I haven't the damndest idea."

He'd found the admiral's personal harmonic among Glenn Hamilton's things in her tent. Nox did not know his brother well. They had only met a few times. Nox had come into being only after the eldest Farragut son left home to save the world.

"Where are you?" John asked.

"I am absolutely nowhere," Nox said. "Headed home."

Big John could be naïve but he was no idiot. He knew which home Nox meant. The place everyone goes at journey's end. Nox saw the fear cross John's face. "Don't."

Nox twisted a hard smile. "You know how they say it's never too late to turn back on a wrong road?"

"Yes."

"They're wrong. Ever read *Lord Jim*?"

Apparently he had. He said, "You don't have to die, Nox."

"But you know I do, O Best Beloved. I'm kind of looking forward to it."

He saw big John trying to talk, with nothing to say. *He does know it.*

And there are the tears. Big John Farragut was an unrepentant crier. Nox didn't know how he got away with it, but no one ever called him weak. Nox couldn't even say John Alexander Farragut wasn't Superman. Because he was.

Even Superman can't save me.

Nox had no idea why he called. He'd thought something would come to him. Nothing did.

"Good-bye, John."

* * *

Merrimack was still two hours outside of the Zoen star system on the return journey from the cloke home world when Tactical's coffee went splashing through the deck grates, the cup rolling.

"Captain!" Marcander Vincent sang out. "Found your pirates!"

He posted images on all the monitors.

"Where?" Calli demanded.

"Just sublighted at the outer edge of the Zoen system. Near the clokes' Ark."

"And we can *see* him?" said Dingo. They shouldn't be able to see the Xerxes unless he wanted to be seen. "Has to be a decoy."

"He's got company," said Marcander Vincent.

"Company other than the Ark? What kind of company?" Dingo leaned in to see the one-man waspish ship with the Xerxes. "Is that—?"

"A Roman Striker, sir."

"Bulldust!" said Commander Ryan. "Rome made another patterner?"

"Or Rome wants us to think they have," said Calli, who didn't believe it.

Tactical reported, "Striker and Xerxes are moving in lockstep. The Striker has a hook on the Xerxes."

"I didn't think you could get a hook on a Xerxes," said Calli.

"*We* can't," said Ryan. "If it can be done, it would take a Roman patterner in a Striker to do it."

"Where is *Gladiator*?" Calli demanded.

"Orbiting Zoe, sir."

Calli snapped to the com tech. "Give me Numa."

Red Dorset fed the Roman link to the captain's console.

Calli sent, "*Gladiator*, this is *Merrimack*. Your Striker has hooked a vessel that is the property of a LEN member nation. Deliver the Xerxes into our custody."

Caesar Numa answered Calli's hail in person. His refusal was tranquil. "Under international law we are the arresting agent, and we are taking the pirates of The Ninth Circle into our custody."

"You can take your pirates, Numa. Hand over the ship."

"We made the arrest. We can execute criminals more efficiently than you."

"The *ship*, Numa. You can have your criminals. The *ship* is property of a League member nation. I demand you turn over the *ship*."

"You are not flying an Italian flag, Captain Carmel. I will not discuss disposition of the Xerxes with anyone other than a valid claimant."

Calli slammed off the com. Yelled at it, "You frumious toad!"

"I'd've paid money to see you say that to his face, Captain," said Commander Ryan.

"I may yet," she said. "I can't let him get the Xerxes. If he reels that Xerxes in, he'll keep it."

"He already has it."

"No, he doesn't. Not while there are pirates inside it. What is *Gladiator* doing now?"

"Status unchanged. Orbiting Zoe. *Gladiator* is not heading out to meet the Striker at the edge of the system. The LEN pirate hunter *Windward Isles* is moving out."

"What direction are the Striker and the Xerxes traveling?"

Tactical responded, "The Striker is dragging the Xerxes by an energy hook in the direction of Zoe. That would be toward *Gladiator*. But they're a couple of billion miles out yet, and they are *not* moving very fast. The Xerxes is resisting. I'm reading a lot of energy output from the Xerxes."

The Xerxes was digging in its virtual heels.

"That's going to be a long tow," said Commander Ryan. "If the Striker is hauling the pirates to *Gladiator,* he won't make it until sometime after Judgment Day."

"Captain!" Tactical cried.

"Say something, Mister Vincent," said Calli.

But already she saw it on the monitors. The Striker's slow progress was slowing down more. Drastically.

The pirate ship had fought the towing Striker to a near standstill.

Then their direction reversed. The larger Xerxes dragged the smaller Striker by its own energy hook in the direction the Xerxes wanted to go.

The Striker struggled, not letting go.

"What's happening here?" Calli demanded. "Who has whom?"

"It's the Striker's hook, sir. But the Xerxes is setting the course at the moment," said Tactical. Then noted, "*Gladiator* has launched Accipiters."

Accipiters were fast Roman attack ships. That would indicate some concern on Numa's part, even if the battlefort *Gladiator* did not break from its orbit around Zoe.

"Is this real?"

Commander Ryan said, "The Xerxes can't realistically go anywhere with that ball and chain on it. The pirates are just delaying the inevitable."

The pirate ship flashed its visual image—the last thing men saw before they died. The Xerxes appeared engulfed in a bright hologram of an enormous leopard, a silent roar issuing from its red-dripping mouth. The skull and crossbones flag stood posted on her bow alongside the molten circled IX travesty of a Roman standard. The bloody scrawl across the leopard-spotted hull read in Italian: Abandon All Hope.

He's changing the color of inevitability, Calli realized.

The leopard didn't intend to go far.

She could see which direction the locked pair of ships was going.

"He's hitting the Ark."

"*Suicide?*" said the XO.

"Why not?"

The pirates were going to die. They could still choose how.

The com tech reported, "Captain, I've got the LEN here. Screaming."

Apparently one of the several international ships denied

landing rights on Zoe was sending a live feed of events at the edge of the star system back to Earth.

"League HQ wants to know why we aren't stopping the Xerxes from flying into the Ark."

Calli asked the com tech, "Is the LEN's concern for the Xerxes or for the Ark?"

"Not sure, sir."

Calli took up the caller. "Sir, on LEN orders, I don't have anyone near the Ark. *Merrimack* is two hours out from the star system, best speed."

Purple words issued from the com.

Calli shut him off and hailed her rear guard. She had left two Spit boats with two squadrons of Swifts behind in the Zoen star system. "Colonel Steele! Scramble Swifts! You have trade at the edge of the star system. Hit the Xerxes!"

The way Swifts docked with a Space Patrol Torpedo boat, the Swift's cockpit opened up onto the deck from below, so the docking bay looked like a plot of fourteen open graves.

Colonel Steele jumped down into the cockpit of his crate. He automatically grabbed down for his displacement collar.

Colonel Steele barked lots of alien words. "Where's my fugging collar!"

It was supposed to be in his cockpit, stowed next to his seat for immediate grabbing. He let everyone know it wasn't here. Going to bust some erk down to dog washer when he got back to *Merrimack*. It was the erks' job to have these crates prepped before they left the *Mack* and ready to go in the blink of an eye—which was too much bloody time as it was.

"COLLAR!" he roared again.

Rhino's voice: "Heads!"

Heard something making a rattling slide across the deck toward him. Steele caught the displacement collar as it dropped down from overhead.

He snapped the collar on and hauled his canopy forward over him.

Back to task. Could bludgeon erks later.

TR Steele had no sympathy for the ugly aliens he was

rushing to save. But Steele was hot to kill pirates. Roman pirates all the better.

His Bull Mastiffs loved to shoot the guns. And they hated to lose a battle.

If this operation saved an arkload of plague rats, well, that's the decision from upstairs. TR Steele's Marines never never never threw a fight.

* * *

The Xerxes was gaining speed, still moving in the direction of the Ark, dragging the Striker with it.

Calli hailed *Gladiator*. "Numa, stop them."

"Our Striker is making a lawful arrest, Captain Carmel."

"You're losing! Both those ships are going to crash into the alien Ark!"

"So much concern for creatures you call latrines," Numa chided.

"There's a difference between refusing the clokes access to Zoe and allowing someone to kill their Ark," said Calli. "That Ark is their world. They built it, they're living on it, and they have a right to it."

"Well for them," said Numa.

"Goddammit, Numa, it's genocide!"

"Why are you swearing at me, Captain Carmel? That is *Our* Striker attempting to arrest *your* pirate ship before it can destroy the alien Ark. What are you doing about it?"

"Make your Striker let go! Those pirates don't want to destroy the Ark! You know they don't. They just don't want to be taken alive! They want you to let go! You have the power to end this. Order your Striker to let go!"

"Grandiose of you to imagine Caesar is in your chain of command," Numa said and cut the connection.

Calli slapped the com off. She composed herself and spoke to her exec. "This is a show. I know how this will end. At the last instant the Striker will miraculously find the power to reverse direction and carry the Xerxes away, the Ark will be spared, and the LEN will *thank* Numa for stealing their Xerxes."

I think that's how Numa intends it to go.

She was not going to let it go that way.

Tactical reported, "Squadrons in range, Captain."

Calli issued orders, "Wing Leader. Wing Leader. Wing Leader. This is *Merrimack*. Hit the Xerxes. Hit the hook."

Steele responded: "Aye, aye, *Merrimack*. All ships. All ships. Open fire. Hit the Xerxes. Hit the hook."

Beam fire from multiple Swifts glanced off the energy hook surrounding the Xerxes. So many hits, so nothingness of damage, Kerry Blue just wanted to step outside and kick the target. She couldn't possibly have less effect.

Cain said it: "Wing Leader, we can't get a clean shot at the Xerxes! The Striker's hook is just making a double field around the target!"

The patterner's Striker had an unbreakable hold on the Xerxes, but the Xerxes was winning the tug-of-war, picking up speed. The joined pair were getting awfully close to the gargantuan Ark awfully fast.

For the Swifts chasing the pair, that Ark was taking on the dimensions of a mountain range.

Kerry Blue fired on the pirate ship. Hit it. Hit it a whole bunch of times. Did nothing. Absolutely nothing.

Heard the captain's voice on the com, "Steele! Hit the Striker! And if Numa's Accipiters get in your way, hit them too!"

Heard Thomas' voice, with joy: "Aye, aye, sir!"

Captain Calli on *Merrimack* watched distant battle play out on monitors, the Xerxes dragging the Striker ever closer to the Ark, faster and faster.

I am playing chicken with my Marines' lives. The Swifts cannot survive a close-in blast.

Calli thought out loud, "The Striker will let go of the Xerxes before it's too late. It has to."

Commander Ryan said, "The Striker will only let go if Caesar orders him to let go. Otherwise he'll hold on to the death."

Marcander Vincent, seated at the tactical station, reported, "Assuming the Ark takes an antimatter hit from either the Striker or the Xerxes, then by best estimate our Swifts will be within lethal distance in seven seconds. Five, four."

The Swifts flew inside the Ark's outriggers. The outriggers spread out for miles. But that was far too close to any matter-antimatter detonation for a Swift to maintain its inertial screens.

"Three, two, one. All Swifts are now within the range of zero survivability."

Commander Ryan said, "Don't let them in there, Captain. Get them out."

"This is a charade," said Calli. "Numa won't allow the Striker to take the suicide plunge."

The Marines fired barrages of beams at the pair. "Hit!"
No effect.

"Hit!"
No effect.

"GrettaaaaaaaaH! WILL you just DIE?"

The Xerxes was speeding in now, the Striker clinging.

"When that thing explodes, the Swifts' fields *will not* hold."

"Caesar wouldn't sacrifice a patterner just to take out a pirate ship," said Calli.

Commander Ryan said, "Didn't you once tell me Numa hates patterners."

Calli blinked wide.

He does.

Calli pounded on the com, "Steele! Squadrons! Wear off! Abort! Abort! Abort!"

The captain's voice hammered in Kerry's helmet. As close to screaming as Kerry Blue ever heard Carmel sound when she wasn't on fire. Got everyone's attention.

Kerry muttered, reversing hard. "I'd'a had him."

The Striker kept its death grip on its captive. The Xerxes towed its captor, accelerating—

And pierced the alien hulk like a missile.

Both ships disappeared inside.

Captain Carmel barked: "All Swifts! All Swifts! Get clear of the Ark! You are too close."

"Trying to," Cain Salvador grunted. Realized, late, "This thing has a gravitational pull."

Not a strong one but significant when he was trying to accelerate through the light barrier.

FTL was not happening. And Cain needed to be out of here yesterday. They all did.

Steele bellowed, "Slam it to the gate. Move! Move! Move!"

Kerry Blue: "Moving, aye. Like a slug!"

Steele: "Energy fields to the stern!"

Cain: "We're about to get a push. Either to FTL or the hereafter."

Kerry Blue: "See you on the other side."

The Ark erupted, volcanic. Almost seemed to contract for a split instant from an internal event of cataclysmic intensity. Fissures formed in the hull all around the colossal structure, like landmasses breaking. And the whole thing heaved outward, revealing its core.

Lit up like a new sun.

Someone yelling on the open com, sounded like Kerry Blue, running ahead of the blast. "*YeeeeeAhhahaha!*"

"Oh—" Calli gaped speechless for several moments before the many images, grasping for a strong enough word. "*Farragut!*"

Held her breath until a voice sounded over the Marine com. At least one of the Swifts made it away alive.

It was Colonel Steele. "Wing! Call in by the numbers!"

"Alpha One, here."

"Alpha Two, I think I'm here."

"Alpha Three, here."

Cain: "Alpha Four not present but accounted for."

Carly was back on *Merrimack*, getting reacquainted with her arm.

"Alpha Five, aquí."

"Alpha Six, I'm in the wrong neighborhood."

"Alpha Seven, I'm in the middle of flying crap."

"Baker One, I'm in Kerry Blue's neighborhood."

"Baker Two, I got the whole state of New Jersey running up my tail."

"Baker Three, I'm *in* New Jersey."

"Baker Four, here."

"Baker Five, where am I supposed to be?"

"Baker Six, here."

Charlie and Delta Flights called in. Every man jack and jane alive.

Colonel Steele called out coordinates for his scattered squadrons to muster.

Calli demanded of Tactical, "Mister Vincent. Give me status of the Ark. Status of the Xerxes. Status of the Striker."

"Status of the Ark is smithereens," said Marcander Vincent.

The Ark threw off chunks the circumference of city blocks at relativistic speeds, each jetting steam from many fractures into the vacuum. Powerplants the size of buildings became projectiles.

"The core got annihilated," said Marcander Vincent. "The rest of it—well, there's the rest of it."

Parts of the titanic mobile world spewed in every direction. Giant plates ripped away. Pulverized bits blew out in colossal sand storms. Continued explosions erupted in the largest of the scattered pieces as nuclear furnace cores cracked open to perfect cold. Burning gases lit the vacuum in brief flashes for miles.

Merrimack, still hours away from the show, was getting her visual resonant feeds from the Spit boats. "Survivors?" Calli asked.

"That kind of hit?" said Marcander Vincent. "The clokes got flattened down to the thickness of a micron in about a trillionth of a heartbeat. They never felt a thing."

"God rest their squiggy souls," said Dingo Ryan.

Tactical went on, "It wasn't the collision that did all this. The kamikazes were probably alive right up until the antimatter release dead center of the Ark. Sir, it was a single annihilation event."

Calli felt a chill. *A single event.* "What exactly are you telling me, Mister Vincent?"

"There was only one antimatter source. The rest of the explosions are coming from within different pieces of the Ark."

There should have been two antimatter blasts if the Xerxes dragged the Striker in with it.

"You mean the Striker let go before the Xerxes self-destructed."

"Yes, sir. I've got a trace image suggesting the Striker may have passed *through* the Ark and got away intact."

He played back an enhanced computer scan of the ejecta from the initial blast. Something shot straight out the other side of the Ark, moving too fast to be propelled only by the explosion. In fact the plot moved *ahead* of the explosion. Marcander Vincent tapped at the replay. "That is definitely a small ship moving under its own power."

"Do we know for sure *which* ship?"

Strikers were tough to detect, but they didn't have the perfect stealth of a Xerxes. This ship left a trace.

"It's returning the energy profile and trail signature of a Roman Striker."

The Striker got away.

Calli breathed, "Numa, you bastard."

The patterner lived. Calli wondered if Caesar would be pleased or disappointed.

"Will that shock wave from the annihilation hit Zoe?" Calli asked.

"Won't affect the planet, sir. The shock wave has three and half billion miles to diffuse before what's left of it gets there. Zoe is on the far side of the sun from this action. The light flash will get there in about five hours but the Zoens won't even notice it."

The Swifts of Red and Blue Squadrons had gotten clear of the flying wreckage and were returning to their Spit boats.

The Roman Accipiters had already turned around and were headed back to *Gladiator*.

Gladiator never left its orbit around Zoe.

Merrimack was still over an hour outside the star system.

Numa held all the high ground.

"Take us down from threshold," Calli ordered. The race was lost.

She signaled *Gladiator*.

Caesar deigned to take her call.

"Why didn't your Striker let go sooner, Numa?" She knew he had been monitoring everything that just happened. "What was the point of playing chicken with the Xerxes? You lost the Xerxes and annihilated the alien Ark."

"We did not annihilate the Ark. And don't pretend to value the aliens," said Numa Pompeii. "The pirates inadvertently did you and humanity a favor by killing the creatures and themselves. Survival is for the fittest. Not just the strongest. 'Fittest' also includes the useful and beautiful. The clokes are none of those things. We are."

"Are you speaking in royal plurals again, Numa?"

Caesar Numa Pompeii said, "You will survive, Callista."

Captain Carmel sent her report to the admirality. It was concise to the point of being abrupt. Just bald facts. She was too angry to put any insight or observation into it.

The cloke Ark had been murdered while she was off trying to save the cloke home world. It wasn't the loss of cloke lives that angered her. She did not love them. It was the losing.

"Commander Ryan, you have the deck."

The Marine guard at the hatch came to attention as Captain Carmel left the command platform.

Calli collected her Legal Officer in person. She leaned in the hatchway and swirled a half bottle of Scotch. "Mister Buchanan. This has to die."

"Aye, aye, Captain."

Rob Roy rose from his workstation, where he had been watching the death of the Ark and of the Xerxes play out on the monitors. He followed Calli to the Captain's Mess.

The assassination of the Scotch was underway. The condemned had been seriously wounded to begin with. Calli finally said, "It appears that the pirates would rather die than be taken captive." She ran that thought up like a trial balloon. She expected some resistance.

And got it. "That is the *appearance*," Rob Roy agreed. Something wasn't right in the *appearance*.

"Did they have other options?" Calli said. Then spoke her real suspicion aloud, "Was The Ninth Circle working under the covert command of Caesar this time?"

Rob Roy advocated for the devil, "If Caesar commanded the pirates, why would he make them squander the Xerxes?"

"That doesn't help me," said Calli.

Rob Roy poured her some reinforcements.

Calli said, "Numa wanted the clokes out of his universe and the pirates dead." A light sheen of sweat made her appear to glow when she was drinking. "Why?"

Still on the side of the devil, Rob Roy challenged, "Why would you think that's what Numa wanted?"

"Because it's what he got."

Rob Roy couldn't think of a counterargument.

Caesar Numa had a bad habit of getting what he wanted.

"You are a frighteningly lucid drunk, Captain."

Calli capped the bottle. "Take me home."

Calli had been played. Knew it. She didn't know to what end. She couldn't bring herself to mourn the death of disgusting aliens, but the cloke Ark had come under suicide attack, and she could do nothing but watch.

Watch.

Was that what Numa needed her to do? Watch?

Had to be.

What did he need me to see?

What did I really see?

Merrimack had returned to Zoe when Tactical reported, "Captain. I have multiple displacements appearing on the planet. *Gladiator* is putting legionaries on the ground."

"Not while I'm here."

Calli Carmel crossed the command deck to look over Tactical's shoulder. She looked to the com tech. "Mister Dorset. Get me the Self."

Caesar did not deign to take her hail.

On a public resonant link a Roman broadcast from the planet showed the Praetorian Guard stabbing imperial eagles into the ground and claiming the world in the name of the Senate and People of Rome.

Numa Pompeii asserted his right to the planet with great bluster and authority. He cited international law.

Calli glared at the monitor. "That's not right," she said. "He has no right."

"Are you sure?" said Commander Ryan.

"No. That's why I'm checking his sources." On the intracom, "Mister Buchanan!"

Rob Roy, the Legal Officer, was already checking Numa's citations. He told Calli, "Short answer. He's wrong. Flagging this planet is against international convention."

"What's my legal remedy?"

"You have a legal and moral obligation to defend the convention, Captain Carmel."

"In plain Americanese, Mister Buchanan?"

"Shoot him."

36

STANDING AT THE REAR of the command deck, Colonel Steele visibly brightened, a hard kind of brightness. TR Steele hated the peace.

Calli asked her Legal Officer, "Under which flag am I shooting?"

"Ours. This world is under extraplanetary assault. You have jurisdiction."

Someone in the control room muttered low, "Hot damn!"

Calli was shouting. "Commander Ryan! Change out the flags."

"Aye, aye, sir!"

"Get this green shit off of me!" Calli tore off her LEN armband. The green LEN flag came down from the command deck and from the ship's external mast. The Stars and Stripes flew alone.

"Battle stations."

Merrimack launched all her Swifts, both of the SPTs, and the long-range shuttle, and sent them into Zoe's atmosphere.

Caesar would not fire on an antimatter engine in the atmosphere of a world he wanted to own.

Calli ordered displacement jammers activated planetwide to prevent *Gladiator* from displacing down any more men and equipment than he already had on the ground. The jammers also prevented Numa from retrieving the soldiers he already had deployed on world.

Then Calli ordered, "Mister Ryan. Fire on *Gladiator*. Fire everything."

Captain Carmel had no expectation of damaging *Gladiator* with the barrage, but it would keep Numa's troop carriers and fighter craft inboard and away from her Marines.

Merrimack's Swifts were safe from Roman fire as long as they remained in Zoe's atmosphere.

The Swifts still needed to guard against an energy hook from *Gladiator*. A hook could snuff them.

Merrimack's guns hammered at *Gladiator* to keep its energy locked up on itself.

Gladiator didn't even try to deploy a hook. It didn't need to. The Swifts' weakness was their very short range in atmosphere. Without the cold of space around them, the small fighters rapidly overheated.

Surfacing out of the atmosphere would leave the Swifts vulnerable to *Gladiator*'s guns.

Gladiator could wait for its targets to come up to cool.

Captain Carmel sent the Swifts to the arctic on the winter side of the world.

"Tracking."

"Tracking, aye."

"Locate all Roman ground units."

"Roman ground units located, aye," said Tracking. "Twelve plots." Then he added, "Roman ground units have deployed shield domes." He thought the captain intended to strafe.

"Targeting. Acquire the Praetorian unit who planted Caesar's eagles. Acquire the eagles."

"Targeting, aye. Targets have an energy dome over them, sir."

"Target the dome."

"Targeting, aye. Praetorians, eagles, energy dome acquired, aye."

"Engineering!"

"Engineering, aye."

"Ready hook."

"Engineering, aye. Hook ready and standing by."

"Hook the target."

* * *

The Praetorians were arrayed in full ceremonial armor. They had posted Caesar's eagles on the planet for the glory of the empire. They saw flashes in the day sky. Someone was shooting upstairs. But they were safe under an energy dome.

A sudden jolt threw them to the ground.

No.

The ground was rising under them.

A pseudopod of energy, extending from *Merrimack*'s inertial field, jabbed down to the planet surface, enclosed the Romans, their shield dome, and the ground they stood on, and pulled them *up*.

Imperial eagles canted over. Roman standards wobbled. The ground became loose and crumbly under the guardsmen. They lay flat forward for a dizzying ride a quarter way around the globe.

Merrimack set them down in darkness, not gently. The energy hook dissolved.

Wind felt like blades. Breath iced in their lungs. They narrowed their eyes to slits. Blowing ice collected on their lashes. They had come from a temperate zone. They were not equipped for arctic operations. Their energy dome was still active, but it was an umbrella. They were vulnerable at ground level.

A wind-whipped spray of glassy particles sent them all crouching low again. They heard engines.

Not friendlies. These were United States fighter craft.

Incoming beamfire at ground level took out the dome generators. Now the guardsmen were open to the sky. Bitter wind was dry and cutting. The place was dark except for the auroras and starshine lancing off the glittering snowpack.

The Swifts set down in a blizzard of ice crystals that made tinny sounds on the guards' bronze helmets, lifted their formal tunics and stung their bare legs. Cold metal armor felt sticky.

The Swifts' canopies slid back. Figures in full environmental gear, including heated suits, emerged from their cockpits. The Marines' personal fields glinted around them. Their splinter guns presented muzzles first.

One figure climbed atop his fighter's fuselage. The host of stars were icy bright around him. The American's merry grin was visible through his faceplate. He called down through his helmet speaker. "Freeze!"

The Praetorian decurion raised his hands. "Oh, you're a laugh riot, you are, Yank."

Tactical spoke what Calli had already noticed. "*Gladiator* is not returning fire."

This was a bad sign.

Numa Pompeii always takes the war home.

Caesar was going to hit her from behind. Only she didn't know how.

It came quicker than she expected. Red Dorset turned from his station at the com. "Captain. Incoming call on the resonator. It's Admiral Farragut."

Already?

"Give it to me."

Red Dorset sent the link to the captain's console.

"Yes, sir?" Calli said wearily into the com.

"You've been undercut," Admiral Farragut told her. "The order came down from the President. *Merrimack* is to take no more action without direct orders."

"Can you give me the direct order, John?"

"No," said Admiral Farragut. "No one is saying you lacked authorization or you did anything wrong. They're just saying stop."

"Does the President know Numa caused the destruction of the cloke Ark?"

"From here it looked like Roman ships tried to save the Ark."

"That was staged."

"I believe you. No one else will. They won't want to."

"Numa will take over the world," said Calli. "You know if you let Rome in, you've given them the world."

"Cal? I think he *has* it. You lost this one. Don't make me give your ship to the Dingo."

"John, you know I can't lose to Numa!"

"You did, Cal. If we hadn't just got off a war, we might have got someone to make a stand. The pols don't want to spend lives on this. They don't see Rome as a danger to Zoe. It's over."

She had arguments. Kept from voicing them. "Aye, sir."

In a moment the admiral came back, "Cal?"

"Yes, John?"

"Do you know what happened to my brother?"

Dingo Ryan issued the order for the Marines to release the Roman prisoners.

The Marines had been holding the Praetorians in a Spit boat at the pole. Colonel Steele turned the Romans out to the arctic night, then ordered the Swifts aloft. The fighters lifted in a blast of ice crystals.

Merrimack had not turned off her jammers. With the jammers still in place, *Gladiator* could not displace the stranded guardsmen off the polar ice pack.

Asante commented over the com, "A little *cold*, isn't that?" There was a distinct grin in his voice.

"They can walk home for all I care," said Steele.

Cain sent, "Sir? Can we salute?"

The Yurg sent, "You know, show respect."

"Proceed," said Colonel Steele.

The Swifts executed a low fly by, scarcely higher than a rooftop, over the Praetorians. Vicious winds and sonic booms trailed in their wakes.

As the Swifts rose out of the atmosphere, *Gladiator* launched a transport toward the planet, probably to collect the freezing guardsmen.

Cain sent over the Marines' open com, "Colonel? Can we go back down and salute those guys too?"

"Can we?" said the Yurg.

"Can we?" said Kerry Blue.

"Colonel?" said Cain.

Guessed Colonel Steele didn't like that idea. He wasn't responding.

All flights were returning to *Merrimack*.

Colonel Steele, leading Red Squadron, wasn't adjusting his course for the approach.

"Wing Leader. This is Alpha One. Are you there, sir?"

Steele did not answer. He did not change course or speed.

"*Merrimack. Merrimack. Merrimack.* This is Alpha One. I have lost contact with Wing Leader. Colonel Steele is not answering his com."

"Wing Leader. Wing Leader. Wing Leader. This is *Merrimack*. Respond."

Nothing.

Hailed Cain instead. "Alpha One. This is *Merrimack*. Bring your squadron in to the flight deck."

Steele's com was out. He was having systems problems. Meant he would come in last.

Alpha and Baker Flights rode their beams in to *Merrimack*'s starboard wing. They touched down, clamped down, rode the elevator down. The upper flight deck of the starboard wing was clear for Steele's approach.

Marines climbing out of their Swifts on the hangar deck all looked to the empty slot.

Rhino said, "Where's the Old Man?"

Steele should have circled round for his approach after everyone else was inboard.

"Captain?" said Commander Ryan. "Steele's not coming back."

"Overtake," said Captain Carmel. On the com she sent, "Colonel Steele, if you can hear me, shut your engine down."

The Swift did not deviate course or speed. The engine stayed hot.

Tactical said, "We have a runaway."

"Bring him in. Assume incapacitated pilot," said Captain Carmel.

Dingo Ryan got on the intracom. "Displacement. This is Command. Ready rapture for Colonel Steele. Execute when ready."

"Command. This is Displacement. No go. Negative correspondence. I can't get a read from Colonel Steele's collar. The Colonel's displacement collar is turned off or damaged."

"Whatever incapacitated Steele took out his collar too," Ryan told the captain. "What *got* him?"

Marcander Vincent said, "Nothing. Nothing hit him."

"Check him," Calli ordered the specialist next to Marcander Vincent. If Vincent missed something, Calli was going to send him down, no matter what she promised John Farragut.

Then she was on the com: "Medical Department. This is the captain. Report to cargo bay one."

To her XO: "Mister Ryan, shut that Swift down, hook him, and get him in here. Cargo bay one."

"Aye, aye, sir."

Ryan issued the override signal that remotely shut down the Swift's engine. At the same instant *Merrimack* closed a full hook around the runaway.

Engineering reeled the Swift into the designated cargo bay.

The moment the cargo bay pressurization lights showed green, the inner access hatch opened. Fully suited medics ran inside, and scrambled atop the Swift's wings. Marines thronged into the bay after them. The Marines stood back at the bulks, out of the medics' way, craning to see.

The Swift's canopy frosted over opaque.

The erks hadn't even popped the Swift's canopy, and already the medics' faces looked altogether wrong.

Carly, escaped from sickbay, circled her reattached arm around Kerry Blue.

The erks dragged the canopy open.

The Marines' low mutters rumbled through the compartment.

"They didn't wait for the pressure light."

"Why didn't they wait for it to pressurize?"

"What are they doing?"

The medics were stepping down as if from a funeral.

When the medics cleared, Marines surged forward. Those still in their environmental suits climbed up the space-cold wings and looked into the cockpit. The mustard-suited erks moved aside for them to see.

No one was talking.

Carly, first one up, turned away from the cockpit. She looked down from the wing, her face stricken.

Kerry Blue cried, "*Is he alive?*"

Carly's eyes were wide and helpless. Carly said, "I don't know."

Kerry Blue advanced. The Marines parted for her and helped her up onto the wing to see for herself.

The cockpit was empty.

Captain Carmel signaled the displacement department over the intracom. "Did you execute rapture?"

Displacement responded, "Negative. Negative rapture.

We did not get correspondence. We did not initiate. Rapture not attempted. We can't even try now. Target's collar signature has ceased registering."

"I need to know what happened," said Calli. "I need to know yesterday."

Already the erks were pulling the landing disk from Steele's cockpit. They handed it down to the displacement techs, who took a reading on the spot.

The disk's tracking record indicated a displacement event occurred from this disk at the instant Steele's collar signature ceased to register.

Displacement notified the captain, "Steele *did* displace." *Some*where.

Or nowhere.

Successful displacement required three correspondences—the displacement collar, the remote landing disk, and the sending/receiving chamber. It was three or nothing. Without all three, the traveler was thoroughly gone. And thoroughly dead. There was no margin for error in human displacement.

Grasping for anything, Calli hailed *Windward Isles*. "Ram! Do you have Colonel Steele?"

"Sorry?" Captain Singh did not understand the question.

Calli had hoped it was Ram Singh who displaced Steele out of his cockpit.

There were other ships orbiting Zoe now, mostly Asian scouts and news services. They had been underway here since Dr. Minyas' announcement of the discovery of alien DNA.

Calli was not going to ask any of them if they had displaced her Marine. None of them could possibly have *Merrimack*'s displacement harmonic.

Commander Ryan said, "Rome has our displacement harmonic."

Tactical clutched at his console. "Oh, God, do we have another mole?"

"Rome doesn't need a mole," Commander Ryan said. "We left LDs all over the LEN expedition site. Rome could have got our displacement harmonic off one of those."

Calli hailed *Gladiator*. "Numa, where is my man?"

"You misplaced one?" Numa said lightly.

"Don't foxtrot with me!"

"Perhaps you should be more careful with your men."

Calli slammed off the com and turned to Rob Roy, who was standing at the rear of the command deck. "Did you notice he didn't deny it? That means he doesn't have him."

Rob Roy had noticed. "I'd have thought the opposite. He's dodging the question because he *does* have Steele."

"No. He's dodging the question because an outright denial would require Numa to admit that he doesn't know where Steele is. When Numa doesn't know something, the best he can do is make you think he knows. When Numa actually says the words, 'I don't know,' it's a lie."

"That's labyrinthine."

"That's Numa Pompeii. He doesn't know where Steele is."

"That's rather terrifying, sir," said Rob Roy.

Captain Carmel collected her Marines. They looked to her like lost dogs needing an alpha. Calli was as angry as any of them over the loss of Steele. *I can't replace that man.*

The Marines needed their captain to be invincible now.

She couldn't tell them she would bring Steele back, but she promised them she would find out what happened, and if there was a human agent behind it, she promised them that agent would die.

Her Intelligence Officer, Bradley Zolman, was looking into the possibility of Roman kidnap, but he advised her that the more likely answer was that Steele's displacement equipment had malfunctioned, and he accidentally displaced without correspondence. That would not be kidnap. That would be fatal.

Everyone wanted it to be kidnap.

And everyone was afraid to use the displacement equipment now.

✳ ✳ ✳

Caesar Numa issued an Imperial Mandate. *Merrimack* must withdraw from the Zoen star system and take her Marines with her.

Calli got Numa on the com to tell him personally, "Caesar, I cannot leave. I am under your mandate to take my Marines with me. You *know* I have a man unaccounted for."

Numa said tiredly, "You sound like you've been sleeping with a lawyer. Don't start another international incident. You can be removed from command. Send the particulars of your AWOL Marine to my adjutant. He will look into it."

"Colonel Steele is not AWOL!"

The attitude shift was as palpable as a pressure drop before a storm. "Steele?" Numa said. "*Adamas*?"

Adamas was Rome's name for the colonel. *Adamas* was the Latin word for *steel*. "It is Adamas whom you lost?"

"You know that!" said Calli.

Numa wouldn't say he knew. He wouldn't confirm that he hadn't known. But he dropped the boredom facade. Numa told Captain Carmel earnestly, "I will use best efforts—best efforts—to determine the situation of your man. You must promise me something in turn."

I must? This was a deal with the devil. "What?" said Calli.

"Check your own house."

Her house. What was her house? The *Merrimack*? The United States Naval Fleet?

Calli shook her head, confused. "Check my house for what?"

"Roman moles."

She felt as if she were having tea with a March Hare and a dormouse. "But you are Rome!"

Numa's chest expanded to its most broad. His voice rumbled absolute royal authority. "Yes, We are."

And Calli suddenly knew what he was telling her.

Shit.

He was talking about an alternate Rome. A challenger to Numa's supreme power.

He meant Romulii.

"You're looking for Romulii," said Calli. "You're looking for them *here*."

Not just in Perseid space. Not just in the Outback. Numa was looking for Romulii on Zoe.

Riddled with nanites, Romulus, former Caesar, currently existed in an induced coma. Effectively dead. Or sleeping like a King Arthur, the once and future king.

The Romulii were making straight the way for their true Caesar's return.

This planet, Zoe, was a place of miracles. Zoe would make a fine place to stage Romulus' resurrection—with or without Romulus.

Calli had to wonder: Was Romulus really still sleeping?

It would be just like Romulus to take something of profound cosmic significance, like a second Creation, and turn it to personal gain.

Roman moles suddenly sounded likely.

In both their houses.

A choice between Numa and Romulus was a choice between the devil and the devil. Calli fought the idea, hard. There had to be another choice. She couldn't see one at this time.

She had to wonder, was Numa just sowing discord in making her look for moles? Trying to get her to suspect her own people? Or was he genuinely concerned about his comatose rival's spy network.

Adamas had been Romulus' gladiator.

A sudden outlandish thought struck her. "You *don't* think the Romulii killed Steele?"

She wanted Numa to react with surprise or a laugh. He didn't.

"Kill?" said Numa. "Not likely."

"*Kidnap?*" said Calli. The idea was crazed. Numa must laugh now.

But he didn't. "I don't dismiss *any* possibility, especially ones I don't want to believe." He had dropped the royal plurals. He was talking to her man to man. The focus of his eyes was hard. "Check your house."

Kidnap was a preposterous conspiracy theory. A displacement equipment malfunction was vastly more likely than kidnap by Romulii.

All reason and evidence pointed to horses, and Numa was telling her to look for zebras. She should tell him to go to hell.

"I will," Calli said.

When she turned off the com, Commander Ryan said, "Captain, does this incident remind anyone of other displacement equipment we found where it had no business being?"

"I have not forgotten, Mister Ryan."

Dingo was talking about the displacement disks left in space among the stations of Port Campbell. She had said at the time it had the look of someone preparing the way for a blitzkrieg through the Boomerang.

"Are you going to share that information with Caesar?" Dingo asked.

"No," said Calli.

"Reason, sir?"

Calli's mouth spread wide and tight. "Because they could be his disks."

She inhaled as if to say something else. Didn't.

"Captain?" Dingo prompted.

"Does it seem possible that Numa could not find a way to make Romulus dead if he actually has custody of Romulus?"

"But he does have custody. CIA has surveillance all over that installation. It's in the heart of Roma Nova. Romulus is there."

"Is he?" said Calli. "There was something Numa wasn't telling me. He's lost Romulus."

"Are you telling me or guessing, Captain?"

"I'm betting you he has."

Dingo considered this for several moments. Said, "I bet you're right."

Captain Carmel and Commander Ryan accompanied the ship's Legal Officer, Rob Roy Buchanan, to Colonel TR Steele's compartment to supervise the opening of Steele's private locker.

Rob Roy lifted the universal key.

"No."

The three officers turned.

Outside the hatch stood Flight Sergeant Kerry Blue. She appeared strangely calm, her face clear. She hadn't been crying. She stood with her weight on one foot. Kerry Blue never came to attention or even to ease unless you ordered her.

Kerry Blue told the captain, the XO, and the Legal Officer, "He's not dead."

That the colonel and the flight sergeant had an off reservation relationship was common knowledge. Everyone knew it. It was everyone's secret. No one reported it, and there had been no under-the-deck grumblings of favoritism. Morale was high among the Fleet Marines, so Captain Carmel chose not to know about it either.

But now Kerry Blue was holding up an official proceeding, and it was time to put the Marine in her place. "Flight Sergeant. This is not fair to the colonel's next of kin. They need to know."

"His next of kin knows he's not dead," said Kerry Blue.

Calli turned to her task. She nodded to the ship's Legal Officer, poised at the locker. "Pop it."

Rob Roy took the universal key to TR Steele's locker and opened it. He looked through Steele's personal effects.

Marines who had wills kept them in their lockers. Rob Roy found Steele's. He expanded the legal document.

The lawyer's eyebrows lifted as he read.

The XO read over Rob Roy's shoulder. "Right, then," said Dingo.

Rob Roy closed the will, replaced Steele's things into his locker and closed it for the voyage home.

Calli, standing back at the hatch, questioned, "Mister Buchanan?"

Rob Roy said, sounding faintly surprised. "The colonel's next of kin *knows*."

Calli turned around toward the corridor. Kerry Blue had already withdrawn.

Calli turned back to her officers and let herself look astonished. "Since when? When did this happen?"

"From the date on the certificate, we were in Port Campbell," said Rob Roy.

"It's an Ozzie contract," said Dingo. Sounded as if he approved.

"Mister Ryan. Have Mo check the Marine over."

"You think Kerry's ill?" said Dingo.

"I think she's lost it," said Calli.

"Because she thinks Steele is still alive?"

"Because she thinks she *knows* Steele is alive."

Rob Roy demurred. "Doesn't mean she's crazy. Tales of psychic connections between loved ones are universal. They've never been proved. But." He ended with a shrug.

"I don't believe in it," Calli said.

"Well, we know *we* don't have one," Rob Roy admitted. He could read Sanskrit better than he could read Calli's mind. "But I can't insist it doesn't exist. Jose Maria believes in it. Smart man, Jose Maria."

"Jose Maria believes in the biblical God," Calli said.

"It doesn't matter what Kerry Blue or my Aunt Martha believes," said Dingo Ryan. "Steele is either dead and we'll never find him, or he's not dead and we need to find him now, now, now."

Calli had to reconsider. Even throwing out the idea of a psychic connection, maybe a degree of doubt was still in order. "That man has died more than most. He may even hold some kind of record. I don't want to count Steele out if there's *any* hope at all. But really. What are the odds?"

"The odds?" said Commander Ryan. "The odds say Adamas really carked it this time."

Calli's nodded. Whether Steele vanished because of accidental equipment failure or intentional sabotage, the end was the same. Kidnap was an unreasonably exotic idea.

Calli ordered, "Have the boffins tear the colonel's crate apart. And I want the displacement gear sifted down to nanite scale. I'm not ready to declare. And what the hell, we already know his next of kin can wait."

37

MERRIMACK was still in orbit around Zoe when Lieutenant Glenn Hamilton received a summons before the captain.

Glenn had been dreading this review. Afraid she didn't mask it well.

Dingo Ryan was glib enough. It wasn't his career on the line. He winked as if he knew something. "So you went native ashore, Hamster?"

Oh, hell. Was that what the captain told him?

"No," said Glenn. "I went human."

Dingo said, "That never really works among aliens."

Glenn kept her mouth shut, her lips pressed in a tight line. It had not been her finest hour.

Glenn left the command deck and marched toward her doom.

Merrimack was alive around her. Hatches banged open or shut. Water trickled in the conduits. Boots clanged on ladders. Lifts hissed. Voices murmured, shouted, laughed. So many voices. Glenn Hull Hamilton loved this ship. She was going to miss it.

After what Dingo had said, she was pretty sure she was getting a reprimand for her actions on world. The delay in *Merrimack*'s departure would give her a place to go if she wanted to quit rather than take a reduction in rank. Had to be why Carmel hadn't left orbit yet.

Glenn entered the briefing compartment. The captain was there and waiting. There was no Marine guard inside the hatch. That was a good sign. It meant no one was expecting Hamster to go parabolic when she received the news. And there was no Rob Roy in here. Absence of legal counsel was a great sign. Glenn hoped it was a great sign anyway.

Calli bade Glenn sit across from her at the table.

Glenn sat, rigid. The captain passed a data capsule across the table.

Glenn took it, questioningly. "Sir?" It had a Navy seal on it. Had to be a reprimand. An official one at that.

The captain said, "I'm making an assumption here. I don't want that to look like I'm pushing you out the air lock."

Glenn saw what she had in her hand. Not a rep. Far from it. Captain Carmel had made an official recommendation for Lieutenant Glenn Hamilton to be given her own command.

That meant a transfer to a ship that didn't need a xeno-linguist.

Patrick had been holding her back.

Patrick was staying on Zoe.

There was nothing holding her here now.

Be careful what you wish for.

"Thank you, sir."

Cal gave her head a minimal shake. "You're ready. You've been ready."

Glenn displaced to the LEN expedition camp.

The LEN scientific expedition were allowed to stay on world for now—by leave of Caesar Numa and under Roman supervision.

It was before dawn in this time zone. But *Merrimack* was leaving. It was now or never.

Glenn had signaled ahead. She told Patrick to meet her at the edge of the sleeping camp.

Patrick's eyes did the quick head to foot when she thunderclapped into existence on the landing disk.

Patrick saw his wife was in uniform. She hadn't brought any belongings with her. He didn't look awfully surprised. He did look awfully disappointed.

Glenn stepped off the disk. She moved in close, laid her

hand on Patrick's chest, her head bowed. She told him what he already knew. "I can't stay." She had to whisper, because her voice didn't work.

"I don't want a divorce," said Patrick.

"I don't either." Tears burned to get out. She was not going to cry. "I don't want to separate, but that's what's happening."

"I don't want a legal separation," said Patrick.

Glenn sniffled, lifted her head. "Neither do I."

"This isn't going to work," said Patrick.

Glenn nodded silent agreement. *Probably not.*

But there was no need to force it.

Patrick said, "The pack keeps asking for you."

He had been out with the foxes again.

Glenn said, "They get over their losses quick."

"They keep asking."

"Patrick, don't you make me cry." She held in her tears.

It was still dark. She looked up to the half starry sky at the rim of the Milky Way. Patrick followed her gaze. He said, "Make up a constellation with me?"

"Um." He'd thrown her off guard. She said, "Okay." It was something to keep her from crying. Glenn pointed out the groups of stars she and Nox had already named. "There's Akela. That's Nag and Nagaina. That's Zam-Zammah. Those are Nox's. There's the *Merrimack*. Statue of Liberty. And that's—okay that's an ice cream cone."

"An ice cream cone?" Patrick chided.

"I felt like ice cream," Glenn snapped, almost crying, almost smiling.

"What about that group of stars." Patrick pointed. "From big blue there to that tight pair five degrees down, over to the reddish cluster."

"I don't think we did anything with that," Glenn said. She sniffled.

"That's not taken?" Patrick said.

"No. That's yours. Give it a name."

"Glenn Hull."

She caught in her breath. She couldn't think of anything to say.

Patrick was pointing up. "And how about those stars. Next to you. The five red ones. Are those taken?"

She shook her head.

Patrick named them. "That's Princess."

Glenn threw her arms around him, cried into his ear, "Patrick, don't let the clokes take over Zoe. Don't let those monsters take root on this world."

She was not sure how she expected him to do that. There had been too much talk of letting the surviving clokes stay on Zoe.

She felt Patrick's palm on her back. He said, "I thought I'd put the clokes' fate into the paws of whose world this is."

Glenn pulled back, blinked at him. "The foxes?"

He gave a shrug. "You know what they say. Dig up a clutch of cloke eggs you stop the clokes for a day. Teach a fox to dig—"

Glenn gave a wobbly smile. "You don't need to teach a fox to dig."

"Teach a fox to dig up ugly ugly bad bad . . ."

You stop them forever.

Anyone who wanted to preserve the clokes would need to relocate them. Zoe was *not* going to sustain cloke life.

Tears broke out. Glenn smiled, sniffed. She held him tight. Her fist closed on the back of his shirt. "Patrick Hamilton, I am going to miss you."

* * *

As *Merrimack* left the Zoen star system, Glenn brooded over the lost soul that was Nox.

Nox had done evil ghastly things, and she had no business feeling fond of him. At some point she knew she would decompress, get her head clear, and find the ability to loathe him. For now she felt loss and waste.

What was a devil but an angel gone wrong?

"How does one become so twisted?" she wondered out loud.

She was killing a bottle of Kentucky bourbon with Captain Carmel and Rob Roy Buchanan in the Captain's Mess. The bottle had belonged to another John Farragut.

Rob Roy suggested, "When you cast people out from society, they're going to exist outside of society. You make them outlaws. Punishment may make the victim feel better, but as far as teaching a lesson to the offender or making an example of him, punishment accomplishes the opposite of what you like to think it does. Jesus had the right idea, but the Old Testament is so much easier to follow."

"There was a lot to the man," said Glenn. "I would have thought Rome could do more with him than toss him out as trash."

"Yes," said Calli, her voice hard. "You would think."

Glenn told Calli, "The Xerxes didn't need to crash into the Ark. Nox didn't need to ride the Xerxes in. He didn't need to be aboard."

"No, he didn't," Calli agreed.

"He could have bailed."

"He could have," said Calli.

He could have. "But we didn't see any life craft from the Xerxes. Ambassadorial ships have great escape boats. The pirates didn't use them."

Rob Roy recounted the facts. "Antimatter detonated inside the Ark. We saw the Striker fly out. And there is no chance the pirates were somehow aboard the Striker." He paused on that one. "Is there?"

"No," said Glenn and Calli together.

The Striker was physically too small.

And after more consideration Calli questioned, "Why the hell would Numa sacrifice the Xerxes?"

"He didn't," said Glenn. "Not on purpose. I'm sure he thought the Striker would win the tug-of-war with the Xerxes."

"The patterner *lost?*" said Calli, eyebrows high. "That doesn't fit the kind of patterner we both know."

Now that she thought of it, Glenn had to agree. "Augustus would never have lost that battle."

Patterners never lost their grip. Not accidentally. When a patterner lost, he had a reason.

"And even after the Striker lost its hold, the Xerxes might have survived a collision with the Ark," said Calli. "I don't know why the Xerxes detonated. There was no need for that either. A Xerxes' containment system should have survived impact. I think."

But it hadn't survived. It was an incontrovertible fact that antimatter had detonated inside the Ark.

That meant the pirates committed suicide and took the alien Ark with them.

"Maybe Nox's Circle just wasn't that familiar with the ship's controls," Rob Roy offered. "Or maybe they wanted to go out with a big bang."

The Xerxes was a valuable piece of equipment. The patterner had tried to salvage it but couldn't overpower pirates hell-bent on freedom or death.

The patterner tried to stop them.

Patterners don't lose.

A new thought struck Glenn. "Why was there a patterner at Zoe?"

"I'll do you one better," said Calli. "Why is there a patterner at all? I never expected Numa Pompeii to let another patterner be constructed. Ever. You'd have thought Numa would have learned better from the last one."

Glenn nodded into her shot glass. "Nobody wants another Augustus."

"Amen," said Calli. She downed a shot. Drew a breath with an inward hiss.

"The pieces still don't fit," said Glenn. "The picture is wrong. We're missing something."

Calli circled back to Glenn's first thought. "Nox did not need to ride the Xerxes in."

That left the question: So *did he?*

* * *

The patterner Cinna turned to his brothers. "Welcome to the band of the officially dead."

The pirates of The Ninth Circle had never expected to be breathing while dead.

Faunus' thick brows contracted. He took count of his brothers. Nox, Pallas, Nicanor, Orissus, Leo, Galeo. All of them were here in the control room of their Xerxes, *Bagheera*.

Faunus turned to the thing that looked like their late brother, Cinna, with a vertical knife hole stabbed in the front of his tunic. Cinna was wearing black, so you couldn't see how much blood was on him. He appeared as a slender youth, handsome as all of them used to be, no more than seventeen. His black eyes were as old as the sphinx guarding the Great Pyramid.

Faunus spoke. "What just happened?"

"A show," said Cinna.

Even now all the *Bagheera*'s monitors displayed images of the clokes' FTL Ark continuing to erupt from internal detonations, turning the parts of the Ark that survived the initial antimatter blast inside out. "Not that," Cinna added, watching the exploding images, his face smooth as dark marble. "That's not a show. The death of the alien Ark was real."

"Where's the Striker?" said Nox.

Cinna nodded toward the images of multiple explosions. "In there."

Wreckage from the alien Ark spewed like galactic shrapnel. The flashes would have blinded the brothers if not for the radiation filters built into the Xerxes' viewports.

The Striker had made the suicidal plunge into the Ark and released antimatter into the heart of it.

The Xerxes was solidly underfoot.

Leo blinked at the continuing explosions. "I thought it was going to be us."

Cinna said, "It was meant to look as if this ship went in."

"Looked like it from this angle," said Galeo. Shuddered.

Nox shut his eyes. He could still see the lights of the titanic alien ship hurtling close, fast, its mass filling the view, obliterating the stars, heaving up like the ground at the bottom of Widow's Edge. Nox, his brothers, his leopard, were going in.

The Xerxes plunged into the Ark.

Flashed the most fleeting energy signature of a Striker as it came out the other side.

Leaving the Striker at the heart of the Ark to open its antimatter containment core.

To all appearances, it was the Xerxes that died in the suicide plunge, and it was the Striker that got away.

"Everyone would expect me to escape," said Cinna. "Patterners have that reputation. And the leopard needed to die."

That part of the show, the death of the leopard, required a sacrificial lamb, something that could penetrate to the heart of the alien Ark and make an explosion on a magnitude of a Xerxes. Cinna had to sacrifice his Striker for that.

Cinna had controlled his Striker by resonant command from on board the Xerxes *Bagheera*.

A res signal on a secret harmonic was undetectable, untraceable. Resonance left no trail.

Being at point zero of the antimatter release, the Striker left no debris to tell a different tale.

"If the leopard had to die, why not just send the leopard in?" said Faunus. "Not complaining, mind you." He was happy to be breathing. Astonished, but happy. He still had his machete too, and that was astounding.

"A Striker is aging technology. This ship," Cinna knocked on the Xerxes' control console with a black-gloved hand. "Is the latest. Caesar wants his patterner to have the latest."

There it is.

So that was why Nox and his brothers were still here. For the moment.

It hadn't been feasible for Cinna to ballast the brothers along with his doomed Striker. They wouldn't fit in it. The Striker was a one-man craft.

The brothers had been left in place, on board the Xerxes, for the duration of the show.

Now they were excess mass.

They were all armed. They could try to kill Cinna a third time.

Cinna touched gloved fingers to the vertical slit in his tunic at his midriff. His face looked pinched. He told Nox, "This does not feel good."

Nox asked, "Do we get the grisly revenge now?"

Cinna's inhuman eyes moved across each of his brothers in turn. Nox. Pallas. Nicanor. Faunus. Orissus. Leo. Galeo. Cinna answered, "Are we still a squad?"

38

THE DRY PALE SKY was hazy over Sector Primus on the Roman world Phoenix. Small moons stretched overhead from horizon to horizon like a string of broken pearls. Satellites gleamed hard bright white like daystars. Imperial Intelligence could be watching.

One could hope.

But the patterner told the brothers no one was watching. "There will be no deus ex machina," said Cinna.

Nox waited with his brothers in a level area halfway up the massif. Gray contorted trees hemmed in a circle, and there were flat rocks inside the ring on which to sit.

Cinna was calling them up one by one to the Widow's Edge. Orissus had gone first.

Orissus had been hard on Cinna when Cinna first joined the squad. Orissus was always hard.

At the snap of twig from the path, Nox, Pallas, Nicanor, Faunus, Leo, and Galeo stood up, expectant.

Cinna came back alone. Orissus was nowhere to be seen.

Cinna stepped into the circle of trees. He called up Nicanor next.

"Where's Orissus?" Faunus demanded.

Cinna kept his silence; his basilisk glare fixed on Nicanor and waited to be obeyed.

"Well, then," Nicanor said, stepping forward, chin up, back regal. Nicanor was the lordly one of their number. Nicanor followed Cinna out between the twisted gray trees. He walked with great dignity.

No one sat back down.

The brothers' talk turned to murmurs. "He's fucking with our minds," Faunus said.

"It's working," Leo said, nerves unraveling.

"Cinna never liked Orissus," Pallas whispered.

"You don't think he really made Orissus jump," said Galeo.

"I'm trying not to think at all," said Nox.

Faunus whispered, hardly louder than breathing, "Do we kill Cinna?"

"Already did," said Nox. "Twice."

They hushed.

Cinna came back alone. He pronounced the next name. "Galeo."

Galeo turned a three-sixty, as if there might be another Galeo in the circle. He cast lost looks to his brothers.

And followed Cinna out between the twisted trees.

The brothers stopped talking altogether.

It took longer this time. That was a good sign. Maybe. It took longer to reel up a netted jumper than it did to let one fall. Did Cinna really let Orissus fall?

The net deployment used to be automatic. No one ever dropped.

And where was Nicanor?

Cinna came back alone again.

He regarded each of the four remaining in turn.

He looked so very young. He looked so very old. His face was lineless, with little expression. The look in his eyes was something between a basilisk gaze and a thousand-yard stare. His black eyes moved from Nox to Pallas to Leo to Faunus. He looked past them, through them.

He nodded at Leo.

Leo threw back his head and howled. Cinna waited like the grim reaper. Leo followed Cinna, still giving voice to raging howls. The sounds diminished as the two climbed away to the heights.

Nox found himself reaching for the sounds. He needed to hear Leo. At last he was listening hard to only the gritty wind.

Nox, Faunus, and Pallas remained.

Faunus sat on a rock. He'd taken up a stick and was jabbing at the dirt with the end of it.

Pallas stood by a tree, its scaly green foliage so dark it was nearly black.

Nox tried to collect his thoughts. Then tried to obliterate them. He needed to make his mind a perfect blank. The universe was unfolding, not perhaps as it should, but the way it was hell-bent on unfolding. *It is what it is. It will be what it will be.*

Cinna came back—alone—to collect the next brother.

Faunus' patience tore. He jumped up from his rock, threw his stick aside. He bellowed, "Me! Take me!"

"Very well," said Cinna and turned to lead Faunus away.

Nox and Pallas clasped hands as if arm wrestling. They squeezed bone-mashingly tight, in case it was the last thing they ever did. They released. And waited.

After a lifetime, footsteps approached. Sounded like a single set.

And so it was.

Cinna appeared between the trees, alone.

He faced the two who remained. "You."

Cinna pointed at Nox.

Pallas cursed.

Nox advanced to his fate. He looked back to Pallas. "Be seeing you."

Pallas' face was tight. He gave a single nod.

Nox marched up to the height in Cinna's footsteps. He did not hear any voices from up there.

Because no one was there.

He arrived to only the wind on the lonely summit.

Winged creatures circled on the air above the hardpan. They were rot-colored carrion eaters. Phoenix's equivalent of vultures.

Nox looked over the edge. He expected it by now. Funny how that didn't lessen the sense of shock. Horror still knotted his guts. He swallowed hard and stinging. Rasped, "Oh, you son and heir of a mongrel bitch."

Cinna had earned his revenge, but Nox could still resent him for actually taking it. Nox blinked fast. Refused to cry. He backed away from the edge.

"It's still broken," Nox said, his voice rough.

"What is broken?" said Cinna.

"The net's automatic deployment is still broken. We didn't know it was broken when we sent you over."

"It's not broken now," said Cinna. He held up a switch. "It's manual."

Manual. And Cinna had let them all drop.

"We didn't drop you on purpose," said Nox, resentful.

"End's the same," said Cinna.

Yes, the end was the same.

A song started playing in Nox's head, a gentle Christian hymn, all out of place. It was the wrong damned circle. Nox's loved ones were not in the glory. The musical loop had started in his brain, and he couldn't get it out of there.

His voice came out hoarse. "You got a switch, FDG? Don't net me."

The patterner looked curious. "FDG? I don't know that one."

"It's Americanese," Nox snapped. "Stands for Dead Guy." Nox turned toward the brink.

Cinna spoke at his back. "Do you actually want to die, or is this an attempt at reverse psychology?"

"This is no reverse nothing. I'm running away again. Just drop me."

"If it *is* reverse psychology, then you lose," Cinna advised him. "No one disobeys a Farragut."

Nox took his place on the cliff's edge. Looked down. Well, yes, there they all are. The bloody carnage below welcomed him. Nox spread his arms. "O, My Brothers, I am coming."

Will the circle be unbroken, by and by, Lord, by and by?
He launched himself into a beautiful dive.

The wind rushed at his ears, his nostrils; his heart raced in instinctive terror as the bloody ground came hurtling up.

Then there was a sting of ropes against his skin, pressure on his face and chest, the nauseating reverse and a springy jouncing up and down.

The net had deployed.

Nox screamed in his mother tongue. "Son of a bitch! Son of a bitch!" He thrashed like a cat in a bag.

The bouncing settled, and he felt a tug from above. The other hidden mechanism had deployed to reel him up.

One arm and one foot sticking out through the thick netted mesh, Nox was rising. The bloody ground moved away from him. He struggled to get all his limbs inboard. He caromed lightly once or twice against the ragged rock face, spun. His breaths heaved. He braced himself.

This is a psych. He's toying with me before he kills me. He's going to drop me again. For real this time.

The winch turned. Nox was near the top. As he rose over the edge he met Cinna's black eyes. Nox glowered back at him.

The winch stopped. Nox dangled there just over the cliff. He would not repeat himself. He silently dared Cinna with all his wrath, *Drop me.*

Cinna seized the net and swung Nox over to solid ground. Cinna pulled a cord that let him out of the net. "Watch your step."

Nox stood up and stepped out in a quivering rage, snorting.

Cinna turned blandly and walked down the path that led to the waiting area.

Nox paced, looking for a good rock with which to bash Cinna. Or maybe he should just push him. Maybe he could grab him and jump. Or maybe just jump and be with his brothers. That's where he was headed anyway.

After an eternity he heard Cinna returning up the path with their last brother, Pallas.

Pallas hiked up with heavy tread over the crest. He met Nox's gaze. Nox tried to ward off the brightening hope on Pallas' face to see a brother alive. Nox gave a grim shake of his head.

But Pallas had seen Nox and assumed that Cinna was netting people. Pallas looked around for who else was up here.

There was only Cinna and Nox and Pallas.

Pallas looked over the edge, scuttled back from the mess below. "Ho! Who is that?"

Nox, furious and crying, answered him, *"Who don't you see up here?"* He was past trying to contain his tears.

Pallas seized Nox in a brief pounding hug. Pushed apart hard, wheeled around, and hurled himself over the edge.

Nox thought his own heart would stop. But it continued

its merciless hammering inside his chest. He was still cruelly alive with this monster when all his brothers were dead.

He ran to the edge. He didn't want to watch, but he had to. He needed to see it. He didn't want Pallas to die alone.

Far below, something shot out from the rock face. A spreading honeycomb blossomed wide, then folded back in on the dropping figure, closing around it. The net stretched down long. Bounced back up.

The net had deployed. Nox could see Pallas moving within it.

Nox gasped, his vision blurred, dizzy between crushing relief and rage.

The retrieval mechanism was drawing Pallas up. Nox stayed on hands and knees, breathing grief and fury.

The net's arm swung over solid ground. Pallas emerged from the net, shaken, sad, composed.

Pallas' demeanor made Nox pick up his *dignitas*.

Nox stood up and faced Cinna. Nox spoke thickly, "It is just us three then."

Cinna said, "There are eight in a squad."

Pallas and Nox exchanged puzzled looks. Eight? Where were the other five supposed to come from?

Cinna signaled someone to come.

Gritty footsteps sounded, approaching. Boot soles on sandy rock. Pallas and Nox turned toward the sound.

Cinna didn't look. He knew who was coming.

Nicanor, Faunus, Leo, Galeo, and Orissus hove into view, hiking up the rocks.

Pallas caught in a breath, astonished.

Nox turned away. He looked over the cliff.

The red pools and broken bodies at the bottom of the cliff vanished before his stinging eyes.

Pallas stared as his brothers returned from the dead. Pallas' eyes were nearly round, pooling tears. His lower lip quivered. He asked them, his voice shaking, "Are you real?"

Nicanor gave a couple of uncertain blinks with a tentative smile. He didn't understand the question. "Aye. Why? Aren't *you?*"

Pallas threw his arms around Nicanor, hugged him

fiercely. His face mashed against his brother's ear. He pounded his fist against Nicanor's back. Pallas hugged them all, Leo, Galeo, Orissus, Faunus.

Cinna had netted them. All of them. They were real. They were alive.

Nox stood apart, hugging no one.

His brothers' voices overlapped in a blur of baritone sound, trading stories of their jumps. Their voices trailed to silence as each caught sight of Nox, his face fixed in a gargoyle glare.

Nox turned to Cinna. Spoke, deadly cold. "Your turn."

"I had my turn," the patterner said.

Color poured into Nox's face. Nox breathed fire. "*Do you not trust your brothers?*" And he thrust out a demanding palm.

Cinna gazed back at him.

Cinna and Nox stood locked in a stare down. Cinna dead calm. Nox vibrating.

Cinna moved first, smoothly. His hand came forward. He lightly placed the net deployment control into Nox's hand.

Expression blank, Cinna turned and walked off the cliff.

His brothers swarmed to the edge to watch the drop.

Nox stayed where he was, standing perfectly still. He knew what he had to do.

Drop him.

The row of brothers looking down over the cliff reared back like one beast. "Ho!"

And they laughed.

The net had deployed.

They watched as the netted bundle bounced up and down and twisted round one way, unwound, and twisted round the other way.

Orissus cranked his head over his shoulder to see Nox. Orissus snorted. "I wasn't sure you were going to catch him."

Nox looked down to his hand, his fingers depressing the control trigger.

"My hand slipped," Nox said. He passed the control to Pallas. Let someone else reel the cur up.

Pallas moved the switch that activated the retrieval assembly. The mechanical arm lifted up. The winch turned. There was a dry squeak to it.

As the bundle rose above the cliff edge, Nox glared at the patterner balled up in his net, still dangling over the edge. Cinna seemed calm to the point of boredom, resting with his back rounded against the rope bag, his knees folded up against his shoulders. He waited without pleading.

Nox said at last, "Bring him in."

Pallas turned the control to swing the net over solid ground. Sand in the metal gears squealed.

Cinna disengaged himself from the ropes and stood up before his brothers.

The patterner was a strange being. So very like them. So very not, with eyes that appeared to be looking both inward and out. The cables extending out of his forearms and out the back of his neck made him look alien.

Faunus asked Cinna, "Did you know Nox was going to net you?"

"How could I?" Cinna said. "*He* didn't know what he was going to do." Opaque eyes slid to Nox.

A motion like a tic tugged at Nox's mouth. He admitted, "I didn't."

Nox had made up his mind while Cinna was falling. Actually, there'd been no mind to it at all. Nox's hand just squeezed. Some brain cell sent that message, but it wasn't a conscious one. Nox thought he meant to drop him.

All their rage had guttered out. Each of them felt it. Something thoroughly burned out was settling on the cliff top. The ashes of fear.

"*Now*," said Nox. "Now, we are a squad."

Cinna asked his brothers, with a nod at Nox, "How did he get to be your mouth?"

Pallas shrugged, his head turning slowly side to side. "He just starts talking."

"I was dropped on purpose," said Cinna.

"I swear we didn't mean to," Nox said wearily.

"I didn't say it was *your* purpose," said Cinna.

Nox's mouth hung open. He couldn't speak. Leo and Galeo exchanged glances.

Nicanor spoke, "*Whose* then?"

"I wish I knew," said Cinna. "When I returned to the cliff

to replace the net's motion sensor with the handheld switch, I found the net deployment mechanism had been sabotaged. Someone jammed a rock into the works. The simpler a deed is, the harder it is to find its pattern. My death may have been a conspiracy, and I don't have access to a database that would reveal it to me. It may have been some bored kid with a rock. I don't know if the failure of the net was specifically targeting me or if I was simply the next sod to jump. Either way, I was murdered."

A bored kid with a rock would not explain how Cinna got picked up from the bottom of the cliff in time to save his life. Or how he lived at all. The impact from that kind of fall should have sprayed his brains over the whole province.

"You find out who did that to you, Little Brother, you let us know," said Nox. "We can get real creative on him."

"I am counting on that."

"And what about us?" said Nox. "Why are we still alive?"

"You—we—are The Ninth Circle of Hell," said Cinna. "And we are dead. Never forget that. We don't exist. We haunt by leave of Caesar Numa."

"*Why?*"

"Caesar needs a free hand," Cinna said.

All became clear.

No one would be hunting them any more. There was no bounty on dead men or on an annihilated spaceship.

Spacefarers could be as superstitious as ancient mariners. The implausible sightings of the leopard ship would be dismissed as ghost stories. The actions of the Circle could be attributable to no one. Especially not to Caesar.

Because we are dead.

Credible people had watched them die.

The Ninth Circle existed at Numa's will.

And all the broken pieces fit together. The brothers had everything they wanted. Well, not everything. Not half. But the main thing, the thing that made them whole. A purpose. A belonging. A reason for living.

They started down the path together. Orissus singing a drinking song, Faunus playing along on his panpipe made of cloke bones. Nox and Pallas tried to dance to the tune, but the way was too rocky. They stumbled a lot. Cinna walked with them.

And it became their motto, never to be spoken outside the Circle:

Semper Pro Roma / Numquam Nomene Sua
Always for Rome / Never in Her Name

RM Meluch
The Tour of the Merrimack

"An action-packed space opera. For readers who like romps through outer space, lots of battles with gooey horrific insects, and character sexploitation, *The Myriad* delivers..."   —*SciFi.com*

"Like *The Myriad*, this one is grand space opera. You will enjoy it."   —*Analog*

"This is grand old-fashioned space opera, so toss your disbelief out the nearest airlock and dive in."
       —*Publishers Weekly* (Starred Review)

THE MYRIAD   0-7564-0320-1

WOLF STAR   0-7564-0383-6

THE SAGITTARIUS COMMAND
          978-0-7564-0490-1

STRENGTH AND HONOR
          978-0-7564-0578-6

THE NINTH CIRCLE
          978-0-7564-0764-3

To Order Call: 1-800-788-6262
www.dawbooks.com

DAW 48

S. Andrew Swann
The Apotheosis Trilogy

It's been nearly two hundred years since the collapse of the Confederacy, the last government to claim humanity's colonies. So when signals come in revealing lost human colonies that could shift the power balance, the race is on between the Caliphate ships and a small team of scientists and mercenaries. But what awaits them all is a threat far beyond the scope of any human government.

PROPHETS
978-0-7564-0541-0

HERETICS
978-0-7564-0613-4

MESSIAH
978-0-7564-0657-8

To Order Call: 1-800-788-6262
www.dawbooks.com

DAW 161

S. Andrew Swann

DAW 123

CJ Cherryh

The Foreigner Novels

"Serious space opera at its very best by one of the leading
SF writers in the field today." —*Publishers Weekly*

"Her world building, aliens, and suspense rank among
the strongest in the whole SF field. May those
strengths be sustained indefinitely, or at least
until the end of *Foreigner*." —*Booklist*

To Order Call: 1-800-788-6262

www.dawbooks.com

DAW 8

Edward Willett

"Their moral dilemma is only on of the reasons this novel is so fascinating. The Selkie culture and infrastructure is very picturesque and easily pictured by readers who will want to visit his exotic world." —*Midwest Book Review*

"Willett is well able to keep all his juggling balls in the air at the same time....It's a good story, a great mate to the first volume." —Ian Randal Strock at *SF Scope*

The Helix War
Omnibus:
Marseguro *Terra Insegura*
978-0-7564-0738-4

And don't miss:

Lost in Translation
978-0-7564-0340-9

To Order Call: 1-800-788-6262
www.dawbooks.com

DAW 177